W9-CRX-367

IN THE COURT OF THE KING
TREACHERY RULED . . .

Lady Serena, whose sapphire eyes and rare beauty not even King William could resist,

Lord Gyles, who was sure he had tasted every pleasure and experienced every sensation life held . . . until he met Serena,

Lady Beda, sultry and diabolical wife of Gyles's dead brother, who would stop at nothing until her plans for Gyles and Camden Castle were realized,

Richard, whose unquenched passion for his childhood sweetheart, Lady Serena, would drive him to disaster.

THIS IS
COURTLY LOVE

A tale of love in a breathtaking era, a time of courageous knights, perilous jousts, royal intrigue, when passion reigned supreme.

ATTENTION: SCHOOLS AND CORPORATIONS

WARNER books are available at quantity discounts with bulk purchase for educational, business, or sales promotional use. For information, please write to: SPECIAL SALES DEPARTMENT, WARNER BOOKS, 75 ROCKEFELLER PLAZA, NEW YORK, N.Y. 10019

**ARE THERE WARNER BOOKS
YOU WANT BUT CANNOT FIND IN YOUR LOCAL STORES?**

You can get any WARNER BOOKS title in print. Simply send title and retail price, plus 50¢ per order and 20¢ per copy to cover mailing and handling costs for each book desired. New York State and California residents add applicable sales tax. Enclose check or money order only, no cash please, to: WARNER BOOKS, P.O. BOX 690, NEW YORK, N.Y. 10019

Courtly Love

by Lynn M. Bartlett

WARNER BOOKS

A Warner Communications Company

WARNER BOOKS EDITION

Copyright © 1979 by Lynn M. Bartlett
All rights reserved.

ISBN 0-446-91120-8

Cover art by Elaine Duillo

Book design: Helen Roberts

Warner Books, Inc., 75 Rockefeller Plaza, New York, N.Y. 10019

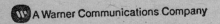 A Warner Communications Company

Printed in the United States of America

First Printing: September, 1979

10 9 8 7 6 5 4 3 2 1

For Joe, who understood
the midnight writing sessions;

and for Andrea, who spent
so many hours watching me type
and never complained.

Contents

Courtly Love

{ PROLOGUE }
The Betrayal

1

"I'll not wed him!"

The angry words rang through the halls, causing the servants to glance knowingly at each other and to depart hurriedly for a different part of the castle. The argument between Lord Geoffrey and his daughter Lady Serena-had begun at breakfast and now, shortly before the noonday meal, neither party had surrendered to the other; and knowing the stubbornness of both, the battle could rage late into the evening.

Lord Geoffrey was seated behind a massive oak table upon which numerous papers were strewn. A fine looking man who had lived a full life in the five and forty years God had seen fit to grant him, Geoffrey, his dark hair flecked slightly with grey, allowed his brown eyes to flash angrily back at his daughter. At seventeen, Serena was a portrait of her mother at the same age. Her taffy brown hair shot through with gold hung to her waist and her sapphire blue eyes glared defiantly back at her father.

"I'll not wed him!" she repeated in a calmer voice. "You promised me that my marriage would be a love match—I was to wed whomever I chose. You swore to my mother on her deathbed that I would not be forced into a political marriage. Will you now break that holy oath? You know Richard and I . . ."

"Richard no longer is of any concern to you, nor you to him. You shall be wed to Lord Gyles of Camden. All the negotiations are completed." Geoffrey tapped the papers before him. "There is nothing else to be discussed, these arrangements are final, Serena. Richard would never have accepted you on these terms, Lord Gyles has."

Serena snatched the papers from her father and began to read them—no small accomplishment, since few people could read and women were not educated at all. Her delicately arched brows pulled together in a frown.

"But, Father, this cannot be right! These say that all I bring with me as a dowry are Mother's dower lands. What of the gold and silver I know you've had saved for me these many years? Surely that's not . . ."

"There are many expenses in a household as large as this, Serena," a purring feminine voice interrupted. "Really, Serena, you should be more considerate of your father's position."

"Aurelia, my pet." Geoffrey left his seat to guide his wife to a chair.

Serena watched the beautiful blond woman coldly. How things had changed when Father had remarried. The household Serena had managed since her mother's death three years before had been taken from her charge and it seemed Father had no time either for herself or her brother Bryan. Aurelia had been pushing her toward any available male who visited Broughton. Before Aurelia had come, Father had been content to allow Serena to choose her own suitors. Serena's eyes narrowed angrily, emphasizing their upward slant.

"Was this marriage your idea, Aurelia? I cannot believe that Father would choose Lord Gyles for my husband without being influenced by someone else. If I remember correctly, your sister was married to the lord's half-brother, Kier, wasn't she? It was never known how Kier happened to be riding alone the morning he was killed, was it? As for expenses incurred by this household, I would remind you that I well know when coin must be spent and on what items." Serena studied the richly clad form of her father's wife—she could not and would not think of her as a stepmother. "It suddenly comes to me how my dowry was spent. 'Twas used to clothe your back, Aurelia, was it not? The bolts of material that have constantly arrived here . . . of course." Serena eyed her father with dismay, and the good man flushed slightly under her uncompromising stare. "Is this how you carry out your promise to my mother?"

"Serena, there is much you must understand. . . ." Geoffrey's voice trailed off as Serena raised a tiny hand.

"I do not care for explanations or excuses, I wish only a share of that which is rightfully mine. From you, Aurelia, I want the key to the storage room where you keep the bolts of cloth. And from you, Father, I want your word that I may have anything in that room that attracts my eye." Aurelia moved as if to speak, but subsided into tight-lipped silence when her husband nodded. Serena flashed them both a cold travesty of a smile as she stepped to Aurelia and extended her hand. "The key, Lady Aurelia, if you please. Thank you." Serena thoughtfully weighed the key in the palm of her hand. "Very well, Father, the battle is over and well met by both sides. Only tell me why Lord Gyles is willing to accept so poor a bride when Richard would not."

Her father's flushed face turned a deeper hue of red. "He is wealthy enough, Serena. He has no need of more coin."

"And he is a bastard." Aurelia's voice cut across her husband's. "Being merely a bastard—even though his father saw to it he would be Lord of Camden if his legitimate, first-born son died without leaving issue—there are few who would wed him."

Serena paled and her eyes pleaded with her father for denial, but he stood with bowed head studying the floor. "There is no need to be so blunt with the lass, Wife. I would have told you, Serena, when the time was right."

"When, pray, would that have been?" Serena's blue eyes shot sparks into the room. "On my wedding day?

'Tis bad enough I may not take a husband of my own choosing, but this—to be wed to a nameless bastard who would have naught save for his half-brother's death. Whatever have I done, Father, that you would humiliate me in this cruel manner? Have I done you some grievous wrong that you now set to right by marrying me to some nameless cur?" The pain in Serena's heart was so intense that she had to take several deep breaths before she could continue. "Never fear, my Lord Geoffrey, I shall honor this arrangement to my dying day, or his. But hear you this, and heed my words well." Serena's voice was so low they had to strain to hear as she continued. "When the day comes that I am wed, I shall no longer be your daughter, save in name only. Any children I may bear will never know their grandsire, for I will never set foot in your home willingly again. If you should find it necessary to visit Camden you shall be treated as befits your station, but you will find no daughter's love from me. For the present, keep your wife out of my way, for I will brook no further interference from either of you. If you will excuse me, I shall now seek out what my dowry has purchased, for I would not want my husband to find my wardrobe lacking." Serena bent into a deep, mocking curtsy and swept from the room.

Aurelia gave her husband an angry look as she jumped to her feet and poured herself a goblet of wine. "The chit needs a good hiding, Geoffrey, and I'll not have her pawing through my materials!"

"Guard your tongue, woman, that chit you speak so harshly of is my daughter. And the precious materials and trinkets you pleaded and pouted for were bought dearly with coin that was rightfully Serena's. 'Tis only just she have a share of them." Geoffrey spoke slowly, each word seemingly wrung from his throat. He had no doubt that his daughter meant every word she said. He sighed deeply, he had not meant to injure his daughter's pride nor force her into a marriage that would turn her so fully against him. Geoffrey cast a glance at his high-born Norman wife. Perhaps it had been a mistake for him to marry again—another injustice Serena doubtless held against him. His first wife—Serena's and Bryan's mother —had been a beautiful Saxon maid of sixteen summers when they had wed and within a year Bryan had appeared, lustily crying his anger at a cold, indifferent world. Serena was born two years later and from the time she could crawl, had followed Bryan like a shadow. Geoffrey had even indulged his wife's whim and allowed Serena to study with Bryan under the tutelage of a monk. The girl had a quick, seeking mind and soon outstripped her brother in their studies. Much to Bryan's chagrin, Serena also wheedled her way into his private lessons of horsemanship, self-defense, and battlefield tactics. Yes, Geoffrey reflected, both children had flourished well until that fateful day ten years before.

The year 1066—by the Christian calendar—had seen the bastard Duke William set foot on English soil, and with him came death and destruction. Geoffrey had fought at Hastings, and when the bloody battle was over, had surrendered his sword and sworn allegiance to William. This he did not out of fear, but for the sake of his family's preservation. As he saw old friends and comrades-in-arms hunted and killed like animals, Geoffrey grew more and more confident that his choice had been the best course for all concerned. And William had proved a just and fair ruler, not at all the cruel Norman the English Saxons had feared.

Geoffrey slumped into a chair near the fire. To what end had his plans come? His son rebelled at every turn, fighting both his father and the Norman rulers, and now Serena, his beautiful, treasured daughter, had disowned her family. Well, perhaps by evening Serena's temper would cool and she would reconsider her words, but Geoffrey could tell by the rigidity of Aurelia's body that she would not forget what Serena had said.

"Do not take Serena's words to heart, Aurelia," Geoffrey said. " 'Twas her anger speaking is all."

Aurelia turned to her husband. "She hates me, Geoffrey. She has ever since we were wed, and I'm not a favorite with Bryan, either. I had hoped that Serena would be pleased with the match I arranged, but I can see I've only given her more cause to dislike me. What a twit—she should be pleased to have a husband with such wealth, not like—" Aurelia stumbled suddenly to a halt, realizing her error. "I mean, that is . . . I . . ."

"You mean you wish you'd married a richer man, and perhaps a little younger as well, rather than my father, don't you, Aurelia?" Bryan stood in the entrance, his blue eyes flashing in the same way as his sister's. "Just why did you marry my father? Because you feared you'd die a shriveled up spinster? Or was it to better your life by lowering ours? I know all about your fine Norman family, madame. A grand name and title, but no money in the coffer to pay for their support. So it was decided you and your sister should marry wealth. Pity your sister's husband died so suddenly—well, perhaps she can find another soon. This one may even live long enough to give her a child if . . ."

"Enough, Bryan!" Geoffrey growled. "You will show your stepmother the respect she deserves."

Bryan bowed mockingly to Aurelia while he addressed his father. "I am, Father. Aurelia has always received the respect she demands from me. Your pardon, I came to ask Serena to go riding." He turned on his heel and strode from the room.

Aurelia poured herself another goblet of wine as Geoffrey slumped deeper into his chair and studied the fire.

Serena knelt on the stone floor surrounded by bolts of material, her old nurse Nellwyn unraveling more cloth for her young mistress's inspection. The anger had spent itself, leaving Serena with a sense of having been betrayed and used. Tears flooded her eyes and trailed miserably down her cheeks. How could her father do this to her? He had promised her! A pair of leather boots came into her blurred vision and Serena looked up into her brother's face.

"You'll ruin the velvet, Serena, have a care." Bryan teased gently. He crouched beside her and swept her hair from her face. "Why the tears, sister? Has our darling Aurelia upset you again?"

Serena shook her head miserably. "Not this time. Oh, Bryan, I'm to be married in a month." At his frown she began to cry again. "I don't even know the man who is to be my husband—I've never seen him! And of course Aurelia thinks the match is perfect." She sobbed bitterly.

"But Richard—" Bryan began.

Serena shook her head vehemently. "I have no dowry! Aurelia spent it all on . . . on this!" She spat as her hand indicated the room. "All I have are mother's dower lands to bring to my husband. But I shall have my revenge on Aurelia. She beggared me for these materials and she will pay dearly! She'll not have anything left to choose from in this room. What I do not use I'll destroy!"

"Serena, calm yourself!" Bryan shook her roughly. "Now tell me everything that's happened." Words poured over each other as Serena recounted the morning's events while Bryan listened in an angry silence. After a moment's silence he snorted in disgust. "Gyles the bastard. A Norman like the fair Aurelia. Well, no Norman pig will bed my sister; I'll see his head parted from his shoulders before he tries!"

"No, Bryan! 'Tis not that he is a Norman or even a bastard that matters most to me. 'Tis the fact I was not given a choice, nor was his proposal even discussed with me that rankles." Bryan rose, his hand still clenched on his sword hilt and anger glinting in his eyes. Serena tugged on his arm. "Bryan, what purpose will killing him serve? If you are caught, you would have to pay the wergeld. Could you face serving his family for the rest of your life?"

"If not me, then you, Serena. As his wife your lot will be little better than a slave. I have seen him, Serena. He has no respect for women. I have seen the bastard heartlessly ignore the following day the same woman he bedded the night before. He has no honor, Serena, and I'll not stand idly by and see you play his whore!"

"Bryan, that's enough! Even if he has no honor, I do. I told Lord Geoffrey I would honor the arrangement and I shall. Do you believe I shall cater to his every whim? If you do, you do not know me well. I shall be his wife, not his harlot! He is not wedding my mind, only my body. *Only my body,* Bryan, do you understand? He can take all the women he wishes, I shall not care. And if I am lucky, perhaps God has had the wisdom to make me barren, so that after a year or so I can return to my dower estate. Whatever, Lord Gyles will never possess me totally."

"And what of Richard? What part of you can he claim as his?"

Serena shook her head, the golden streaks in her hair catching and reflecting the sunlight from the open window. "None, Bryan. He has no . . . no right. He can claim nothing of mine and he dare not take what I do not offer. He will understand."

"Nay, Serena, he will not. He has claimed you as his own since we were children; far too long for him to give you up docilely. He may even contest Gyles's fitness as your husband."

Serena paled. "He must not, for should he win, even then I fear Father would simply marry me to someone else." She sighed and leaned out the window. "I wish I had been born a boy. Men have far more freedom than women. Why is it that simply because I wish to decide my own fate, everyone gets upset? I can rarely slip past Father or Aurelia in your old shirt and altered pair of leggings to ride as I wish. Instead I am forced to ride at a sedate pace, on a sidesaddle, and with an escort! I thought Aurelia would swoon the day she found me in my suit of mail, sword in my hand as I went to join you in your lessons. That night she lectured me for hours on 'the proper deportment of a lady' until I thought I would scream! Bah! I should have run her through! 'Twould have saved our family much in the way of sorrow."

Bryan laughed as he tugged a curl. "I begin to think I should pity the Norman bastard. Tell me, do you plan to sleep with your sword on your wedding night to insure he gives you the proper respect?"

Serena's blue eyes twinkled with mischief. "Nay, my dear brother, only with my sharpest dagger."

{ BOOK I }

A Marriage of Convenience

2

Snow fell gently from leaden skies as the procession from Broughton neared the castle of Camden. Serena shifted in her saddle and glanced over her shoulder to locate Bryan where he rode with Richard. Seeing her look, Bryan raised his lance in salute and gave his sister a reassuring smile. Richard looked at Serena with a naked anguish and longing that tore at her heart. Why had her father insisted upon Richard attending her wedding? A warning to them both, Serena guessed. Her father's—no, Lord Geoffrey's—way of telling them both that she now belonged to another man.

In the past month, Serena had kept every promise she had made herself. Her father she unfailingly addressed as Lord Geoffrey, although his eyes had pleaded with her for understanding. Serena's revenge upon Aurelia was complete when—after Serena had returned the key—she went to the storage room and found it empty. Aurelia's enraged shriek had echoed through the castle and shortly thereafter Serena was summoned to the chamber Lord Geoffrey shared with Aurelia.

"You little vixen!" Aurelia's voice had been shrill. "What have you done with my materials, the trimmings? The room is bare, there is not so much as a scrap left!"

Serena had given her stepmother an innocent look. "Whatever do you mean, Aurelia? I was given permission to take whatever I needed, since 'twas my money that purchased the lot." Serena spread her hands. "My need was great."

"But . . . but there were colors that would not suit you in that room, several bolts that were chosen purely to compliment my complexion. Surely you didn't use those?"

"Of course not." Serena had affected a wounded tone.

"Well, then, what did you do with them?"

"Do with them?" Serena chewed on a long fingernail as she pondered the question, then flashed Aurelia her sweetest smile. "Why, since the colors did not please me, I burned them."

Bryan had choked back a fit of laughter that was entirely missed in the face of Aurelia's anger.

"Burned them!" Aurelia fairly screamed the words.

Serena shrugged. "Everyone else seemed determined to decide the disposition of my dowry, so I thought it best to lend a hand." She smiled brightly. "Was there anything else you wished?" Lord Geoffrey shook his head. "Then if you will excuse me, I have some fittings left on my gowns, and packing I must attend."

A sneeze shook Serena from her reverie, and she gave her nurse a sympathetic smile. "Poor Nellwyn, this journey's not been easy on you, has it?"

"Ah, child, me old bones ache, and I be chilled through and that's a fact. How much farther before we reach that accursed Norman's castle, lamb?"

"Hush, Nellwyn, the accursed Norman will soon be my husband." Serena giggled, belaying the stern command of her words, for Nellwyn knew full well the extent of her charge's dislike of the forthcoming marriage. "If you'll raise your old head, I believe that's Camden directly in front of us."

The four towers of Camden rose high above the stone rectangle of the castle proper. The windows were tall, narrow slits made for the purpose of defense; an archer made an insignificant target when in position by the openings. From the top of the walls and towers long wooden shafts protruded. Their use—Serena knew at once—was to support huge vats of boiling oil, which could be poured down on attackers. Guards were spaced at even intervals along the walls, and all carried the English long-bow, that weapon having proven more effective at a long range than its Norman counterpart, the cross-bow. Serena's brow furrowed as she studied the castle. It was perfectly situated for defense as it sat upon the crest of a hill. Undoubtedly there were numerous wells within the walls, an armory, graneries, and buildings to house animals as well as the serfs who would flee from their farms to the safety the castle offered during time of war. Serena lifted her eyes and scanned the walls, seeking the unknown man who was to be her husband among the unfamiliar faces gazing down at the procession in rapt attention. Leaving Nellwyn to grumble about the discomfort of her saddle, Serena touched a heel to her horse's flank and rode back to join Bryan and Richard.

"Serena?" Richard covered her hand with his, as she joined him. "You've been avoiding me. We haven't had a chance to talk since your marriage was announced."

"I've not been avoiding you, Richard. I've been busy, 'tis all. Besides, what do we have to discuss?"

"Why did you accept his proposal? You know we often talked . . ."

"Don't, Richard, please! I'm sure Bryan has told you the matter was taken out of my hands, and your father would never have accepted me with such a small dowry. It doesn't matter now, anyway. Oh, don't make this worse than it is already. What's done is done, and there's no help for it!"

Her fears had suddenly caught up with her, and Serena sought refuge in Bryan's teasing banter.

"The one on her left is Bryan, Serena's brother. The other is Richard. I believe he hoped to wed the girl." The woman stepped from the window to begin dressing. "Go ahead, Gyles, take a look. Aren't you anx-

27

ious to catch a glimpse of your blushing bride?" she laughed and slipped the kirtle over her generous curves.

Gyles shrugged as he belted his sword over his tunic. "I'll see her soon enough, and from the description you gave me, the lass has little to commend her." But he crossed to the window and squinted dark green eyes against the glare of the snow, as if hoping to see through the hood that hid Serena's features from him. "There's little enough of her from what I can see. How old did you say she was, Beda?"

"According to Aurelia, she just passed her seventeenth birthday." Beda studied Gyles's profile. "A Saxon virgin for your wife, Gyles. My sister and I arranged everything beautifully, don't you agree?"

"You always seem to get everything you want, Beda. On that point I agree. It was Kier's bad luck that you didn't want him I suppose." Gyles's voice held a bitter undertone.

Beda rubbed her now fully clad body against Gyles. "Ah, Gyles, how could I settle for him once I set eyes on you? I'll never forget the day you came here, so cold and arrogant in your manner, so openly disdainful of us all. But there was a chink in your armor, brave knight, and I found it. Do not forget our agreement."

"Do you threaten me, Lady Beda?" Gyles raised his eyebrows.

Beda's hand caressed the broad expanse of his chest. "Threaten? Never that, Gyles. I mean only to warn you. I doubt the fair Lady Serena will take kindly to having your bastard son raised under this roof."

Gyles's hand caught in Beda's white-blond hair, as he pulled her head back. "Bastard or not, he is my son and he goes where I do. No one threatens Alan or mistreats him."

"Of course, Gyles, I understand. It was Kier's misfortune that he chose to teach Alan a bastard's place in this world when he did. Gyles, you are hurting me!" This last emerged as a gasp.

Gyles's hand had tightened in her hair, briefly, but

now Gyles pushed her from him roughly, as if he could no longer bear her presence. "I do not remember Kier's death, I do not remember killing him as I've told you before!"

"I know, Gyles. That is the basis for our . . . arrangement, is it not? I have sworn that my husband drowned after he was struck by a tree limb. In return for that, you have agreed to see to my personal . . . ah . . . contentment and well-being. 'Tis a fair agreement, Gyles, we both have what we most desire. You have your freedom, your son, and now a wife; and I at last have a man to fill my bed instead of a pleading jackass. I am even willing to share you with your wife. Young as she is, I doubt she will think it amiss that you do not seek her company every night."

Gyles's green eyes clouded. "You cannot really expect me to play the part of your stud after my marriage, Beda. The idea is absurd."

Beda paused at the door that joined their bedchambers, her eyes flashing contempt. "But I do expect it, my handsome bastard knight. And if you don't do exactly as I say, I will see to it that the hangman stretches your neck. Then what will become of your son?"

Serena drew her mount to a halt and watched the tall, slim man descending the steps. His shoulders and chest were broad and tapered down to a flat belly, slim hips, and muscular thighs. His walk was steady and relentless, like a cat stalking its prey, one hand resting easily on the hilt of his sword. The thick, black hair glittered darkly against the white of the snow that fell upon his head, and his brilliant green eyes seemed to look through rather than at his guests. Serena gave a small shiver beneath her blue velvet cloak when she saw the small scar that curved down from the middle of his cheek to the corner of his mouth. Dark eyebrows the same color as his hair arched slightly at Serena as if he could sense her scrutiny, but she could not be sure, because at that moment Gyles strode forward to greet Geoffrey.

"What say you, sister, do you find the groom to your liking?" Bryan's voice was low, but Serena caught the hint of anger in it.

"He's so old, Bryan!" Serena murmured in dismay.

"Nay, Serena, only one and thirty. Still young enough to keep a new wife flat on her back in bed, I've no doubt."

"You're being crude, Bryan, and I'll not stand for it. Either keep your untoward comments to yourself or go away from me. You'd better keep that wineskin hidden. You know Aurelia doesn't approve. I have enough to worry abo—" Serena's voice died in her throat when she saw Gyles and Geoffrey approaching.

Bryan noted his sister's pallor and its cause and threw Gyles an angry look. Which is this one, thought Gyles, rejected lover or protective brother? He sneered silently as he watched Bryan lift Serena from her horse and set her upon the ground. Apparently he was not to be allowed to touch his future wife more than necessary before the wedding. Serena dropped into a deep curtsy when Gyles halted before her.

"Rise, Lady Serena. Welcome to Camden." Gyles extended his hand to help Serena to her feet and found himself staring into the loveliest face he had ever seen. Huge blue eyes generously fringed with long, sooty lashes looked at him unwaveringly, the delicately shaped rosebud mouth was slightly parted to reveal even white teeth and the corners of her lips turned upward into a small smile.

"Thank you, m'lord." Serena strove to keep her voice even as she gazed entranced into cloudy green eyes. The man had a magnetism about him that was undeniable. Her cold hand was enveloped by his large warm one and Serena found herself wondering what it would be like to be securely held against that broad chest surrounded by strong arms. Yet . . . she felt or sensed that he was angry, but at what . . . or was it whom?

Aware that all eyes were focused upon them, Gyles dropped Serena's hand and addressed her father. Serena turned and stroked the soft muzzle of her horse, all too conscious of Aurelia's high-pitched laughter floating back to her from the entrance of the castle. A hand grasped the bridle and Serena looked up into Richard's tightly drawn face.

"Serena, I—" Richard stopped abruptly, an apology in his brown eyes. He quickly walked away.

Serena was puzzled but relieved at Richard's sudden departure. Her nerves were strained to their limits and she feared that if Richard continued with his entreaty and imploring looks she would burst into tears. What she couldn't see was the warning look Gyles had bestowed upon Richard while they talked. Arranging a tryst with her lover already! Women were all alike, harlots the lot of them! This young girl for all her innocent looks was just like the rest. All the women he'd bedded had been married and none—least of all Beda—felt any guilt at cuckolding their husbands. Well, his wife would not put horns on his head, of that he would make certain. Gyles went to Serena's side and drew her hand through his arm and led her to the castle entrance.

"I'm sure you must be tired and chilled after your journey. I'm afraid there are people you must meet before you can retire to your chambers. You will be expected to attend the evening meal, but you needn't stay for the entertainment afterward if your weariness proves too great."

Serena glanced up at Gyles, wondering at the harsh note in his voice. Now what have I done? He speaks as if he hates me and we just met.

The four women on the stairs turned as a body and fixed their eyes on Serena. Aurelia's sister, Beda, was simple to identify by her coloring and her resemblance to Aurelia. The other two women were the old lord's wife, Lydia, and his daughter, Mara. It was plain to see that both resented Gyles's presence and the fact that he was now lord of Camden. But Serena was sure that she had missed something in the exchange between Beda and Gyles. There was a certain predatory gleam in Beda's pale blue eyes when she looked at Gyles, and he treated her with a mocking formality that hinted of intimacy.

"Serena is tired, I'm sure. Mara, show her to her

chambers." Gyles made the merest sketch of a bow and turned to join Lord Geoffrey.

Mara threw a look of disgust at her half-brother's back as he disappeared into the castle. "You will have to excuse Gyles, he's dreadfully lacking in manners. But you'll find that out for yourself." Serena said nothing, so Mara continued chattering as she led Serena through imposing, high-ceilinged halls and corridors. "I really don't know what Father was thinking of. 'Twas bad enough when Kier was alive, but now that Gyles is lord of the manor he's positively insufferable. I've had your chambers made up in the women's quarter; you have a beautiful view of the lands, and 'tis one of the coolest rooms in the summer."

"That's very nice, Mara, but I thought . . . well, I shall be sharing Gyles's chambers starting tomorrow." Serena's cheeks burned hotly and she avoided Mara's gaze.

Mara threw Serena an odd look. "Oh, yes, of course. Well, we shall see. In the meantime, Gyles said these were to be your rooms. Here we are."

The door to the chamber was open, and Serena's breath caught in her throat. A fire crackled in the huge fireplace, the large bed was covered with an emerald green velvet that reminded Serena of Gyles's eyes; tapestries hung on the walls, and wardrobe chests lined the outer wall. Serena dropped her cloak onto one of the chairs by the fire, scuffing the rich fur pelt beneath her feet as she did so.

"There is a private chapel in here." Mara opened a door and pointed. "There is a friar in the village so you can make arrangements for him to say Mass or hear your confession at your convenience. Is there anything you wish? No? Well then, I'll see you at the meal. One of the servants will come for you. I suggest you try to rest; you will need it before the night is over." With a faint smile Mara withdrew, the door closing softly behind her.

Serena threw herself upon the bed and pouted at the ornately carved headboard. What kind of a household

32

was this? Mara and her mother obviously hated Gyles; there was a strange undercurrent between Beda and Gyles; and she, Serena, was to marry this cold, remote man. Gyles himself, well, that looked like another problem. Was he attracted to her, Serena wondered? The top of her head barely reached the middle of his chest, and she knew it would take little effort on his part to lift her in his arms and carry her to his bed. Serena's eyes widened at the thought. What was she thinking of?! How could she even consider. . . . She didn't even know Gyles, and, yet, what would it be like to have that lean body pressed firmly against her own? Would those green eyes soften when he gazed down at her? How would his lips feel as they played freely over her own mouth? Enough! Serena's mind screamed at her. Rest now; time enough later, to sort out your thoughts.

The great hall was filled with the smell of roasting meat and the sound of the knights' ribald laughter as they speculated about Gyles's future wife.

"I've heard she's little more than a mite." One grizzled veteran laughed, and at Gyles's silence and raised eyebrows he continued. "White as linen, too, one of those fine ladies who are afraid the sun might damage their precious skin. All in all, she doesn't sound like a tasty morsel for you." The surrounding men laughed in agreement as Gyles's preference in women was well known among his men, but one by one the laughter died in their throats.

Serena waited at the bottom of the stairs, her head held high upon the delicate column of her throat as she fixed the source of the jest with an unwavering stare. Her pale blue gown clung to the unmistakable curves of her body and accented the creamy texture of her skin. Serena's blue eyes shot sparks at the man as she advanced to the table.

"Pray go on with your story, sir knight, I am sure you had not reached the most interesting part." Although the words were sweetly spoken there was a challenge in Serena's tone and the man reddened and dropped his eyes to the table. A teasing grin played at the corners of Serena's mouth. "Ah, my good knight, did your mother never warn you that a tiny dog will leave the largest bite? But rest assured, if you are as brave with your sword as with your words, I shall never fear for my protection here at Camden."

The circle of men guffawed loudly and the abashed knight—Serena learned later his name was Edward—loudest of all; at that moment pledging silently to protect the tiny mistress from any harm.

" 'Tis your plan to win the loyalty of my knights with your womanly charms, Serena?" Gyles's eyes had turned cloudy in his anger and Serena shrank inwardly. "Beware then, for not all men are easy victims to a pair of swaying hips and rounded breasts."

Serena's eyes widened in astonishment. "M'lord, you do me a great injustice! I seek no one's loyalty or love, for that must be freely given or it means naught. 'Twas not my wish to marry you, for that was taken out of my hands, but I wish only to make the best of the arrangement. So *you* beware, m'lord, for not all women fall at the feet of an arrogant, strutting stallion!" Serena whirled from him to cross the hall and stand between Bryan and Richard, her color high and her temper flaring.

She had left his side so quickly that Gyles had no time to give voice to the sarcastic reply that was on his tongue. Serena was not the insipid creature Beda had led him to believe; she had pride, a temper, and a cutting edge to her tongue. Somewhere in the back of Gyles's mind a warning rang out that his wife would not allow herself to be used as a mindless pawn. Even now her back was presented to him, and Gyles watched as she tossed off a goblet of wine without a pause. Gyles smiled inwardly; Beda had planned to retain control of the household after his marriage, but he had the feeling little Serena would change that if she had a mind to.

"Serena, what happened? Gyles looks like he's ready to run someone through." Richard studied her angry face. "Did he insult you?" Richard's hand dropped to his sword.

"Oh, for God's sake, Richard, don't be stupid! What are you planning to do, challenge him? He'd cut you down in a trice and then sit down to his meal. Ah, this whole situation is impossible!" Serena's knuckles whitened around the goblet.

"Serena," Richard murmured as he drew her free hand to his lips. "Let me—"

"Stop it, Lord Gyles is coming." Bryan deftly removed Serena's hand from Richard's. "I've no desire to see my sister made a widow before she's a wife, nor to lose my best friend. Serena, behave yourself," Bryan warned and then both he and Richard were gone.

Serena's eyes narrowed wickedly, but she kept her back defiantly turned to Gyles's approach. She sensed his presence behind her and knew her defiance served only to anger him further, but she needed time to compose herself. If he hoped to make a fool of her before his household and guests, he would be mistaken. Serena drew a deep breath; her temper was now under control and she would show Gyles just how sweet and charming she could be if it killed her! What Serena didn't see was the possessive look in Gyles's green eyes as he watched the retreating back of her one-time suitor.

"If you are ready, Serena, it has been a long day for my men and their hunger is great." Gyles looked down and his gaze was immediately trapped by soft blue eyes. He became suddenly aware of Serena, the gentle curves of her body, the creamy texture of her skin, the subtle fragrance that assailed his senses with more force than a battering ram.

"But of course, m'lord," Serena said demurely. "How thoughtless of me to delay the festivities." She offered her hand. "Will you lead me to sup, m'lord? I should like to learn more about your family and household lest in my ignorance I offend." Serena slanted a glance at Gyles from beneath her lush brown lashes as she glided by his side.

"Hah!" Gyles barked as he handed her into a chair. "I've no doubt, Serena, that you care not whom you offend."

Serena pouted. "Surely, m'lord, you mistake me for someone else? Beda perhaps!" The last had a slightly malicious note, as Serena had already felt the bite of Beda's tongue when they met. She turned from him and bent her attention to Richard who had managed to seat himself beside her.

The meal did little to improve Gyles's spirits, as he was caught between Beda's mocking looks and the fact that Serena ignored him completely in favor of the Saxon. When the last of the meal was cleared away, Gyles realized that Serena was no longer at his side but had wandered with Richard and Bryan to examine the weapons that decorated one wall. He watched with rising ire as first one, then another, and then another of his knights began to flock to her like moths to a flame, and soon he could hear her gentle laughter bubbling over their heads.

"Your bride is most charming, Gyles. Aren't you going to fight your way to her side to win her favor?" Beda's voice was a silken purr as she watched him closely.

"She could charm the skin from a snake," Gyles muttered. "I've no intention of joining her retinue; what's one man more or less to a woman of her kind."

"Poor Richard, I fear he may never get over his loss." Aurelia's voice was a duplicate of her sister's. "Have you noticed, Lord Gyles, how he hangs on her every word? I warned my dear husband many times of the danger of allowing those two easy access to each other, but Serena has always managed to have her way. Why, she even swore to Geoffrey that Richard had done no more than kiss her. Of course, I never believed her."

Gyles ignored the two women's innuendos, concentrating instead on watching Serena and Richard. Richard's bright golden head bent often to Serena, yet as far as Gyles could tell they exchanged no yearning glances. Richard treated her with the respect she was due; and while it was plain to see they held each other in tender regard, neither acted with an intimacy born of sharing a bed. So Serena was an innocent, ignorant of a man's touch and body; and he, Gyles, who had privately sworn never to marry, would soon take her to wife. His finger absently traced the scar on his face as he watched the sparkling creature across the room. As if she sensed his scrutiny, Serena's eyes found him and she stood rooted to the spot, unable to move or speak as those brilliant green eyes impaled her while Gyles walked slowly toward her.

" 'Tis time you were abed, Serena," Gyles mocked. "For I wish you well rested for tomorrow. I vow you will get little sleep tomorrow night."

Serena's eyes flashed but she had no time to retort because Gyles was already propelling her up the steps to her bedchamber. He stopped outside her door but made no move to release her, only tightened his already painful grasp on her wrist.

"There was no need to be so crude, m'lord. If you felt I acted improperly there are other ways to remove me from a situation such as that. And would you mind releasing my arm before you break it!"

Gyles complied immediately and with such force that Serena fell against the door. Gyles raised his hands to the wood on either side of her, his look cold and bone-chilling.

"I ought to break your neck for the way you've behaved. Now listen well and remember: This castle is mine, these lands are mine, and you are mine!! You belong to me—or you will tomorrow—and no one else! Do you understand?"

"I don't belong to you! I'm not a possession! I—"

Gyles's large hands came down on her shoulders with bruising force, and he shook her so hard that Serena's vision blurred. "Do you understand?" Gyles bellowed.

"Y-yes," she stuttered, suddenly afraid of the look in his eyes.

"Good." Gyles released her and opened the door to her chambers. "Sleep well, Serena."

Serena slammed the door behind her with as much force as she could muster, and as an afterthought she petulantly dropped the bolt as well. The audacity of the man. Possession indeed! He grew more arrogant by the minute. Serena pulled off her gown and jerked the ribbons from her hair. She stood before the fire clad only in her shift and began to comb the tangles from the gleaming brown and gold mass. Reluctantly she admitted that perhaps she had forced Gyles too far with her outrageous flirting tonight, but there was something in his manner that caused her temper to flare the minute he appeared. Besides, he had no kind words to spare for her either. All of his attention was bent upon the Lady Beda. Serena slipped into the bed and stared into the flickering shadows on the wall. This would be the last night she slept alone, probably for a very long time, because Gyles would no doubt expect her to produce as many sons as she was capable. Serena drifted into a restless sleep that was tormented by a pair of green eyes and a face that bore a wicked scar, while across the castle the occupants of two adjoining rooms were wide awake.

Gyles rose from the bed—magnificent in his nakedness—and stood before the fire. He could feel Beda's gaze on him like a living thing; predatory in its nature, always demanding more and more and yet never satisfied.

"Which chamber have you chosen, Beda? 'Twould not do for me to stumble blindly around the women's quarters in search of you."

"My dear Gyles, I have no intention of moving to another chamber. Let Serena keep Lydia and Mara company, for I have no desire to do so. I have occupied the same room since I came here as a bride and it is still mine as I am Lady Beda of Camden."

"Only until the vows are spoken tomorrow," Gyles stated softly. "I doubt my new wife would take kindly to our having an adjoining chamber, although it would be easier on me. At least I wouldn't have to prowl the castle as I ran from one bed to the other. By the way, does my wife come first, or were you planning to alternate nights?"

Beda had left the bed but now paused on her way to her chamber. "Really, Gyles, at times such as these your lack of breeding does show. You really are quite vulgar—and common."

Gyles shrugged and returned to his bed, wrinkling his nose in disgust as he found Beda's perfume still lingered on the pillow. What a trial. Beset by Beda on one side and Serena on the other, the only bright spot in his life right now was Alan. At the age of three the boy enjoyed tagging along behind his father, constantly asking questions: "Why?" and "What's that?". Just wait until Serena discovered his illegitimate son! That would send her into a rage. She really should have been allowed to marry Richard, Gyles mused. At least they seemed to get along with one another. Good God, what did he need a wife for, anyway. How had he allowed himself to become so entangled in Beda's web? There had to be some solution to these problems; his own ego would not allow him to be treated as if he were a stallion put out to stud, his only worth to be found in his body. Gyles would not allow himself to be used in that manner.

Her wedding day dawned dull and overcast, with the sun only occasionally breaking through grey clouds. Serena's spirits sank even deeper; she nervously paced her chamber. Pausing to smooth her gown or pat her hair she waited to descend to the guests gathered below. At intervals she alternately raged at her fate or meekly accepted it, and this inner conflict showed on her face. Serena's brows were drawn into a frown and her lips curved downward in sullen resignation. Nellwyn entered and found her young mistress gazing at the fire, while one dainty foot beat a steady tattoo on the stone floor.

"Well, lamb, 'tis time. They all be waiting for ye down below, and yer husband has a most anxious look about him. No doubt he'll keep ye with babe for many years to come, and I'll have me hands full raising yer wee ones. Best thing for ye, lamb, 'twill put an end to yer wild and boyish ways, so ye'll be forced to act like a young lady should."

"Perhaps he will be incapable of giving me children. How then will you earn your keep, Nellwyn?" Serena retorted.

The nurse shot her mistress a sideways glance. "Aye, I think he'll give ye many babes, Serena. He has the look about him. Now come, they all be waiting."

It was all Serena could do not to turn and run when she entered the great hall and saw Gyles calmly accepting the congratulations of the wedding guests. When he saw her he dared to grin at her in that superior manner that made her want to slap his handsome, arrogant face. But as she remembered his harsh words about her being one of his possessions, Serena raised her chin a notch in determination. Very well, she could be just as charming and nonchalant as he! Obviously the marriage meant little or nothing to him the way he was flirting with Beda. His own sister-in-law! That was too much! Serena made her way to Gyles and slipped between him and Beda before either of them could protest. Beda gave Serena a look that could have killed her and Gyles's eyes grew quite cold until they looked like polished green stones. Serena ignored him and focused instead on Beda.

"You will excuse us, will you not? Bryan wishes to share a bit of wine with us before the ceremony." Serena's voice was quite sweet, but her eyes shot daggers at Beda who turned and stamped off. Serena watched with satisfaction.

"Ah, Serena, are you jealous of me already? I had not thought so by your actions last night." Gyles mocked her.

Serena gave him her most dazzling smile as she tucked her hand through his arm. "I assure you, m'lord, I care not with whom you dally, but *not* on my wedding day. Today you will play the part of a loving, devoted husband or I shall make such a scene as you have never witnessed, I promise!"

Gyles's scar showed white against the rest of his face. "I see. And you?"

Serena laughed softly. "But I am your most loving and devoted wife, have I not told you so? I see I have not; then allow me to show you." She raised herself on tiptoes and pulled Gyles's face down to hers to place a gentle kiss upon his lips. "I see my kiss displeases you, m'lord, but you must understand I have had little experience. Will you teach me later, m'lord?"

Something flared in Gyles's eyes and he growled, "No, Serena, by God I shall teach you now!" His arms went around her as he pulled Serena's delicate form from the floor into a crushing embrace. Gyles's lips burned against hers and she gasped when his tongue forced its way into her mouth, but try as she would, Serena could not escape the painful hold Gyles had on her. Then, suddenly, she stopped struggling and instead lay passively against Gyles's hard body and let him do as he pleased; while into the back of her mind crept the thought that the kiss would be even more enjoyable if she responded. But before she could, Gyles loosed his arms and deposited Serena back on the floor, realizing that if he continued he would not be able to face his guests for some time. But while Gyles's face showed no emotion to reflect his thoughts, Serena stood gazing up at him, her face slightly flushed, her eyes soft and hazy. She felt dizzy and breathless; what had happened to her? Richard's kisses had never affected her like this, but then Richard had never dared to kiss her in this manner, either. Of a sudden, Serena was aware that the hall had quieted and all eyes were focused on them. Her color heightened all the more.

Gyles grinned mockingly as he bent toward her to tease one of the curls that hung down Serena's back. "You learn quickly, Serena, I think I shall enjoy this night above most, for you are proving your willingness to become my possession."

Serena's lips parted in silent rage but before she could regain her voice, Gyles had led her to kneel before the priest to recite the vows that would bind her to him for the rest of her life. Tears sprang to her eyes as Serena watched her young girl's hopes of a love match die when Gyles's voice rang clear and strong through the hall. It was over. A few words spoken and she was Gyles's wife, his property, with no will or mind of her own. A thing he owned and that was all. Gyles frowned as he studied Serena, watching her blink back the tears that stood in those clear blue eyes. Now what was the matter with the woman? By the saints but she was unpredictable; her moods changed faster than any woman he had ever known. One minute she was fighting him tooth and nail and the next she looked as if she would burst into tears if he but looked at her.

But Serena had regained her composure and when she took her seat beside her husband at the table, she was able to smile graciously at her guests. It was when she caught Richard watching her with such obvious longing and anguish written on his face that Serena murmured something under her breath and left the table. Gyles stiffened in anger and he made to follow her, but Beda pulled him back to his chair and refused to loosen her grip. It was from Beda's side that Gyles watched with growing rage his wife's progress through the hall. The younger men seemed all too eager to claim the one kiss that was their right and Serena was whirled from one pair of arms to another until she collapsed dizzily against Richard. Without a word his lips claimed hers in a hotly passionate kiss and when Serena forced herself from his grasp she was trembling.

"Don't—don't ever do that again! You have no right—"

"I did once, Serena, I had the right to claim all of you once, and I should have. Remember the day we went riding alone? I could have taken you then and you wouldn't have stopped me. But for your sake I held back, I wanted you as my wife in name before you became my wife in fact. I should have bedded you and given you a child, then your father would have been forced to allow us to marry. Instead, I am forced to watch a bastard fondle you and share the same roof as he, while he spreads your thighs and takes your maidenhead!"

"Do you think I do not wish it otherwise? Men!" Serena spat. "You're all alike, thinking only of a woman as she is in bed! I have feelings too, I have a mind as well as a body, but no one seems to realize that." At the agony in his eyes Serena relented. "Forgive me, dearest

42

Richard, but 'tis done. There's nothing we can do. You will soon marry and we will both build new lives."

Richard shook his head. "No! If I cannot marry you, I shall have no wife."

"You're being foolish, Richard. We must live out our lives as best we can. You'll find someone else, someone you can care for, I know you will."

"But what of you, Serena? Married to a man you do not love, what of your life?"

Serena cast a hurried glance toward Gyles. "My life is with him now. I can only trust in God and pray that He will grant us some small measure of happiness. I must go now, Richard. I will rise early enough to see you off on the morrow."

The afternoon melted into evening, but its passing was barely noticed within the castle. There the revelers ate, drank, and were entertained by a traveling group of mummers who performed magic, juggling, and some fortune telling.

" 'Tis said the old hag's predictions often come true, Serena." Gyles bent to his wife. "Why not allow her to look into your future."

Serena shook her head. "My fortune was told once before, and today put the lie to those words. I shall not allow myself to believe in childish fantasies any longer, but will make my own destiny however I may."

"You are far too young to harbor such bitterness."

Serena turned to gaze into her husband's eyes. "I am not bitter, m'lord, merely practical. My life was altered and I had no voice in the matter, but I have accepted that. What else is there to be done? I shall make the best of what God sees fit to grant me, more than this I dare not hope for."

Gyles did not reply, so both returned their attention to the juggler in front of them. The evening grew late and finally Nellwyn motioned to Serena that it was time for her to retire, which she did to many a ribald comment and raucous laugh. Once in her chamber she was quickly stripped of her gown and in its place was put a nightgown of fine linen. Nellwyn removed the ribbons from Serena's hair and brushed it until it flowed about her like a curtain of brown-gold velvet. As Nellwyn escorted her to Gyles's chamber, Serena kept her mind blank, trying not to dwell on how Gyles would use her.

Once inside the door, with Nellwyn no longer at her side, Serena's eyes and thoughts flew to the bed. She walked hesitantly to it and tested the softness first of the ticking and then the pillows. Serena paced to the windows, but the shutters were closed and barred and as she had no desire to let in the winter chill, she found nothing there to distract her. At last she poured herself a goblet of mulled wine and curled in a chair by the fire to study the flames. I can but hope he will be gentle, Serena thought, and if he finds me willing to act the part of a loved wife, perhaps he will not be displeased with me. I will honor with all my being the vows exchanged between us and try to bring him some measure of happiness.

Having made this promise to herself, Serena's heart lightened. Their first kiss had been most enjoyable—so perhaps Gyles was also skilled enough to deny her body the pain that accompanied the consummation of a marriage. Unconsciously, Serena found herself listening for the sound of her husband's footsteps, but Gyles walked so softly that she didn't hear him approach, and when the door was thrown open and he entered the room, Serena flew from her chair. Gyles gave her a brief glance before he closed the door. When he turned back to her, Serena smiled timidly.

"Would you like some wine, m'lord?" At his nod she hurried to bring him a goblet, completely unaware of the appreciative light that came into his eyes as she stood silhouetted in front of the fire. Her body was clearly outlined by the flickering light, and Gyles was as tantalizingly reminded of her daintiness as if she stood nude before him.

"Have you decided to become my obedient possession, Serena? You are much changed from the defiant lass who supped with me." Gyles studied her as she returned to the chair.

"I am your wife, m'lord," Serena said simply.

"To do with as I will?" Gyles's tone had become harsher.

Serena fought down the fear rising inside her and nodded.

"So you will then agree to be my whore, Serena?" Gyles sneered. "Having been purchased by wedding vows will you come whenever I command? Will you do whatever I tell you to? Will you bear my sons every year without complaint? You should give me strong heirs and beautiful daughters, although 'tis to be hoped they will not inherit their mother's sharp tongue!"

Serena's eyes flashed blue sparks and she rose defiantly from her chair. "How dare you speak to me like this! I am not a brood mare you've purchased nor some harlot you've found for a night's dalliance!"

"You are my wife, sworn to obey me!" Gyles's voice rose.

"Your wife, yes, your whore, never!" Serena's tone matched his.

"You will do as I say!"

"Only if I am so inclined!"

"You are a stubborn bitch!"

"And you are an arrogant bastard!" Serena's hand flew to her mouth and her eyes widened in dismay. "M'lord, I—I'm sorry, I did not mean—"

Gyles's rough voice cut her off. "You did not seek to wed me, but did you ever consider that I may not have cared to wed you? If I had had a choice, I most certainly would not have taken *you* to wife! You will not obey me in anything else, but in this you shall. Get out. You may be my wife, but the thought of consummating this marriage revolts me."

"My goodness, don't tell me you two have done nothing but argue?"

Serena gasped and whirled toward the sound of Beda's voice. The older woman stood in a doorway Serena had not noticed before; clothed in a filmy night-gown, her blond hair unbound, Beda's appearance was angelic. Serena's eyes grew larger as Beda continued into the room and proceeded to make herself comfortable while Gyles merely shrugged and seated himself by the fire. Serena looked back at her husband, then at Beda, and as realization began to dawn, her stomach twisted and churned, the bile rising in her throat. The silence grew between the three until Serena thought she would go mad. No wonder he had not been eager to find a wife!

"You—" Serena choked out, "you're disgusting. Both of you." Serena flew to the door, wrenching it open with such force that it slammed against the inner wall of the chamber; she fled through the hall to her room. Once there, she bent over the chamber pot and retched until she was so weak her legs threatened to give way. To think she had been ready to offer herself to him, had actually resigned herself to being his wife. Serena stumbled to the bed and threw herself full length upon it. How could she have been so blind? The looks exchanged between Gyles and Beda; the way she clung to his arm and managed to be at his side whenever she could. Why hadn't she noticed earlier—she, Serena, who had always been so sensitive to other's feelings? Had Kier known he was being cuckolded by his own half-brother? How sickening; not only was she to be an unloved wife, but unwanted and untouched as well. In an unusual fit of self-pity, Serena buried her face in her pillow and cried.

"Was there a reason for your unwanted appearance, Beda, or are you just here to cause trouble?" Gyles had not stirred from his chair, yet a more sensitive person would have sensed the suppressed violence in him. His fingers tightened around the goblet and the scar on his cheek whitened beneath the bronze of his skin. "You didn't expect me to play the devoted lover tonight, I hope, because I won't."

"I hadn't really thought of it," Beda lied. "But

46

since your bride seems to have flown . . ." She left the thought unfinished.

Indeed Serena has flown, Gyles thought. Why had he felt that sudden urge to lash out at her—to hurt her and destroy her pride? If Beda hadn't interrupted them, Gyles knew he would have taken Serena by force—if force was necessary—in order to wound her more deeply. But for a brief moment he now remembered, there had been a willingness, almost a curiosity in Serena's eyes when she looked at him. And Gyles had found that the sight of her scantily clad body had excited him more than any other woman's. Beda came to stand before him, and Gyles felt disgusted with her, their arrangement, and himself.

"Well?" Beda's voice had turned husky and she arched her back, displaying her breasts to Gyles's view.

"Return to your chamber, Beda. I cannot find it in my heart or body to bed you this night—or any other night for that matter. Seek your pleasures elsewhere, for I will no longer supply them."

Beda's eyes narrowed. " 'Tis your choice, of course, but two things I would remind you of. Serena will not consent to share your bed after what she witnessed here— if that is what you are thinking. And what of Alan? What will happen to him when it is discovered his father is a murderer?"

"My son will be cared for, so you can no longer hold that knife to my throat." The bluff he had been considering these past weeks suddenly found its way to Gyles's tongue. "As for myself, if your accusation should reach the king's ear, I shall tell the truth and trust in his fairness. I'm tired of your game, Beda, and I will play it no longer. If I were you, I would retire to my dower estate, as befits a widow."

"Are you ordering me to leave, Gyles?"

"I'm telling you what would be best for everyone concerned. You're still young enough to marry again, surely—"

"I'm sure it would be most convenient for you if

I left Camden," Beda spat, "but I won't. I have no desire to remarry, either. So I'm afraid you'll have to put up with me. I won't move to another chamber; we'll see how long it takes before you come crawling back to me." Beda flounced from the room.

The fire had burned down to embers before Gyles finally found sleep in his large, empty bed.

3

"You don't know how our lives changed when *he* came here. When my husband was alive—" Lydia's voice droned on.

Serena sighed inwardly as Lydia began her usual vitriolic tirade against Gyles. She bent her head over the tapestry she was making and wondered again at the hatred that seemed to permeate this household. Among the family Gyles had no allies, for it appeared that even his relationship with Beda had changed in the four months Serena had been his wife. Beda still found every opportunity to seek him out, but Gyles seemed uninterested and lost no time in setting her from him. As a result, Beda's tongue was sharper than ever and Serena often felt its malicious edge. What she had done to deserve Beda's hatred Serena did not know, for she had not usurped Beda's position in any way; neither within the hall nor with Gyles. Oh well, at least here in Lydia's chambers she was safe from another unwarranted attack, as it seemed Beda had never and would not condescend to visit her mother-in-law.

Serena found herself longing for the peacefulness of Broughton; even when Aurelia was at her worst, Serena had been able to escape by seeking out Bryan's company. Here she had no one except Nellwyn who was no comfort at all since she detested Camden more than Serena did herself. What will become of me? Serena wondered desperately. Am I to spend the rest of my days like Lydia, sewing on tapestries that will never be finished much less grace a wall? Will I never be loved or have children to hold and comfort and love? Serena looked down and saw to her disgust that she had ruined the piece she was working on. In despair she folded away her sewing and rose to leave.

"Why, Serena, where are you going? I was just about to order a light repast served to us here. 'Tis so much nicer than having to dine in the hall with *him*." Lydia's face wore a bemused expression as Serena opened the door.

"No—thank you. I have been thinking of planting a herb garden, and on my walk yesterday I noticed some old flower beds. If no one minds, I should like to put them to use." Serena looked from Mara to Lydia and noted the expressions of distaste that came to their faces. It was obvious that neither cared in the least to dirty their hands with such menial labor. That was all well and good; they could stay in their rooms and play the martyrs and rot, but she was not content to spend the rest of her days in that manner!

Once in her room, Serena donned her oldest gown and caught back her hair with a bit of ribbon. From one of the chests she removed a finely tooled leather-bound book and from another chest a tray of seeds. Descending to the kitchen she obtained the tools she would need whereupon she slipped as unobtrusively as possible past the knights who were entering the hall to partake of the midday meal. When at last she reached the dilapidated flower beds, the warm spring air and sun had revived her spirits to the point that she set about cleaning the neglected earth with a vengeance. Serena barely noted the passing of the sun overhead as she pulled out weeds and turned the soil with a hoe to expose the rich black earth below. The soil was warm and felt pleasant to the touch. With her long, slender fingers she deftly poked shallow holes into which the seeds could be deposited.

Suddenly, Serena felt that she was being watched, and she pivoted swiftly on her knees to find a small boy studying her curiously.

"Hello." Alert hazel eyes sparkled as a shy grin spread over his face. "I'm Alan. What's your name?"

Serena released the breath she realized she had been holding. Had she really expected her husband to seek her out? "Serena."

"Oh! so you're Lady Serena." She was just about to ask what he meant when, in the way of all children, Alan's mind went directly to what fascinated him. With a stubby forefinger he pointed behind her. "What's that?"

With the back of her hand, Serena pushed back a tendril of hair that had tumbled over her forehead and smiled. "I'm planting a garden."

"Are you going to grow carrots? Horses like carrots, you know."

"This isn't that kind of garden. I'm planting seeds that will make people well."

"Oh." Alan's face was crestfallen. "Is somebody sick?"

Serena laughed. "No, Alan, at least not that I know of. But if someone does fall ill, then I may be able to help them. I'll tell you what." Serena continued as she saw Alan was still disappointed in her choice of gardens. "If you will help me, we will plant some carrots, but only if you promise to take me along when you feed the horses."

Alan nodded in vigorous agreement and fell to his knees beside Serena. He was like a pup digging for a bone and had soon covered himself as well as Serena with dirt. When all the beds had been worked, Serena retired to the shade of a tree with Alan close on her heels. She wiped her hands on her skirt, and Alan following suit, cleaned his on his shirt. He watched eagerly as Serena opened her book and began flipping through its pages. His face grew puzzled as he watched her.

"What's that?"

The question had been asked so often that afternoon that Serena wanted to laugh, but seeing Alan's serious expression she answered in the same vein.

" 'Tis a book that I've kept since I was a child. I've written down what herbs are used for what ailments, the growing times for each, and what they need to grow well." Serena flipped a few more pages. "Back here are different potions for fevers and wounds and the like." Serena offered him the book and Alan accepted it eagerly, his hands caressing the leather reverently.

"My father says that when I am older I will learn to read and write."

Serena smiled but said nothing. The boy was bright, intelligent; but he had no chance for an education as the child of a serf. What a waste! But . . . an idea grew in the back of her mind. Perhaps Gyles would allow her to keep the child as a page, and that way she could see to his education. Serena dropped an assortment of seeds in Alan's chubby hands, and they returned to their work.

"Where do you live, Alan?"

"Here." Alan was more intent upon putting the seeds in the ground than with answering questions.

"Yes, Alan, I know you live in the village, but where?"

"Here!" The small boy's voice was exasperated as he pointed to the castle. "My room is up there." The finger moved, indicating a room near Gyles's chamber.

"Does your mother work in the castle?" No doubt that was the case, Serena thought with a smile, and Alan —in the way of children—was embroidering upon reality.

"My mother's dead." The tiny voice held no grief. "Father said she died when I was born." Again the grin. "Father says I look like her."

As she studied his face more closely, Serena thought Alan greatly resembled someone else. The gnawing thought grew in the back of her mind: If the nose were a bit longer, the face leaner, the eyes green instead of hazel. . . . No, it wasn't possible! And yet, why hadn't she seen Alan before? Had he been purposely hidden from her? And if he had, it could only mean . . . Any doubts were dispelled when Alan scrambled to his feet and hurled himself toward an approaching figure with a glad shout.

"Father! Come see what we've done." Alan tugged on the large, outstretched hand with all his might.

The broad shouldered figure drew closer, and Serena found she hadn't the strength to rise from her knees to her feet as she stared, mesmerized, into a pair of dark green eyes. They had not seen each other alone nor spoken more than a formal greeting to each other since their aborted wedding night. Now, suddenly, they were alone with a small boy who would surely sense there was something amiss between them. Even while these thoughts flew through her mind, Serena could not help admiring the rugged handsomeness of Gyles's face and the lithe, animal grace with which he walked. Serena was acutely conscious of her own disheveled appearance; her face was lightly flushed and smudged with dirt, her hair uncombed and her gown plain.

Gyles, however, found no fault in his wife's appearance. Her hair tumbled about her in riotous curls that trapped the sunlight and reflected it in golden brilliance; her gown—damp with perspiration—clung to the delicate curves of her body, outlining her so well that she could hardly have revealed more had she knelt naked before him. Serena's blue eyes sparkled in the sunlight as she stared up at him, and Gyles felt his body begin to give in to his starving appetite. If Serena had been some simple serving girl and if Alan hadn't been there, Gyles would have thrown her to the soft grass and eased the ache in his loins. As it was, Gyles imposed an iron will on his passion and greeted her casually, wondering why she hadn't yet attacked him about his son.

"Serena." He released Alan's hand and the boy scampered off to resume his planting. "I thought you passed the days with Lydia and Mara making tapestries and embroidering linens." Gyles squatted on his heels beside her and examined her handiwork. "You've done quite well. Is it your intent to masquerade as a common lass occasionally?"

His sarcastic remark went unanswered as Serena asked what was uppermost in her mind. "Alan *is* your son, m'lord?"

Gyles glanced at the boy before he replied. "Alan! 'Tis time you went inside." As the small boy unwillingly trudged back to the castle, Gyles turned to Serena. "He is my son—why ask such an obvious question, Serena? Do you think I would deceive a child?"

"Why not? You've deceived others!" Serena retorted. Then she continued more softly. "Why did you not tell me you had been married before? I could have understood more easily your desire not to wed again."

Gyles laughed, but the sound was harsh and there was no amusement in his eyes. "What makes you think I was wed to Alan's mother? One does not need marriage vows in order to make a child!"

Serena's eyes widened. "B-but, I thought—I mean, the way Alan spoke . . ." Serena cast about for words to conceal her embarrassment. "Did Alan's mother die in childbirth?"

Gyles sighed and rose to his feet. "What difference does it make? And why should it matter to you, Serena?"

Serena gained her footing stiffly. "I do not mean to pry, m'lord, and I am sorry if I have offended either you or Alan. You have not answered my questions, so I assume you do not care to discuss the subject further. Why you hid Alan's presence from me I do not know, but I wish you had not. He is a handsome child, bright and intelligent; I should like very much to know him better, but I suppose you will not allow me that small pleasure either. I hope you have a competent nurse for Alan, m'lord, for 'tis obvious even to a blind man that he greatly needs and desires a mother! Good day, m'lord!" Serena whirled to follow Alan, but instead two strong hands came down upon her slender shoulders and she was spun around to face Gyles.

Serena's eyes shimmered with unshed tears, and Gyles regretted his cutting words of a few moments ago. Serena *was,* after all, his wife and she *did* deserve answers to her questions—even though Gyles was not in the habit of explaining anything to anyone. "Alan is mine—my bastard son. Do not flinch at the word, Serena, for that is what he is in the eyes of the world. His mother was a lady of . . . some consequence, married to a man who preferred fighting in Normandy over tending his estates in England. If you don't mind, I will spare you all the details. When the lady found she was with child, she was angry and bitter, threatening to kill herself rather than have the incident known, and . . . other alternatives. I finally persuaded her to retire to a convent and there bear my child. It was agreed that I would raise the child and no one need ever know." Gyles's eyes suddenly turned a muted, cloudy green. "When Alan was born, she wouldn't even look at him or touch him. She treated him as if he were the devil's child or carried the plague! To her Alan was something loathsome, vile, beneath her contempt—certainly not deserving of any affection from her. Do you wonder that I thought it best to tell him his mother was dead rather than the truth?"

Serena said nothing as she collected her seeds and book, then returned to her husband's side. She tilted her head back in order to gaze directly into Gyles's eyes. "I believe you did the right thing, m'lord. The boy had no part in his conception nor did he have a choice in selecting his father or mother, yet he is the one who will have to bear the taunting words and cruel jests of others. 'Tis kind of you to spare him that pain for as long as possible, yet there will come a day when Alan will have to be told."

Gyles nodded silently, for he knew that day was fast approaching, and he was not sure what words he would use to crumble Alan's world. Some of Gyles's inner turmoil must have showed on his normally impassive features, for Serena, her eyes still watching him intently, gave him a gentle smile.

"You have loved and protected Alan for this long, m'lord, when the time comes he will remember that. He will not turn from you when he learns the truth."

55

"What I have done, I did because I sired him and because of that I am responsible for him. Nothing more," Gyles said gruffly.

"Does love frighten you so much that you must use other words in its place? Love is a strength, m'lord, not a weakness."

"Love is for fools!" Gyles sneered. "Have you no further questions, Serena? Does not your inquiring woman's mind long to know who Alan's mother is so you can add more gossip for Lydia and Mara to spread?"

Serena's smile faded, but her reply was soft and without malice. "That is of no importance to me, m'lord. Why should it be?" Defeated, Gyles could find no answer as he stared down into her eyes and saw a smile curve her lips once again. "Then you have no objections to my being Alan's friend?" Gyles shook his head, completely bemused at the softness his son had brought out in his wife—she who was more than able to match Gyles's own anger when she chose.

At odds with himself and Serena, Gyles raised her chin a trifle higher with his finger. "You have my leave to retire to the castle, Lady Serena."

Serena dipped into a swift curtsy, but when she rose her eyes mocked him. "Thank you, m'lord."

Serena gave her hair a final pat and walked toward the stairs. She detested mealtimes because they forced the antagonists of the household into direct confrontation. She would have preferred to take her meals in her room, but she refused to give Beda or Gyles the satisfaction of knowing that these gatherings brought her nerves to the breaking point. A tug on the back of her skirt brought Serena up short, and she turned to see Alan watching her solemnly.

"Why aren't you at the table, Alan? I'm sure the meal has already started."

"Father didn't say I could. Will you take me with you?"

Serena considered him for a moment. "Did you eat

in the hall before I came, Alan?" He nodded, and Serena sighed inwardly. How many restrictions had been placed on Alan because of her? "Come along then. From now on you and I shall dine together."

Happily, Alan grasped Serena's hand and nearly skipped along beside her through the corridor and down the steps. When they entered the great hall, all conversation abruptly died and Serena noted that Beda half rose from her seat at the sight of them. Recently, Beda had taken to occupying the chair next to Gyles that was rightfully Serena's; tonight was no exception. Serena didn't mind, for it meant she was spared the scathing remarks Gyles usually heaped upon her, and she was only too glad to find a seat elsewhere at the head table. Now Serena gently pulled Alan to the table and into a seat next to her, after which she concentrated on filling first his trencher and then her own. The conversation resumed, but when Serena looked up from her food, she found both Gyles's and Beda's gazes upon her. Gyles's look told her nothing, but Beda's eyes blazed with malevolence. Serena lowered her head to attend to Alan's questions and to her food. As the meal progressed it became increasingly obvious that Beda drank far more than she ate. Her voice became louder and more shrill, until no one in the hall could pretend not to hear her. Beda reviled everything about Camden and when that subject was exhausted she turned her attention to the occupants of the castle, beginning with Lydia. That poor woman flushed under the cutting edge of Beda's tongue and as soon as she had fled from the hall in tears it was Mara's turn. Mara paled, but before Beda could complete her tirade, Mara rose and with great dignity left the table. At their tables, the knights shifted uneasily as they realized Beda could now direct herself to the one person she had meant to insult all along. Serena also realized that fact and sat with her hands tightly clenched in her lap. Alan looked from one adult to another, not understanding why his father didn't make Beda stop shouting; he was not allowed to speak like that in front of Gyles.

57

"And, of course, there is the fair Lady Serena. Still so pure after four months as a wife. Mayhap 'tis your pallor that disgusts your husband, or perhaps you are too thin. Poor Lady Serena, should I tell you how to attract your own husband? 'Tis not so difficult as you may think. And once having enticed him to your bed, I could teach you well how to please him."

Serena stared at her trencher, feeling sick and humiliated beyond belief. It had been an open secret that Gyles had not consummated their marriage and that he and Beda had been—and probably still were—lovers. But to have the matter openly bandied about was a different matter entirely. The knights were glancing nervously at each other and would not look at her, while Gyles sat as if he were carved out of stone; his scar had already whitened and a muscle in his jaw had begun to tic.

Why doesn't Serena fight back, Gyles wondered? It wasn't like her to remain so silent; her face so drawn that her blue eyes looked twice their normal size. Alan was nervously plucking at her sleeve and Serena slipped an arm around his small shoulders with a shake of her head to warn him into silence.

"She looks positively maternal, doesn't she, Gyles? Does mothering come naturally to you, Serena, or does it apply only to motherless bas—"

"Enough!" Serena's voice rang through the hall as she rose from her seat with such violence that her chair fell back with a crash. "Alan, go to my room. Do you know where it is? Good, tell Nellwyn that I sent you. Now go," Serena said softly and gave him a gentle push toward the stairs. She watched until the boy was out of sight, then turned back to face Beda.

"So protective of a bastard, Serena! Could it be that *you* are his mother?" Beda sneered as she advanced upon Serena.

"If I were, Lady Beda, you would now be picking yourself up from the rushes on the floor. Say what you like to me, for I can defend myself, but *never* let me find you tormenting the boy!" Serena's features relaxed as she brought her temper under control and an amused smile played on her lips. "Is there anything else you had to tell me, Lady Beda?"

The two women stood facing each other with only a small space separating them. Beda was taller than Serena by a full head, yet the smaller woman stood straight and tall before her, apparently completely unafraid, which angered Beda further.

Serena raised an eyebrow at Beda. "Ah, well, as you seem to have lost your tongue. Perhaps we can continue our conversation at some later time." Serena's look encompassed both Gyles and Beda. "Have a pleasant evening, Lady Beda." She turned and mounted the stairs. It was Gyles's shout that warned her, and Serena turned to find Beda, a dagger in her raised hand, only a few feet from her.

Driven past all endurance, Beda saw Serena as the foil to her plans. Her life had been running smoothly until she had allowed Aurelia to talk her into having Gyles marry Serena. Aurelia had sworn the girl would cause no problems at Camden and so far Serena had caused nothing but trouble! Their greater plans be damned, for Beda would rid herself of Serena's presence once and for all.

Serena read the resolve in Beda's drunken stare and tried to sidestep the blow, but her movement was not quick enough, and Beda's dagger buried itself in the fleshy part of Serena's shoulder just above the collarbone. With her good hand, Serena caught Beda full in the face and shoved her backward down the stairs where she sprawled in a drunken heap.

Gyles stood at the foot of the stairs, a horrified look on his face as he stared at his wife. The left side of her bodice was becoming rapidly stained with blood, and she leaned weakly against the cool stone wall. Vaguely, Serena realized that Gyles was beside her, and she forced her eyes open. She despised the sudden weakness in her legs and the way the room seemed to be spinning inside her head. Tentatively she forced her right hand upward until she could touch the hilt of the dagger. Her fingers came away sticky with her own blood and a buzzing began in her ears.

Nellwyn screamed, "Aiyee! Serena, child! What've ye done to me poor lamb?"

Alan's small face appeared from behind the nurse's skirt and his eyes grew round with fear.

"Nellwyn, take Alan back to his room and stop your screeching! I'll be all right, 'tis nothing." Serena's words sounded unconvincing even to her own ears, and to prove the truth of them to her nurse and the boy she reached up and pulled the blade from her flesh, her stomach churning at the sickening, grating sound it made against the bone as it came free. A spurt of blood followed its removal, and Serena felt a pair of strong arms come around her as she swayed dizzily. She looked up into Gyles's concerned green eyes and managed a wan smile. Her tongue felt swollen and it seemed forever before her stiff lips would respond to her wishes.

"I do not wish to swoon here, m'lord. Please . . . would you mind helping me—" The world dimmed and darkened completely, as Gyles felt Serena's legs buckle. She collapsed limply into his arms.

Consciousness returned slowly to Serena, until at last her eyes focused on the ceiling of her room. She could hear people moving quietly about and talking in hushed voices, and she found herself wondering how many hours she had lost to that sudden blackness that had enveloped her. She must have made some slight movement, for Nellwyn's face was immediately above her.

"So yer back with us, lamb. High time, too, for ye've wasted the better part of a week." As Serena reached up to touch her shoulder, Nellwyn nodded. "Aye, the bleeding's stopped, and 'tis not such a bad wound for all the blood that came out of it. Ye scared me near to death, and Alan, poor little tyke, has been crying since he saw ye. Said ye were going to die like his mother did, and wouldn't listen to Lord Gyles when he said ye wouldn't. Ye'd better see him, lamb, before he floods the castle."

Serena smiled. "Help me up, Nellwyn, so I can get dressed, then get the boy. And get rid of those women, the way they're staring at me makes me nervous. Well, what are you waiting for?"

"Do ye not want to ask about Lord Gyles? 'Twas he who carried ye to yer own bed and saw to the tending of yer wound." Nellwyn looked at her charge slyly. "Aye, well, I can see yer too proud to ask, so I'll tell ye anyway. He's been with ye every minute and he just now left to eat."

"His concern is touching." Serena spat out the words to conceal the wild leaping of her pulse at the mention of her husband. "And you are meddling again. I shall dress myself, since you seem to have forgotten my orders, so you and the others may take your leave. Bring Alan to me and something to eat also."

It took longer to dress than Serena had thought because of the stiffness in her left arm. But it moved easier as she forced herself to use the arm, and she could manage quite well when she combed her hair. Nellwyn returned with a tray of food and Serena fell upon it ravenously while Nellwyn watched approvingly. Just as Serena finished, there was a light rap on the door.

"Take the tray away, Nellwyn, and bring Alan in. And there's no need for you to hover about—don't look at me that way, I'm not a baby anymore and I'm perfectly capable of dealing with one small boy!"

"Aye, that ye be, but can ye deal with the lad's father?" Nellwyn asked with a knowing smile.

Serena's eyes widened in anger and Nellwyn beat a hasty retreat, for she knew full well her mistress was quite capable of a harsh rebuke when she felt her old nurse had overstepped the boundaries of familiarity.

Alan entered the room cautiously, as if he were afraid of what he might find. To his child's mind, the beautiful lady with gold streaked hair had been mortally wounded by Beda. Why else would she have lain so still and unmoving with her face as pale as the linens on her bed? His father's repeated assurances had done nothing to quiet the fear that had grown with each hour that passed and Serena had not awakened. Alan's happiness knew no bounds when he saw Serena sitting in a chair by the fire, and he could only stand and stare as he watched a smile spread across Serena's face.

"For shame, Alan! Nellwyn tells me you've been hounding her all day, and now you won't even greet me?"

With a glad cry, Alan ran to her side and buried his face in her skirt. Serena felt his tears dampening the material of her gown and although the movement cost her much in the way of pain, she lifted Alan onto her lap to still his sobs.

"There's no need to cry, Alan. Everything is fine. Hush now, little one." She rocked him gently and ruffled his black hair.

Alan raised his head and rubbed the tears from his eyes with his small fists. He touched Serena's shoulder tentatively. "It doesn't hurt anymore?"

Serena smiled down at him. "It hurts, but not badly. I've received worse falling out of trees."

"When I grow up, I'm going to be a knight just like my father, and I'll protect you. I won't let anyone hurt you again," Alan said vehemently.

Alan was suddenly lifted from Serena's lap and swung high in the air by a strong pair of hands before he was set on the hearth. Serena's gasp subsided when she saw Gyles looking down at her, a mocking smile on his lips.

"I did not mean to frighten you, Serena, but Alan should have been abed long before this. Nellwyn is waiting to take you back to your room, Alan, so bid goodnight to Lady Serena and be off with you."

With a last smile for Serena, Alan did as he was told and scampered into Nellwyn's waiting arms. Gyles turned back to his wife, who had risen from her chair.

"You need not remain standing, I give you leave

to be seated." Gyles folded his long body into a chair and smiled at Serena.

Serena's temper flared. "You give me leave!" She sputtered. "You come in unannounced and have the audacity to——" the words choked in her throat as she remembered Nellwyn's words. She studied Gyles's face from beneath the veil of her lashes. There were circles under his eyes, giving evidence to the fact that he hadn't slept for many days and nights.

Gyles seemed not to notice Serena's abrupt silence. " 'Tis my home, Serena, and I may go *where* I wish, *when* I wish. Do you dispute that?"

"No, m'lord."

"And are you telling me I am not welcome in your chambers?"

"No, m'lord."

"Then sit down!" Gyles roared for Serena was so pale he feared she would swoon. Serena obeyed so quickly that Gyles felt the first true amusement he had experienced in years. "You are feeling better?"

"Yes, m'lord. The shoulder is a bit stiff, but it moves well so I doubt there is any permanent damage. Is . . ." Serena frowned, unsure of her next question. "Lady Beda . . . is she . . . well?"

"Beda enjoys the best of health," Gyles muttered. "Unfortunately for everyone." Serena looked at him in surprise as he continued, "I am sorry, Serena, for not realizing the extent of Beda's anger. I should have stopped her when she began insulting you. Believe me, I never meant for you to be humiliated in front of others because of me, nor did I think that Beda would do anything as insane as attacking you." Gyles reached out and brushed his fingers lightly over Serena's injured shoulder. "Though I was forced into this marriage—for reasons you do not know and probably would not understand—I would not have you hurt." A small laugh. "My son is better with words than I am. As best I can, I shall see to it you are not hurt again. A word of caution, Serena, avoid Beda as much as possible, her attack on you—"

"I think she has meant to do me harm since I arrived." Serena completed the thought for Gyles. "I do not know what I have done to make her hate me."

"You are young and quite beautiful, I believe that is reason enough. You have usurped her position as lady of the manor, and she finds it impossible to accept that simple fact."

"M'lord," Serena began hesitantly, "was it your desire to wed Beda?" Gyles looked at her so oddly that her eyes slid away from his. "Please . . . I do not mean to pry, I only wish to understand my position. It is clear that I am neither wanted nor needed at Camden and—it would be easier for everyone if I were not here. If you desire it, I will retire to my dower estate."

"Alan needs you—he has grown quite fond of you in such a short time and I will not permit you to destroy what happiness he has. You are my wife and you will remain here!"

"Yes, m'lord." She refused to look at Gyles again and she heard him give a snort of disgust before he stormed from the room. Serena caught her bottom lip between her teeth to still its trembling. So things were to continue as they were. Nothing had changed. Nothing! Serena had thought that just for a moment Gyles's eyes had softened when he looked at her. Even if it had only been desire she had seen, Serena would have welcomed it. At least Gyles, her husband, would have wanted her for *something*. A virgin wife Beda had called her, and it seemed she was to remain so. The thought disturbed her greatly. Gyles's first kiss had awakened strange thoughts and yearnings in her young body; they had frightened and excited her. Serena admitted to herself, at last, that she desired Gyles—the man she had been forced to marry and had detested on sight. He had aroused passions in her that he refused to see to a finish. The devil take him! She was no wife to him nor would she ever be; she was less than nothing in his eyes. Well it would not remain that way, she would see to that! Since he seemed to dislike women with spirit, she would play the gentle wife; where he thought to find anger there would be only tender regard; where before Gyles had encountered stubbornness he would be met with compliance. Serena would weave a net about him so slowly and with so much care that Gyles would find himself ensnared before he realized it!

4

Spring was suddenly gone and summer descended upon Camden with a vengeance. The sun lavished its warmth upon the fields during the days, but the nights often brought refreshing showers that cleaned the air and brought a welcome relief to Serena. Accustomed to the many shade trees surrounding Broughton, Serena resented the openness of the land around the stone walls of Camden. Her only respite from the wilting heat came when she would take a horse from the stable, gather up Alan and a light lunch, and ride a short distance to a spring-fed pond which was concealed from the road by dense undergrowth and an abundance of trees. If Serena found the heat unbearable, it was far worse to remain indoors. Beda—whom she avoided as much as possible—treated her with contempt; while Lydia and Mara had begun to avoid her. Undoubtedly Serena assumed, it was because of her own change in attitude toward Gyles. She shrugged it all off. As far as she was concerned, neither cost her any peace of mind. What did worry her was that Gyles continued to be impervious to her charms. Apparently he did not consider her attractive enough for his tastes, for the only time he sought her company was when she was with Alan. Since the night she'd finally awakened after her injury, Gyles had not again visited her chamber.

Now Serena sighed and sat back on her heels. She

had decided to weed the garden before the heat became too bad and she glanced behind her to see how Alan was faring. Oblivious to everything, he was working his way down the rows of carrots, taking great care to uproot any offending growth that would deny the carrots their share of the water. With each day that passed Serena grew more fond of the lad, and she found herself longing more and more for her own children and a husband who would love both them and her. And the deeper that longing grew the greater grew the desperation that she would have neither. Serena was seized by a sudden jealousy of the woman Gyles had lain with and given a child. Had it been within her power, Serena would have made Alan her own, but only Gyles could do that and she dared not approach him on the subject. Only the king could legitimatize Alan, and then only if Gyles petitioned him to do so. Well, perhaps Gyles had some other plan for his son. Serena desperately hoped so, for she often caught herself thinking of Alan as if he were her own son.

Sparkling blue eyes squinted upward to study the sky. Not a cloud in sight and the afternoon promised to be scorching. Serena lifted the heavy mass of her sun-lightened hair from her neck and rose to her feet. She did not want to spend the rest of the day back in her chambers, alone with her thoughts.

"Alan, would you like to go with me to the pond?"

"Now?" Alan looked dubiously at the rows of carrots.

"The carrots won't die, you can finish weeding tomorrow. Go inside and ask Nellwyn to fix us a basket for lunch. I'll get a horse from the stable."

As the pair cantered away from the castle, Serena was blissfully unaware of the rider approaching the castle from the opposite direction. Alan was seated in front of her, so the knight saw only Serena's back, as he spurred his horse on faster. The horse's hooves clattered in the courtyard and brought a groom out of the stable. He caught the reins that were thrown to him and was about to bid good morrow to the rider but the words died unspoken before the harsh look in the rider's green eyes.

"Who saddled a steed for Lady Serena?" Gyles shouted the words.

The groom took a step backward and stammered, " 'T-'twas I, m'lord."

"Why did you not accompany her? I left orders that none of the women should ride alone!"

"B-but Lady Serena never allows a groom to go with her, m'lord. Every groom we did send after her, she promptly lost, so after a while we just gave up."

"You mean to tell me that none of the men can track one small chit of a girl?" Gyles advanced upon the groom who backed nervously away and swallowed convulsively. "Bah! I am surrounded by fools!" He snatched the reins from the groom and remounted. "I'll deal with you upon my return!"

Serena chewed on a piece of bread smothered with honey as she watched Alan play in the shallow water. The boy was trying diligently to swim, but he succeeded only in getting water in his nose and mouth as he sank beneath the surface of the pond. When he regained his feet for the third time he glared at Serena and splashed from the pond to throw himself on the bank.

"You promised!" Alan said reproachfully.

Serena smiled. "I said I would teach you to swim only if you waited a while after you had eaten. You went in the water far too soon."

Alan's face crumpled as tears threatened. "I'm sorry, Serena."

Serena's tender nature could not bear to see the child in tears and she relented. After all, Alan was just a boy and he had little enough to look forward to at Camden. "Do you promise never to do this again?"

At his eager nod, Serena rose and pulled off her gown. Clad only in her thin undergarment, Serena scooped Alan up into her arms and waded into the water. Setting him in the shallows, she began her instruction. "The first thing you must learn to do is float: Lie back across my arms—don't be afraid, I won't let you sink. Now put your arms straight out. That's right, you're doing fine. Now I'm going to take my arms away, so keep

68

your back straight and your arms out. Good, good!"
Gradually she withdrew one arm, and when Alan had
adjusted to that, Serena drew back her other arm. The
lack of support frightened Alan; he forgot all Serena's
instructions and began to thrash wildly as he sank
beneath the surface of the water. Hastily, Serena bent
down and pulled Alan upward, but not before he had
lowered the water level by several mouthfuls. Alan's
arms fastened themselves around Serena's neck, soaking
her thoroughly, as he gasped and choked.

"You must try again, Alan."

"N-no!" Alan sobbed and tightened his arms.

"If you don't, you will never learn, Alan. I know
'tis frightening, but as long as I am here, nothing will
harm you. You're not hurt are you?" Alan shook his
head. "You see? Swallowing a little water won't hurt
you," Serena chided. "Now, let go of me, and we'll try
again. On your back, arms strai—" A twig snapped, and
Serena snatched Alan back to her as she turned toward
the bank.

Gyles sat astride his horse, his green-eyed gaze pinning Serena with its intensity. As he watched her, Serena's expression changed from one of fright to relief.
She lowered Alan back into the water and smiled up at
Gyles, unaware of the fact that her garment clung damply to her body, leaving little of its assets to his imagination. A tightening began in Gyles's groin and he shifted
on the saddle to relieve his discomfort. The movement
didn't help and the sensation grew stronger, while he
gazed at Serena, forcibly reminding him of his monkish
abstinence the past months. The reminder served to
heighten his already flaming anger, and Serena was a
convenient outlet. She noticed the darkening of Gyles's
features, but bent upon her new strategy, she deliberately ignored it and waded slowly toward the bank. Several tendrils of hair had escaped the knot on the top of
her head and they curled willfully around her face, as
the sun struck the gold in her hair. Gyles found himself
momentarily dazzled by her appearance. For an instant,
Gyles was reminded of the fairy tales he had been told

as a child about a water nymph rising from a lake, incredibly beautiful, incredibly delicate. Gyles shook himself mentally; now his mind was betraying him as well as his body. But the way Serena walked toward him, her hips swaying ever so slightly, and stood beside his mount gently stroking the horse's neck. Gyles had an unobstructed view of the delicate swell of her breasts, could see the nipples puckered from the cool water.

Serena noted where her husband's gaze had traveled and smiled. "Welcome, m'lord, I did not think anyone knew of this place save Alan and myself. Have you eaten? There is meat and bread and a flagon of wine left if you hunger. Pray dismount, m'lord. I fear Alan has persuaded me to teach him to swim, but I am sure you will make a far better tutor than I. Alan and I—"

"I have more important business to attend to than teaching my son to swim or listening to my simple-minded wife's empty chattering. You were told not to ride without a groom, yet you have deliberately disobeyed my order! I cannot spare the time to track you all over the countryside! Henceforth, when you ride you will take a groom or you shall not ride at all! Does that make any sense in that empty head of yours, m'lady?"

Serena ground her teeth in mute anger. She would not allow herself to be provoked into an argument! "I am sorry if I have displeased you, m'lord, 'tis only that I sought a place where Alan and I might be free from prying eyes and sharp tongues." Serena spoke quietly and kept her eyes downcast, so Gyles could not see the flashing anger in them. "Since you so command, I shall bring a groom along whenever Alan and I decide to swim. We will not venture forth alone again."

Gyles could have roared in sheer frustration. The last thing he wanted was his wife exposed as she was now to any man she would arbitrarily pick to accompany her! Did she have so little common sense? Or was it possible that since he hadn't consummated their marriage, Serena had decided to take a lover—any lover?

Serena's changed attitude these past weeks had not escaped Gyles's notice, and he had wondered at the way she so boldly flaunted herself beneath his gaze. Gyles's knights had taken note of the change as well, and his temper flared whenever he chanced to intercept the admiring glances and compliments that were directed at Serena. Serena herself appeared totally unaware of this as she continued to chat with the knights and laugh at their rough jests. There was little Gyles could do to discourage Serena's behavior short of forbidding her to leave her chamber, and that action would make Gyles the brunt of many a derisive comment. But he would see to it that she welcomed no other man to her bed.

Visions of Serena's delicate body being invaded by a common servant swirled through Gyles's mind. He could picture all too well rough hands touching that smooth flesh, a calloused hand reaching upward to cup a small breast, Serena's thighs being brutally parted as she thrashed beneath a gigantic, hairy body. . . .

"M'lord?"

Gyles wrenched himself free from his imaginings to find Serena gazing up at him questioningly. Of their own volition, his hands had clenched themselves into fists and Gyles's face had contorted into an angry mask. Even the bravest of his men would have quailed in the face of his rage, but Serena looked at him quite calmly. Why wasn't she shrinking from him in fear, begging his forgiveness for what he knew she was planning? Slut! Whore! For all her pretended affection for Alan, Serena was no different than the others. He would see her game foiled—take a lover would she! When he finally regained enough control to speak, Gyles's tone should have frozen Serena where she stood.

"When you desire to ride, Lady Serena, tell me, and I shall accompany you," he said tersely. " 'Tis not my wish that you should brazenly display yourself to every man of Camden like a strumpet displays her wares—no matter how much you would enjoy doing so."

Serena gave Gyles an innocent smile. "Your pardon, m'lord, I meant only to obey your wishes, not upset you." Her satisfaction deepened as Gyles's jaw began to work. He might not want her as his wife, but Gyles was

71

not about to allow any man to encroach on one of his possessions; that much Serena had known and played upon. And it had worked—far better than she could have hoped for, in fact. Serena let his biting words pass; Gyles was a proud, arrogant man and for some reason she could not fathom, he seemed to have a violent dislike of women—especially her. Gyles still remained astride his horse, anxious, it appeared, to be off. But Serena hadn't finished with him yet. Being sure to keep her eyes demurely lowered, she said, "May Alan and I complete our swim, m'lord? I fear the day is far too warm for me, and I would enjoy passing the afternoon here."

Alan joined Serena with his plea to be allowed to stay, and groaning inwardly, Gyles agreed. His self-control was most sorely tried by Serena's appearance and he could foresee nothing but frustration for the remainder of the day. Nevertheless, he dismounted and seated himself on the blanket Serena had brought and watched as Alan's instruction continued. As the sound of their laughter rang clearly over the water and onto the bank, Gyles felt suddenly excluded from their fun—and this exclusion brought an unfamiliar pang to his heart. Serena had momentarily halted Alan's lesson, and the two of them capered in the pond, splashing each other with water, while Alan tried futilely to catch hold of Serena's leg to drag her beneath the water. Laughing, Serena eluded Alan and swam farther out into the pond where Alan knew he could not follow.

"Not fair, Serena, not fair!" Alan wailed. He turned to Gyles in mute appeal.

Unhappy with his role of spectator, Gyles sprang to his feet and stripped to his loincloth. Serena stopped swimming and trod the water as she watched Gyles bend down and whisper to Alan. The boy nodded in vigorous agreement and then Gyles began to swim toward Serena. As Serena realized Gyles's intent, she gave a small shriek and she heard Alan laugh. Watching Gyles, Serena knew she could not hope to reach the opposite bank, for he was by far the faster swimmer, but there was the chance she could avoid him. Taking a deep breath, Serena sank beneath the surface and struck out at an angle that would carry her off to Gyles's right. She swam until she was sure her lungs would burst before she surfaced. Serena sucked in several deep breaths of air before her ankle was seized in a vise-like grip and she felt herself being pulled downward. Frantically her arms flailed about her and her hand made contact with Gyles's head. Serena's fingers tangled themselves in his hair and she gave a vicious tug. Gyles's hold loosened for an instant, and Serena kicked her foot free and struck out with her other foot, which made contact with Gyles's chest. She shot upward. When Gyles surfaced beside her, Serena was angry enough to give him a thorough dunking, but seeing the carefree grin on his face, she could do nothing but laugh back at him.

For his part, Gyles felt more light-hearted and younger than he could remember. His anger with Serena for her imagined betrayal of him dissolved, as her blue eyes sparkled at him. How could any man—least of all himself—resist her teasing look? Gyles made as if to push Serena back into the depths of the pond, but out of sheer self-preservation, Serena wrapped her arms around Gyles's neck, so that if she went under, so did he. Gyles relented and instead playfully splashed a light spray of water against her cheek.

"You nearly drowned me." Serena laughed.

"I? Who was it that nearly sent me to the bottom of the pool? Nay, Serena, I think 'tis I who was nearly drowned." He felt Serena's arms slip from his neck and resisted the overpowering urge to pull her back against him. His world seemed lighter somehow—it was comfortable here with his wife and son, with none of the usual bitter undertones that were common at the castle. Gyles watched Serena floating beside him, her gold-streaked hair fanned out in the water around her. Gyles recalled his earlier mental accusations against his wife and wondered at them. Did he really believe that Serena sought to betray him? No, that was not possible. Although Gyles knew little enough about Serena, he did know that honor and faith were highly important to her. Serena would not break the sacred vows she had taken, for she would not shame herself in that manner. For all the harsh treatment and insults she had endured at Camden, Serena had not reviled him; had not, in fact, even spoken to him about the injuries done her—especially by Beda.

That thought brought a frown to Gyles's face. Serena had been horrified and sickened when she learned about them—and Gyles had to admit he could not blame her. Had Serena forgotten? Or had she chosen simply to ignore the facts? Either way, Serena had never thrown it in his face or questioned him about it. She seemed quite willing to be his wife if he so desired, but by no means was she forcing a decision upon him. Serena was unfailingly polite whenever they met—a most welcome respite from Beda who alternately threatened and cajoled in the misguided hope that Gyles would return to her bed. Finally, aggravated beyond his endurance, Gyles had taken to bolting his side of the door that joined their chambers. At the time Gyles had thought that if Serena lay behind that door he would have it torn from its hinges instead.

Serena paddled back to Gyles and wondered at the frown that had replaced his smile of a few moments before. She cast a glance at the bank to assure herself that Alan was out of the water, and then turned back to Gyles. His eyes rivaled the leaves above in their greenness, and his skin had turned to a deep bronze during these summer days. Serena had often watched as he and his men held practice sessions with their weapons. Now up close, she could see the firm, rippling muscles of his arms and shoulders, which before she had seen only from a distance. Serena had little enough to judge by, but she knew instinctively that Gyles was indeed a magnificently built man. She had no difficulty understanding why—if Bryan had not been lying—the women at court found him so appealing. What would happen if she went to him now and placed a gentle kiss upon his lips? Would he put her from him? Or would Gyles take her in his arms and whisper the endearments she yearned to hear from his lips? There were so many unanswered questions.

Gyles was looking at her and smiling. At least he

seemed to have removed the curtain from between them, and that was a start, Serena told herself hopefully.

"You look pensive, Serena. Does something trouble you?" Gyles's voice was soft and low, with a gentle note that Serena had never heard before. He allowed so little tenderness to touch his life, she thought sadly.

"No, m'lord," she answered quietly. Then she smiled teasingly. " 'Tis only that I grow weary and must beg your leave to return to shore, for if I do not, I fear you shall be made a widower."

Gyles laughed, and stretching out one arm, caught her to him. "Then shall I ferry you back, m'lady? In truth, 'twould not be a difficult task, for I think you weigh little more than Alan."

The moment was precious and Serena was loathe to let it go, so she lay passively against Gyles's chest and let him bear both their weights. Gyles seemed to be of the same mind, and Serena could hear the steady beat of his heart in her ear. Hesitantly, she raised one hand up over the dark mat of hair on his chest until her arm was around his neck. The water sparkled as if inlaid with jewels, the wind rustled softly through the trees and time hung suspended for them—trapped around their bodies as they lightly touched, drifted apart, and came together again. From the woods came the trilling of a bird, the only sound that broke their splendid isolation. Both felt the need to speak: Gyles to refute his earlier angry words, and Serena to tell of the strange, new emotion that she had discovered in her heart. But neither could find the words, and instead they held tightly to each other, expressing their thoughts in unspoken communication.

Eventually, it was Serena who broke away and smiled shakily at Gyles, whose face wore a puzzled expression. "We . . . we must go, m'lord. 'Tis late, and there is the joust tomorrow and the guests."

Gyles nodded, not trusting his voice, for he, too, had been inwardly shaken by their contact. Something about this girl stirred the very depths of his soul, and it was not just desire. He had had this feeling before: when they were arguing; the day they had discussed Alan; and especially during the long days and nights he had kept his vigil by Serena's bedside and feared—yes, Gyles could admit that much to himself—feared for her life. He drew a deep breath and put a teasing note in his voice. "I shall race you to the shore, Serena. Are you game? You do swim very well for a woman, but . . ." He allowed his voice to trail off.

Serena rose to the bait. "A challenge? But, m'lord, you must make the contest more interesting."

Gyles raised an eyebrow. "A small wager on the outcome, Serena? Will that make the contest worth your while?" Serena nodded. "Very well, then, what do you wish if you win?"

Serena's eyes danced with deviltry. "To be allowed to take part in the lists tomorrow."

"What!"

"I was going to anyway, but now I have risked my chance, for if I lose, I shall not participate." Gyles still wore a dumbfounded expression as she continued. "Since my wager is quite dear to me, m'lord, what will you wager that is equally dear?"

Gyles stared at her and then shook his head as if to clear it. "Serena, surely you are not serious about the lists! Even if you were trained in the art of combat you would stand no chance against veteran knights. Any of my men, even the weakest of them, could accidentally do you a grievous injury. I will not allow—"

"The wager, m'lord, or the challenge is void," Serena warned. "And if the challenge is off, I participate as I planned, even if you deny me your permission."

"Oh, very well," Gyles groaned. "For my wager, I choose—" His mind raced frantically. "I choose that you begin, as of the end of this race, to occupy your rightful place at Camden as my wife. And you will start by having Beda removed from the chamber next to mine and installing yourself in her place."

Serena paled, and Gyles thought for a moment that the price was too high. Actually, if he won, Gyles would have accomplished two ends. He would be relieved—at least to some extent—of Beda's noisome presence, and

Serena would be closer to him. The afternoon had caused Gyles to realize that he did, in fact, desire Serena as his wife. She would be his talisman against all that was ugly and sordid in his life. Her mere presence could bring him a peace of mind he had never thought to have. Serena still had not spoken and Gyles watched her closely. "Well, Serena, what say you? Do you agree to the wager?"

Numbly, Serena nodded. The wager was more than she could have hoped for—to gain her rightful place beside Gyles! Yet, she also desired to participate in the mock battle. If Serena won, she lost; and if she lost, she won! Which course to take? "Aye, m'lord, I accept your terms. Do you give the signal or do I?"

"By all means, let us be fair. You give the word, Serena. 'Tis only just since I challenged you."

Serena nodded. "Now!"

Both struck out for the shore. Serena concentrated completely on keeping abreast of Gyles. As she had observed, he was a powerful swimmer, and he effortlessly began to pull ahead of her. Serena drew upon her reserves and once more was even with Gyles. The process was repeated again and again until Serena weakened and suddenly realized that Gyles only toyed with her, prolonging the game. He could easily have outdistanced her from the start, and could now be sitting on the bank if he so desired.

A glance over his shoulder showed Gyles that Serena was lagging behind him, but her jaw was set in a determined line. "Yield, Serena! You cannot win!" Gyles called back.

"Nay!" Serena shouted and for her trouble swallowed a mouthful of water. Damn but the man was irritating! Gyles's laughter floated back to her, and she saw that the long strokes of his powerful arms had already carried him to the shallows and he was now wading to the shore. Frustrated, Serena stopped swimming and let herself sink beneath the water. What difference did it make whether Gyles won? It had been a light-hearted contest, made in jest, and whatever the outcome, she gained.

What was she trying to prove? And to whom, Gyles or herself? Why could she not feel content with the thought of being Gyles's wife? For most women, that would be enough. What was she searching for?

When she surfaced, the first sound Serena heard was Gyles calling her name. Did his voice sound frantic or was her mind—already confused by the questions that chased each other around—playing tricks on her? She paddled easily to the shallow water and then walked to the bank. Gyles waited for her, his legs slightly apart, arms folded over his chest. His eyes were flashing angrily at her, and Serena wondered what had caused him to lose his bantering mood.

When Serena neared Gyles, his hand shot out and she was pulled roughly against him. "What were you playing at out there?" Gyles asked angrily. He lifted Serena off her feet until their eyes were level with each other. "I thought you had taken a cramp and could not gain the shore."

Serena looked at him in wide-eyed astonishment. When she gazed into those green eyes, all defiance drained from her and the questions that had plagued her earlier seemed completely unimportant. "Did I frighten you, m'lord?" Serena asked softly.

Gyles did not reply, but Serena felt his arm tighten around her. His free hand rose and brushed an errant strand of hair from her face. When Gyles spoke, his voice was oddly strained. "Never . . . ever . . . do that again, Serena. I'll not allow you to escape our wager so easily."

But I do not wish to escape, Serena wanted to say. Why couldn't she speak those words? Why did pride chain her tongue, when Serena's heart told her that the words would greatly ease things between herself and Gyles? And why was he staring at her as if he could read her thoughts?

"You will carry out your part of our bargain." It was a statement, not a question, and Gyles searched Serena's face for a sign that she would refuse.

Serena's eyes dropped away from his; surely he

could look directly into her soul and see the inner turmoil there. "The bargain will be met, m'lord, though I daresay Beda will prove most difficult."

Gyles returned Serena to the ground, then gently cupped her face between his hands. "If Beda proves troublesome, I shall deal with her. Take no chances, Serena. Remember her dagger."

"You need not remind me, m'lord. I remember full well her anger." Serena glanced behind Gyles to see Alan running toward them. Reluctantly, Serena pulled Gyles's hands away from her face. " 'Tis time we left, m'lord, the day grows short and I fear we have neglected Alan."

Alan threw himself into his father's arms. Gyles lifted the boy to his shoulders and offered his hand to Serena. A small smile curved her lips as her fingers interlaced with her husband's and the trio walked back to the picnic site. Serena's kirtle was still wet and she debated removing the garment before she donned her gown, but Gyles and Alan were waiting impatiently for her, so she quickly shrugged the garment over her shoulders and hurried to the horses. Gyles lifted Serena into her saddle, then mounted his own horse and seated Alan before him. The ride back to the castle was spent answering Alan's questions, and he soon had Serena and Gyles laughing at his inquisitiveness. They were still chuckling when they reached the stables, and the grooms who ran out to hold their mounts glanced at their Norman lord in surprise. The grooms were not the only people who were interested in the return of the lord and lady of the manor. Nellwyn and Beda waited on the steps of the castle— the old nurse with a satisfied smile on her lined face, and Beda with her face contorted into an ugly mask.

Serena noted the killing looks Beda gave her, and she was suddenly overcome by a feeling of pure terror. Serena's legs trembled and her hands turned to blocks of ice. She retained enough control to send Alan off with Nellwyn before the confrontation with Beda. Gyles sensed Serena's fear and slipped an arm around her shoulder, readying himself to intervene should Beda threaten Serena in any way. Her uneasiness receded a

79

bit, and Serena drew a deep breath to steel herself and steady her nerves.

But matters were taken out of her hands as Beda launched full force into an immediate attack on both of them. "Where have you been? Your guests have been arriving since noon!" She gestured toward the field where pavilions were being set up. "I have had the entire responsibility of welcoming your guests and quartering the lords and ladies here in the castle. You, Lady Serena, should have been here to attend to these matters; after all, though you are *not* a wife, you *are* the lady of the manor and you do have duties to attend—"

"You need not remind me of my duties, Lady Beda, I am quite aware of them, I assure you," Serena said quietly, though a slow flush colored her cheeks, for she had forgotten the grand scale of the lists Gyles had planned. "And from this moment on, I plan to relieve you of the duties I have so thoughtlessly thrust upon you." Serena motioned one of the servants to her as they advanced into the hall.

Beda glanced sharply from Gyles to Serena as she caught the new authority in Serena's voice, and her eyes narrowed until they were little more than slits at the sight of Gyles's hand resting lightly on Serena's shoulder. Something had happened.

"See that Lady Beda's things are removed from her chamber at once." Serena broke into Beda's thoughts when she addressed the servant. "And have my belongings placed in their stead. Beda, you may have my former chambers if you wish; the room is quite pleasant."

Beda glared at Serena. "What do you think you're doing?" she hissed. "I have no intention of giving up my chamber!"

"I fear you have no choice, Beda. The rooms you occupy are not yours, but belong to whoever bears the title Lady of Camden." Serena stole a quick look at Gyles before she continued. "I have waited for you to gracefully relinquish that which is no longer yours, and I feel I have been more than patient. But your time and my patience have run out, and so I tell you now that I will no longer be kept from my rightful place."

"I will not——" Beda began.

"You will do as I say, Beda, and not cause a scene in front of our guests, or I will have you confined to your chamber." Serena advanced upon the older woman, feeling quite pleased that at last she could do what should have been done when she first became Gyles's wife—and with Gyles's approval. "Heed my words well, Beda, for your own sake." Serena warned.

One look at Gyles told Beda that there was no help to be had from him, at least for the present. So she whirled and mounted the stairs that led to the upper floors.

"She's gone to find Aurelia, no doubt."

The familiar voice caused Serena to spin about and the next moment she was being twirled around in her brother's arms.

"Bryan! Oh, Bryan!" Serena was laughing and crying at the same time. "I'm so glad to see you! How long have you been here? How long can you stay? Are you riding in the lists? Will you . . ."

"Stop! Stop!" Bryan grinned down at her. "Will you never stop badgering me with questions? You have done so since you were first able to speak, and I was greatly hoping your marriage would change that." Bryan looked closely at Serena, and the bantering tone disappeared from his voice. "All is well with you, Serena?" He spoke quietly, for though Gyles had turned to speak to other arrivals he was not out of earshot.

Serena lowered her eyes. "Yes, Bryan, of course."

"We have heard," Bryan continued, "that you two, the marriage . . . is not complete."

Serena colored. "You should not speak of such things, Bryan, and especially not here."

"Is it true?" Bryan persisted.

"True or false, 'tis none of your concern, Bryan."

"Richard is here, Serena, and he wishes a private word with you. He has sent me——"

"Are you both mad? Have you taken leave of your

81

senses entirely?" Serena whispered angrily. "I cannot—and will not—meet Richard alone! You must tell him—"

"My greetings, Bryan."

Gyles had returned to them so quietly that Serena nearly jumped at the sound of his voice. When his hand came to rest lightly on her shoulder, Serena was sure that he could feel the wild beating of her heart and she searched his face for some sign that he had overheard the conversation with Bryan. But Gyles was smiling at Bryan, so Serena relaxed and suddenly became aware of her mussed appearance. As soon as she could, Serena would have to escape to her new chamber and change, for more guests were filling the hall with each minute that passed. She returned her attention to the conversation and winced inwardly as she noted the stiffness with which Bryan spoke to Gyles. Bryan was looking daggers at her husband and Serena feared that soon he would drop any pretense of cordiality and intentionally insult Gyles.

"Tell me, Bryan," Serena intervened smoothly. "Will you participate in all the events?"

Bryan tore his gaze from Gyles and understood instantly that he had been outmaneuvered. His anger had reached its limits and he snapped at his sister. "Of course I am! What a stupid question!" He ignored the pained look in Serena's eyes as he continued. "What of you, sister dear? Will you participate as well? Or are you now content to let some knight carry your colors? Serena always took part in the combats at Broughton, Lord Gyles, except for the lance combat. She was far too light and was constantly being unhorsed. Even so, Serena persisted until Father finally forbade her to enter the joust. With a broadsword or longbow, however, Serena is most accomplished. Why, when we were small, she often threatened to kill the first Norman cur she set eyes upon. 'Tis to her undying shame that she appears to have forgotten—"

A hand clapped hard against his shoulder cut off Bryan's speech and he turned to glare at the source of yet another interruption. Richard glared back at him before releasing Bryan's shoulders and bending to kiss Serena's hand. Bryan snorted and stalked away.

"Serena, you are more beautiful than ever," Richard murmured, then raised his head to salute his host. "Your pardon, Lord Gyles, for greeting your lady first, but I would have you remember that we are old friends." Gyles inclined his head slightly as Richard continued. "Be patient with my friend," Richard nodded at Bryan's retreating back. "I fear he indulged himself with his wine-skin far too often during the journey. 'Tis a fault of his for which Serena can vouch." He bowed and made his way after Bryan.

Serena stared at the floor, embarrassed to the very depths of her soul for her brother's behavior. Everything had been going so well! What must Gyles think of her now? Would he turn from her now and again become remote and arrogant? She had hoped so desperately for him to want her as his wife.

While Serena's thoughts were in a turmoil, Gyles's were surprisingly clear. That Serena had not wanted this marriage, he had known, but that she shared Bryan's hatred of Normans was something new. Gyles had heard rumors concerning Bryan's activities and he wondered if Serena had a part in her brother's schemes. If he invited her to share his bed, would he awaken some night to the feel of a cold blade at his neck? Serena had been so pliant this afternoon—why? What was she planning? To have Bryan under his roof was bad enough, but he also was plagued with Richard's presence as well. Did Serena plan to kill him and then take Richard as her lover? What did Serena hide behind those blue eyes of hers?

Gyles was of a mind to confront her with his accusations, but he checked the impulse. "Go and change, Serena, before you take a chill. I will see to our guests." Serena turned her face upward to his and he frowned at its paleness. "And for the love of God, put some color in your cheeks and try to smile, or I'll be accused of beating you! I would hate to be challenged either by your brother or that erstwhile Saxon swain of yours," he snapped.

The evening was a nightmare that seemed to last forever for Serena. She moved through the guests with a smile fixed on her lips. She answered questions and made conversation without being aware of what she said. Gyles spoke not a word to her and in fact avoided her completely. Serena's only comfort was that he treated Beda the same way. Serena's nerves were stretched so taut that she felt like screaming when she found herself trapped between Richard and Bryan. Bryan had made free with the ale and the last vestiges of control had vanished.

"My sister, the Norman whore!" He saluted her with his drinking horn. "Where is our most gracious host, your husband? The Normans! They rape first our land and then our women. Does he please you well, sister? The nights are far too short for him I'll wager." He subsided back into his ale and Serena nearly dashed the horn from his lips.

Serena drew a shaky breath. "Perhaps you had best take Bryan outside, Richard, before he causes trouble."

"Serena, he didn't mean anything. You know what he's like when he drinks. Do not blame Bryan, for I understand well how he feels." Richard moved closer to her. "Is it true that your marriage is not complete, Serena? The Norman has not touched you?" Serena's eyes blazed at him and she started to move away but he caught her arm. "If 'tis true, Serena, there is still a way for us to be together. Petition for an annulment, Serena, the Church will surely grant it."

Serena pried Richard's fingers from her arm and hurried from him. Across the hall Aurelia and Beda watched her departure with pleased expressions.

"Everything is going quite well, Beda, don't you think?" Aurelia smiled at her sister.

Beda nodded sullenly. "Except for Serena. I thought this afternoon that our plans would come to naught, but now"—she glanced speculatively at Gyles—"I'm not sure."

"You have kept them apart?" Aurelia asked worriedly. "There won't be any offspring from this union?"

"I've done my best!" Beda hissed.

"Yes, especially when you attacked her! You nearly destroyed everything with that idiotic move. I'll tell you once more—first Geoffrey and Bryan, then Serena and

Gyles." Aurelia sighed. "Stop pouting, Beda, you'll have Gyles for quite some time. You must get me more of those herbs before I leave. My supply is nearly gone."

"Tomorrow, while everyone is at the tournament." Beda cast a smug look at Aurelia. " 'Tis thoughtful of Serena to keep such a liberal supply of what we need, as well as a book to tell us how much to use." The two sisters exchanged smiles and settled back comfortably in their chairs.

Thankfully, the evening ended early as all the guests wished to be well rested for the lists the following day. Serena retired gratefully to her chamber. The pleasant afternoon seemed years ago now, and Serena could have wept for her stillborn hopes. There was no sound from Gyles's chamber and Serena assumed that he had sought out Beda's room. She fell into bed, emotionally drained, but sleep eluded her as her mind continued to race. What had happened, Serena asked herself again. A few ill-chosen words, and all her plans had been destroyed. Damn Bryan and his fondness of wine! Was she never to live her life without others' interference? She heard the door to Gyles's chamber open and close, and Serena lay quietly listening to the sound of his movements in the room. Would Gyles at least come to her to discuss Bryan's rashness and Richard's thoughtless actions? If he did, Serena was sure she could repair what damage had been done. But the night grew older and Gyles did not come, and Serena nearly cried in her despair. Instead she rose from the bed and opened the trunk that held her armor. Carefully, Serena removed her mail, armor, shield, and weapons and began to polish them by the flickering candlelight. She had been a fool to believe Gyles could be won by soft words and willing compliance, but she would be a fool no longer.

At breakfast the next morning Serena was silent and withdrawn and Gyles marked with interest the deep shadows beneath her eyes. Serena picked at her food and finally pushed it away, drawing Gyles's attention.

"If you are ill, Serena, perhaps you should remain inside." The mocking concern in his voice made Serena long to tear at his handsome face with her nails. Gyles saw the brief flash of her anger and, smiling, he continued. "You do look a bit feverish, m'lady, I fear you took a chill after our swim yesterday. Yes, I believe 'twould be best if you kept to your chamber until you are better."

It was impossible that she could have taken a chill in yesterday's heat, Serena thought, and Gyles knew it, but she merely shrugged. "As you wish, m'lord. I had planned to spend the day abed."

Serena rose and left the hall, her departure noticed by none save Richard to whom she gave a slight nod. She gained her chamber, but did not enter, listening instead to the cacophony of voices diminish as the guests left the castle. Only then did she hurry into the room and bar the door behind her.

Gyles watched the tilting with little interest, awaiting his turn with the lance. The riders were good, but so far few had shown any style at tilting; instead they appeared content to charge pell-mell at each other without taking careful aim with their lances. Well, Gyles shrugged, that was the difference between seasoned fighters tempered in battle and untried boys.

His turn came, and Gyles mounted his horse, a strong stallion that had served him well for three years. The horse pawed eagerly at the earth, sensing the upcoming excitement. At the far end of the field, Gyles could see his opponent—the well-polished armor glinting brightly in the sun, as he adjusted his sheld, snapped closed his visor, and extended his arm for a lance. Gyles did the same and both men waited for the signal to charge. A banner dropped and Gyles set his spurs into his horse's sides. The cheering of the crowd barely carried over the din of thundering hooves as Gyles settled his lance more securely in his grasp. All the weapons used today had been blunted and their blades covered, so no mortal injury would befall the contestants. Gyles watched his adversary approach and felt a flicker of admiration. The man wavered neither to right nor left and his lance—angled across his body—was pointed directly at the center of Gyles's shield. It appeared to Gyles that his adversary was slightly off balance, the weight of the lance carrying him too far to the inside of his horse. Gyles adjusted his own lance so that it would catch the upper right portion of the shield. At the instant before they met, the knight pushed his shield up and out, and Gyles's lance skittered harmlessly skyward while the other's lance caught fairly on Gyles's shield. Braced as he was for a hearty blow, Gyles was surprised by the light contact of the lance and had no trouble retaining his seat. He reached the end of the field, tossed aside the used lance, deftly caught the new one thrown by a squire and wheeled his horse around. The other knight was already charging full-tilt across the green, and for a moment Gyles was taken aback by the size of his opponent. It was strange that he hadn't noticed before how small the knight appeared in contrast to the horse. Gyles's mount surged forward, but Gyles's actions were purely automatic, his mind concentrating instead on the knight—armor had a way of deceiving the eyes because of its bulkiness, it could make a large man appear smaller than his normal size and the opposite was also true, and yet . . .

The distance between the two had rapidly diminished and at the last minute, Gyles altered the angle of his lance so that it caught the knight square in the chest instead of the shield. A muffled "oof" came from behind the visor, and the knight neatly somersaulted backward over the rear of his horse. The lance flew uselessly from his grasp and the knight hit the earth with a thud and an alarming clatter of armor. As he galloped toward the end of the field, Gyles caught sight of the squires racing from their places on the sidelines to aid the fallen knight to his feet. By the time Gyles turned his horse and returned to the site of his victory, the knight was being led into one of Lord Geoffrey's pavilions. His shield lay against the side of the tent along with the unused lance. Gyles rode to the pavilion and dismounted. The shield caught and held his attention, and he knelt to study its logo.

Divided into three parts, it bore no resemblance to any of the coats-of-arms Gyles had seen before: the upper half of the shield was divided into two equal parts, on the left a white rose bloomed, the petals painted in such perfection that they appeared real, green leaves perched delicately on gently curving, thornless stems; the right showed the sword Excalibur protruding from the stone from which King Arthur had freed it, and proclaimed its owner's Saxon heritage; the complete lower portion of the shield was devoted to the image of a bolt of lightning twisting and tearing its way through a cloud. The colors used also fascinated Gyles, for they were not the bright, vivid colors typically used, but were instead muted tones of green, blue, and gold that gentled the senses rather than assaulted them.

Gyles rose and hefted the lance. It was lighter by far than those normally used, and with a frown Gyles tested the shield as well. It, too, was of less weight than it should have been; well made and sturdy, it was true, but the shield was still too weak to withstand an assault of any duration, for it would surely bend and crack under the repeated blows of a broadsword.

"Serena was far too light—she was constantly unhorsed." The echo of Bryan's words burst into Gyles's mind. "Far too light . . . constantly unhorsed; far too light . . . constantly unhorsed . . . unhorsed . . . unhorsed . . . unhorsed." Serena! Gyles made for the flap of the tent, but found the way blocked by a grinning Bryan and an ashen-faced Richard as they exited.

Bryan glanced at the shield and lance that Gyles still held and the grin deepened. "I can assure you, Lord Gyles, that yon knight admits his defeat; he is of no mind to continue the contest, as you seem wont to do."

Gyles replaced the weapons. " 'Tis an unusual logo, not familiar to me," he said as he straightened.

Bryan threw back his head and laughed, "Did you not know? 'Tis Serena's own coat-of-arms. Did she never show it to you? Odd, for she is inordinately proud of it."

Gyles pulled the helm from his head and brushed the mail coif back from his face. Serena! He should have guessed; she had acceded too readily to his request to remain in her chamber. No wonder Bryan was laughing; Serena had made a fool of him! If it was ever discovered that he had tilted with a woman, and his own wife at that . . .

The wickedly curved scar whitened as the corner of Gyles's mouth tightened. "I should like to see my wife!" Gyles growled.

"Serena?" Bryan looked puzzled. "She's at the castle! Oh, no!" He began to laugh. "You think Serena is here? You think Serena was . . . that she jousted. . . ." He dissolved into helpless gales of laughter and sank to the ground.

"There's no cause for hilarity, Bryan!" Richard snapped. "Godwin might have been badly injured." Some color had returned to Richard's face and he addressed Gyles. "The shield is Serena's, as you know." He hesitated before continuing. "When—before Serena left Broughton, Godwin was her sparring partner, since he was the only man near her size. He has always carried Serena's shield in the lists she herself did not take part in."

Gyles had watched Richard carefully as he spoke. The younger man did not meet his eyes, and his speech, somehow, did not ring true. "I would meet Godwin." Gyles said.

Richard glanced briefly at Bryan who had recovered and was gaining his feet. Bryan shrugged. "Of course. Godwin will be honored, m'lord." Turning, he led the way into the pavilion.

A young man lay on the pallet, and by the dim light that filtered through from the outside, Gyles judged the lad to be no more than twenty. Godwin was nude save for his loincloth, and Gyles bent to examine what slight damage his lance had done; his brown, lean fingers gently pressing the unmarked skin covering the breastbone.

"There seems to be no serious damage," Gyles said as he straightened. "Is there much pain?"

"N-no, m'lord." Godwin stammered.

Gyles's eyes probed the corner of the pavilion. "Was your armor badly dented?"

Godwin stirred uneasily. "No, m'lord."

"His squire is seeing to his arms, m'lord." Bryan broke in smoothly. "By tomorrow no one will be able to tell where your lance caught him."

Gyles nodded and left, and as he rode from the pavilion, Bryan's laughter floated on the air behind him.

Serena leaned against the wall, her head tilted to one side, as she listened to the minstrel's love ballad. A tiny smile curved her lips and her eyes held a dreamy, far-off quality that unreasonably angered Gyles when he happened to glance her way. Richard joined her and handed her a goblet, and Serena pressed the palm of her hand against his cheek; a gesture that caused Gyles to stiffen and his scar to whiten. Richard bent to Serena's ear and she raised her delicate shoulders in a shrug and laughed teasingly up at him.

Serena had not condescended to speak a word to her husband, but instead had enchanted everyone—at least every knight—that had come within her sphere of influence. Gyles had to admit that Serena was dazzling. Her hair was caught beneath a snood of woven pearls and her dark green dress set off her complexion to decided advantage. Her cheeks contained a hint of color, her mouth the shade of the pastel pink wild roses that grew unbidden in her garden, and Serena's eyes glowed with an excitement that Gyles had never seen before.

Serena was acutely conscious of the burning looks Gyles sent in her direction, but she steadfastly ignored them. Gyles had chosen to condemn her for Bryan's and Richard's behavior—very well then, so be it. If 'twas a marriage of convenience he desired, Serena too could seek contentment elsewhere. He was more remote and aloof than ever before, and Serena damned herself for having let him glimpse the naked yearning of her heart for love. She began slowly, stone by stone, to build a wall about her heart, so that he could not hurt her again.

Where her wounded heart had failed her, Serena's pride did not, and her bearing this evening left no doubt in anyone's mind that she was indeed mistress of Camden. Beda had been relegated to a less obvious seat at the head table and the servants responded willingly and without delay to Serena's every command.

Every movement Serena made was perfectly in keeping with her role, but it seemed she deliberately provoked her husband's ire at every opportunity. She charmed Gyles's friends until every one was willing to happily give his life for her. If Gyles—driven into a savage mood—played the gallant with Beda or any of the other ladies present, Serena retaliated in kind until Gyles came dangerously close to violence as he watched his wife fend off over-eager advances. But what drove Gyles perilously near the breaking point was that whenever Serena passed him, she swept into a deep curtsy and did not rise until he had gone some distance from her. Whenever the act was performed, eyebrows raised among both Normans and Saxons, as well as murmured comments about an unnatural marriage. The evening had progressed in this manner until Gyles avoided going anywhere near his wife for fear she would think of some other outrageous act. Gyles was sure Serena had lost her mind.

On the contrary, Serena knew precisely what she was doing as she set the spur deeper into Gyles's pride. She had been deeply hurt and she had set about to repay Gyles in the same coin. But even though her plans were going well, Serena could not help the sinking sensation in her heart that told her Gyles was lost to her forever.

Serena closed her eyes and rested her head against the cool stones of the wall. Instantly a mental image of Gyles appeared behind her closed lids—Gyles as he had looked the afternoon at the pool; his lithe body tall, straight, and bronzed; his powerful arms holding her against him; the weak helpless feeling that invaded every inch of her being as Gyles lowered his head toward her.

No! Serena's eyes flew open. That had not happened, Gyles had not kissed her that day. It was all in her imagination! She must stop dreaming, hoping.

The minstrel had finished his song and was waiting for some show of pleasure from Serena. Distractedly, she tossed him the gold goblet she held. The minstrel bobbed his thanks and continued on his way.

Richard murmured into Serena's ear, "The man spoke truly, Serena. You are, indeed, a feast upon which no man would tire of dining. Come away with me, my love. Tonight. We can be far away from here by first light tomorrow. Once at Balfour we will be safe; no one could harm us there. We will be happy, Serena, I swear it. As soon as your annulment is granted, we shall be wed. Ah, Serena, you shall be my most treasured wife, and I shall teach you the full measure of a man's love. Our children will play where I once did; and never shall I give you cause to doubt my love for you, for I will worship you day and night."

Serena's eyes were bright with unshed tears. "Oh, Richard, you spin such lovely tales. I only wish that they could come true."

"They can, Serena! They can!" Richard caught her hands urgently. "Come with me, and all these tales will become real."

Serena shook her head. "It can never be," she said sadly. "Gyles would come after us—he would tear Balfour down stone by stone, kill you, and take me back to Camden. Unjust as it may be, I am his wife and he will keep me until death ends this mockery." Serena gave Richard's hands a gentle squeeze. "Marry, Richard," she implored him. "Marry! Forget me, I beg of you, for my sake and yours. Produce heirs for Balfour; find a wife." Richard watched her closely, and Serena's control nearly vanished at the kindness and love that shone in his eyes. "Go away from Camden and never return. I can bring you naught but pain. Go! Oh, please, Richard, go!" The tears began to spill down her cheeks. "Leave me to my own private hell!"

Serena stumbled blindly toward the stairs, but Gyles blocked her path. Automatically Serena sank into a deep curtsy. A band of pain circled her chest and grew tighter and tighter until she nearly choked with it. Serena was being torn to pieces, her soul severed to bits between Gyles, Alan, Richard, Bryan, and herself. Her breath came in short gulps and seared her lungs.

"Get up!" Gyles snarled.

"I—I cannot, m'lord." Serena gasped.

"Rise, Serena, or I will carry you from here!" Gyles warned.

Serena struggled to obey him. The band of pain tightened further, and Serena felt certain she would swoon. Her legs would not obey her and Serena closed her eyes to try to right the suddenly tilting world.

"Will you leave the hall on your feet or in my arms, Serena? Whichever way you choose, I swear you will pay for your behavior this night." Gyles's voice was harsh.

Serena lifted her tear-streaked face and gave vent to the humiliation that bit so deeply into her heart. "Then beat me! Kill me if you will! I do not care! End this hellish existence you have given me. I am weary of your biting words, your spiteful actions." Gyles's hands closed around Serena's arms and he pulled her roughly to her feet.

How could she alter so quickly, Gyles wondered? The evening had been hers; she had beaten him in their unspoken war. There was not a man present who did not adore her, nor a woman who did not envy Serena her grace and beauty. Gyles stared down at his wife, not daring now to release her for fear she would collapse. She was trembling violently, the tremors passing through her body and up his arms. Gyles caught sight of Richard watching them and a violent wave of anger flooded him. So that was what had reduced Serena to tears! He was tired of Serena's former suitor constantly reminding his wife of what might have been.

"We are retiring, *my lady*," Gyles said sarcastically. "And if you make a scene, I will drag you from the hall! Do you understand?"

"Please," Serena begged, the tears flowing freely now. "Let me go. Allow me to find my own peace."

"With Richard? Nay, Serena, not now or ever shall I let you go. You are like a wild mare, you need only to be properly broken."

Serena's temper flared at his words. "You are not the man to do that, m'lord. Better have tried."

"But not in my fashion," Gyles said silkily, and guided her up the steps.

The band of pain diminished, the tears slowly halted as Serena's self-control returned. By the time they entered her chamber, she was in command of herself and she eyed Gyles warily.

"What is it you wish, m'lord? Your husbandly rights?" Serena sneered. "Shall I strip for you or would you prefer to tear the gown from my back?" Gyles's scar showed starkly white against his face. Serena knew her attack was effective and she pressed it home. "Pray tell me how I may pleasure you, m'lord. Shall I rub the weariness from your body? A warm bath perhaps? Wine? No, I can see none of those appeal to you. Then what?" Serena dropped gracefully to her knees. "I am yours to command. Give me an order and I shall obey."

Gyles's features hardened. "How did you pass the day?" He began to wander aimlessly about the room.

"I slept. Alan came to my room and I played with him. I worked on a piece of tapestry." Serena wearied of her game and rose from her knees to seat herself more comfortably on a chair. "Why do you care?"

Gyles ignored the question. "You allowed another to carry your standard and colors. I will not allow you to do so again."

Serena removed her snood and began to uncoil her hair. "Why should Sir Godwin not bear my colors? Are you volunteering to do so? You bear your own so proudly. I cannot believe you would prefer to wear my colors."

"You are my wife, and I will allow no other man to accept such an honor from you." Gyles paused beside the chests that lined one wall. "Bryan tells me you have a set of armor and a coat of mail, I want to see them."

"As you wish." Serena crossed the room to him and opened a chest. She lifted the mail and held it up for his inspection.

94

Gyles turned it over, eyeing the links critically. "Now the armor." He commanded.

Serena nodded and opened the door that led to the private chapel. "I had no other place to store it, I'm afraid. I thought your men would think it odd if I placed it in the armory."

Gyles ran his hand over the metal. "'Tis a fine piece of armor, good workmanship." He lifted it from the floor and found, as he knew he would, that its weight was less than it should have been. Scaled down to suit Serena's size, of course, and light enough so her slight frame would have no difficulty bearing the load of the armor. By the glow of the candle, Gyles could see that Lord Geoffrey had indeed indulged his daughter's boyish whims, for she possessed nearly every weapon imaginable. Gyles replaced the armor and closed the door to the chapel behind him.

Serena had returned to her chair and sat combing the gold-streaked mass of her curls. She kept her back to Gyles when she spoke. "Am I to be allowed to view the lists tomorrow or am I still confined to this room?"

Gyles frowned slightly at her unyielding back. "Do as you wish, Serena, I do not care."

When the door had closed behind her husband, Serena doubled over in the chair as if in great pain.

5

"The lists have been greatly enjoyed, m'lord."

Edward and Gyles stood behind a parapet on the castle wall. Beneath them, the green field was littered with the knights in their polished, glittering armor, and the spectators milled about. The people's clothing formed bright splashes of color against the meadow as did the pavilions with their standards snapping smartly in the breeze. Gyles had not yet donned his armor and his coat of mail showed dull grey in the morning sun.

Gyles nodded at Edward's observation and clapped the older man's shoulders. "You should have competed, Edward. Those callow youths need a good display of arms. Look at the way they hack at each other. None of them would have lasted a minute at Hastings."

Edward chuckled, "I have my hands full just training the young pups you bring me, m'lord. I fear I am far too old to withstand the irritation of being set upon by any of those gallants." He studied the field briefly. "They have set up the targets, m'lord, we had better descend."

But Gyles was watching the archery range below, his scar deathly pale. A knight in a familiar suit of armor had caught his eye, and while he watched, the knight strung his bow and tested its resiliency. Godwin! Again wearing Serena's coat-of-arms on his shield, though Gyles had expressly forbidden her to give him her favor.

Gyles took the steps two at a time, heedless of Edward's shout: "Sir Gyles! Your armor, m'lord."

He burst into Serena's chamber only to find it empty. With a growled expletive, Gyles turned and hurled himself along the passage, down another flight of steps, through the great hall and outside, where he made for the archery range. Godwin was already at the mark when Gyles arrived and he was forced to cool his heels and rage while that good knight loosed his arrows. With each arrow that found the heart of the target, a cheer went up from the bystanders, and once more Gyles was forced into unwilling admiration for Godwin's marksmanship. Of the five arrows allowed, only the last did not find the center, and Godwin raised a gloved hand in a gesture of indifference before he swung around to leave the field.

Gyles made to follow but found his path blocked by Richard who was stringing his bow. Gyles tried to brush Richard aside and as he moved, tangled his foot in the rawhide, which immediately became emmeshed in the links of his mail. Richard swore as he knelt to free the strip of rawhide.

"I know I am your guest, Lord Gyles, but you must have a care. I am delaying the contest because of your clumsiness and I fear your mail is shredding this string. Squire!" Richard called over his shoulder. "Return to my tent and bring me another string. And be quick about it! If you will stop struggling, m'lord, I can free you the sooner."

Gyles ground his teeth in impatience as he watched Godwin's rapidly retreating figure. By the time Gyles was freed, Godwin had disappeared, and Gyles was forced to return to the castle to retrieve his bow, as it would soon be his turn to compete. As he stamped through the great hall, Gyles nearly collided with Serena. Her face was flushed and her eyes appeared overly bright as she sought to go around him.

Gyles's hand shot out, stilling her movement, and she bent into the by now familiar mocking curtsy. "Where have you been?" Gyles snarled.

"With Alan, m'lord. I lost track of time and must

hurry if I am to see Bryan shoot. May I rise?" Serena's voice was breathless.

"You missed Godwin's display then?"

"Godwin? He has already taken part then? How did he fare?" Serena was on her feet now and Gyles could sense the excitement coursing through her.

"Your man fared well. As far as I know he leads the field."

Serena clapped her hands in child-like glee. "Does he really? How wonderful. Please, m'lord, will you release me? I am most eager to be off."

"I can see that." Gyles sneered. "You disobeyed me, Serena. Godwin had your favor again today."

"He asked so prettily, m'lord." Serena's long, tapering fingers came down over Gyles's hand and struggled to loose his grip. "Please, m'lord, I am missing the match!" Serena wailed.

The cold mask of formality and reserve had dropped away and Gyles glimpsed for the first time a side of his wife he had never seen. Serena was young—as he had never been allowed to be—and that youth carried with it an exuberance and vitality she had heretofore carefully suppressed. Serena was vibrant and alive, and Gyles realized she must have felt isolated and lonely when she had been separated from her family and friends, from all that was familiar to her. Gyles had tried to crush her spirit, to subjugate her will to his, and for that he felt a wave of guilt wash over him. Serena thrived on what he was incapable of giving—love, a commodity sorely lacking at Camden.

Distressed, Gyles released Serena's arm. "Go then," he said quietly. "Richard is about to shoot, perhaps you will bring him luck." Beside Serena's innocent enthusiasm he felt old and jaded.

Gyles walked slowly to the steps and Serena watched him go with wide eyes. She was suddenly ashamed of the trick she was playing on him—Gyles tried, for all his arrogance and pride to be a fair and just man, but she had given him little chance to prove himself with her. Serena twisted her scarf in her hands. There was no help for it now, she had begun the conspiracy and must see it through. Serena ran from the hall into the dazzling sunlight.

Gyles raised his bow, sighted the arrow on the target and exerted a steady pressure on the bowstring.

"Hold! Wait! Do not shoot!"

Serena's voice floated through the air, and, turning, Gyles saw his wife pushing her way toward him. Obligingly the spectators parted and Serena raced the last few feet to Gyles. He lowered his bow and looked quizzically at Serena.

"Oh, I nearly missed you!" Serena gasped. "Wear this, m'lord, for luck." She lifted her scarf and tied it about Gyles's arm. As he drew his brows together in a frown she said desperately, "Please, m'lord. I must have a champion."

"You have Godwin."

Serena flushed. "But you are my husband. 'Tis you who should be my acknowledged gallant."

Gyles stared down into the twin pools of blue that were Serena's eyes. "You would allow a *Norman* to bear your honor?"

"Only one Norman, m'lord," Serena murmured softly, and withdrew from the field.

Serena found a place among the cluster of spectators between Richard and Bryan.

"What are you about, Serena?" Bryan asked angrily. "Have you forgotten your vengeance so quickly?"

"Be still, Bryan, he is my husband. 'Tis fitting he wear my colors." Serena's eyes never left Gyles as he loosed one arrow after another.

"Serena?" Richard's voice was anguished.

Serena turned to Richard. "Do not start again, Richard, I beg of you. I can endure it no longer. Between you, Bryan and Gyles, my soul is being ripped to pieces. Be my friend, Richard, and leave it at that."

"I cannot give up hope, my love."

A cheer went up from the crowd, and Serena spun back to the contest. Gyles's arrows had all found the center of the target, and a surge of pride flooded Serena. She did not even notice that Richard left her side, as she started forward to congratulate Gyles, but Bryan placed a restraining hand on her arm.

"You astound me, Serena. What are you playing at now? First you swear you must have revenge and now you play the gentle wife. Decide, sister mine. Which do you desire to be: vengeful or loving?"

"Neither. Both. Oh, Bryan, I know not." Serena looked at Bryan pleadingly. "My head pulls me one way, my heart another. I am confused and beset on all sides. I can find no peace in any decision I make. What has happened to me, Bryan?"

A strand of gold blew across her face and Bryan gently brushed it away from Serena's cheek. What he thought, Bryan did not wish to put into words; for he had the feeling that Serena, his adoring, younger sister was growing away from him. Bryan smiled. "What of Godwin?" He teased lightly.

"There is no reason he should not take part in the mock battle tomorrow. Nothing has changed."

"I'll be glad when the lists are over, my nerves are torn to shreds," Bryan sighed. "Speak to Richard, Serena, his heart has been broken."

"I have. He doesn't listen. He shouldn't have returned to Camden, it only caused him more pain." Serena looked around for Gyles, but he had disappeared from the crowd. Belatedly, Serena remembered that Beda had lauded his victory with a kiss that was in no way sisterly. Was Gyles now in Beda's arms within the walls of her chamber?

"The players have arrived." Bryan's voice jolted Serena away from her thoughts. "Let's go watch them, Serena. We'll find Richard and while away the afternoon. For the last time, Serena, let us pretend that nothing has changed—and then, then you must pick up your life. You are my sister, Serena, and we have inherited strength from our parents; you will conquer your Norman mate if that is what you desire most. And I think it is."

The evening passed in much the same manner as the preceding ones, with some slight changes. Serena no longer dropped to the floor when Gyles neared and Bryan resisted the temptation of the ale kegs. Richard refrained from badgering Serena about an annulment and the hall resounded with the revelers' laughter. The following day would see the mock battle and as the opposing forces had already been decided, the knights took great delight in shouting challenges at each other. With Gyles seated beside her, Serena happily viewed the entertainment.

"Godwin is not present again tonight, it seems. Where does your brave Saxon keep himself, Serena?" Gyles studied his wife's profile with an odd sparkling in his green eyes.

"Godwin is a most pious young man, m'lord. I believe he finds the evening's sport not to his taste." With her head, Serena indicated several couples locked in each other's arms.

"It makes a night pass swiftly." Gyles observed with a shrug as he reached for his ale. "Richard seems to have found a most willing partner," he added.

Serena followed his look. "So he has," she said with little interest, then suddenly sat bolt upright in her chair.

Gyles leaned back in his chair and watched the different emotions chase across Serena's face. "Does it trouble you that he has found another, Serena?"

"No . . . but, the woman—m'lord, she is married!" Serena's voice was shocked.

"So?"

The strange note in his voice caused Serena to turn to Gyles. "But, m'lord, they are committing adultery."

" 'Tis a common enough practice, Serena, the lady was forced into a marriage she abhors, so she finds her pleasure wherever she can." He was speaking not of Richard and his lady, but of himself and Serena.

And Serena saw the analogy. "Her husband, m'lord, does he also take his . . . pleasure outside his marriage vows?"

His green eyes looked away from her blue ones and

concentrated on the guests. "He does. He is a most virile man and his appetite is never appeased."

If Gyles had hoped to shake her, he was successful. Serena's hands were clenched in her lap and she studied them closely. "He finds no comfort in his wife's arms?" Serena asked quietly.

"They have three offspring, all boys. Their duty to each other is finished—and she neither encourages nor discourages him to seek her bed." A pain began somewhere deep in his heart and Gyles had to force himself to continue. "They do not love, Serena, and have made each other's lives unbearable."

"One does not choose who to love, 'tis something that happens without mortal interference," Serena said reflectively. "Would that one could say 'I will love this person and not the other.' But one cannot. Love must begin without pressure and then be tenderly nourished by the lovers. Love should be freely given; it should be shared so that as it grows both people are incomplete without the other."

Serena looked up and found herself lost in Gyles's emerald gaze. He knew! Gyles looked into her heart and saw there what she had only now discovered. Serena had no defense left to her with which to deny the truth she saw revealed in his eyes, and now he could hurt her as he never had before. She began to tremble and her only thought was to escape. Escape Gyles before he forced her to put her emotions into words. His large, warm hand suddenly covered hers and Serena's eyes dropped to study the strong, brown fingers that exerted a gentle pressure.

"You are trembling, Serena, and your hands are like ice. Come, we will retire." Gyles rose to his feet, drawing Serena with him.

Unsteadily, Serena managed to stay by his side as they made their way through the hall and up to their chambers. Gyles did not pause by Serena's door but took her instead to his chamber. He left her side to light a candle and then reached out to pull his wife against him. Serena stood stiffly in the circle of his arms and Gyles began to gently stroke her back. His lips brushed lightly against the top of her hair and Serena shuddered.

"Do not be afraid, Serena, I will not hurt you more than I can help. Do you understand?"

Serena nodded. "Nellwyn told me." She tilted her head upward. "I do not fear the pain, m'lord."

"You fear me?" Gyles's hands stopped their gentling movement and his fingers meshed around the back of her neck. "You needn't, Serena, for I will be as gentle as possible."

"I suppose you've had many women?"

"A full legion at least," Gyles teased.

"Do not mock me," Serena whispered.

Gyles sobered instantly. "Forgive me, I am not used to dealing with untutored virgins." His hands moved and pulled the ribbons from Serena's hair and then twined themselves in the curls.

Gyles's breath was hot upon her neck and Serena raised a hand to the wiry curls at the back of his neck. "I am ignorant, m'lord."

"I do not expect a virgin to know a man's passions," he murmured against her hair. "I shall teach you well, Serena, not only my delights, but your own as well."

Gyles bent and covered Serena's lips with his own as his hands slid down her shoulders and arms before they circled her waist. Gyles's mouth worked on hers, prying her lips apart ever so slowly until his tongue could enter and plunder the recesses of Serena's mouth. Serena felt herself lifted from the floor and clasped tightly against Gyles's chest. His mouth released hers and Serena's head fell back against his arm while his lips traced a burning path down her throat. His breathing quickened and Gyles pressed Serena closer until it seemed no part of her body did not touch his and Serena could feel his desire. His lips claimed her again, a savage repossession that drew her very soul out of her body and into his own. A sweet, urgent need surfaced in Serena, and she returned to Gyles over and over again the kiss he had given her.

She clung to him with all the strength of her tiny body and found herself moving wantonly against Gyles until she was sure the contact of their bodies would take her to the brink of insanity. Gyles pressed tiny kisses against the corners of her mouth and temples and gently lowered her down the length of his body until her feet reached the floor. Unwilling to lose the strange lassitude that permeated her body, Serena lay against Gyles, listening to the deep beat of his heart return to its steady, even pattern.

Gyles's eyes glowed as he looked down at his wife and he cupped her chin in his hand and brought her face upward. Serena's eyes had darkened with passion and Gyles knew she would not resist his advances this night. For the moment Serena was totally his, her will bending to his—but for how long? Would morning find her once again rejecting and repudiating him? Should he take her tonight and force her into the realization that though she might wish it, she would never escape him? What could he use to bind her tightly to him? That her pride forced her to honor the vows she had spoken was not enough for Gyles. He wanted her bound to him so closely that she would never glance at another man.

"What would you have from me, Serena?" Gyles asked huskily.

"Have from you, m'lord?" Serena's eyes grew puzzled and she drew slightly away from him. "I do not understand."

"Jewels? Furs? Name only what you desire and you shall have it." Gyles smoothed the mass of hair over Serena's shoulder.

"There is naught that I desire . . . except . . ."

Gyles sighed. Serena was no different from any of the other women he had taken after all. His hand dropped to his side. "Except what, Serena?"

Serena blushed deeply. "I would ask . . . that is . . . will you . . . for me . . . will you no longer seek out Beda?" Her words tumbled over each other now. "I do not mean to be shrewish, m'lord, truly, but in truth I cannot bear the thought of you in her arms."

It was an enormous admission for Serena, and Gyles recognized it as such. "That I can easily grant you, for as

God is my witness, I have not shared her bed since you and I were wed. Name something else, Serena." Gyles smiled down at her. "What can I give you that you do not now possess?"

Serena shook her head. "Nothing, m'lord."

"Then you must grant me a boon, Serena."

"If it is within my power, m'lord, I shall do whatever you wish," Serena replied.

"My name is Gyles, not 'm'lord.' Say it."

"Gyles." The name was spoken gently, almost shyly, and the sound was most welcome to Gyles's ear.

Gyles bent to place a kiss upon Serena's lips. "And now, sweet wife, the night grows short." He lifted Serena in his arms and strode across the room.

Serena's head rested against his shoulder and she closed her eyes against the rest of the world. The bed was soft and seemed to welcome Serena's weight, but her eyes flew open when Gyles did not join her. He stood above Serena, a half-smile playing on his lips, and she found Gyles had placed her on her own bed.

"Rest well, Serena, tomorrow will be long and tiring." He turned to the door which joined their rooms that still stood ajar from their passage. "One last thing, Serena. You remember the afternoon at the pond?" At her nod, Gyles continued, "You gave me your word on a certain matter."

Serena propped herself up on her elbows and eyed him curiously.

"Your word of honor, Serena, that you would not take part in the lists, remember?" Again Serena nodded. "See that you keep your word."

Gyles woke well-pleased with himself the following morning, and allowed himself the luxury of lying abed before he began the day. Memory of the evening sprang to his mind and Gyles found himself smiling at the ceiling. Serena. She would be his wife in deed as well as in name soon, and the thought brought Gyles contentment despite the warmth that was beginning to grow in his loins. Her ability to meet his own passion with a ferocity all her own astounded Gyles; but he must tred carefully lest he go too far too quickly and frighten Serena with his desire. The suffused warmth turned into a sweet ache within his body and Gyles was sorely tempted to seek out Serena's bed despite his previous resolutions. But Serena had to be tenderly wooed—Gyles knew that now—so that she would not feel she had been bid and bartered for like a brood mare. Oh, yes; when Gyles finished his courtship of her mind there would be no corner of it that would defy him and then Gyles would be free to unleash all of Serena's passion.

Gyles swung himself from the bed and began to gird himself for the battle. Hearing movements outside his door, Gyles called for his squire to enter and soon Gyles descended to the hall to break his fast. Serena was not at the table, and though Giles dallied as long as he dared, by the time he rose Serena still had not shown herself.

A frown crossed Gyles's face; it wasn't like Serena to be late; for all week she had beaten him to the hall every morning. Gyles could think only that Serena had had a change of heart where he was concerned and the thought caused his face to set grimly. Serena had reconsidered and decided upon Richard over her husband. Gyles retraced his steps to seek her out and confront her and nearly ran over Serena in his haste.

Her hair still mussed from sleep fell across her shoulders and over the creamy skin of her bosom, and Serena was clad only in a blue chamber robe as she stood beside a pillar that concealed her from the hall below. She reached out and drew Gyles into the shadow with her.

"I overslept," Serena confessed drowsily, as her blue eyes hazily focused on her husband. "But I could not let you leave without wishing you luck."

Gyles smiled and indicated his scabbard around which was tied Serena's scarf. "Today I carry my gentle lady's colors into mortal combat," he intoned heavily. "And should I mortally stricken fall, 'twill bring me comfort to know she cares."

Serena paled. "Do not speak like that, Gyles, not even in jest!"

"Ah, you remembered, Serena. 'Tis much to my liking to hear my name from your lips." Gyles caressed her cheek with his fingertips and shook his head at her loss of color. " 'Tis only a mock battle, Serena, no harm will befall me," Gyles chided.

Serena's hand sought his and she pressed a kiss into his palm. "You will have a care for yourself, Gyles?"

Gyles smiled indulgently. "Yes, Serena, I will take care. For of what use would I be to you if I were only half a man?" he asked wickedly.

"Gyles!" Serena looked at him reproachfully before her lips curved into a smile. "And try not to be too angry with me, I pray you. I promised Godwin he could bear my standard today, and I cannot in all fairness revoke that honor now."

Gyles sighed and shook his head. "Ah, Serena, which are you: Saxon maiden or Norman wife? In truth you have probably instructed Godwin to remove this poor knight from your life."

"Nay, Gyles!" Serena flew into his arms and pressed herself tightly against him. "I would not! I swear, I would not!"

"Serena?" Gyles was shocked by her vehement denial. "Serena? I but meant to tease you."

" 'Tis not amusing!" Serena's voice caught in her throat. "You are my husband."

Gyles lifted her in his arms. "Then give your husband a token to carry into battle," Gyles whispered hoarsely and his mouth came down on hers. He had meant only a gentle kiss, but the fires that had been so carefully banked now flared and Gyles knew that his mouth was working with a bruising force on Serena's.

Serena—her newly discovered passion blossoming forth—met Gyles's tongue with her own and reveled at its effect, for his hands slid down her back to her buttocks to mold her firmly against him. When at last they parted, it was Serena who was able to speak despite the strangely overwhelming ache in her body.

"The trumpets sound, Gyles, you had better hurry for you will have little enough time to don your armor."

Her blue eyes sparkled teasingly at him. "What you hunger for will be here when you return."

Serena spun from his hold and ran lightly to her chamber. At the door she paused. "I will be watching," she called. "See you do my colors honor!" With a light laugh she disappeared.

Gyles pulled on his helm and surveyed the field as his squire buckled the sword around his waist. It was only mid-morning, but already the heat beat down in shimmering waves. Not the ideal day to be trapped in a suit of amor, Gyles mused. His green eyes scanned the field and he noticed that he would not be the only late arrival. Godwin was hurrying to keep pace with Bryan as they gained the field, and Gyles saw him refuse Bryan's offer of a horse for the combat. Bryan was gesticulating wildly to the younger knight, and then Godwin must have spoken for Bryan's movement ceased and he stood quietly in front of Godwin. Bryan must have begun one last appeal, but Godwin would have none of it and flipped down the visor of his helm and swaggered—that was the only word for it—to his squire to choose his arms.

The shield was slipped over Godwin's forearm and then he selected a broadsword. The mace he discarded as it could not be blunted and its sharp spikes were capable of splitting a man's head with ease. A lighter sword was strapped around Godwin's armor and at the last minute, he reached out and added a dagger to his equipment. Bryan was nearby, going through the same process, but his equipage was suited—as was Gyles's—for a man on horseback. He called something to Godwin and Godwin raised his hands in an indifferent gesture. Richard's banner was crossing the field to where Bryan and Godwin stood arguing and Gyles was surprised by the fierce look on Richard's face. He stepped between Bryan and Godwin but addressed himself solely to the smaller knight. A light breeze rippled over the field and part of Richard's words reached Gyles's ears.

". . . insane . . . I will not allow . . . when Gyles sees you . . . could do with a thrashing . . . still not too old . . .

knight of the realm . . . Lady Serena . . . brother should know better . . . off the field!"

In an action completely out of character, Godwin stamped his foot and Gyles burst into laughter. It appeared Godwin had his own reasons for avoiding the mixed company of the castle. Gyles wondered if Serena knew her former sparring partner's sexual preference. Small wonder Richard wanted him off the field—no doubt he felt Godwin unworthy of his knighting. Gyles dismissed the scene from his mind and mounted his horse.

As was customary, the combatants circled the field so that the spectators could cheer their favorites. Gyles caught sight of Alan waving excitedly to him with one hand while Nellwyn kept a firm grip on the other. The nurse gave Bryan a disapproving glare as he passed and Gyles wondered if Bryan had fallen back into the habit of imbibing too much. Serena was nowhere to be seen though Gyles's green eyes probed the crowd for her. Undoubtedly she was still dressing, Gyles thought, or perhaps she had decided to wait in her chamber until he returned so they could have the privacy he for one so urgently desired. Serena's welcome—Gyles could already see the delicate alabaster body gracing his bed as Serena's eyes beckoned him to join her.

The trumpets blared and the opposing forces took their positions. Gyles's mount stamped and tossed its head, as eager as its rider for the battle to be met. The signal was given and with a roar the knights surged forward. Soon the air was filled with the metallic ring of steel upon steel. Sword met shield, lance found armor, and churning hooves raised clouds of dust that blinded and choked those caught in its midst. The rules of the combat were simple: If a knight was unhorsed he could continue to fight on foot, but once a man lost all his weapons or lost his footing and fell, he was disqualified and must leave the field.

Slowly, one by one, defeated knights trudged from the scene of combat, some suffering bruises but no serious damage. The morning wore on and the participants fell more quickly, for the merciless heat of the sun made the armor unbearably hot, and most of the men actually welcomed their own defeat as it meant they could retire to the shade, doff their armor, and ease their thirst from the kegs of ale and wine.

The field was rapidly diminishing as Gyles unseated his mounted opponent. The man regained his feet quickly and raised his sword to strike, but Gyles's blade caught the hilt and sent it spinning into the air. The knight acknowledged his defeat and Gyles turned to search for another adversary. Rivulets of sweat ran down Gyles's face and into his eyes and he blinked rapidly to clear his vision. It appeared that if he desired another opponent he would have to cross the field, so Gyles spurred his mount in that direction. No other combatant remained on horse as Gyles dismounted and sent his steed off with a sharp slap on its rump. Gyles hefted his sword and advanced toward a knight who was dispatching his larger foe with consummate skill.

Gyles halted and his voice rang clear between them. "Declare yourself, sir knight. Friend or foe?"

The knight turned so that Gyles could see the logo on his shield, and when he spoke, the voice was oddly muffled. "Foe, Lord Gyles. I am Godwin of Broughton. Come, for my blade is eager to bite another Norman shield." And Godwin's sword sang through the air.

Gyles raised his shield just in time, for even with its blunted edge the broadsword would have dented his helm. Caught off guard, Gyles felt himself give ground as Godwin delivered a series of lightning blows that gave Gyles no opportunity to raise his sword, for he was too involved with presenting his shield to Godwin. Gyles immediately recognized that because of Godwin's lesser size he could not withstand the usual grueling, punishing display of arms, and rather than stand firm and allow Gyles's blows to find him, Godwin reverted to dodging Gyles's sword and darting under his guard to land a blow. Though Godwin's blade often found its target, it cost Gyles little, for he was accustomed to the heavier blows of men his own size; yet he admired Godwin's determination. Where many knights depended upon sheer strength to win the day, Godwin had been forced to develop a skillfulness Gyles had not seen before among Saxons. Godwin swung again, and the blade of his sword caught in Gyles's shield. As Godwin worked to free the blade, Gyles slipped his arm from the enarmes of the shield and sent both sword and shield flying off to the side.

In desperation, Godwin drew his light sidearm, though both men realized the futility of the move. Gyles stayed his blow. "Yield, Sir Godwin. You are my wife's man and I have no wish to do you injury. 'Tis finished and you have fought gallantly." Godwin shook his head. "Then I shall end this mockery quickly." Gyles's sword descended and he felt the shield buckle beneath the force of his blow. Godwin's light sword flashed toward him and Gyles brought his sword upward to block the blade's path. The thinner steel bent then broke, and still Godwin did not admit defeat, but instead moved closer to Gyles while they circled each other so that he could make better use of his shortened weapon.

Gyles lifted his sword in both hands and as it began to descend, the light slanted across Godwin's visor, exposing a pair of sparkling, deep blue eyes. Godwin's eyes were brown! The thought flashed through Gyles's mind even as he knew there was no hope of checking the blow, and his sword broke through the shield and glanced off his opponent's helm. Gyles flung his weapon aside with a savage cry as he strove to catch the figure as it pitched forward. His suspicions were confirmed when Gyles felt the slight weight in his arms. He knew, even before his shaking fingers lifted the visor and his eyes beheld the delicate face of his wife, that Godwin had never been his opponent. A trickle of blood started at Serena's temple and cut a path downward across her cheek. Gyles tore the gauntlets from his hands and fumbled for the scarf that hung on his scabbard. He dabbed anxiously at the blood to discover the location of the wound. God, oh, God! Gyles prayed mutely. Do not take her from me, I beg you. Oh, God! Beneath his helm, Gyles was unaware that tears mingled with sweat.

Footsteps pounded toward him and Gyles glanced

up to see Richard and Bryan racing across the field. "Have a care for yourself," Serena had begged him this morning. Serena, Serena. Gyles anguished silently. You would take from me all that I need in life, yourself. Gyles dragged the helm from his head so that he could pass a hand over his eyes, for his vision had suddenly blurred.

Richard dropped to his knees on the other side of Serena's unmoving form; Bryan allowed himself a quick look at his sister and signaled for a litter. Absurdly, the mock battle still raged and the crowd still cheered its champions on. All were oblivious to the tragedy that had taken place and anger was added to Gyles's private anguish. Bryan knelt beside Gyles and gently pulled his hand away from Serena's face.

"Let me, Gyles." Bryan's voice was low, and he deftly blotted at the blood with the scarf.

Gyles studied Bryan's blue eyes, duplicates of Serena's, and rage built steadily within him. "Are you responsible for this?"

Bryan didn't answer, but busied himself with removing Serena's helm. He lifted her head and tugged at her coif. Serena's bright hair spilled onto the field and Gyles groaned inwardly as he remembered how soft those curls were beneath his fingers. Bryan was still dabbing at the blood and now he looked up. "Look to Serena's helm."

"What?" Gyles asked dumbly. This was no time to be concerned with Serena's armor.

"The helm!" Bryan snapped. "Is there a sharp edge on the inside?"

Gyles picked up the discarded helm and ran a finger around its edge. There! A part of the inner rim seam had not been hammered down, but had been left standing. It would cause no discomfort when worn, but a blow to the head . . .

"Well?" Bryan asked sharply.

"Aye, Bryan, there's an unfinished seam," Gyles answered.

"I thought as much." Bryan's fingers parted Serena's tresses at the hairline, exposing a thin cut a few inches above her ear. He gave Gyles a shaky smile. "She'll be fine, Gyles, your blow merely caused her to lose her senses."

"Thank God!" Richard whispered and made to lift Serena in his arms.

"Take your hands from my wife," Gyles ground out. "If you ever touch her again, I will see you dead." Gyles carefully raised Serena in his arms and set off for the castle.

Once inside the comparative safety of Serena's chamber, Gyles allowed the mask he had held so carefully in place in front of the others to slip, and his handsome face contorted in agony. Tenderly, he placed Serena on the bed and removed first her armor and then the mail. He gave a choked laugh when he saw the altered clothes Serena wore to protect her delicate skin from the links of mail. Gently he pulled those from her as well, then found a cloth and water and bathed her, washing the caked blood and grime from Serena's body and face. Gyles left her for a moment in order to search through the chests for a chamber robe, and having found one, he returned and clumsily dropped it over her shoulders and finally succeeded in pulling it down the length of her body.

Serena stirred and whimpered softly when Gyles moved her again to slip her beneath a linen sheet. She quieted immediately and Gyles dropped a light kiss on her forehead when the door opened to admit Nellwyn.

"See to your mistress," Gyles snapped. "When she wakes, send for me." He spun on his heel and left the room.

Outside Bryan waited, and a short distance from him stood Richard. Gyles sent a withering look at Richard then turned to Bryan.

"I want to see you!" Gyles snarled.

Bryan had the audacity to grin at his sister's husband. "Yes, I rather thought you might." He followed Gyles into his chamber.

"Of all the addlepated, senseless, insane tricks to pull!" Gyles thundered as soon as the door closed behind Bryan. He paced wildly about the room, divesting himself of his armor as he worked himself into a towering rage. "Serena is little more than a child, and a woman into the bargain, so I can excuse her behavior on the grounds that she doesn't know any better; but you should have. How long did you think she could have lasted out there?"

Bryan viewed Gyles's agitation calmly and poured himself some wine before answering. "It appears to me, my baby sister held her own quite well. She *was* one of the last on the field, remember. And save for a piece of sharp metal, Serena might still be on the field. I know not how Norman women behave, but 'tis not unusual for a Saxon woman to follow her father or husband into battle. The custom is used less often now, but two and three generations ago, Saxon men viewed this action as the supreme testimony of love and devotion from their women."

"It's barbaric!" Gyles's anger was not appeased. "And stupid. A woman is no match for a man; Serena proved that today."

"Oh? Serena defeated all opponents save you today —without assistance. You must have noticed she relies not on physical strength but skill. And she has had the benefit of fine tutors. As for the practice being stupid, ask my father some day how he met my mother." Gyles's raised eyebrow invited Bryan to continue. "She unseated him in a joust. You see, Serena is her mother's daughter."

Gyles gave an impatient wave of his hand. "It makes no difference, Serena could have been killed today."

"The risks were no greater than when she tilted, Gyles."

"Tilted!" Gyles swung on Bryan and caught the collar of his tunic with both hands. "You were fool enough to help her joust? Who, in God's name, was her opponent? Godwin?"

"Nay, Gyles, 'twas you." Serena's quiet voice carried over the echo of her husband's shouting. Serena stood at the adjoining door, her chamber robe falling in soft folds around her body, one hand resting lightly against the wall for support. Gyles was white-faced with rage as he viewed his wife; his body stiff and unbending.

Bryan smiled. "Well, sister mine, I can see there are no ill effects. I have been trying to convince your husband . . ."

"Yes, I heard you—both of you—as I'm sure the greater part of the castle did. Would you leave us now, Bryan?"

It was a command, not a request, and, accordingly, Bryan drained his glass and retired.

Serena made her way to a chair, receiving neither assistance from Gyles nor a sympathetic look. She folded her hands primly in her lap and watched her husband expectantly. "If you must berate someone, m'lord, 'tis I who should receive the sharp edge of your tongue, not Bryan." Gyles remained silent and unmoving so she continued. "If you are waiting for an excuse or an apology, you will have a long wait, for I will give you neither. I am what I am, and you must accept that."

Still Gyles did not speak, only studied her with his unwavering green gaze, which Serena returned. The silence grew until it filled the room and grated on Serena's ears. Eventually she sighed and rose to leave. "You are a stubborn, arrogant man, m'lord."

"Sit down! I did not give you permission to leave!" Gyles pulled a second chair up to face Serena. He drew his hands over his face before he spoke. "Why?"

Delicate hands with long, tapering fingers spread themselves in a helpless gesture. "I do not think I can explain—and I doubt you would understand if I could."

"I may—why do you try so hard not to be a woman?"

Serena tilted her head, considering, and then shrugged. "Is that what you think—that I wish to be a man?" She was silent for a moment, her eyes fixed on some unseen object, lower lip caught in her teeth. "Perhaps in some respects you are right. I would have others respect me for myself, not merely because I have a passable face or because my body induces lust in some. I have a mind—I think and feel the same as does a man." Tears sprang to her eyes and choked her voice. "Do you think the jests of your men and the old lord's family when

I came here did not hurt me? They did—the words cut deeply—the taunts wounded me more deeply than Beda's dagger. To be treated like . . . like a possession . . . an object to be used at someone else's whim, 'tis a degradation I hope you never feel, m'lord. A woman has as much pride, as much honor as a man, but she is treated as if she had none! A horse is treated with more respect—at least it has a use, a value, which, it appears, a woman does not. A woman is needed only to provide heirs for her mate, after that is accomplished, of what further use is she? None!"

" 'Tis not always that way, Serena."

"No?" Serena cut across his speech. " 'Tis a common practice for a husband to receive an annulment if his wife is barren, as you well know." Tears flowed freely now and her voice rose. "Is that what will happen to me if I fail to bear you children, m'lord? Will I be set aside, cast out, stripped of whatever I could once call mine? The night of our wedding you asked only if I would bear your children, not if I would be happy as your wife. What if I am barren? Will you rid yourself of me? Am I only a womb with attached limbs?"

"Serena . . ." Gyles half-rose from his chair.

"What do you see when you look at me? Do you see a human being who thinks and feels much as you do? Or do you see only a female—a body to be used how and when you wish? What am I to you?"

Her last words were wrenchingly sobbed out, and Serena buried her face in her hands, the gold-streaked hair tumbling forward to obscure her tears from Gyles. Gyles sat frozen in his chair, his mind clouded by Serena's questions and his heart aching for the crushed dreams she had had. He was trying to understand, but he could not. Every woman was content to be a wife; to be protected, to worry about nothing more pressing than what colors to choose for the tapestry she was making, or whether her new gown should be trimmed in fox or ermine. What need had Serena of more? What was it she demanded from him? If he could love her, would it be enough, would whatever drove her from contentment be dissipated? No other woman Gyles had known had troubled him as did Serena, no other had tried to reach his mind rather than his loins; and in doing so Serena had confused him as badly as she herself was confused. Gyles strove mightily to see behind her words and nearly blundered.

"What is it you want from me, Serena? Your freedom? An end to our marriage?"

Serena nearly went to him then, for though he tried to conceal it, there was pain in Gyles's voice. But instinct held her back. Serena brushed the tears from her face with the back of her hand. It was hopeless, he couldn't understand . . . he didn't know.

Gyles studied his hands, wanting to grant Serena what she wished, but not knowing how. Then, suddenly—"The lists. That is why you broke your word? To prove something to me?"

"In part. I was angry, hurt. First Bryan's slurs, then your anger with me. I wanted to strike back, to hurt you as I had been hurt."

"You might have been killed out there!"

Serena shook her head. "Though you may not believe it, I took great care. There is no glory in defeating so small an opponent, m'lord, you were in far greater danger than I. I never intended for you to find me out."

The pieces began to fall into place. "There is no Godwin, is there, Serena?"

"No. 'Tis the name I used at Broughton. Believe me, m'lord, I meant not to disgrace you."

Gyles rose and framed Serena's face with his hands. "There is no disgrace, Serena, you fought well. In truth, I doubt you could ever do anything that would disgrace me. Ah, Serena, will I ever understand you?"

"Will you try, m'lord? Do you want to understand me?" Serena caught his hands in hers. "I wish to know you, not the face you present to others, but the side I am sure you have buried so deeply that no one can reach."

"You will be disappointed, Serena. You have called me arrogant, proud, cruel—to that you must also add stubborn, for that I am—but there is little more to me. If you search for love and tenderness; beware, for they cannot be found in my heart, I have none."

"You love Alan," Serena objected.

"I explained that before." Gyles dropped his hands and moved from her. "'Tis responsibility I feel, nothing more."

"And I? Am I also a 'responsibility' to you? Is that why you raged at Bryan, because you might have lost one of your possessions?"

Gyles turned an anguished face to Serena. "Forgive me," he said thickly. "I wish I could tell you what you want to hear, but I cannot. I cannot!"

Serena went to him then, her slender arms wrapping themselves around his waist. "You will, in time," she assured him. "Wishing to love is half the battle."

"Serena . . ."

Serena raised her face to his. "One final question, then we shall speak no more of this. Do you at least desire me? Will I in fact be your wife?"

Gyles smiled and raised a curl to his lips. "That is two questions, wife, which would you have me answer? Do you wish me to admit to lust?" In one fluid motion Gyles lifted her in his arms and carried her to his bed. His weight followed hers down and Gyles covered Serena's body with his own. "I confess, I desire you," he whispered against her lips, "and were you well, I would claim you now and with such force that you would beg me to cease."

Beneath his fingers Serena's robe fell open and the breath caught in her throat as Gyles explored where no man had gone before. His hands, his mouth, caressed, teased, burned wherever they touched until Serena writhed beneath his touch.

"I . . . I would not ask you to stop," Serena gasped.

Gyles's mouth caught at her breast, tugging gently, teasing the nipples into hard, taut peaks while his hand moved lower over her abdomen until it found the soft hair between her thighs.

Gyles's face loomed over her, green eyes burning

118

with desire. "No more 'm'lord' between us ever. No more separate chambers with a door to hinder my attentions." His lips slanted across hers with a violence born of long denied need. "You will in fact be mine and soon, very soon I will no longer lie alone with an ache for you so deep within me that I come near to losing my mind." Gyles pulled her robe closed and smoothed Serena's hair. "But for now, you must rest. This night will be long and tiring, for you must be the proper lady of the manor despite the fact your head may hurt." He gave Serena a wicked grin, a quick kiss on her lips and sprang from the bed to adjust his binding clothing. "I must see to our guests."

"Gyles!" Serena wailed and pushed herself upright. "You cannot do this to me!"

"Do what, Serena?" Gyles had already poured a glass of ale and stood gazing at Serena, savoring her state of dishabille, his green eyes blazing anew as her movements disarranged her robe.

"You know!" Serena sputtered. She followed Gyles from the bed and stood before him. A tapered forefinger poked at Gyles's chest. "You, Gyles, are a knave! Oooh . . . you, you . . . 'Tis not fair to set me afire and then leave. . . . Gyles, you know what I mean!"

"Are you so eager for my embrace, *ma petite?*"

"Yes!" Serena retorted baldly and Gyles's eyebrows flew upward. "Don't look so shocked, why shouldn't I admit it? Why should I not be allowed my lust as you are allowed yours?"

"Serena, Serena. I think I shall never tire of you for you never fail to surprise me." Gyles shook his head and laughed. "I am leaving because I must, Serena," Gyles said quickly as she opened her mouth to argue. "The combat is over and I must be present to laud the victor; you are fully aware of that. Were it not for that, I would happily remain to deflower you," he teased.

"My Lord Gyles of Camden, you are crude!" Serena gasped, shocked to the core.

"So I have been accused! Aah, wife, you are blushing. Is it now your turn to be shocked?"

"You needn't be so . . . so blunt, Gyles," Serena rebuked him, softly.

"Some women would have found it amusing."

"I did not!" Serena snapped.

"Careful, my sweet, your temper is showing," Gyles admonished, and pulled her stiff body into his arms.

Unexpectedly, Serena yielded. "You are right, of course, Gyles," she murmured against his broad chest. "I have no wish to argue further. I fear I am too sensitive; I beg your forgiveness for my harsh and hasty words." She raised herself on tiptoe and brushed Gyles's lips. His arms tightened, but Serena wriggled free. "I shall rest and join you later." Her blue eyes sparkled as Serena glided from the room.

She leaned against the door and laughed softly when she heard Gyles utter a muffled curse and slam the door as he left the room. She slipped into the bed and closed her eyes. Her head *did* hurt and she could do with a short nap and a bath. Serena's eyes clouded—Gyles would be in the hall by now, surrounded by the other knights and, inevitably, adoring women. The scene was vivid in Serena's imagination. Ah, Gyles, my dearest husband, tonight I shall make sure you have eyes for none other than myself. And I will make you want me as badly as I desire you! Serena drifted into sleep with a bewitching smile on her lips.

Gyles was in a strange mood according to the guests who knew him. He smiled and jested, laughed at the bawdy jokes that made the rounds, and ignored the overtures made him by the ladies present—much to everyone's surprise. Beda attempted to press her attentions upon him, and Gyles brushed her clinging hand away as if it was an insect that annoyed him. His eyes traveled constantly to the staircase—eager, expectant, burning a brilliant green in his bronze face.

"Are you waiting for your bitch of a wife to appear, Gyles?" Beda hissed. "No doubt she's found someone else to occupy your spot in her bed." Beda smiled venomously when Gyles finally turned his attention on her, the scar on his face was white and his jaw tense. Beda leaned toward him to whisper conspiratorially. "I have heard that she welcomes the knight Godwin to her chamber. For that alone you should kill him and divorce her!" Surprising her, Gyles threw back his head and laughed, unshared amusement clear in his eyes. "I should not think your wife's unfaithfulness a source of humor, Gyles."

Gyles controlled his mirth with an effort. "Not that it concerns you, Beda, but whenever Godwin has visited Serena, I have been present. In truth, all three of us are the best of friends." Beda's mouth closed with a snap and she made to depart, but Gyles halted her. "I have received an offer for your hand that I am considering. How look you upon Sir Arthur of Darnley?"

"Gyles, you would not!" Beda's eyes were incredulous. "I have no wish to marry again."

"What you wish does not signify, Beda. When you marry Arthur, all your dower lands go with you and he is most satisfied with the terms of the bargain."

"You are doing this only to be rid of me!"

"True, Beda. One widow here is enough. Hopefully someone will offer for Mara soon."

"Then you and that Saxon slut will have Camden all to yourselves," Beda interrupted.

"Guard your tongue, Beda. Serena is my wife and I will not have you sharpening your tongue at her expense. Besides," Gyles eyed Beda speculatively, "I doubt we shall be alone long, children have been known to happen."

"You think Serena will bear your children?" Beda jeered. "Do not raise your hopes, for her skill with herbs can easily find a potion to keep her barren. No matter how you may sweat over her, Serena will give you no heirs." Beda's words had an ominous ring to Gyles, and he paled beneath his tan. Satisfied, Beda left Gyles to his thoughts.

Determinedly, Gyles pushed Beda's vile words from him. Serena—she was not capable of doing such a thing, even if she bore no love for the child's father. He was sure that Serena did bear him some affection, she had nearly told him so. But Alan's mother had sworn she loved me, Gyles mused, yet she wished to destroy Alan before his birth. Why must I always doubt, why can I not believe in Serena? Must I forever believe the worst of others? Beda seeks only to further her own ends. Serena fights me, true, but only when she feels I am wrong. Serena, Gyles thought desperately, come to me, I have need of you! I begin to doubt what I have found!

As if in response to his plea, Serena appeared at the head of the stairs, her eyes searching the hall for her husband. Her smile when she found Gyles was brighter than the candles that lit the hall, and his fears began to recede. Serena made her way slowly into the hall and to Gyles, pausing now and then to exchange pleasantries, allowing Gyles to feast his eyes upon her. Serena had dressed with special care, choosing one of her gowns that was cut to reveal the soft texture of her breasts. Circling her neck was a necklace of delicate gold links—Gyles's wedding gift to her, which she had never worn—and her hair was caught up to the top of her head with ribbons so that the sun-touched curls cascaded down her back and shoulders. His breath caught in his throat as Gyles watched Serena—hips swaying gently—approach him. She stood looking up at him, her subtle fragrance enveloping him. Serena took the goblet from his hand and sipped daintily at its contents, her eyes never leaving Gyles's face for a moment.

"You are playing havoc on the nerves of every man here, Serena," Gyles told her in a low voice.

"Indeed?" Serena questioned archly. She traced the rim of the goblet with a forefinger. "Does that include you, Gyles?" Serena moved closer, so their bodies almost touched. "Or are you immune?"

"That I am not, for I am human, and your nearness stirs me deeply." Gyles spoke lightly, but his mind warred with his urges for control. It would be a long evening indeed if Serena continued to toy with him in this manner.

"You will turn my head with your compliments, Gyles." Serena returned his cup and brushed lightly against him. "I would stay if I could, but I must be about my duties."

Gyles's hand stayed her. "You are playing the tease, Serena."

"Yes, Gyles, but only for you." Serena eyed him consideringly. "I have decided I am far too unworldly and the remedy of that fate is entirely in your hands. You have often been to William's court, tell me," she smoothed the bodice of her gown, "is the cut of my gown proper?"

Her bosom was daringly displayed to Gyles's devouring gaze, and he groaned, "Proper enough, especially if you are intent upon seduction."

"Oh?" Serena chewed thoughtfully on a fingernail. "And my hair—is it all right?"

"Beautiful, Serena."

"Do you think—"

"Enough, Serena! Spare me the rest of your toilet, I beg of you!" It was all Gyles could do to keep from crushing Serena to him as it was without having her question him about her obvious assets.

Serena laughed, softly, "Gyles, I believe I've caused you to blush."

Gyles's face was, in fact, flushed, but not from embarrassment. "Shall I cause you to do the same?" He grinned down at her. "I can, you know—remember our wedding day? Since then I've learned a great deal more about what can bring the color to your cheeks."

Serena pinkened but laughed good humoredly, "Shall we attend our guests together, Gyles? That should save us both from embarrassment."

The evening passed with Serena never out of arm's reach of Gyles, which caused his men to nudge each other knowingly. The harsh words and strained behavior previously common between Gyles and Serena had disappeared and the glances they exchanged could almost be called loving. Where before Gyles had ignored the men who flocked to range themselves about Serena, he now warned them off with looks that caused their blood to chill.

"What's gotten into him?" one of the younger knights sulked to Edward. " 'Tis impossible to have a word with Lady Serena without being interrupted by Gyles."

Edward had noted his lord's changed behavior and —believing it a good thing—smiled into his ale. "Why should you wish a private word with the lady? She will grant you nothing beyond a smile and a few kind words, despite what you may hope." The younger knight flushed dully as Edward continued. "My advice is to turn your attentions to one of the serving maids; you'll have better luck and less chance of having your head separated from your shoulders."

Seated next to her sister, Aurelia was also asking the same question.

"Well, I don't know what's going on!" Beda replied testily. " 'Tis certainly not my fault he's bewitched with her. You're the one who kept assuring me Serena would never lower herself to bed a bastard, remember?"

"Will you keep your voice down! Geoffrey may be old but he's not deaf!" Aurelia plucked nervously at the material of her skirt. "If you don't do something quickly, we're going to have an additional complication. Beda, for the love of God, stop sulking and start thinking. You had Gyles under your control once, do so again."

"I cannot! Since Serena arrived Gyles hasn't had a word to spare for me."

"Has he bedded her yet?"

"How should I know? I can't very well hide under the bed to find out. Or do you propose I simply ask him?" Beda affected a mocking tone. " 'Tell me, Gyles, do you pleasure yourself with Serena often? Is she warm and willing or do you have to use force?' How is that, Aurelia, do you think he will answer?"

"Oh, close your mouth and let me think!" Aurelia snapped. "If Serena gets with child all our plans will be destroyed. Alan is no problem since he could never inherit Camden—you are sure Gyles made no provision for that?"

"Yes. Gyles plans to send the boy to Normandy.

He has an estate there and Alan will inherit those lands. Camden plays no part in Alan's future."

"Then you must see to it Serena bears Gyles no legitimate offspring." Aurelia paused, considering. "The potions and tissanes you used so effectively on yourself should do the same for Serena."

"But they must be used early enough and their taste cannot be disguised."

"Then she must meet with an accident; push her down the stairs or see she falls from her horse, use your brain for once instead of your body," Aurelia said in exasperation.

"You don't appear to be doing all that well yourself," Beda flashed back. "Geoffrey is still up and about and Bryan doesn't sppear to have fallen under your spell! Geoffrey should have been dead by now and Bryan safely ensconced by your side. You were supposed to be with child; either Geoffrey is not performing his husbandly duties, or you are barren!"

"All right, all right! Let's stop these useless recriminations. All you have to do is prevent Serena from giving birth to an heir. Leave Bryan to me." As one, Aurelia and Beda turned their attention to Serena. Feeling their malevolence across the hall, Serena shivered.

Gyles turned to share a jest with Serena, and the smile faded from his lips when he saw her pallor; touching her arm, he felt her shivering. "Serena?" Gyles bent to her with concern. "Are you well? Is it your head? Is it causing you pain?"

"No, Gyles." Serena's lips were stiff. "I don't know . . . I suddenly feel cold as death." She gave him a halting smile. "I'm fine; I must be standing in a draught. Some wine will help, perhaps."

"I'll get you some." Gyles disappeared and Serena wrapped herself in her arms. Gyles reappeared and pressed a goblet into her hand. "Drink this." Serena drained the goblet quickly and set it aside. "Better?"

Gyles's brows were still knit together with concern and Serena forced a smile. "Yes, much." The apprehensive feeling was still with her and she felt the need to be safely enfolded in Gyles's arms. "I told you that setting my passions ablaze and then refusing to see them to an end was not healthy." Serena's tone was bantering, but Gyles sensed that something was still amiss, so he drew her to him.

"Trying to escape my evil clutches?" Gyles teased.

" 'Twould serve you right," Serena answered tartly. A little color had returned to her cheeks and she let her eyes sparkle up at him. "Perhaps it should be you who escapes me, Gyles. I may be a vixen waiting to tear you into tiny pieces with my hands."

Serena raised a hand to his chest and Gyles caught it in his own as he bent to her ear. " 'Tis my fondest wish that what you say is true, Serena . . . and I will soon find out."

Richard tore viciously at a chunk of pork. "Look at them!" he snorted in disgust. "Serena's making a fool of herself. Were I any kind of man I would have taken her honor long ago."

"And felt the bite of her dagger as well," Bryan retorted. "Let it go, Richard. Let Serena find some happiness." He studied his sister as she sat laughing with Gyles at the head of the table. When he returned his gaze to Richard, Bryan caught sight of Aurelia watching him. "She's at it again," he muttered.

"What?"

"Aurelia." Bryan nodded in her direction. "She's watching me like some damn hawk."

"You know what she wants, Bryan. Why don't you give it to her?"

"Cuckold my own father? Richard, if you weren't so far into your cups, I'd challenge you for that remark. Besides, the idea of bedding that one is repulsive," Bryan shuddered.

"Well, we all have our problems," Richard shrugged. "And this," he added raising his drinking horn, "is our only solace." Bryan also raised his horn in tacit agreement and both proceeded on the road to oblivion.

"You have not exchanged more than a few words with your father since the tourney began, Serena," Gyles reprimanded softly. "He has sought you often, but you seem to avoid him."

Serena glanced in her father's direction. "We have little to say, Gyles. Harsh words were exchanged before our marriage and I doubt there is a way to bridge that gap."

"Because of me?"

"Not you specifically. The words would have been spoken no matter who was chosen for me."

"Ah," Gyles agreed. "So now he pays the price for your bruised pride?"

"Gyles, that's not fair! You know how I feel—"

"Even though the marriage is not as hateful as you thought it would be, still you would punish the man who gave you life? Your pride is too great, Serena."

"*My pride!*" Serena's eyes widened. "Compared to you, I look like humility personified." But Serena contemplated his words. At last she sighed. "You are right, Gyles. 'Tis time I made my peace with him, for in truth he did only what he thought best. But I cannot do so with Aurelia by his side. Will you take her elsewhere, Gyles?"

Gyles's hand covered Serena's. "Of course, cherie, for you I will do anything." Gyles rose and soon he and Aurelia had left the table for the far side of the hall.

Serena left her place to thread her way to where Geoffrey sat. She placed a delicate hand on his shoulder and her voice broke when he turned. "Father? I . . ." Serena fell to her knees before him. "I would ask your forgiveness for . . . for all that has passed between us. My words were spoken in anger, and I—" Serena choked back a sob, "I—"

Serena had no need to say more, for Geoffrey reached down and clasped her to his chest. " 'Tis I who should beg your forgiveness, child, for forcing you to marry against your will. If I could, I would set matters aright, but—"

"Nay, Father, there is no need. All goes well with me."

Geoffrey cupped his daughter's face with his hands. " 'Tis the truth, Serena? You would not lie to me?"

Serena's eyes glistened with tears, saying more than her words. "'Tis the truth, Father. I am happy—you chose well for me."

"I had heard," Geoffrey hesitated, "that your marriage is not complete. Is that true?"

Serena slipped into a chair beside him. "I will not pretend that all was well between Gyles and me at first. But, Father"—she pressed his hands, overjoyed at being able to confide in him as she had done when she was a child—"I have grown to know him and . . . and care for him. Gyles has a son, Alan, did you know?" Geoffrey nodded, a worried look crossing his face. "A bastard child, I know, but Alan is a fine lad; bright, loving, and I have come to love him deeply. I wish you could meet him, Father, you would know what I mean."

"And your own sons, Serena, where are they?" Geoffrey teased and laughed at the color that rose in her cheeks. "I would have grandchildren before I become too old to dangle them upon my knee."

"Soon, Father, I promise you," Serena laughed. "You are too impatient. Besides, you will never be old. You look younger than ever." But concern touched her heart, for there were lines in his face that had not been there before and Geoffrey's usual ruddy complexion held a tinge of gray. "Are you well, Father?"

"Aye, Serena, but the years and old injuries take their toll. I have begun to feel my age, 'tis all." At his daughter's worried look he smiled. "But a grandson or two would greatly improve my spirits."

"As soon as God wills it, Father," Serena promised.

"Serena! How nice!" Aurelia's hands captured Serena's and she placed a kiss on her stepdaughter's cheek. "We have seen far too little of you, dear. Why just last night your father was saying—"

"Yes, well, I have explained to Father how busy I've been." Repelled by Aurelia's display of affection, Serena stood up. "You look well, Aurelia. That is a new gown, is it not?"

Aurelia's sharp intake of breath was a hiss and Geoffrey said warningly, "Serena."

"Your pardon, Father." The words were humbly spoken but Serena stared icily at Aurelia.

Aurelia laughed shortly. "'Tis all forgotten, Serena. And I have long since forgiven you."

"Forgiven!" Serena was brought up short by Gyles who had been watching the exchange with interest.

"You will excuse us, I know. Serena has begged to have her future told by the old seer, and I see she is now free." Deftly, he bowed to Geoffrey and led Serena away. "I know you bear no great love for Aurelia, Serena, but you needn't antagonize her."

"She's a witch, Gyles," Serena said bitterly.

"Don't you mean bitch?"

"That, too! And more," she grumbled. "Ooh, if she were a man, I'd run her through—and her lecherous sister as well! The world would be better for their going."

"Jealous, Serena?" Gyles stopped walking, and, hands on hips, studied his wife.

"Of which one?" Serena, goaded by his calm manner, said flippantly, "My loving step-mother or *your* loving harlot? Which should give me greater cause?" Gyles stiffened and Serena was instantly contrite, but anger overrode that emotion. "Well? Have I need to be jealous of Beda? Answer me, Gyles!"

Instead, Gyles turned on his heel and walked off, while Serena wanted to burst into tears. "Fool!" she chided herself. "You ignorant fool!"

"Wha's s'matter, 'Rena?" Richard stood beside her, bleary-eyed and weaving on his feet. "Yer noble husband find a better piece o' fluff?"

"You're drunk!" Serena snapped. "Get out of my way and go sleep it off somewhere!"

"'Rena," Richard said in a hurt voice. "Aw, 'Rena, don' be mad at me. S'not my fault. You tell 'er, Bryan."

Serena rounded on her older brother to find him as far into his cups as Richard was. "Oh, you're a fine pair!" she hissed.

Bryan either ignored or did not hear Serena's comment. "S'right, ya know, s'not Rich-Richard's fault." He gave her a drunken grin.

"See! Whyn't ya give him the same side of yer tongue ya give me?" Richard began to stagger, his eyes rolled heavenward and he pitched forward against Serena.

"Oof!" Serena staggered under Richard's weight as she struggled to keep him upright. Bryan dissolved into helpless, drunken laughter and Serena nearly cried in sheer frustration. "Richard, wake up! Ooh, you clumsy ox! Wake up!" Frantically, hoping pain would bring him around, Serena delivered a vicious kick to Richard's leg. "Ouch! Oh! damn you, Richard, get off me! If I had a grain of sense, I'd let you drop right here!" Abruptly, Richard's weight was taken from her. "Oh, *thank you*, Edward."

Edward was far less gentle than Serena had been, and simply dumped Richard's limp form in a corner by the hearth. The grizzled knight gave Serena a rakish grin. "Can I be of any further service, m'lady?"

"Nay, Edward, you have done more than enough. My thanks."

Edward shrugged and returned to his table. Serena swung back to Bryan where he sat on the floor. "Get up, Bryan!" she said through clenched teeth. Serena bent down until she could look squarely into her brother's face. "I said, get up," she said menacingly, and Bryan hurried as best he could to comply, while Serena nearly dragged him to his feet. "Now take yourself and Richard out of this hall and don't return until you've regained your senses!" Serena caught his ears in her hands and shook him violently. "Do you understand?" she said furiously.

"Y-yes, Serena," Bryan groaned. "P-please stop, you're m-making me sick." Bryan paled and Serena released him.

"If you must be sick, go outside. And don't forget your friend!" Serena whirled and walked away, her emotions spiraling in confusion. She looked around the hall for Gyles and saw him conversing intimately with Beda. Tears sprang to her eyes and Serena quickly lowered her

130

head to study the floor. Her temper and pride had once again overridden common sense and she wondered what price she would pay for her biting tongue. Serena scuffed a dainty foot against the floor and brushed the back of her hand over her cheek before she dared to look up again. The guests were beginning to retire to their chambers and as Gyles was still talking to Beda, Serena could not see what purpose would be served by remaining in the hall, so she also sought her room.

The chamber was dark when Serena entered and she fumbled about for a few moments before she was able to light a candle. She opened the adjoining door; Gyles's room was also dark and with a sigh she closed the door and moved distractedly around her chamber. Serena tugged at the ribbons in her hair and brushed the heavy mass gently; the golden necklace was placed in a small jewelry chest and Serena ran her fingers lovingly over the delicate links before closing the lid. The gown fell from her shoulders, followed by the kirtle, and Serena rummaged through a clothes chest for a nightgown. She pulled on the first one she found and then realized it was the same nightgown she had worn on her wedding night. Serena smoothed the thin material with her fingers; that night it had been Beda who had kept Serena from Gyles's embrace; would she allow her thoughts of Gyles and Beda to do the same thing now?

The door to Gyles's chamber opened and closed and Serena could hear him moving restlessly around. No woman's voice came from within and Serena breathed easier. She went to the door, but hesitated, her hand trembling on the latch. Will my pride stand between us forever? Serena wondered. He is my husband and I love him! Should not that be enough to overcome whatever would keep us apart? If I give him my love freely, surely we will find some measure of happiness together.

Gyles stood at a window staring at the night, seeing nothing, his head resting on his crossed arms. The adjoining door opened and Gyles wheeled, arms dropping to his sides, to see Serena standing uncertainly in the doorway. Her white nightgown floated about Serena like a cloud, and by the grace of a bolt of lightning, Gyles saw the smile that trembled on her lips.

Serena advanced into the room until she reached the window and Gyles. A light rain began to fall from the ebony sky as thunder rolled over the plain toward Camden. Serena's fingers explored the stones of the wall and Gyles felt his anger ebb away. He understood—how could he not?—for his wounded pride and quick temper had often had distressing results. How often in Normandy had he challenged a man who dared broach the subject of his ignominious birth? Gyles ached to take Serena in his arms and explain the nefarious circumstances that had drawn himself and Beda together, but his pride would not permit such a disclosure. He had yielded enough that day.

"Gyles?" Serena turned from the window. "Gyles, I am sorry. I apologize for my sharp tongue. I meant not to throw your . . . your liaison with Beda at you. 'Twas a cruel and thoughtless thing for me to do . . . and I am sorry. You cannot know how the thought of you holding her pains me. Call it jealousy if you will, for in truth that is what it is, because I love you." Serena's voice broke and when she stumbled on, the words were choked. "I never believed I could feel for a man what I feel for you, and it frightens me and my fear causes me to be foolish and irrational. I fear that some day you will decide to set me away from you and, oh, Gyles, that I could not bear! 'Twould be easier for me to remain here and watch you take a mistress." Tears dropped from her eyes to spot the bodice of her gown. "Oh, that is not true, I would not easily give you up. I would fight her for you . . . I am just so afraid, Gyles! Afraid of you, myself, my own emotions," Serena said miserably. "I wish only to be your wife and make you happy. And I greatly desire to bear your children. Gyles . . ."

Serena was suddenly crushed in Gyles's arms and she could only sob against his chest while he stroked her hair. "I do love you, Gyles, but I fear that one day you will look at me and there will be hate in your eyes and then . . ."

"Hush, Serena!" Gyles placed a kiss on her hair. Her honesty and defenselessness touched him deeply, and he wondered at what had contributed to molding Serena into the woman she was. "Hush," Gyles said again. "You have no need to weep. If I could love, Serena, I would love you." He gave a short mirthless laugh. " 'Twould have been better for you to marry Richard, for I doubt I will bring you happiness. But, Serena, you give me so much. You love my son, and without asking for anything in return you love me. That you anger me at times is true, but before God, there is something about you that stirs me as no other has." Serena's weeping had ceased and Gyles pulled her even closer to him as if he would envelope her slender frame in his. When Gyles spoke, his voice was thick and harsh. "I desire you as I have no other woman, and the ache I have had for you these past months has come close to driving me to insanity. I may not give you love, but I can give you this!" And his lips covered Serena's with a bruising, searing kiss.

Caught off balance by Gyles's sudden attack, Serena felt her body stiffen in shock, and then she tasted the wine on his lips. Had she so offended him with her caustic remark about Beda that he had taken his solace in a wine flask? Remorse for her action filled Serena, remorse and an overwhelming desire to bring to Gyles a peace she was positive he had never known. Gyles was still assaulting her mouth as if it were a keep to be wrung from an enemy's hands or as if she were a harlot bought and paid for for the night.

That thought gave her strength and Serena brought her hands up to exert a steady pressure on Gyles's shoulders. She wanted and needed this union as desperately as he, but it must be shared, not brought about through force. Gyles raised his head with a snap, his green eyes flaring with anger at her resistance.

"What . . ." Gyles started to say, but speech died as Serena covered his mouth with her fingertips.

Serena traced the curve of his mouth while she spoke. "I desire you, Gyles, with all my being, but I will not be brutalized." Recognition showed in his eyes and Gyles gently kissed the fingers pressed against his lips.

"I did not realize, Serena. I shall go mad if I do not have you soon!" Gyles's voice was a groan as he bent to lift Serena into the shelter of his arms.

Their faces were level as Gyles carried Serena to his bed and she looped her arms around his neck so that he had no choice but to accompany her to the mattress. Serena now sought Gyles's lips eagerly, and her own parted willingly for the invasion of his tongue. One of his hands was tangled in her hair and the other sought her curves through the nightgown. Serena pressed as tightly to Gyles as she could, her hands stroking the back of his neck, frustrated because he still wore his formal attire of the evening and there was no bare flesh for her to touch and caress. As if sensing her thoughts, Gyles rolled from Serena to divest himself of his clothing. Her breath caught in her throat as Serena gazed at the symmetrical perfection of his body—his broad shoulders gleamed, bronze in the candlelight; his chest and abdomen were covered with a mat of fine, dark, curling hair that tapered to a thin line running downward . . .

Gyles watched Serena assessing him and mistook the silence that followed her inspection for fear. Serena had risen from her prone position and was kneeling on the bed, her hair falling in glorious disarray about her. If she fled from him now . . . "Am I so ugly, Serena?" His voice was a whisper.

"Oh . . . nay, Gyles," Serena managed to choke out. Her hands reached out to touch, to explore the firm muscles beneath the flesh. "I have never seen . . . I never knew a man to be so magnificent!" Color flamed in her cheeks under his level gaze.

Carefully Gyles pulled Serena to him and drew the gown from her body. The appreciation in his eyes struck a flame in Serena and she pressed herself against Gyles. Their lips met and clung while Gyles lowered them both to the bed. His hands roamed freely, and by his gestures,

Gyles encouraged Serena to do the same. She did not know how to deal with a man, but took her cue from Gyles and allowed her fingers to touch what they might. The muscles of his back and shoulders were firm beneath her touch, his hips slim, his thighs powerfully muscled from years of training and combat. Serena shied away from the most intimate point of contact and contented herself instead with teasing the wiry curls on his chest.

Gyles rolled to his side and his mouth burned a path down her throat and between her breasts. He pulled Serena on her side, before he bent to kiss each breast in turn, until the gentle tugging of his mouth caused her nails to dig into his shoulders. Still Gyles persisted in his glorious form of torture, his mouth placing kisses everywhere, while his knee rode between her legs so his hand could search freely.

Serena tingled all over, from her toes to her now maddeningly sensitive breasts. The ache for him was overwhelming and Serena's hand dropped from his shoulder until she had within her grasp Gyles's own aching manhood. Gyles moaned softly, and fearing she had done him some injury, Serena began to withdraw her hand, but Gyles quickly stilled her movement. Instead he taught her a motion that brought pleasure to them both.

The next kiss was aflame with both their desires and intuitively Serena moved closer to Gyles until he rolled to cover her completely. Her hands went up to feel the play of muscles in his back as Gyles altered his position, slightly, as if to draw away from her.

A small whimper broke from Serena's throat as she arched her body toward her husband. "Gyles . . . oh, Gyles, please . . .," she whispered.

Astride her now, Gyles gazed through passion-filled eyes at Serena's fairness. "I must hurt you, Serena. Forgive me, cherie," Gyles murmured thickly. His mouth came down to cover the groan that escaped Serena's lips as a searing pain coursed through her abdomen. Gyles was still, imbedded within her, not moving until he was certain the worst of the pain had passed.

Serena's eyes burned with unshed tears, the trancelike state she had been in shattered so that she was sure it could not be recovered. So this was how it ended—suffering on her part, while the man above her eased his need! In her innocence, Serena did not realize how wrong her conclusion was until she tried to ease away from Gyles.

"Be still a moment longer, Serena," Gyles's voice rumbled in her ear. "Allow the pain to pass." He kissed the hollow at the base of her neck.

"But . . . is it not over?" Serena blurted out.

Above her in the semi-darkness, Gyles smiled. "Ah, no, fair Serena, 'tis far from ended."

Gyles began to move, slowly, gently, filling Serena until he seemed to have invaded her whole being. What pain there was eased and then disappeared altogether and what replaced it was a sweet, rapturous thrill along with a primitive need that had yet to be fulfilled. With a will of its own, Serena's body met and matched the rise and fall of Gyles's, and when his lips left hers, Serena murmured sweet endearments against his ear, while her hands played along the length of his back. It started so deep within her, this sense of being one, of being united with Gyles, that when the surge of pleasure burst forth into full bloom, Serena's eyes flew open in astonishment and love.

"Gyles!" His name was a bare whisper upon her lips and his quiet, triumphant laugh fell gently upon her ears, while at the same time Serena felt a change in his body. Where before his movements had been gentle, Gyles seemed now to be driven by a passionate violence and Serena welcomed him with all her being. She held him tightly, her mouth playing lightly on his, and she felt it immediately when the first spasms tore through his body. Then he seemed to collapse upon her, and Serena tenderly brushed the errant locks of coal black hair from his forehead.

Carefully, Gyles rolled on his back, taking Serena with him in an iron embrace she could not have broken if she wished to do so. Serena made a column of her fists upon his chest and rested her chin on it while she smiled down at him. Gyles toyed with a strand of hair, wrapping it around his fingers to feel its silken texture.

"I think," Gyles said speculatively, as he gazed into the twin blue pools of her eyes, "that I prefer to meet you here rather than on the field of honor."

Serena's eyes widened in shock before she understood Gyles was teasing. She wriggled into a more secure position on Gyles's chest. "I am not so sure. I think that perhaps you have need of a few whacks now and then to fully appreciate me."

"And you are far too independent and cocky. Perhaps I should beat you regularly to keep you in line." To punctuate his remark, Gyles gave a playful slap to Serena's backside.

Serena switched tactics and began to trace light patterns on his chest. Serena gave Gyles her most innocent and beguiling look. "And what, pray, can I do to avoid such a fate at your hands? Or must I place my trust—not to mention my state of health—solely in your good offices?"

"That," Gyles said ironically, "would be a pleasant change."

"Very well then," Serena leaned forward to place a quick kiss on Gyles's mouth, "so be it. Do with me what you will—my life is in your hands." Gyles stiffened and his face took on such a grim cast that Serena—afraid she had gone too far in her bantering—left the protection of his arms to sit beside him on the bed. "Have I offended you, Gyles?"

"No," Gyles replied quickly. He rose on one elbow to study Serena and trace her jawline tenderly. "Serena, I have no wish to completely rule your life, and if I try, resist me, fight me, do anything but give in to me."

Serena's brows drew together in a puzzled frown. "I do not understand. I love you, Gyles. You are my life, why should I . . ."

"I will destroy you!" Gyles's voice was anguished.

Serena's heart ached with his painful exclamation,

and she drew his arms around her and held his face in her hands. "Nay, Gyles, whatever you may believe now, I know—I know!—you would never hurt me."

Gyles shook his head to negate her statement, but Serena only brought her face closer to his. "Accept what is, Gyles. My love will shield me from any harm."

Gyles's face was still troubled and Serena knew any further talk to be useless. Why he thought he would destroy her Serena did not know, but she was determined to sway Gyles from his dark thoughts. Deliberately Serena eased herself along the length of Gyles's body and nibbled at his lips. She felt his response to her closeness and pressed herself more firmly against Gyles as his hands moved along her body.

"Oh, Gyles, my darling, my love," Serena whispered as Gyles crushed her beneath him.

6

Serena paced along the terrace that enclosed the courtyard where Gyles and his men practiced with their arms. Gyles and Edward roamed through the pairs of dueling men, correcting ill-aimed blows and weak parries. Serena shivered in the cool, late autumn breeze, mentally damning herself for not having worn a cloak. She stopped walking and sat on the low wall, studying the figures below. Her gaze rested finally on Gyles as he strode from one end of the courtyard to the other like a caged animal. He caught sight of Serena and paused, his eyes seeming to cut straight through her as his face set grimly. Tears pricked at Serena's eyelids, but she tossed her head defiantly at her husband and refused to obey the unspoken command that seemed to ring through the air. Serena saw Gyles mouth something inaudible and start across the courtyard to her. She knew when Gyles had reached her side, but Serena refused to look at him.

"You shouldn't be out here, Serena." Gyles's tone was impatient.

Serena nodded toward the courtyard. "You and Sir Edward have your task set before you if you hope to turn the new men into an effective force by winter. Look at the way they hack at each other—they couldn't defend themselves against a nursery full of babes let alone a well-trained band!"

Gyles dropped to the ledge beside Serena, one leg

pulled up to his chest to form a resting place for his arm. "They are learning," he said negligently. "Return to the castle, Serena, 'tis far too cold for you out here without a cloak."

Gyles reached out to assist Serena to her feet, but she snatched her arm from his grasp. "Since you will not permit me to practice, the least you can do is allow me to watch," she snapped.

"We've already discussed this, Serena," Gyles warned her, recalling full well the heated battle of the day before when he found himself sparring with a knight who turned out to be his wife. Gyles had ordered Serena from the courtyard immediately, and that night had demanded the surrender of her armor—a demand she had refused to obey. The argument that ensued had ended with Serena throwing a drinking horn at Gyles's head and stamping from their chamber to the adjoining one, barring the door so Gyles could not follow. "I have instructed Edward that if you attempt to train with him again, he is to bring you to me immediately."

"At Broughton—" Serena began.

"This is Camden, not Broughton, and you are my wife, now, not the spoiled daughter whose every whim is allowed. I will argue no further, the matter is ended!"

Serena whirled on Gyles. "May I at least be permitted to ride?" Her eyes snapped defiance at him, and Gyles could not help admiring the beauty her anger brought forth.

Gyles shrugged. "Ride if you like, but not Demon, and take a groom with you."

Demon was Serena's favorite mount, a chestnut stallion with an irascible disposition, which only she could deal with. "Do you wish to select the horse for me?" she spat.

"The dappled mare should suit your purpose." Gyles rose and stood looking down at her. At last he sighed. "Serena, I have explained to you why I sent Alan to Normandy. The land he will one day inherit is there, and he must learn to love it and the people."

"But he is so young, Gyles! You could have waited

several years before sending him away." Tears clung to her lashes now, and Serena brushed absently at them.

How Alan had wept when Gyles had informed him of his journey. And how Serena had stormed at Gyles in the privacy of their chamber, even though she knew it was not her place to interfere with the way Gyles raised his son. Failing to change Gyles's mind she had wept bitter tears at the knowledge that Alan would soon be residing in far off Normandy and she would no longer be able to hold and comfort him. Unfairly, Serena refused to listen to Gyles when he explained his reasons for sending Alan from Camden. Serena sensed that Gyles had not told her the real reason behind his actions, but she refused to question him on the matter. Perhaps Gyles had never really cared for his bastard son.

"Serena?" Gyles rested a hand lightly on her shoulder. "Perhaps you should visit your father for a while."

"Are you trying to rid yourself of me, also?" Serena questioned spitefully.

Gyles shook his head. "I thought a trip might improve your spirits, 'tis all. Things cannot continue between us the way they have been—surely you realize that. It has been a fortnight since Alan left, and in all that time I have not heard you speak a kind word to me. If you have accusations, then speak them plainly. For I warn you now, I will not abide your shrewish behavior any longer. Either resign yourself to the fact—though you may not believe it—that what I did was best for Alan, or retire to your dower lands." Gyles walked a short distance from her and stood with his hands clasped behind his back. Tell her you fool! Gyles's mind raged at him. Tell her it would have been easier to cut off your arm than to send Alan away. It had torn at Gyles to send his son from him, but it would keep Alan safe should Beda decide to accuse Gyles of Kier's death, which she had begun again to threaten to do. Alan was safe, but what of Serena; would she suffer if Beda succeeded? No, Gyles assured himself, Serena could always flee to her father and brother for their protection.

"Gyles?" Serena's small voice broke into his thoughts. "Is it your wish that . . . that I leave Camden?"

Gyles turned and eyed her impartially. "The choice is yours. You have until this evening to decide."

Serena watched Gyles return to the courtyard before she turned to seek the warmth of the castle. The great hall was deserted—Mara and Lydia were in their solar, the servants had retired to their homes until the evening meal, and the empty room seemed to mock Serena's loneliness. A shrew, Gyles had called her. Well, had she not the right to be angry and rage at unkind fate? Everyone, it appeared, was wanted by someone, except herself! No, Serena corrected herself, that was not entirely true. Alan had loved her and Gyles—despite whatever stopped him from loving her—did need her, even if he was too stubborn to admit it. Serena could tell by the look in his eyes whenever they were alone that with every day that passed Gyles enjoyed her company more.

Footsteps sounded behind Serena and she turned wearily, resenting the intrusion.

"Where is Gyles?" Beda greeted Serena rudely.

Serena's chin lifted a notch. "My husband is with his men in the courtyard, they are holding practice with arms this afternoon."

"Gyles was supposed to come to my chamber after the noon meal," Beda said sullenly.

Serena's hands clenched at her sides. "I will remind him of it when he returns. Or perhaps you would care to tell me whatever troubles you instead of bothering my husband."

Beda's shrill laughter echoed through the deserted hall, causing the hair on Serena's neck to prickle. "What I have to say I will say to Gyles, and no one else." Beda moved closer to Serena. "You have known Gyles for less than a year—do you truly believe you have any influence over him? If so, you are a fool. Gyles and I have been . . . friends . . . since he arrived at Camden five years ago. I know him better than you can ever hope to, Serena." Beda stood directly in front of Serena now. "What will you do when Gyles tires of you? He will, you know, just as he quickly tired of his conquests at William's court. If you wish to save yourself from their fate, take my advice and leave here, now. Take what you can and return to your father. You can rest assured that Gyles will not trouble himself to follow you—and should he try, you have my word that I shall detain him."

"How kind of you, Beda," Serena said drily. "But you will not have to exert yourself on my behalf. In fact, I would not dream of inconveniencing you." A tight smile flickered across Serena's face as Beda stiffened. "So, in the event you have forgotten your place here, pray let me remind you: Your chamber is in the women's quarters." Serena advanced upon the older woman and Beda steadily retreated before the warning that flashed in Serena's blue eyes. "And *I* assure *you,* Beda, should I discover that you have at *any time* lost your sense of direction within the castle walls, I shall derive the greatest pleasure in seeing you safely back to your rooms!" Beda opened her mouth to retort, but Serena cut her short with an impatient gesture. *"Good day, Lady Beda!"*

Serena watched Beda's unhurried ascent to her chamber with narrowed eyes. Of all the unmitigated nerve! Serena's anger rose—if ever anyone deserved a good hiding or thorough instructions in morality it was Beda. And if Beda thought for an instant that Serena would gracefully accept Gyles taking a mistress—

Masculine voices and laughter broke into Serena's thoughts as the knights filed into the great hall to warm themselves by the fires and quench their thirsts with ale and wine. Gyles brushed by Serena, filled a horn with ale, drained it, and then turned a critical eye on his wife.

"I thought you were going riding," Gyles said casually.

That remark snapped the slender thread Serena held on her anger. " 'Twould appear that you are the one who has been doing most of the *riding,* my lord!" Serena ground out. "One of your mounts waits for you in the women's quarters, and the other is only too happy to take your kind advice and absent herself from your presence. Good riding, m'lord!"

143

Serena whirled and disappeared up the stairs to her chamber while Gyles looked after her in confusion until the meaning of her words struck him. With an oath he set down his horn and then strode resolutely to the women's quarters. At Beda's door, Gyles did not pause to knock, but flung wide the portal without warning so that Beda, indulging herself with a scented bath, shrieked and her servant scurried into a corner.

"How dare you!" Beda gasped.

Gyles ignored her. "Leave us!" Gyles instructed the servant with a jerk of his head. As the door closed behind the girl, Gyles turned his attention to the woman who still lounged in the water. "You, madame, deserve to be flogged."

"Whatever for, dearest Gyles?" Beda asked innocently. She rose slowly from the tub and made a great show of finding a cloth to wrap herself in. Her breasts hung like overripe melons and Gyles turned away, repelled by the over-generous endowments when he compared them to Serena's delicate form. Beda wound the cloth around her and perched on the edge of her bed. "Don't tell me our precious Lady Serena came crying to you about our conversation."

Gyles's interest was pricked but he concealed it. "My wife said that you wished to see me."

"My wife, my husband!" Beda mimicked. "Do you never address each other by your Christian names? In truth, Gyles, I am amazed that you haven't sent your wife scurrying back to her father yet. Surely that skinny child doesn't give you any pleasure! Your taste—as I remember—runs more to well-fleshed females."

"Such as yourself?" Gyles asked.

Beda lay back on the bed and stretched. "How kind of you to remember. Tell me," she slanted a look at Gyles, "have you decided to renew our arrangement?"

"Not if I were dying and it would save me!" Gyles snorted.

"That could be arranged, my churlish knight," Beda mused aloud. "No. Not you, but, perhaps, Serena. She does lead quite a reckless life at times, you know. Especially that steed, Demon, that she rides; I'm surprised Serena hasn't been thrown yet. If you place any value on her dower lands, you should watch her more closely. Accidents have been known to happen. Remember poor Kier—" Beda twisted on the bed and propped herself up on her elbows. "I did hear that Serena planned to go riding, didn't I? I am glad that Alan is in Normandy—it would have been tragic if Serena had met with an accident while Alan was with her. Don't you agree, Gyles?"

Gyles stood as if turned to stone, the curved scar on his cheek showing starkly against the rest of his face. He had to swallow several times before he could force his voice through the constriction in his throat. "Speak plainly, Beda. Are you threatening Serena's life?"

Beda gave a shrill giggle. "Why, Gyles, how could you think such a thing? I but meant to caution you, 'tis all." Abruptly her face hardened. "And now, leave my chamber."

It took only two strides of his long legs to carry Gyles to the bed and jerk Beda to her feet. "I have never hurt a woman, but in your case, Beda, I am sorely tempted to make an exception."

Beda laughed. "You haven't the nerve, Gyles. If you abuse me, I have only to call upon my brother-in-law's protection."

"Do you believe my father-in-law would come to your aid?" Gyles sneered. "Geoffrey would think first of his daughter, not his wife or her kin. Remember that should any injury befall Serena. And heed this also: Sir Arthur has contracted for your hand and I am still considering his offer. Do not force me into a rash decision, for your own sake."

Serena drew her mount to a halt in order to cast a quick glance over her shoulder. The groom who had accompanied her from the castle was some distance behind, and Serena clucked softly to Demon urging him off the road into a dense thicket. Soon the groom cantered by Serena's hiding place. She gave a muffled laugh before emerging from the thicket. Serena turned Demon back in the direction from which they had just come and rode until she found the faint path that would carry her into the forest and the small stream that ran through it. The leaves had long since surrendered their vibrant hues to the bitter, overcast weather of an English November and now lay in sodden piles upon the ground. Trees lifted naked limbs like skeletal fingers high into the sky, waiting silently for the first heavy snow to sever them from the trunks and send them crashing to the ground.

Serena dismounted and led Demon to the stream, then settled herself upon a cushion of leaves beneath a sturdy oak. Demon raised his head and snorted at his mistress.

"What's the matter with you?" Serena asked peevishly. "I have enough trouble today without you adding to it." Demon eyed her curiously and gave an arrogant toss of his head. "Oh, go back to your master; you and he deserve each other." A final snort from Demon and he retired to graze calmly on what grass could be found, while Serena attempted to dampen her anger.

Serena rested her head against the tree trunk and watched the clouds float through the overcast sky. The weather matched Serena's mood and she bit her lower lip in vexation. Beda. Gyles and Beda. Together. Serena's own wedding night and Beda had been present then. And yet Serena could not believe that Gyles was unfaithful to her—she was positive she would know if Gyles sought another's bed, especially Beda's. Gyles might not love her, but neither did he bear any great affection for Beda. But there was something that flickered in Gyles's eyes when Beda was mentioned—if Serena had to put a name to it she would call it fear. Serena frowned. Gyles afraid of Beda? Impossible! Or was it? Gyles avoided Beda, yet she made every effort to seek him out. Why? To resume their former relationship—was that what Gyles feared? Again, why? Gyles was no man's or woman's puppet who would mindlessly bend to another's will. Yet . . . Gyles had had an interview with Beda before and shortly thereafter Alan was sent to Normandy. Why? The explanation Gyles gave Serena was simple enough, yet Serena felt certain there was more to it. Gyles's decision had been so sudden, almost as if it had been forced upon him.

A bolt of lightning streaked through the sky followed closely by a rolling clap of thunder that brought Serena to her feet with a start. The heavens opened suddenly, and Serena found herself soaked to the skin before she could take a step toward her mount. Demon's eyes were rolling, the whites seeming to fill the sockets and it was only then that Serena remembered his fear of storms.

Serena approached the skittish beast cautiously, speaking constantly in a low, gentling tone. Demon backed farther away and Serena cursed silently. Serena extended her hand. "Easy, boy, steady . . . come here, Demon. Come on, boy. We've got to get back home . . . and once we're there, I'll see you get a nice handful of oats. Come on, Demon . . . easy now. . . ." Her fingers closed around the trailing reins. She drew the reins over Demon's head and had just settled her foot in the stirrup when another clap of thunder rumbled through the trees and Demon reared. Serena's foot slipped from the stirrup and the reins were jerked from her fingers as she tumbled full length against the earth. Before Serena could regain her feet, Demon bolted from the clearing and was soon out of sight.

Serena stood carefully, assuring herself that at worst she had only a few bruises. For the first time, Serena regretted having eluded her groom. Well, there was no help for it now, and she couldn't get any wetter than she already was. It would be a long walk back to Camden.

When the storm broke over Camden, Gyles was in the midst of a rare display of temper, and the brunt of his anger was the hapless groom who had had the misfortune of accompanying Serena. The rafters of the stable echoed with the sound of Gyles's voice and the crashing thunder and the snorting of uneasy horses.

"Well," Gyles continued in a quieter vein, "the only thing to be done is to try and find my lady. And you"—he pointed a long forefinger at the unfortunate groom—"will accompany us. Edward, gather twelve of the men.

Tell them what has transpired, and have them make ready to leave within a few minutes. At least Serena is riding a gentle mount, that is something we can be thank —Yes, what is it?" Gyles snapped impatiently to the groom who had dropped on one knee in front of him.

"B-beg pardon, m'lord, b-but your lady . . . that is, her steed . . ."

"Get on with it, man!" Gyles said impatiently.

The groom swallowed nervously and hurried on. "Lady Serena is riding the stallion, Demon, m'lord."

Gyles's face darkened and a muscle in his cheek began to tic. "I left instructions—ah, the devil take it. Edward, set out as soon as you can. And as for you"— Gyles faced the groom—"you lost my wife, and 'twould be to the betterment of your hide if you found her again!"

The groom needed no further urging and was astride his horse before Gyles could draw the bridle over his own mount. With a final exasperated look at Edward, Gyles led his mount out of the stable only to be brought up short by the sight of several men trying to calm a terrified Demon. The empty saddle brought back Beda's ominous words with a vengeance and a shaft of fear stabbed at Gyles's heart. Gyles hesitated no longer, but threw himself upon his horse and drove his heels hard into its flanks.

At last! Serena thought wearily as she neared the grey walls of Camden. Her hair was plastered to her head and back and the material of her gown clung tightly to her body. Her cloak hung over one arm; she had grown far too warm with it on and the damp wool had only served to encumber her steps. Serena hoped that her groom had not told anyone of her precipitous actions, it would only serve to anger Gyles and add to his worries. She really shouldn't have taken Demon out to-day, especially against Gyles's expressed wishes, but then, that was precisely why she had selected Demon. It went against her nature to be told what she could and could not do. The sound of a horse's hooves churning up earth caused Serena to look upward and through the downpouring rain. Much to her dismay, Serena saw Gyles coming toward her. So the groom had talked after all, and judging by the look on Gyles's face as he drew closer, Serena's interview with her husband was going to be far from pleasant.

Gyles halted beside Serena. "Enjoying your walk, my lady?" His green eyes raked her from head to toe, and though Gyles smiled, the smile did not touch his eyes.

Serena bent her head and studied the wet grass. Above all she did not wish to quarrel with Gyles, so she said nothing.

"Your silence is most appropriate, as is your demure attitude. I can but hope this will continue." With one fluid movement, Gyles bent and swept Serena onto the horse, in front of him. "I will be forever in your debt if you will hold your tongue until we gain the privacy of our chamber. After that, you may bite, scratch, kick and scream; but you will be the proper lady in front of our servants."

Serena snuggled closely against Gyles, letting the heat that emanated from his body warm her. "Yes, Gyles," she murmured obediently.

Their return was met with silence and a few of Gyles's men glanced at Serena with a mixture of apprehension and pity. Gyles fairly dragged Serena from the horse and pulled her roughly along behind him up the steps into the castle and to her chamber, calling for hot water as they went. His grip was excruciatingly painful, and to struggle only caused more pain. So Serena gave up and let him have his way with her. Gyles nearly threw Serena into the room, and closed the bedroom door with a slam that could be heard in the great hall.

"You are, without a doubt, the most infuriating, exasperating woman it has ever been my misfortune to meet!" Gyles roared down at Serena.

Serena smiled and began to strip the wet clothes from her body. Serena knew, his anger was caused by his concern for her. She could not blame him, and neither would she fight with him. There was a knock on the door and servants were admitted to pour steaming water into the tub. Gyles subsided temporarily into tight-lipped silence. When they were alone, Serena lost no time in settling herself into the water. Gyles paced the room while Serena sank deeper in the tub to drive the chill from her bones.

"Were you thrown?" Gyles asked abruptly.

"No. Demon was frightened of the storm and bolted," Serena answered easily.

"You were not to ride him. Did I not forbid it?" Gyles's voice rose.

"Yes, Gyles. But had you allowed me to ride astride rather than forcing that odious sidesaddle upon me, I should have ridden him with greater ease." Serena rinsed the soap from her body and rose. "Would you hand me that linen, please?" Gyles angrily complied, hurling the cloth at her. "Thank you," she said and stepped from the tub, walking toward the fire to dry herself. "There is no need to shout at me, Gyles, I can hear you quite well. I am sorry I disobeyed your wishes, but my punishment has already been meted out, has it not?"

Gyles regarded her silently before he nodded reluctantly. Even if he wished to punish Serena for her disobedience, Gyles knew he could not bring himself to do so. She looked so delicate standing before the fire— so tempting. It had been a long time since Serena had last come to him, and Gyles felt himself responding to her nearness. Serena was tousling her hair with a linen and before Gyles could stop himself, he had reached out to touch one of her gold-flecked curls and rub it thoughtfully between his fingers.

Behind the curtain of her towel, Serena smiled. If nothing else, Gyles did desire her. Serena was ashamed of the way she had treated Gyles since Alan's departure. He was only doing what he thought best for his son. The towel dropped from her fingers and Serena looked up into Gyles's intense green gaze.

"Forgive me for doubting your judgment, Gyles. 'Twas wrong of me—and cruel." Serena reached up to touch the scar on his cheek, something she had never done before. Deliberately she traced its path. "I have

150

missed you these past nights, Gyles. This room is far colder than yours . . . and I have grown accustomed to having you beside me when I awake."

She was in his arms then, and Gyles bent to place gentle kisses on her lips and neck. "I must tell you," he said at last, "why I sent Alan away." Gyles seated Serena in a chair, and seeing the serious expression on his face, she remained silent. Gyles drew a deep breath and began.

"There is much you do not know of me, so 'tis important I start at the beginning. I was born in Normandy; the old lord and his family are Norman as was my mother. My early life is of little importance; my mother was a serving girl in the castle, and because of the lord's position, I was sent to one of his friend's estates to begin training as a squire. When I had earned my knighthood, I returned. My mother was dead of the fever and my father had a legitimate heir, Kier, who had been born shortly after I had left. There was nothing to bind me there, and William was gathering an army to cross into England, so I joined William. Understand, Serena, I bore no grudge against your people, but I had to make my way in the world." Gyles seated himself on a stool in front of Serena, and caught her hands in his. "I was— and still am—a bastard. I was entitled to nothing from my father and I could not foresee spending my life in the service of someone else. William offered the chance of a small fief, and I had nothing to lose and everything to gain. William was victorious, and I was granted a small estate in Normandy, where I lived peacefully for five years."

"Aside from Alan's birth," Serena put in.

Gyles's face softened. "Yes, Alan. I have often reproached myself for his birth, 'twas my wish never to force my lot on another, but—" Gyles raised his hands helplessly. "I could not allow his mother to deny him life. And after his birth, when I held him, touched him, watched him grow, I swore he would not endure what I had had to. Then my own past caught up with me. That part you know already, my father's wish that his blood line continue to hold these lands was agreed upon by William and I was summoned to remain at Camden until Kier should sire a son." Gyles stood and began to pace the room. "Kier hated me and my son. It seemed we quarreled constantly, and Kier lost no opportunity to insult and badger Alan. Alan deserved nothing, so my half-brother believed. He would have made my son his servant—and a servant only learns his place by repeated beatings. I came upon them one day—Kier had sent me out with a patrol to find a band of thieves that was plaguing the area. We found them easily, and upon our return to Camden I learned that Kier had whipped Alan for entering the great hall during a meal. Kier and Beda had gone riding, so I followed and found them resting by a stream." Gyles pressed the heels of his hands over his eyes. "I was blind with rage, I struck him, we fought—and then, I don't know! Kier must have struck me on the head. Anyway, I lost consciousness. When I awoke, Kier was floating in the stream—dead. I had killed him. I don't remember it, but I must have murdered Kier. If it became known, I would have been executed or, at the very least, exiled. There was Alan to consider, he was only two. Beda offered me an arrangement. She would swear Kier's death was accidental if I would . . . agree to become her lover."

Serena was frozen in her chair. "But . . . then why did you wish to marry?" she whispered.

"I didn't! I never wanted a wife!" Gyles raged. "I wanted no one else to complicate my life or Alan's. 'Twas Beda's suggestion, for as the estates fell to me I would have need of a legitimate heir. God! How I hate all women and their cunning, devious minds. What need had I of a wife?" Serena paled, her blue eyes enormous, and Gyles went swiftly to her side. "Nay, Serena, do not think that. Those were my feelings before I met you. I admit I resented you at first, our marriage was forced upon me as it was upon you. I would have resented any woman I married, not just you. And then, the night of our marriage—I shall never forget how you looked at me, at Beda. It sickened me as I know it did you. Believe me, Serena, I have not touched Beda since we were wed. And now . . . now she threatens to expose the fact that I murdered Kier if I do not return to her bed. That is why I sent Alan away, and why you must leave as well."

Gyles stood at the hearth, arms braced against the mantle, and Serena felt the tears spring to her eyes. She wet her lips several times before she spoke. "Is it your wish that I return to my father?"

Gyles's shoulders slumped. " 'Twould be safer for you should Beda decide to accuse me," he said haltingly.

Serena rose and touched Gyles lightly on his shoulder. When he turned, her eyes searched his face earnestly. "That is not an answer, Gyles. I shall speak more plainly. Do you no longer want me? If so, tell me and I shall leave; but if I go, I promise you I will be back. I will not leave your side forever."

"Serena," Gyles pulled her into his arms. "You are being foolish . . . if I should be taken—"

"If that happens, be assured I will run all the way to my father's lands. I am not foolish nor even very brave. You are my husband, my life is with you. And if that means fleeing England or proving Beda is lying, then so be it. She is lying, Gyles, I know it and you must also. You may have quarreled with your half-brother, but you did not murder him. One way or another we shall force Beda to tell the truth."

"You believe me? God's truth, Serena, I do not remember." Gyles drew a shaky breath, then laughed harshly. "Beda thought you would leave me when you found out about Alan. Instead, you gave him love, became his mother, protected him." Serena's loyalty and devotion had touched something deep within Gyles, and it was as if an emotional dam had burst. Feelings Gyles had not believed he possessed found their way to the surface to flood his heart and brain. "And you loved me though I offered you nothing in return. I tried to drive you away, I was close to hating you for a time because of your innocence—I was never allowed that luxury." Gyles crushed Serena against his chest. "I am a selfish man, Serena, I do not wish you to leave me, yet I cannot place you in any danger. I never thought to find a woman who would discover the way into my heart. You are dear to me, Serena, more precious than anything I own. I would move heaven and earth to stop that which would take you from me. You alone can twist a blade deep into my heart with a harsh word or cause my day to be brightened with a smile, and that disturbs me greatly."

Tears rolled down Serena's cheeks as the words she had waited so long to hear were spoken by Gyles—but there were unspoken words as well. Gyles's pride would not allow him to ask Serena to stay and help him, but the plea was there all the same. Gyles's arms had become almost unbearably tight around Serena, and—as if their minds touched in that instant—Serena suddenly realized that Gyles was afraid. He was afraid for Alan, for Serena, and not least of all, for himself. Instinctively, Serena knew what she must do and say.

"Gyles," Serena said quietly. "Will you allow me to stay? I cannot return to Broughton. My father would send me straight back to you; and I will not retire to my dower estate. Camden is my home, Gyles, will you not allow me to fight for it, and you?"

"You are stubborn," Gyles said with a brief smile. Then he sobered. "Never leave me, Serena, for without you I am not whole."

Serena wrapped her arms around Gyles's neck and pulled him downward. "Nay, Gyles, I shall never leave you, not so long as I have breath in my body." Serena began to caress Gyles, and she admitted to herself that she had missed sharing his bed.

For his part, Gyles felt his long restrained desire burst forth, and he kissed Serena savagely. He swept her from her feet and carried her into his chamber, pausing only to close the adjoining door. Serena slipped from his arms and, while, Gyles watched, slowly unwound the towel that covered her. Gyles hurriedly shed his clothes and they came together with a ferocity that drove all considerations—save the need to become one—from their minds. With a show of urgency she had never displayed before, Serena pulled Gyles to the bed. Serena's need inflamed Gyles's passion further and he rolled on top of her, anxious to possess Serena immediately.

"No, Gyles! Not yet!" Serena said, breathlessly.

Confused, Gyles rolled to his back, then his breath escaped sharply as Serena followed him. She kissed him deeply while her fingers explored his firmly muscled body more daringly than before. While Serena had been well-pleased with Gyles's ardor, she had never dared to take the initiative in their love-making, but had done only what Gyles had instructed. Gyles's words this afternoon had changed all that, for Serena realized that she had withheld a tiny portion of herself because she had never been sure what Gyles's feelings toward her had been. Now she felt the need to give Gyles as much pleasure as he had given her. Duplicating Gyles's actions with her, Serena pressed her lips softly against the places her hands had already touched. Gyles's breathing became labored as Serena's hand closed around his hardness; he arched his hips upward and he groaned softly.

"Serena!" Gyles said with a harsh urgency.

She smiled, then moved to lay astride Gyles, fitting her contours closely against him. Gyles drove into Serena with a savagery that caused her to gasp before she felt him begin to move within her. Soon Serena moved with an urgency all her own as she felt the by now familiar tension build within her. Gyles's movements, too, had altered, and together they began to scale the mountain that would lead to their complete fulfillment. As a wild cry escaped Gyles's lips Serena felt the ecstasy burst within her. Quivering with spent pleasure; entwined together, they drifted into contented sleep.

7

Autumn grew colder, the winds sharper as they howled around the guard towers of Camden, and Serena directed the preparations that would make the castle as snug as possible during the winter. Tanned animal hides were stretched taut over windows and arrow slits, wooden shutters were placed over the hides and Serena insisted that curtains be made out of heavy material and hung in front of the shutters. Serena had been appalled that this had not been done before. She had enlisted both Mara's and Lydia's skills to make the curtains. How she had secured their co-operation Gyles did not know, and he had no desire to find out.

Trees were felled, limbs and trunks cut to acceptable size and hauled back to the castle—under Serena's watchful eye. The wood was distributed to each room and the excess stored in the lower level of the castle in the keep where it would remain dry. When Gyles complained that the space the logs occupied might be needed for poachers or other offenders, Serena rounded on him and told her husband that if he wished to remain well-fed and warm during the cold months to come he should leave her to attend to her duties and occupy himself elsewhere. Edward stifled a laugh as his fearsome, arrogant overlord made haste to comply with his wife's demands.

The larder also fell under Serena's intense scrutiny, and she conferred with the cook and the cook's assistants as to the seasoning and preserving of the different meats. Since game would become difficult to find after the first snowfall, Serena burst in upon Gyles and his men as they indulged in a leisurely evening bout of quaffing ale, and informed them that on the morrow they would bring into Camden an assortment of venison, quail, boar, and such small game as could be found. She ignored their groans of protest, and flashed them a saucy grin and a reprimand about keeping late hours when they must rise early. What meat could be stored would not last the winter; so the livestock the serfs gave in payment for their taxes were driven into a quickly erected stable so that a fresh supply of meat would be close at hand.

One by one, Serena checked off items on the list she had made, until at last, one evening in their chamber, Serena collapsed into a chair with a sigh of relief. It was finished. Camden would withstand the cold weather better than it had before. The parchment fluttered from Serena's limp fingers—she was tired from the weeks of hectic activity. Gradually her eyes closed and her head rested against the back of the chair.

Gyles entered his chamber with a light step, pausing on the threshold when he caught sight of Serena curled in a chair by the fire. Gyles shut the door as quietly as possible, a tender expression softening his features when his wife stirred, sensing his presence.

"Serena?" Gyles shook her gently. Sleep blurred eyes flickered open and he smiled. "I'm cold, wife, come to bed and warm me." Gyles carried Serena to the bed and stripped first her, then himself. When he turned back, Gyles discovered that Serena had curled up and returned to her exhausted slumber. The bed sank under Gyles's weight and he pulled the covers over them both. Serena snuggled up to Gyles and his arm fell about her waist, as he placed a kiss upon her lips. "Sleep well, cherie," Gyles whispered.

The loss of warmth beside her brought Serena fully awake and she sat up, pulling the linen sheet over her exposed breasts. Gyles was feeding another log to the fire and he straightened and gave Serena a brief smile.

157

"I was going to wake you when the chill was driven from the room. Nellwyn is waiting for you in the hall. One of the village women is in travail and is having difficulty—she requires your skill with herbs."

Serena slipped quickly from the bed and hurried to the fireplace to dress. Gyles collected the chest that contained her medicines and Serena's cloak. "Did Nellwyn say how long the woman has labored?"

Gyles nodded. "It has been a full day." Gyles cast a worried glance at Serena. "Perhaps you could tell Nellwyn what herbs to use." A birthing as prolonged as this was not pleasant, and Gyles was concerned that his tender-hearted wife could not bear to watch such suffering in another.

"Nonsense, Gyles. If I can be of help, I shall go gladly. Go back to bed." Serena wrapped herself in her cloak and hurried from the room.

The hut was stifling when Serena entered, and the stench that assaulted her nostrils was overpowering. A woman not much older than herself lay on a thin pallet, her face ashen, lines of pain etched deeply around her mouth. The woman's husband knelt beside her, his hands holding hers with an intensity that caused his knuckles to whiten. The stricken look on the man's face when he raised his eyes to Serena's tore at her heart. The midwife came forward out of the shadows.

"I've done everything within my ken to bring her child into this world alive," the midwife said in a hushed voice. She raised her hands in despair. "What more can we do?"

Serena's bottom lip caught in her teeth. When she spoke, her voice was equally low. "Perhaps if I gave her a potion to relieve the pain for a bit, she would regain the strength she needs."

The midwife considered this. "It could do no harm," she said at last. "But 'twould be of more help if you could make something that will increase the length of the pains. It may already be too late; I fear the child may be dead by now."

"Then we must try to save the mother. Is it too late for her as well?" Serena asked hurriedly.

The midwife gestured in despair. "I do not know."

Nellwyn had already busied herself placing clean linens beneath the laboring woman and soothing both the woman and her husband. Now she returned to Serena and the midwife. "We'd best hurry, lamb, for her strength cannot last longer." Nellwyn seemed completely calm, and Serena was reassured by her presence.

Outside the wind howled and tore at the hut while the trio set about their work. The husband settled into a spot by his wife's head, where he would not obstruct the ministrations of the three women. Setting water to heat in the fire, Serena selected three different leaves from her chest and ground them into a fine powder. When the water was warm, Serena added it to the powder and brought the mixture to the young woman.

Serena knelt beside the pallet and raised the woman's head until it rested in the crook of her arm. Pain-filled eyes looked up at her beseechingly and Serena tried to smile. "This will ease the pain you feel," Serena explained. "It will also increase the contractions so your child will be born soon." Serena held the bowl to the woman's lips and she drank willingly, eager for anything that would end the torment she was in. When the bowl was emptied, Serena nodded to the midwife to do what she could to aid the child's entry into the world.

The night dragged on; snow began to fall, driving through the cracks in the hut's walls. The woman moaned and twisted on the thin mattress, catching Serena's hands in a crushing grip when the spasms reached their peak, until Serena was certain her fingers would be broken. How long could this go on, Serena wondered as she felt the pressure on her hands begin yet again. Outside, dawn was breaking, but the only indication of that to the people in the hut was a lessening of the grayness that surrounded them. The potion had long since worn off, and Serena dared not give the woman another. Shrill cries burst from the woman's lips and Serena longed

159

to rush from the mean hut and escape to the protection of her own room. Perspiration soaked both the woman and the pallet on which she lay, and her cries became inhuman, animal whines that pounded against Serena's ears until she was near screaming herself. And still the torment continued.

Gyles sat, chin in hand, studying the pieces on the chessboard, his brow furrowed in concentration. A grin split his features, suddenly, and his long, lean fingers lifted a piece from the board and then replaced it in a different square. "Checkmate," Gyles laughed at his opponent. Gyles's smile faded as Nellwyn passed through the hall and made her way toward Serena's chamber—which Serena now used only to store her clothes. Gyles lost no time in following the nurse. He found her searching through one of Serena's trunks. "Nellwyn?"

Nellwyn started, then relaxed, clutching a parcel to her ample bosom. "Aye, m'lord?"

"Where is your mistress?"

Nellwyn's eyes shifted to the floor. "My Lady is still in the village. She bade me return and fetch one of her gowns."

The nurse was maddeningly uninformative—whether deliberately or not, Gyles did not know—but Gyles was determined to learn how Serena had fared. "Is Serena tending the child?"

"Both the babe and its mother, m'lord," Nellwyn said slowly. "Ye must have a care with me lamb when she returns. She has seen much during the night and it may have changed her."

Gyles felt a prickle of fear. "They are both dead?" Nellwyn nodded. Without hesitation Gyles strode to his own chamber and returned, swinging his cloak over his broad shoulders as he went. "Serena will have need of me; I shall go with you."

Nellwyn looked doubtful, but there was nothing she could do. So she led Gyles through the storm to the hut where Serena waited. The scene that greeted Gyles drew him up short. The lifeless infant lay on a clean piece of linen; its tiny body had been washed so that none of the debris of its birth still clung to it. Indeed the babe looked to be sleeping. Serena was kneeling beside the mother's pallet, smoothing the damp hair off the woman's face. When Serena turned she seemed unaware of Gyles's presence; only beckoning to Nellwyn to come forward. The midwife had stripped the woman's soiled clothes away, and Gyles now realized why Serena had sent for another gown.

The midwife took the gown from Nellwyn and then spoke to Serena. "Your nurse and I will see to what else needs to be done, m'lady. There is no need for you to tarry here." Serena rose stiffly. "Perhaps, m'lady, if you could send for the priest?"

Serena nodded. Then she went to the man who sat rocking to and fro on the hearth. Her hand rested gently on his shoulder and he raised a tear-streaked face to her.

"She was a good lass, my Ellen," he said thickly. "Never a mean word for anyone." He began to sob and Serena knelt beside him, seeking a way to comfort him, though she knew none was possible. "Why?" The man asked brokenly of Serena. "Why?"

Serena shook her head. "A priest would say 'tis God's will . . . but I . . . I do not know."

Abruptly the man buried his face in Serena's lap and wept uncontrollably while she stroked his hair tenderly, her own tears spilling from her eyes. Gyles moved into the room and carefully covered the infant; sheltering the tiny, perfect body from view. He turned his attention to the woman and the sight of her tortured body. Gyles knew a fear so great that it turned his heart to ice and his limbs to water. The woman's form was chilling in its similarity to Serena's; long, delicate limbs, slim torso, a tiny waist that a man could easily span with two hands, and above all, narrow hips, which, while they could entice a man to lust, were far too small to accommodate a child of any size. Before his eyes, the woman's lifeless face became Serena's, the raven hair that tumbled over the pillow turned to golden brown.

The man in her arms had quieted, and Serena now

161

noticed Gyles as he stood, his gaze riveted on the lifeless form at his feet. Serena's tears stemmed from the frustration she felt at being unable to do anything to save the woman and her child. Childbirth was the natural way of things, and it was a rare case indeed where the babe was presented backward into the world as this one had been. Serena had assisted Nellwyn many times with a birthing when she lived at Broughton and this was the first time she had seen a woman die in travail. Serena knew that if Nellwyn had been summoned earlier, both babe and mother would now be living. The simple fact was that the woman had been allowed to labor too long and had exhausted her reserves of strength. Had Serena arrived sooner, the potion she had made would have brought the child into the world quickly. The midwife was not to be blamed, for she was young and had never witnessed a breech birth before. Inwardly, Serena railed at unkind fate and her own helplessness, but she had no fear for herself should she ever be blessed with carrying Gyles's child.

Serena slipped into her cloak, then went to stand beside Gyles. His face was rigid with tension and when she touched his cheek lightly, Serena was startled by the anger that clouded Gyles's green eyes when he swung to face her. "Let us go, Gyles, there is naught left for me to do here." Gyles stared, unseeing, down at her. Frightened, Serena tugged at his arm. "Gyles, we must leave him to mourn in peace. Gyles, please!"

The urgency in Serena's voice brought Gyles to his senses and with a curt nod he led Serena from the hut and back to the castle in total silence. Serena mounted the stairs, pausing when Gyles did not accompany her, but instead halted and gazed up at her.

"Rest, Serena. I shall wake you for the evening meal." Serena reached out to touch him, but Gyles backed away. "When Nellwyn returns I will send her to you to see if there is anything you need." Gyles wheeled and walked through the great hall and outside.

Hurt and confused, Serena retired to their chamber where she fell onto the bed to stare at the ceiling until sheer exhaustion forced her into sleep.

162

The snow had fallen, leaving its silver coat over the lands and buildings of Camden and Serena, with Gyles riding beside her, viewed the sparkling display with undisguised delight.

"Isn't it beautiful!" Serena breathed.

Gyles gave a snort of laughter. "It's freezing cold, the wind is blowing straight through my cloak, and you think it's beautiful!"

Serena flashed a grin. "It is beautiful," she insisted. "When Bryan and I were small we used to have a snowball fight after the first snowfall. Nellwyn would always be calling for us to come inside, and how angry she would become when we refused. Once we even pelted her with snow until she retreated and let us tire ourselves out." Her eyes softened. "Gyles, does it snow in Normandy?"

Gyles reached over and gave Serena's hand a light squeeze. "That it does, *ma petite*. Do not fret, Serena, Alan is having his chance to play in the snow."

Serena covered Gyles's hand with hers. "I miss him terribly, Gyles. When can he come back to us?"

"Arthur and I are still negotiating over Beda's hand. Once she is safely wed, perhaps, then." A gust of wind blew over them and Gyles studied the sky. "I believe we are in for another storm, Serena. We had best return."

Gyles covertly watched Serena as they rode to Camden. The cold air had brought a rosiness to her cheeks and nose that enhanced her delicate beauty. Gyles frowned as a creeping warmth spread its tendrils through his groin. Since that ghastly birth, Gyles had clamped an iron will on his passions and eased himself infrequently with Serena. He had not yet resorted to dallying with other women, but he sensed that Serena attributed his lack of attention to that reason.

Serena's thoughts were running parallel to Gyles's. His sudden withdrawal of affection had at first angered, then confused Serena. In every other way Gyles had not altered; they rode, talked, and played chess, but when evening came, Serena could feel the reserve in Gyles rear up like a living thing. And in the past months Gyles had taken a decided interest in whether Serena's time came regularly. If she was late, Gyles was unapproachable until the cramps began and she retired to her separate bed for the duration. There was no way Serena could hide her time, for the discomfort was usually so great that she spent at least two days in bed, dosing herself with a potion that allowed her some ease. During these days, Gyles was unfailingly kind, often sitting beside her for hours at a time, seeing to her every need. But once it was past, Gyles again reverted to his odd behavior, and his greatly cooled ardor upset Serena.

These thoughts occupied both husband and wife during the ride to Camden, and both had lost the light mood that had prevailed during their outing. It had begun to snow before they reached the castle and it was with great reluctance that Gyles followed Serena to their chamber. Her surprised look embarrassed him, and he stood uncertainly within the door.

"I must change from this damp clothing," Gyles explained unnecessarily.

"Of course," Serena said in a shaky voice; then turned her back as she proceeded to strip from her own wet gown. She stepped to the fire to warm herself as she dressed, and from the corner of her eye Serena watched as Gyles padded from chest to chest to select dry clothing. Her own long-starved appetite grew at the sight of her unclad husband and of their own volition, Serena's legs carried her across the room to Gyles.

Gyles did not hear Serena approach, and his first awareness of her presence was when slender arms wrapped themselves around his waist and soft lips nibbled at his back. Gyles did not turn, but tried instead to fight down his steadily rising need. "Serena," Gyles said softly.

"Um?" Serena moved around him until she buried her lips in the curling hair on his chest. Her hands stroked his firm, muscular back, and Serena raised up on tiptoe to ply Gyles's mouth with her own.

Gyles brought his hands to Serena's shoulders, but she ignored their pressure, instead darting her tongue cunningly against his, as Gyles felt his resistance weaken.

"Serena!" Gyles said again, this time pleadingly; but

Serena's hand had already found his impassioned manhood and imprisoned it within her grasp and Gyles willingly followed Serena to his bed.

Neither had the need for preliminaries, but instead immediately strained against each other mindlessly for fulfillment. Serena nearly wept when she felt Gyles withdraw suddenly and violent spasms tore at his body as he spilled himself over her abdomen. Frustration welled up within her, and with a muted cry, Serena struck out at Gyles and rolled from beneath him to the edge of the bed.

"Cherie?" Green eyes begged for understanding and Gyles closed his hands around Serena's arms. "Serena, please!"

Serena flew from his touch, her eyes flashing. "What has happened to you?" Serena cried.

Gyles's hands balled uselessly in the bed linens as he fought back the impulse to tell her what terrified him. "Nothing!" Gyles said hoarsely.

"Gyles, please!" Serena fell to her knees beside him. "I can't go on like this! You . . . you've changed, I can't reach you any more. You rarely touch me, Gyles, and when you do, the look in your eyes and on your face makes me feel as . . . as if . . . as if you can hardly bear to look at me." Serena's hand touched his and Gyles jerked away as if her touch burned him. "Gyles, what have I done? Please, Gyles. Please talk to me, tell me what's wrong."

"There is nothing wrong, Serena, 'tis just your imagination," Gyles said coldly.

"Imagination!" she sputtered. " 'Tis not my imagination that you waste your seed nor that I no longer find pleasure in your arms. Is it Beda? Has she threatened you again? Oh, Gyles, you're breaking my heart, do you not see that?"

A knock on the door silenced Serena, and Gyles called out angrily, "What is it?"

"There is a royal messenger below, m'lord." Edward's voice was muffled by the thick oak.

"God's blood!" Gyles ground out. "I'll be down shortly, bid him eat and drink." Gyles threw himself from

165

the bed and began to dress while Serena, huddled on the bed, watched. "Are you coming?" Gyles asked shortly.

Serena tossed her head with a disdainful sniff. "I think not. Would you be so kind as to send Nellwyn to me, please?"

"As you wish," Gyles relented. "Serena, is there anything I can get for you?"

"A husband who loves me would be pleasant!" Serena said tartly. "But failing that, only Nellwyn."

It was late when Gyles returned to his chamber, his brain clouded by the over-abundance of ale he had consumed during the course of the evening. Serena's wounded feelings weighed heavily upon him, yet Gyles dared not tell her of his fears. Serena's time was several days overdue already and Gyles's nerves were badly strained. If Serena did get with child, she must not be tormented by the same devil that rode his own mind, but must believe that the birthing, while painful, would be completely normal. Serena must not be afraid! Weaving slightly, Gyles pulled off his clothing and drew back the curtains of his bed; perhaps by now Serena had forgiven him. But his bed was empty, the coverlet neatly pulled up to the pillows, and with no indication that anyone had reposed there. Green eyes went swiftly about the room to find the adjoining door closed. Gyles tied a robe hastily around his waist and tried the door only to find it barred.

"Serena?" Gyles rapped loudly on the panel. "Serena, open this door!"

"Go away," came her reply from within.

"Serena, open this door, or by God, I shall break it down!" Gyles roared.

"That I would not doubt," Serena's voice sneered at him. But Gyles heard the movement in the chamber and a moment later the bar was lifted from the door. When the panel opened, Gyles caught a glimpse of Nellwyn as she plodded from the room, and then, when his eyes had adjusted to the dimly lit chamber, he saw Serena sitting in a chair by the hearth. "The door has been opened, at your most courteous request, Gyles. Now what is it that is of such urgency it could not wait for the morrow?"

Gyles shifted uncomfortably. "Since you did not leave your chamber this evening, I thought what news the messenger carried might be of interest to you."

"It must certainly be good news that brings you willingly to my presence," Serena said coolly. She rose to pour a goblet of wine, which brought a lifted eyebrow from Gyles. Serena gave him an icy smile. "Well, dear husband, I am waiting eagerly for your news."

"Very well," his tone matched hers. "We are commanded to journey to London in ten days' time and there reside for the time that remains until the new year."

Serena drained her cup and refilled it immediately. "How pleasant. I take it that I must accompany you."

Gyles nodded. "You will attend the queen while we are in residence. The command is from William himself, Serena. He greatly admires your father and wishes to meet both daughter and son."

"But in a different order, I'll wager. Bryan will not take kindly to being ordered to present himself at a Norman court. Father will have the devil's own time keeping Bryan out of trouble." Serena sipped thoughtfully at yet a third cup of wine. "I'm sure the court will prove a most amusing diversion for both of us, Gyles." With a wicked narrowing of her eyes Serena added, "Think of all the old acquaintances you will be able to renew. And how convenient for you that I will be safely out of your way for much of the time. Tell me, is Beda also included in this invitation?"

Gyles's back stiffened. "Yes. As are Lydia and Mara, though I doubt they will attend."

His words had a definite slur and Serena suddenly realized that her husband was drunk and she laughed. "What a fine family we make. What an impression we shall give the court." Serena drew herself up to her full height. "Yes, your highness," she intoned with mock solemnity, "my husband and I are truly enjoying our stay at court. Oh, no, sire, we do not mind in the *least* that we rarely see each other." With an eloquent wave of her hand Serena indicated an imaginary hall filled with people. "As you can see, sire, Lord Gyles has availed himself fully of the amusements found in your court." Serena leaned toward the invisible figure conspiratorially. "If the truth were known, sire, my good lord has not graced our bed since our arrival at court. Could you perhaps find it in your heart to recommend one of your retinue to me, your highness? I would take care that he not interfere with my attendance to your lady queen." Serena dropped into a curtsy and abruptly pitched forward on the floor, the goblet falling from her grasp to roll aimlessly about.

A great deal of the ale Gyles had consumed had worn off during Serena's diatribe and he went swiftly to raise Serena from the floor. As her head rolled limply against his arm, Gyles smelled the wine on her breath mixed with the bitter smell of herbs, and knew instantly the cause for her unusual behavior.

Serena's eyes fluttered open and she laughed weakly. "I see I must swoon before you deign to take me in your arms."

"Your time?" Gyles asked softly.

Serena gave an imperceptible nod. "Does it please you that I do not carry your seed within me? Fool! Did you think I do not know why you spill your seed wantonly against the bed linens? Do you believe I am so stupid as to not realize that you do not wish me to bear your child? The one thing I would ask from you and that you deny me. I would ask for your love as well, but that I know you are not free to give, so all I beg for is your child. Am I so horrible that you wish not to sire a child on me? Have I some flaw that makes you fear our babe would be flawed as well?" Serena struggled from his embrace. "Yes, my time has come!" she screamed viciously at Gyles. "And, no, I shall not need you to sit by my bed and comfort me this time. I want no part of you now. Do you hear me? None! Now leave, get away from me! Out of this chamber! I have no wish for your false consideration! If you cannot treat me with kindness and respect when I am well, I certainly do not want you to make a harlot of yourself when I am ill!" Her anger suddenly evaporated. "Leave me! If there is any mercy in your heart, Gyles, go away!" And then Serena collapsed like a puppet whose strings had been cut.

Gyles easily caught Serena before she fell full length to the floor and carried her to her bed. Then he strode to the door and found Nellwyn waiting in the corridor as he had known she would be.

"Lady Serena has need of you," Gyles told her shortly. Nellwyn nodded in understanding and followed Gyles to Serena's bedside. "You know what to do for her?"

"Aye, m'lord." Nellwyn covered Serena, then inspected the pitcher of wine by the bed. "Did she behave strangely, m'lord?"

"Yes," Gyles nodded. "Screaming at me one minute, swooning the next."

"Aye, well, she took too much of the herbs she mixed in this wine 'tis all." At the sight of Gyles's rapidly paling face, Nellwyn gave his arm a reassuring pat. "Me lamb will be fine, but she'll sleep like the dead this night."

Gyles passed a hand over his eyes. "You heard, Nellwyn?"

"Aye, that I did." Nellwyn considered him before she continued. "Did me lamb speak the truth? Do ye not wish her to have yer child?"

"Not just mine, any man's!" Gyles paused, unwilling to put voice to the fear within him.

Nellwyn was puzzled. "She'll be a fine mother, m'lord, ye need have no fear on that account."

"My God, do you think I do not know that?" Gyles agonized. " 'Tis my fondest dream that we should have a child—indeed a nursery full of them—but if I must choose between the two—"

"Choose? Why must ye choose? Yer both young and healthy. Serena comes from good stock, the lands are at peace—"

"Because she will die! And I will have killed her as surely as if I put a knife in her heart!" Gyles cried in a strangled voice.

Nellwyn's shock was obvious. "Yer pardon, m'lord,

but yer not making sense. Why would Serena die because she had a child?"

"Like the woman in the village," Gyles insisted. "Serena is built the same way; her hips are too narrow."

Nellwyn shook her head. "Nay, m'lord, the woman died because she labored too long without help. Serena—"

"Serena will die! She barely survives her woman's time, how could she endure a birthing?" The terror Gyles had choked back for so long now washed over him in waves. "I will not be the instrument of Serena's death!"

"But, Lord Gyles . . ."

Gyles had already left the room and Nellwyn stood looking at the space he had vacated, a bewildered expression on her face. Gradually a knowing gleam sparked in her eyes and Nellwyn chuckled as she returned to Serena's side.

"Ah, lamb, 'tis a fine, loving man ye married. Now all we need is to convince him yer not as fragile as ye look. Aye, lamb, we'll have a long talk tomorrow ye and me." And Nellwyn settled herself comfortably by her charge to see the night to an end.

When Serena finally awoke, she instantly regretted having to leave the sweet dreams behind, for awareness brought pain. She rolled to her stomach and delivered a solid punch to the pillow. "Nell-wyn!"

Her nurse was instantly beside her. "Here, lamb, I've brought ye the wine. Come sit up now, lass, and drink this."

"Aagh! I wish I were a man." Nellwyn pushed the pillows none too gently behind her back, and Serena said petulantly, "Have a care, Nellwyn, I'm not a sack of flour."

"Nay, but ye be acting like a spoiled child," Nellwyn told her charge sharply. "And for as smart a lass as ye be, ye've not an ounce of sense. Now ye just listen to me," she said when Serena made to speak. "I've a few things ye should be after knowing, and yer not too old or too big for me to take ye over me knee! Just hold yer tongue and let me have me say."

Gradually while Nellwyn spoke, Serena's features

lightened and by the time the nurse had finished, a huge smile graced Serena's face. "Nellwyn!" Serena clasped her nurse's hands. "Oh, Nellwyn, thank you. Now, this is what I want you to do . . ."

{ BOOK II }
A Prince of the Realm

8

Gyles cast a glance over his shoulder, assuring himself that his entourage was close behind him. His gaze rested upon Serena where she rode beside one of the younger knights—Justin by name—apparently enjoying whatever tale he was regaling her with, and Gyles bestowed a withering look on the pair. Annoyed, Gyles turned to his squire.

"Bid my lady wife come to my side," Gyles growled. "You shall ride beside Sir Justin for the remainder of our journey."

"Yes, m'lord." The squire wheeled his horse and rode back to the middle of the column to deliver his message.

It was not long before Serena drew abreast of Gyles and smiled winningly up at him. "Thank you for asking me to ride with you, Gyles, I was growing quite lonely back there."

Gyles snorted but made no reply. In the ten days allowed them to pack and travel to London, Serena's behavior had totally bewildered Gyles. The morning following that disastrous evening, Nellwyn had come to Gyles and informed him that Serena was awake and feeling better if he cared to see her. Gyles had approached her chamber with great misgivings, but had relaxed when Serena had smiled warmly.

Gyles had taken the delicate hand she extended and

raised it to his lips. "You look well. How do you feel, Serena?"

"I am fine, Gyles, a bit groggy from the potion I took last night, but other than that, I am quite fit."

Gyles had sat on the edge of the bed. "Serena, for my words yesterday, I apologize."

Serena had been puzzled. "Your words . . . I am sorry, Gyles, but I do not remember. Did we argue?"

Serena's eyes were soft, with a gentle glow, and Gyles had pressed his lips upon hers. " 'Twas only a small misunderstanding, Serena, of no great importance."

Serena had given him a small smile. "I have been thinking about Christmas, Gyles. Would it be possible or us to hold some sort of festivities for the children here? A repast for them and perhaps some games for them to play?"

"I will see that Lydia and Mara attend to it. You do not remember that we must be at court within ten days, but Lydia and Mara have chosen to remain behind."

Serena's face had fallen, but she accepted the news calmly. The tisane she had swallowed had given her the appearance of a small kitten wanting to be cuddled, and Serena curled against Gyles with a sigh, resting her cheek on the palm of his hand and she drifted into a quiet sleep.

As the days of preparation passed, Serena had returned to share Gyles's bed but had said nothing of his abstinence. Indeed, she seemed totally oblivious to the fact as she and Nellwyn packed and sewed the necessary items for their journey. At first Gyles avoided their chamber until he was certain Serena would be asleep, but after a week, he actually began to enjoy once again the quiet, private hours he spent with his wife. His only trial both at Camden and during their journey was when Serena, seeking warmth, molded herself against him in the night. Several times Gyles had come fully awake to discover his hands tracing the soft curves of Serena's body, and Gyles had cursed himself silently for his body's betrayal.

But the past two days, Serena had taken to riding beside Justin, and Gyles had privately wondered if Serena's indifference lay in the fact that one of his own men was satisfying her needs.

"You will no longer devote your attentions to Sir Justin," Gyles told Serena abruptly.

Serena looked at her husband in surprise. "I did but ride with him, Gyles," she chided.

"For two days! I saw the intimate conversations you carried on!" Gyles growled.

To his surprise, Serena laughed up at him. "Gyles! I have asked you repeatedly to tell me of William's court, and you have repeatedly refused. Sir Justin has been kind enough to enlighten me somewhat." Serena's voice lowered and she moved her mount closer to Gyles. "Surely you are not jealous."

Gyles's face hardened and the thin line of his scar whitened against the wind-rubbed red of his cheek. He leaned over and grasped Serena's wrist painfully. "You are mine, my wife, and I'll not have you encouraging some man into a dalliance."

Serena touched her lips to the lean fingers that circled her wrist. "'Tis the furthest thought from my mind."

Gyles relented and wrapped the folds of Serena's cloak more securely around her. "What is it you wish to know of the court?"

Serena's first impression of London was one of total chaos. People crowded the streets, making it impossible for the mounted column to continue with any speed, and more often than not, Gyles was forced to call a halt so that a herd of sheep or swine could pass in front of them. Roving peddlers plied their trade, adding to the confusion, calling out the prices of their wares in shrill tones that carried easily over the general hubbub. Brightly painted stalls nestled together on the sides of the streets, and it was from this vantage point that wealthier merchants sold their goods. Cloth, baubles, lace, armor; all could be purchased on the streets. For a nominal fee, one could purchase meat—fresh slaughtered, roasted, or

177

cured—wines from England or Normandy, pastries freshly baked and stuffed with those fruits the bakers had been farsighted enough to preserve, which, Gyles informed Serena, would soon disappear during the course of the winter.

Women, too, were available for a few coins. The strumpets Serena easily recognized on her own from the bold, inviting looks they bestowed upon the men in the retinue. Gyles particularly came under their ribald scrutiny and jests, and from the knowing looks one or two of the women gave herself and Gyles, Serena knew that Gyles had dipped into his purse more than once during his last stay in London. Surprisingly, the thought did not disturb Serena—after all, Gyles was a man of vigorous appetites and she could not fault him for sating his needs, so long as he had not continued those activities since their marriage. Fidelity was not the norm between spouses, but Serena expected it from her mate and would countenance no deviation from the wedding vows by her husband. A quick glance at Gyles showed Serena that this daylight confrontation with his one-time bedmates had caused a dull flush to creep from his neck and into his face.

Seized by a fit of deviltry, Serena said with mock concern, "Gyles, are you not feeling well? Your face is quite flushed. Have you caught a chill?"

Gyles shifted uncomfortably in his saddle. " 'Tis the wind," he said gruffly. "It rubs the cheeks quite raw."

"Of course," Serena murmured solicitously. "I have a cream that will heal the chafed skin, and when we are settled, I shall apply it to your cheeks."

Gyles turned an even deeper shade of red under Serena's uncompromising stare. "You can see the castle from here." Gyles pointed over the tops of the buildings.

Serena's face fell. " 'Tis not as large as I had imagined."

Gyles laughed. " 'Tis large enough, Serena, from here you can see only the upper stories. One day I shall take you to a hill where you can look down rather than up at the castle and you will see how grand it actually is."

Serena was still disappointed. "If you say so."

Gyles's lips thinned in anger. "What did you think to find, Serena, all of London overshadowed by a castle? Towers so high they pierced the clouds and continued into the heavens? Walls lined with fur-trimmed guards that would herald your arrival? 'Tis time you grew up and faced life as it is rather than view everything through those romantic dreams you still cling to."

At his unkind words, Serena's chin began to tremble. "I see life most clearly, Gyles, but that need not stop me from wishing it different, or trying to change what I believe is wrong. Had you answered my questions at Camden rather than dismissing them as trivial, we should both have been spared your anger. And that, Gyles, I see very plainly," Serena said softly.

Her quiet rebuke stung Gyles into a pensive silence. Serena was right, of course. With no knowledge of London or the court, how could she form an accurate picture of what to expect? Indeed, no woman Gyles had ever known could face life as straight-forwardly as Serena did. When problems arose, she faced them head-on, without resorting to tears and wails concerning her lot in life, and she always sought a sound, logical solution. She was an admirable, independent woman, this lass who had been forced into his life, and as Gyles studied her delicate profile, he felt an overwhelming thankfulness in his heart that God had seen fit to grant him such a mate.

The column had wound its way through the streets and was approaching the bridge that crossed the Thames when Serena drew her mount up short with a horrified gasp.

"Don't look!" Gyles told her sharply and made to shield Serena's eyes.

Serena batted his hand away and stared, transfixed, at the gory sight in front of her. Three disembodied heads floated grotesquely on pikes directly above the bridge, their eyes staring sightlessly at passersby, the skin falling in lax folds from their cheekbones. The heads had been pelted with dirt and refuse and the bodies that had once obeyed the commands of the now-deteriorating brains must have suffered nameless agonies before death gave them release, for the mouths gaped open in eternal, silent screams. Even as Serena watched a carrion crow dropped from the sky to light upon one of the skulls and sink its beak into a blind eye.

"Gyl-Gyles, what—what could they have done?" Serena's throat was so dry she could barely speak.

"Treason, most likely. This is the usual punishment. Their bodies have probably been drawn and quartered."

Serena blanched and pressed her hand to her mouth. An awful vision of Gyles undergoing the same fate passed through Serena's mind, and she forced herself to choke out a final question. "What is the sentence for murder?"

Gyles turned his head deliberately to the grisly spectacle before answering in a toneless voice. "Exile at the least; at the worst, the same as that." He drew a deep breath, then reached out to squeeze Serena's shoulder reassuringly. "Do not dwell on it, Serena, for it will not happen." Serena was as pale as the snow on the ground and a shudder passed over her. "Are you able to control your mount?" Gyles asked.

Serena raised her head in a defiant gesture Gyles knew all too well and nodded. "Let us get away from here as quickly as possible and I will be fine!"

As Gyles had said, there was no fanfare to greet their arrival at court, but when Serena excitedly surveyed the furnishings of the royal court, any disappointment she may have felt quickly evaporated. The housecarl led them through hallways lined with tapestries and around the men and women who darted from one room to another, apparently on important business for their lord—or perhaps the king himself! The richly dressed people, Serena assumed, were there at the king's request as she was. She wished she had had the time to rearrange her hair and change from the travel-stained gown she wore. Following the housecarl through a seemingly endless maze of corridors and arches, Serena recalled her earlier statement about the castle's size and she laughed inwardly. All of Camden and Broughton could easily fit within these walls and neither had such rich appointments. Small tables and chairs sat outside nearly every doorway and knights bearing the royal standard on their chest guarded the entrance to every corridor they passed through. At last Serena gave up trying to retain her sense of direction and was only too glad when they reached their chamber.

The servant bowed from the room and Serena pulled the cloak from her shoulders and capered about the room. "I have never seen anything like this! Look, Gyles," she lifted a candlestick, "solid gold!" Serena fingered the curtains of the bed. "And the threads of this brocade are silver—real silver—and the coverlet, Gyles, what kind of fur is this?" Serena demanded.

"Mink. Imported from France because of its softness and warmth," Gyles informed her.

Serena bounced on the bed to test its softness. "Did you notice all the tapestries, Gyles? Do you have any idea how long it takes to make one hanging? All of Normandy must have been sewing for years! Look, even the floor is covered with pelts!" Serena kicked off her slippers and curled her cold toes in the fur. "Surely, 'tis a sin to be surrounded by such luxury, so I shall have to say a penance for enjoying it so much." She grinned up at her husband and fell back upon the bed to rub her cheek against the soft fur.

Gyles looked down at her in amusement. "I can well imagine that you will demand I purchase some of these luxuries to return with us to Camden."

Serena laughed. "Nay, Gyles, 'tis fine for the court, but I should not be able to live with it constantly, for in truth, it does make me feel ill at ease. Mink did you say?" Gyles nodded then gave a shout as Serena's foot shot out and tripped him so that he fell beside her on the mattress.

Instantly Gyles's arm caught Serena to him and he began to tickle her unmercifully while she responded in kind. Soon both were laughing helplessly and Serena's head came to rest upon his shoulder.

"You, Serena, are a vixen, and totally beyond my comprehension."

Serena giggled happily and placed a kiss on his cheek. "And you are a brute to attack someone much smaller than yourself."

Gyles's arm tightened and he pulled Serena beneath him. Her face was tinged with pink from their play and her hair had escaped its ribbons as it tumbled around her shoulders. Serena's eyes widened while she looked up at him and they held a soft glow, her lips parted slightly in invitation and Gyles lowered his head and touched her lips in the tenderest of kisses. A knock at the door jolted them apart and Serena leaped from the bed as if scalded.

Gyles rose and quickly rearranged his tunic. "Enter," he called.

A small boy in the dress of a page came hesitantly into the room. "The Lady Serena is bid to accompany me to the queen," he said in a high, piping voice; the words obviously learned by rote, for his brow was furrowed in concentration. "Her Majesty regrets that she must call so soon upon your services and sends her most profound apologies to Lord Gyles and yourself."

Serena had recovered her poise enough to smile at the page. "You may wait outside for me. I shall not be long."

When the door closed behind the page, Gyles began to laugh while Serena hurriedly changed her gown and began to brush her gold-flecked curls into order.

"What, pray, do you find so amusing, Gyles?" Serena frowned over her shoulder.

"You!" Gyles gasped and collapsed into a chair. "You jumped as if you'd been bitten."

"Well, it might have been someone else—perhaps even the queen, and what would she have thought!" Serena said furiously.

A smile still played on Gyles's lips when he answered. "The first lesson of court life: The queen does not come to you, cherie; you go to her. Second lesson: Matilda and William have three sons. How do you think that happened; by their having separate beds? Even at his age now, I'll wager the king still has enough strength to give Matilda a good toss now and then."

Serena whirled, her fingers busily knotting a ribbon

182

in her curls. "Gyles! You are speaking of your sovereign lord to whom you are pledged——"

"I speak of a man and a woman, Serena. Titles do not alter that fact." Green eyes inspected her critically. "Your hair isn't quite right. Come here and let me fix the ribbon."

Serena did as he asked, but fidgeted nervously, trying to inspect the line of her gown. She turned this way and that until Gyles pulled her firmly onto his lap and told her in a voice that brooked no disobedience to sit still. His hands finally fell from Serena's hair and she rose so that he could inspect her appearance. Her gown was of pale blue, shot through with silver threads, ribbons of the same color as the gown held the silver snood in place and the gold highlights of hair gleamed through it so that Serena's appearance was ethereal in its delicacy. Gyles sat, stunned by the beauty of the vision in front of him. "Well?" Serena demanded. "Am I presentable?"

Gyles nodded slowly. What could he say? Serena looked as if she could sprout wings and float above all the lowly mortals of the court. Such loveliness would undoubtedly turn the heads of the men at court, and Gyles felt a prickle of fear for Serena's safety. He rose and walked with her to the door of their chamber. "Be careful, Serena. Speak not to any man—be he squire, knight, or lord—alone."

Serena looked at Gyles in surprise. "But . . ." She stopped at the serious look on his face. "As you wish, Gyles. I shall say not a word unless I am surrounded by the queen's ladies or until you are by my side."

Gyles bent and gave her a light kiss. " 'Tis for your own good. Now go, the queen is waiting."

Serena hurried after the page, lifting her skirt so that she could stay apace with the boy and not lose him in the maze of corridors. As a result, Serena arrived flushed and breathless at the queen's chambers and had no time to compose herself because she was immediately admitted to the queen's presence.

"The Lady Serena, formerly of Broughton, wife to Gyles, Lord of Camden, Wolcott, and St. Clair."

Serena dropped to the floor, fighting silently to regain her breath, and listened as the page retreated and closed the door behind him. Serena remained on her knees, unmoving, not daring so much as a quick glance through her lashes. Surely the queen did not intend to leave her kneeling on the hard stones of the floor!

"Do you speak our tongue?"

The warm, maternal voice startled Serena and she nearly lifted her head to reply, but caught herself in time. *"Oui, Sa Majesté, peu ou point."* Serena switched to her native language. "My tutor preferred Latin but he had some small knowledge of your Norman tongue, which he passed on to my brother and myself."

"You had a tutor, Lady Serena?"

" 'Twas my brother's tutor, actually; a monk from the abbey at Broughton," Serena replied.

"Bien! You are more suitable than any of the other Saxon women who have attended me. But, rise, rise, my child, and come here so I may see you more clearly."

Serena obeyed and was surprised to find Matilda flanked by two young men. Matilda smiled warmly and beckoned to Serena. "Come, child, you need not fear I will bite you; nor, I promise, will either of my sons."

"Now you see how our father won so easily at Hastings, Mother, these Saxons have as much courage as a sheep!" The older of the two men looked at Serena with contempt, his brown eyes glittering with derision.

Serena—with some difficulty—bit back the sharp retort that sprang to her lips and gave Matilda a small smile. "I am most honored at having been granted the priviledge of attending you, Your Majesty."

Matilda chuckled. "Bah! When I was your age, Lady Serena, I would have preferred the intrigues of the young men at court rather than waiting upon an old woman." She bestowed a withering look upon her older son. "As for you, William, you will treat my ladies kindly, as they are gently bred, or you may absent yourself from my chambers."

Serena turned her blue-eyed gaze on William. He

was short in stature but of a stocky, firm build, which Serena knew would turn into a paunch as he aged. William's coloring did not add to his attractiveness, for his face seemed constantly suffused with blood, as if he would fly into a rage at the least provocation—as, indeed, he often did. His features appeared to be constantly set in cruel, cynical lines and when angered, as now, the veins stood out in William's forehead, so that Serena could see the pulse beat in his temples. His eyes burned into Serena and her throat constricted with a fear she had never known. William advanced upon her and Serena yearned to back away from him, but pride stiffened her back and forced her to meet his gaze.

"You forget your place, Saxon! 'Tis unmannerly to look so upon a member of the royal family without permission." William bore down upon Serena, a hand upraised as if he would strike her.

"And far worse for a gentle lord to threaten a mere woman!" Serena retorted without thinking, then as realization dawned, her eyes widened in horror.

"A nation of sheep, eh, brother?" The slender youth who had remained silently watchful during the exchange now came to where Serena and William stood, his brown eyes bright with laughter. He took Serena's hand and bowed over it. "I apologize to this lovely ewe for my brother who has the manners of a goat." His grin was infectious and in spite of her situation, Serena found herself smiling back at him. His voice lowered so that only Serena could hear his next words. "I commend you on your courage, fair lady, but warn you to caution, William will not take this lightly. Mayhap if you were to apologize . . ."

Serena's deep blue eyes thanked him and she turned to face William. She recalled now that Gyles had told her of William—nicknamed William Rufus for his reddish coloring—and his violent temper. "My apologies, your highness. I have the fault of speaking before I think."

William snorted. "That will soon be remedied by your stay here, among your betters."

"Tsk, tsk. William, you *do* have the manners of a

goat. A beautiful woman humbles herself before you and all you do is berate her. I, madame, have better manners, I assure you. My name is Henry." Henry bowed once again over her hand and this time his lips pressed firmly against her fingers.

Serena gasped softly as her pulses leapt at the gentle touch of this prince and Henry's eyes smiled down into hers, acknowledging the flare of reaction. As if he were loath to do so, Henry slowly relinquished her hand and Serena appraised him through the lowered veil of her lashes. Her overall impression was that of darkness; a dark brown tunic trimmed in ermine and embroidered with gold thread, dark hair straight and close-cropped in the Norman fashion, a naturally swarthy complexion made even darker by hours spent in sun and wind, and above all else, dark, flashing eyes that engaged all who chanced to look into their depths. But for all his darkness, Serena did not find Henry's appearance oppressive or foreboding, she saw in this prince, who was the same age as herself, a light-hearted vitality that transmitted itself to her like a physical shock from his slender, whipcord body.

Henry was far different from his brother in temperament, Serena thought, yet both men were arrogant in their own way. William demanded respect by virtue of his overbearing manner, while Henry won the loyalty of those he met with a straight-forward manner and unstudied charm. Oh, yes, Henry was a charmer, William Rufus a bully, and both had inherited their father's magnetism and energy, which they exuded in waves.

"I do not require you to teach me how to deal with a woman, Henry," William was saying. "Nor have I need for your advice on any other matter!"

Henry smiled insolently at his brother. "I take back my words; you are not a goat, William, you are a——"

"Henry! William!" Matilda came forward and delivered a stinging slap to each of them followed by a tirade of French. "Now out, both of you. What an impression you have made on this poor innocent, I cannot imagine; but you will both make amends to her. I have not yet decided how, but you shall both regret abusing my woman." Matilda gave both sons a push to the door and stood silently until it closed. Then she turned to Serena. "Come, child, let me look at you."

Serena obeyed, standing quite still while Matilda circled her, chin in hand, appraising her newest lady-in-waiting. "You are a tiny thing. Are you well?"

"I enjoy the best of health, Your Highness," Serena assured her.

"Bon! I require my hair to be dressed. Are you capable?"

"Yes, Your Majesty."

"Then let us begin. Come."

While Serena brushed and curled the queen's greying but still lovely blond hair, Matilda kept up a running stream of conversation. "You must forgive my sons, Lady Serena, William has spoiled all of our children shamefully and I fear it shows. 'Tis hard for them, being the offspring of a man such as the king. There is naught William has said he would do that he has not accomplished, and our sons must naturally feel they must achieve even greater feats. Henry is a good boy, although I worry about him. Being the third son, he will inherit very little. Normandy will fall to Robert, of course, since he is the eldest and William will receive England. Oh, my dear, I am sorry. Do you hate my husband as some of your countrymen do?"

"No, Your Majesty, I do not hate the king nor the Norman people as a whole." Serena replied honestly, although her pride burned at the thought of her beloved England being handed over so carelessly to one such as William Rufus.

"Ah, but I had forgotten, you are married to one of my husband's bravest knights. Gyles has not visited the court in, ah . . . let me think . . . two years? How long have you been married?"

" 'Twill be a year in January, your majesty."

"Ah! and no little ones?"

"No, your majesty." Serena reddened.

"But soon, yes?" Matilda asked with a twinkle in her hazel green eyes. "Your husband—you are happy with him?" Serena nodded. "It is a rare thing for one to be completely happy in a marriage. When the envoys came from the Duke to offer for my hand, oh, the scene I created! But afterward"—Matilda's eyes softened in remembrance—"William was like no other man I had known. He has a terrible temper, it is true; and such pride, so unwilling to bend, to understand that a person may reach out to give him loyalty and affection freely, with no thought of reward." Matilda blinked rapidly, recalling suddenly Serena's presence. "I am sorry, *ma petite*, for a moment I forgot . . ."

Serena said nothing as she patted a final curl into place, though she felt Matilda watching her in the mirror. She knew little of court life—that fact Gyles had made painfully clear—but she doubted the queen fell to conversing so freely with her women, particularly one so recently arrived at court. Some of her doubts must have shown in her face for Matilda gave a soft laugh and turned to face Serena.

"And now you are wondering if the queen has taken leave of her senses, are you not, child?" Matilda asked with a smile. "I assure you, I am in full possession of my faculties. As you will soon learn." Matilda continued in a sterner vein, "Very little is done at court without a purpose being served—and your attendance upon me does have a purpose. It is no accident that we are alone or that I hoped to gain your confidence by striking a chord within you by the similarities between our husbands. Do not pale so, Lady Serena, I do not mean to frighten you nor do I mean you any harm. In truth you are younger than two of my daughters."

Serena placed the brush she still held on the table and folded her shaking hands to still their trembling. She moistened her dry lips, but when she spoke her voice was calm. "What is it you wish of me, Your Highness?"

Matilda laughed in genuine amusement. "Child, you have more courage than most men I have known! Come, sit down here." Matilda indicated a chair by her side. "The time for pretense is over then; I like you, so from now on there shall be only the truth between us. My husband instructed me to include you among my ladies—because of your brother."

"Bryan? But why?" Serena's eyes were wide with alarm.

Matilda's lips pursed in thought for a moment. "Your brother has no great love for my husband or his rule. No? There are many young men such as your Bryan, Lady Serena, and it is not my husband's desire to destroy the flower of England's manhood. You must believe that. But neither can he allow traitors to spread dissension throughout the land. The king greatly desires peace in the kingdom; it has only been five years since Wales was brought under his rule and more worries must not be added to the burden he already carries. And his burden is great." Matilda's eyes grew sad as she sat wrapped in her thoughts, then she sighed wearily. "I have no love of politics or of intrigue, Lady Serena. I care only for my husband and children, and now I find myself torn between them as well. Do you know of Robert, our eldest son? No? Then I shall speak of him so you may understand my husband's position more clearly. Robert is our first-born, the heir to Normandy's throne. During my husband's frequent absences, Robert rules in his stead. All was well 'til Robert came to England last year and demanded—demanded!—independence and full authority for himself in Normandy.

"My husband refused, of course, and Robert took ship back to Normandy where he and his allies tried to storm Rouen and failed. There was no other course left to William: He issued orders that Robert be arrested. But our son and his fellow rebels had already fled into France. Have you any idea what it cost William to declare his own son a rebel, a traitor? Despite what you may have heard, Lady Serena, my husband is a just and honorable man; he has shown mercy to those who have opposed him numerous times. William has no desire to spill blood senselessly, that I earnestly pray you to believe, but he will brook no interference with his rule. Rebels must be dissuaded from their purpose or he will be forced to deal harshly with them—be they Saxons who wish a Saxon king for England or Normans who desire a different Norman to rule Normandy. If your brother is involved in these rebel activities, and my husband believes he is, there is still time to save him from the executioner."

"You are asking me to betray my brother!"

"Nay, child, nay." Matilda leaned forward intently. "To save him, and your king. If Bryan is captured during a raid or arrested while he is spreading treason, there will be no choice left to William but to order his death."

Serena's bottom lip caught between her teeth. "If I do as you ask, what assurance have I that no harm will come to Bryan?"

"William will give you his solemn oath if you wish; but for now you have my word that your brother will be safe."

"Very well, Your Highness," Serena decided. "I shall do as you ask. What will you have of me?"

"Persuade your brother to give up his activities before he is discovered. Bryan is also at court now, so you will have many opportunities to speak with him."

"I shall do my best, Your Majesty. I have no desire to see Bryan's head on a pike." Serena rose. Everything had been so carefully arranged: her private audience with the queen, Matilda's pretended confidences of her marriage. Oh yes, Gyles had been right, Serena did indeed have much to learn of court life. "Your Majesty, did Gyles . . . my husband, did he know of the king's reason for our summons to court?"

Matilda looked up in surprise. "Gyles was summoned because he has been absent too long from court. I would guess that he did not attend us last year because of your pending marriage."

"Then you will no longer wish me to attend you?"

"*Au contraire,* little one. You appeal to me far more than any of my other ladies, and I would be devastated should you not wish to serve me." Matilda's eyes sparkled, yet it was clear to Serena that Matilda meant what she said. "Now, child, you would not disappoint an old woman, would you?"

Matilda was charming; Serena found herself liking her, for she was a kind woman who had not altered when she became queen. She was a woman concerned primarily with the welfare of her husband and children and very little with the affairs of state except when it directly affected her family. Perhaps it was because Matilda treated Serena more like a daughter than the wife of one of her husband's lords, but for whatever reason, for the first time since learning that she would go to court, Serena looked forward to her stay. Serena sank down before Matilda and put her hands between the queen's in the accepted gesture of servitude.

"If it please you, Your Majesty, I shall be most honored to wait upon you."

"Bien," Matilda said quietly. This Saxon lass was indeed special. When Matilda had learned that Sir Gyles had wed, she had been surprised . . . and shocked as well, for she remembered Gyles and his previous behavior at court all too well. A bastard like her husband, Gyles carried in his heart a burning anger against all women and had bedded the women of court not only because of a physical need but also, Matilda thought, because he enjoyed being able to ignore them completely the following day. One small piece of revenge for the lifetime of shame he endured because of one woman's moment of weakness. That Matilda could well understand, for her own husband labored under the same black stigma of bastardy, yet William's reaction to his illegitimate birth had been completely different from Gyles's. Throughout the years, William had remained faithful to her, never allowing another woman to know his favor; yet at the same time William was unfailingly polite and courteous to those women who lived at or visited the court.

Matilda studied Serena as the young girl worked the snood into place on the queen's hair. Such an innocent, young thing to be wed to such as Gyles. Yet, there was strength beneath that delicate exterior, Matilda sensed; strength Serena would need aplenty to survive a marriage to Gyles. A pretty child, Matilda mused, but how had Serena come to the attention of the lord of Camden; and more puzzling still, what quality did Serena possess that could persuade Gyles to wed her? Was it possible—

just possible—that that fierce Norman knight had found his heart's ease in this beautiful Saxon lass? Matilda gave a slow smile to Serena as she stepped back to survey her handiwork.

"Do not frown so, Serena, you will ruin your lovely brow." Matilda indicated a looking glass on the table beside her and Serena handed it to the queen silently, waiting nervously while Matilda scrutinized her reflection. "Lovely, child. Now, in the wardrobe you will find a gown of burgundy velvet and slippers that match."

Serena complied and soon Matilda was fully dressed save for the gold circlet that was her crown. Serena reached for it, then hesitated, uncertain whether she was allowed to touch the symbol of authority.

"*Vite, vite!* Above all, William detests tardiness," Matilda urged. Serena snatched the crown from its resting place without a second thought and secured it firmly atop Matilda's hair. "Good," Matilda sighed. "I am ready. Come, we shall collect the rest of the ladies along the way."

Matilda kept Serena by her side as they hurried through the halls to gather the remainder of her entourage and rushed the rest of the way to the banquet hall. At the entrance, Matilda came to an abrupt halt, patting her hair and smoothing her gown to assure that her appearance was perfect. When she turned to Serena, Matilda's face had assumed a regal air, but a hint of warmth still glinted in her green eyes.

"I know you wish to sup with your husband, Lady Serena, so I give you my permission to do so. But I shall require your assistance when I retire. *D'accord?*"

"*Oui, Sa Majesté,*" Serena agreed. "*Merci.*"

Matilda's eyes twinkled. "Then run along and enjoy your first evening at court. And, Lady Serena," Matilda halted Serena in mid-turn. "Do not break too many hearts."

Serena strolled among the clusters of people in the hall, anxious to find Gyles, yet eager to explore the new and exciting world of William's court. So many people! Serena's eyes widened in anticipation. There was much to be learned and experienced here: People from all parts of the continent had come to pay their respects to William. Even with her limited knowledge of the French tongue, Serena could hear the different dialects that were being spoken. She must remember to ask Gyles about that! William and Matilda had entered the hall, but were not seated at the table so Serena had some time yet to locate Gyles. Serena glanced around the hall and nearly stamped her foot in frustration. As tall as he was, Gyles should stand out even in this overcrowded room, but Serena could not see him.

"Are you lost, Lady Serena?" A harsh voice beside her caused Serena to jump. William Rufus stood so closely by her side that Serena could smell the wine on his breath as he regarded her appraisingly from heavy-lidded eyes. "My mother is not here to protect you now," William sneered.

Serena's chin lifted. "I do not require protection, Your Majesty. I am quite capable of doing that for myself."

"Are you indeed?" William's knuckles caressed her jawline. "You are far different from the other Saxon women I have met. At least you do not smell as badly as most."

"I regret I cannot say the same for you," Serena snapped then smiled as William's face went rigid with anger. Serena leaned toward him and spoke with great precision. "You are in need of a bath, William Rufus, and I, mere Saxon woman that I am, find you offensive."

William's hands clenched at his sides. "You are insolent, madame, and you take a great risk. For your words alone, I could have you flogged!"

Serena's smile did not waver. "Do as you please, Your Highness, I am sure the court would be very impressed by that display of your power."

William's fingers caught Serena's wrist. "No one else would ever know," William threatened.

"And my husband?" Serena asked softly.

"Would not dare interfere with a royal order," William sneered.

"How convenient." Serena forced a lightness she

did not feel into her voice for the benefit of a passing lord. "Now I know the secret of your attraction to women —you threaten them with the power of your royal position." But Serena was thinking, God help us if this man becomes king! She glanced around and nearly fainted with relief when she saw Gyles making his way to her from across the room. "My husband is coming, Your Highness. Shall I introduce you?"

"We have already met." William released her wrist and stamped off.

Serena lost no time in hurrying to Gyles. "Where have you been? I have been looking all over the hall for you."

Gyles held the hand Serena extended and smiled down at her. "I encountered some old friends, cherie, and stopped to pass the time. How fared you with the queen?"

"Quite well, I think, but I shall tell you of that later. She has released me from any duties until she retires so I may spend the entire evening with you. You must show me everything, Gyles, and introduce me to your friends."

"Nothing would please me more, Serena, but 'tis impossible tonight. The king has called a council after the meal." Gyles dropped an arm about Serena's shoulders. "I am sorry, but we will be here for a long time and there will be many opportunities for me to present you. Ah, 'tis time for the meal. Come."

While they ate, Serena was acutely aware that she was being watched and looked up, expecting to find William Rufus glaring at her, but instead she intercepted a look between Gyles and the most striking woman Serena had ever seen. The woman's raven hair showed blue-black through the gold of her snood, her complexion was as pure as milk and her black eyes were as slanted as those of a cat's. When the meal was over and she rose, Serena was awed by her perfect stature, for the woman was taller than herself by a good head and shoulders, and although she appeared the same age as Gyles, her willowy figure bore none of the disfigurements of childbearing.

"Gyles," Serena tugged on his sleeve when the woman had turned from the table. "Do you know that woman?"

"Which one?" Gyles asked disinterestedly.

"Don't be stubborn! The one who kept looking at you during the meal. The beautiful one with the black hair." Serena nodded her head toward the woman. "Well, *do* you know her?"

"Yes," Gyles answered shortly.

"For heaven's sake, Gyles, must I drag it out of you? What is her name?"

"Her name is Elspeth, she is very rich. I met her at court several years ago, and she has recently been widowed. Does that satisfy your curiosity?" Gyles said curtly.

Serena regarded her husband with icy curiosity. "I beg your pardon, Gyles! I did not know her identity was such a secret. And as my questions seem to affront you, I am certain you will be glad to be relieved of my companionship for the remainder of the evening. *Adieu,* m'lord."

"Serena, wait!" Gyles rose along with her.

"For what?" Serena snapped, then pulled her dignity around her injured feelings. "The king is leaving, Gyles, should you not attend him?"

The hand Gyles had stretched out to Serena fell uselessly to his side. "I shall wait for you in our chamber."

"You needn't bother," Serena told him coolly. "I shall try not to wake you when I return."

Gyles made one last effort to soothe her affronted pride. "I should like to hear about your first day in court."

Serena's anger ebbed away as Gyles took her hand and raised it to his mouth, kissing each of her fingers in turn, his green eyes growing quite warm as he stared down at her. "If you are still awake when I return," Serena agreed, "I should like to tell you of my day."

Gyles bent to kiss her cheek. "Try not to be too long, cherie. Come to me as soon as you can; I shall be waiting." And then he was gone, leaving Serena wondering whether she was still angry with him for his brusque remarks or if she had already completely forgiven him.

All thoughts of her husband were wiped from Serena's mind as she was caught from behind to be held in a crushing embrace.

"Serena, dearest sister!" Bryan laughed at her as she struggled to be free. "I see Gyles has not succeeded in subduing your spirit."

Serena shook herself free of Bryan's arms and grinned back at him. "You need a good lesson in manners, Bryan. Nellwyn failed miserably with you." But she took the arm he offered and they proceeded to wander through the hall.

"When did you arrive?" Bryan asked when they had found a secluded corner.

"Only today, but I have already met the queen and am serving as one of her ladies."

"Perhaps you can teach these oafish Norman women some of your charms."

"Bryan," Serena rebuked him. "The queen is a most gracious woman and she speaks most highly of the king."

"Did you expect she would not?" Bryan glared. "Look at the way these pompous Normans strut about."

"Bryan, please!" Serena said nervously. "You mustn't say things like that! It could get you into trouble."

Bryan eyed her suspiciously. "I am speaking only to my sister; how could that be dangerous? Unless she has forgotten her Saxon heritage as so many others have."

" 'Tis of no use trying to make me feel guilty, Bryan, because what I say is for your own good." Serena placed a hand on Bryan's arm. "Will you calm yourself and listen to me? The queen asked me to speak to you—"

"The queen!" Bryan snorted. "What are you supposed to make me do—fight for William? Well, he will wait a long time for that to happen."

"Bryan, I don't wish to fight with you. Please, only listen to me."

Bryan sighed and drew his sister a goodly distance from the majority of the people. "Serena, I have no desire to fight with you either, but I am certain I already know what you are to tell me. It is what father has been saying to me for the past year, is it not? You never took sides before your marriage and I ask you to do the same now."

"Only listen to me, Bryan," Serena pleaded.

Bryan smiled affectionately. "You are stubborn, sister. Very well, say what you will if 'twill put your mind at ease."

"I don't know what you have been doing, Bryan, but I can well imagine. A raiding party here and there; inciting others to treason; revolt against William. Am I fairly accurate?" Bryan nodded reluctantly and Serena drew a deep breath. "And what have you accomplished? Nothing! Nothing has changed, Bryan. Be reasonable; eleven years have passed since William defeated Harold at Hastings."

"Murdered would be more like it," Bryan said grimly.

"No, Bryan, William was the victor of a fair battle and you know that is the truth. You also know that William's claim to England's throne was every bit as valid as Harold's. 'Twas Harold who caused the loss of so many Saxon lives by his refusal to accept William as the successor to the throne."

"Edward was half-Norman himself, that pious monk! Who else would he select, having no heir of his own? For twelve years Harold loyally served and protected this realm—'twas right and just that he should be our king."

"Right or wrong, Bryan, William was named as successor, not Harold!"

"There were no witnesses to that, Serena, only William's word that Edward chose him."

Serena passed a hand over her eyes. "All right, I will grant you that point. But William was the victor and thus gained the right to the throne."

"His throne is drenched with Saxon blood, Serena! Can you forget that?"

"Bryan, I was only seven at the time and you were but nine. Be reasonable, how much do either of us remember about Edward or Harold?"

"I do not have to remember them in order to dislike being ruled by a Norman pig! Do you not wish for a king of our own people? I do! I wish to see a Saxon once more on England's throne."

"How will you accomplish that? And who will ascend the throne? Edgar the Atheling—a weak, sickly boy who has never even seen England? There are others who covet the throne as well, but that way brings destruction; brother set against brother, as each does battle to see his favorite wear the crown. Would you deliver England to such a fate? It is futile, Bryan! Have we not seen more than enough bloodshed as we grew up?"

Bryan rounded on Serena, his dark blue eyes flashing into hers. "Yes, "I've seen enough bloodshed—enough to last me the rest of my life! I have seen decent, kind men stripped of their lands and Norman lords put in their place. I have watched as William's brave knights dragged our countrymen out of their castles and out onto the green to be tortured before—if they were lucky—the knights killed them. Shall I tell you what the Normans do, Serena? They heat their daggers until they show red-hot, then the prisoners are stripped of their garments. They lay their blades upon the prisoner's naked skin until his flesh is peeled off in strips. Do you know what happens to a Saxon man if he dares to look upon a Norman lady? They castrate him, Serena. If a Saxon woman gazes at a Norman man, he can have her—"

"Stop, Bryan! Were any of our fine, Saxon laws any better? We killed starving serfs for killing game that would feed their families. Was that fair? We beat our housecarls as if they were beasts if they were slow in obeying an order. Was that just or merciful? Norman or Saxon, it makes no difference. Both can be cruel. Are we any better, Bryan? Are you just when you raid villages and slay innocent men, women, and children? Or does your end justify such atrocities!" Serena halted, her breast heaving in anger and concern for her brother's life.

Bryan stared at her, his mouth hanging open. "I have killed no innocents," he said slowly.

"Not yet, but you will eventually, won't you?" Serena shook Bryan by his shoulders. "Won't you? Some of your men already have, haven't they? How long will it take before you become as bloodstained as they are?"

"Don't, Serena," Bryan croaked.

"How long, Bryan?" Serena asked sharply. "How long before you become as beastial as you claim the Normans are? Will I some day awake to find you holding a blade to my children's throats because they have Norman blood running through their veins? Will you kill me because I married a Norman?"

Bryan was appalled. "I would never harm you or yours, sister. I would turn the blade upon myself before I would permit that."

"That is what you say now, but will it be true a day, a week, a year from now? What do you think will happen to our family if you are arrested for treason? You and I are young and strong, but our father is not. He would not survive imprisonment. And if, by some miracle, you were released, where would you go? Your lands would have been gifted to some Norman lord the moment you were taken."

"What would you have me do, Serena, turn my back on all I believe? Do you think so little of me?"

"Nay, Bryan, just the opposite. Our parents taught us never to take the coward's way out. If you want to fight for our people, then fight! But not with a sword and armor, not by committing treason. Father is part of William's council, and when he dies, you will take his place. There you will be able to do much good for England. Fight if you must, but do it peacefully." Serena reached out and grasped Bryan's hands. "Dearest Bryan, I have no wish to see your head on a pike. I beg you to consider your actions."

Bryan pulled Serena into his arms for a quick hug. "I shall think on your words, but I make you no promises —yet."

Serena smiled. "More I cannot ask, Bryan. I know you will not disgrace our family; for if you do, Aurelia and her kin will fall heir to Broughton, of that I am certain." With great satisfaction, Serena noted the change that came over Bryan's features at her words. Well, a small white lie could do no harm, Serena thought. Bryan was fiercely possessive about Broughton and would do everything he could to keep it intact for his own son. In that respect Bryan and his father were similar. She had given him enough to ponder, so Serena deftly changed the subject. "Did Father come with you?"

Bryan took her arm and once again they circulated through the hall. "No, but Aurelia—as you would guess—insisted on coming without him. Did Beda accompany you?"

Serena nodded. "Oh, Beda wouldn't have missed this if both of her legs were broken, you can depend on that. As you can imagine, the trip here was anything but pleasant."

"Father will be disappointed that he did not see you." Bryan frowned. "Could you come home for a while, Serena, after your stay at court?"

"Father?" Serena asked with a slight tremor in her voice. "He's not well, is he?"

Bryan shook his head. "He is not ill, yet neither is he well. It is as if he has no strength or will. He needs you, Serena; he speaks of you often."

"I will speak to Gyles. Oh, the queen is retiring." Serena reached up to kiss Bryan's cheek. "Will I see you tomorrow?"

"I'll come to your chamber. Good night, Serena."

It took considerably less time to divest the queen of her clothing than it had to dress her, and this time Serena was not alone with Matilda, but was nearly lost in the flurry of a dozen other women trying to find favor with the queen. Serena eased herself out of the maelstrom and busied herself folding away the discarded royal garments. Serena had thought that once the queen was ready for bed her ladies were excused to their own chambers, but such was not the case. Until Matilda gave them leave to retire, her ladies-in-waiting remained in her chamber to provide entertainment and conversation. And such conversation!

Serena's face burned bright red as the ladies fell to discussing the attributes of the young lords who were visiting the court. Even Matilda contributed her observations to the ribald comments, and Serena was astounded to hear the queen speak in such earthy terms. What was it Gyles had said? Matilda was a woman and bearing a title did not alter that. The conversation became even more blunt as the women began to describe, in intimate detail, what commended their newest lovers to them; yet it was obvious that no one but Serena was the least embarrassed by the conversation. And she realized with horror that she might be expected to add her observations to theirs. What could she say? Serena had known no other man but Gyles and she could not bring herself to speak of him.

Salvation came from an unexpected quarter, for just then the woman Serena had admired during the evening meal breezed into the queen's bedchamber. Elspeth dipped into a brief curtsy then moved forward to be warmly embraced by Matilda.

"Lady Elspeth, it has been too long since you were last with us!" Matilda pulled Elspeth down beside her. "I was grieved to learn of your recent loss."

"That is kind of you, Your Highness." Elspeth's low, cultured voice floated through the room to Serena. Surely no other woman on earth was so perfect!

Serena edged farther away, so that she could have an unobstructed view of Elspeth and in the process, bumped into one of the other women.

"Oh! I beg your pardon." Serena turned to face a woman just slightly older than herself.

A wave of a delicate hand dismissed Serena's apology. "In view of the circumstances"—she nodded her head toward Elspeth—" 'tis perfectly all right. I am Lady Catherine."

Serena returned Catherine's smile and said, "My name is Serena."

"You are Saxon, are you not?" As Serena's chin lifted, Catherine continued in her natural blunt speech—which, surprisingly, never offended those she met. "I meant nothing by that remark, Lady Serena, except to comment on your heritage. The question will be put to you many times during your stay, so I advise you to become accustomed to it."

"I imagine you are right," Serena said with a small sigh. "But it does become wearying to be asked that so often. It makes me feel as if I had the plague!"

Catherine's crystal laughter caused Serena to grin in spite of herself. "You are right, of course. Come, let's find a nice cozy corner where we can talk." When they were seated with a goblet of warm wine each, Catherine asked, "Is this your first time at court?"

Serena nodded. "My father and brother have been here before, but I was never allowed to join them."

"Small wonder! No doubt they feared for your honor, for I noticed throughout the meal that even the crown prince's eyes strayed often to you." Serena wrinkled her nose in distaste and Catherine laughed. "That, I take it, is for our dear William Rufus?" Serena nodded. "Well, I don't blame you; he is such a bully."

"Have you been to court often?" Serena asked as she sipped her wine.

"Every winter for the past four years, since I was fifteen. I loathe crossing the channel—'tis so choppy, and I fear I am not a good sailor. I detest being tossed about in the water like a toy. Tell me," Catherine leaned forward, "are you married?"

"Indeed, yes," Serena answered with a bright smile. "My lord fought with our king at Hastings."

"You are wed to one of us—a Norman? Well, it should come as no surprise, as lovely as you are. I suppose you had many suitors." There was a touch of sadness in Catherine's voice.

"Nay, only two. A lad I had known all my life, and my husband who I did not meet until the day before we were wed. And you?"

Catherine gave a small, wistful laugh. "That is why I am packed off to court every year, to find a husband. My family has nearly given up hope, I'm afraid. Nineteen years of age and still a maid."

"You will find someone," Serena assured Catherine. "You are far prettier than I—I'll wager the men simply beat at your door day and night."

Catherine grimaced. "That they do, but none bear a proposal of marriage." Catherine looked slyly at Serena. "However, I saw one tonight with whom I would not mind dallying."

"Oh?" Serena's eyes flashed with mischief. "And is there some way I can be of service?"

"Yes." Catherine pounced immediately on Serena's offer. "You can introduce me to him."

Serena looked at Catherine blankly. "But I know no one here save for my husband . . . and my brother."

"And which was the one you spoke so long with after the meal?"

"Oh, that was my brother," Serena said offhandedly, then her eyes widened. "Bryan? You wish to meet Bryan?"

"So that is his name." Catherine mused. "It suits him most admirably, don't you think?"

"Indeed I do. But . . . *Bryan*?"

"He's not married is he?" Catherine asked worriedly.

Serena laughed shortly. "Not that I know of. He . . ." Serena paused. It had never occurred to her that Bryan was attractive to women. Undoubtedly her picture of her older brother differed radically from Catherine's. And perhaps if Bryan was occupied with Catherine he would have less time and energy to devote to treason. "I'll introduce you tomorrow," Serena decided.

"Splendid!" Catherine squeezed Serena's hand in genuine delight. "You must speak of me in glowing terms so that he cannot wait to meet me."

"Rest assured," Serena laughed. "For when I have done, Bryan will be happy just to beg a smile from you."

"We shall get along famously, Serena," Catherine announced. A spate of laughter from the queen drew her attention and Catherine's brown eyes narrowed. "Have you had the dubious pleasure of meeting Lady Elspeth?"

"Not yet." Serena tilted her head to one side. "She is lovely, isn't she?"

203

Catherine shrugged. "On the outside, perhaps, but inside she's ugly as sin."

"I cannot believe that. Anyone so beautiful could not possibly have a dark soul. Do you know her?"

"To my eternal misery, yes. I met her the first time I came to court." Catherine's mouth pursed in disapproval. "Elspeth's husband was alive then, but he was off somewhere engaging in his favorite pastime—war. I suppose it was partly his fault that Elspeth was so unhappy, and when he returned the scandal had died down, but he still took her back to his castle—almost by force—then left her there while he went back to his silly war. She was forbidden to receive guests or go anywhere save for the cloister that she supported. He made her a virtual prisoner and now look at her—parading about in her mourning gowns when everyone knows she's ecstatic because he died."

Gossip was as intregal a part of court life as was romance, and Serena, already caught up in Catherine's story, prodded her new friend on. "What scandal, Catherine? No, wait, let me guess." Serena chewed on a fingernail. "Elspeth finally met the man she loved here at court and when her husband found out he was furious and dragged her off. And . . . and her lover killed himself out of remorse. Is that close?"

Catherine shook her head. "What a vivid imagination, Serena. But, no, that's not precisely what happened. Elspeth was no more in love with her paramour than I am with your English winters. She was attracted to him, yes, and although I was only fifteen and everyone was very silent when I was around, it was common knowledge that they spent the nights together. And the mornings. And the afternoons. In the end, they were both tiring of each other, so when Elspeth's husband appeared, I think she was happy enough to leave. After all, he was quite wealthy and Elspeth has a taste for finery. As for her lover, I don't know, but I'm sure he didn't kill himself. I remember he was very handsome, the type that could make a woman melt if he wanted her to. I haven't seen

204

him since then, but I would know him if I ever saw him. My mother was with me then, and she made certain I met only the eligible young men."

"And he wasn't? Was he married?" Serena persisted.

Catherine frowned. "I don't know. No one ever told me. All I knew was that I wasn't supposed to speak to him. Oh, look. There's the signal from the queen. 'Tis time we all retired. William hates for her to be surrounded by her women when he comes to her."

Serena rose with Catherine. "I wonder how the council went?"

"What council?" Catherine laughed.

"Why, the one held tonight, of course."

Catherine shook her head. "The first council is to be held the day after Christmas as it always is. The king insists that everyone enjoy themselves before they battle the affairs of state. You must have misunderstood. Who told you that?"

Serena's brow creased. "I . . . I must have overheard it at the meal."

"Well, I pity the poor man who spent this evening waiting in the council chamber."

"Yes," Serena said absently as she walked beside Catherine to her chamber. Had Gyles been mistaken or had she not heard him correctly?

Catherine was bidding her goodnight and Serena vaguely replied to Catherine's suggestion that they meet the following morning before attending the queen.

There were no candles lit when Serena entered her chamber and the only light came from the small fire. Gyles sat in front of the hearth, his face all planes and angles in the flickering shadows, his expression brooding. The room was cold and Serena shivered, then hurriedly placed more wood on the fire. Flames leaped up greedily to consume the new logs, and as the warmth began to creep into the room, Serena gratefully sank into a chair and tugged at the ribbons that held her snood in place.

"How was the council, Gyles?" Serena's small voice sounded quite loud in the silent room.

"What?" Gyles sounded preoccupied. "Oh, that. There won't be a meeting until after Christmas." He lapsed back into a bleak silence.

Serena closed her eyes and expelled the breath she had been holding. Gyles rose and poked aimlessly at the fire. "How did you pass the evening, Gyles?"

"In the same inane fashion everyone at court does: chess, conversation . . ."

"Beautiful women?" Serena added teasingly.

Gyles swung on her. "What makes you say that?"

"I did but jest. You are very sensitive this evening, Gyles."

Gyles strode about the room preparing for bed. "I am sorry to be so abrupt, Serena. I dislike court life intensely." Gyles threw himself upon the bed. "And we have at least another month to spend here."

Serena dropped a nightgown over her shoulders and slipped into bed beside Gyles. "I thought you enjoyed the court."

Gyles sat up and drew the curtains around the bed, enveloping them in total darkness. "Well, I don't." He muttered as he relaxed upon the pillows. Serena pressed her chilled body full-length against his side, her slender hand resting in the dark thatch of hair on his chest. Gyles sighed and slid his arm beneath her shoulder, his long fingers caressing the silken skin beneath her nightgown. "How fared you with the queen? Were you properly respectful?"

Serena's breath fell warmly upon his shoulder. "She is such a kind woman; she made me feel quite welcome and at ease." Serena chewed thoughtfully on her lower lip before she continued. "The queen bade me speak with Bryan . . . 'twould seem he is involved in some way with those who would depose William."

Gyles felt himself warming beneath Serena's touch and he had to work to keep his voice level. "And did you do so?"

Serena nodded slightly and in doing so, a strand of hair fell upon Gyles's chest. "I spoke to him, though I don't know if it did any good. Bryan is so stubborn,

Gyles! If he doesn't listen to me, he'll find himself in William's dungeon yet."

"Perhaps 'twould help if I spoke with him," Gyles offered.

"Hah! 'Tis kind of you, Gyles, but Bryan would not listen to you." Serena placed a kiss on Gyles's neck. "Besides, I think I have found the solution. Her name is Catherine; I believe Bryan will be far too involved to worry about something as insignificant as William's crown."

Beside her Gyles chuckled. "Are you trying your hand at matchmaking, Serena?"

"No, indeed," Serena replied indignantly. "In fact, 'tis Catherine's idea totally. She spied Bryan tonight and thought him very favorable." Serena struggled upright and peered through the darkness, trying to see Gyles's face. "And, Gyles, you would not believe what Matilda's ladies discuss behind closed doors! Men! I vow that every man at court was the subject of heated debate tonight, and *not* in delicate, refined terms, either. Even Matilda joined in. Gyles, you should have heard, there is one lord here at court who—"

"Serena, please!" Gyles's laughter cut across her speech. "I have no desire to hear any details." Gyles rolled to his side and pulled Serena back down beside him. "And what, pray, did you contribute to the conversation?"

"I, for once, had the intelligence to keep my thoughts to myself. And, compared to the other women, Catherine and I were the only ones who don't have a vast amount of experience," Serena said primly. Gyles began to nuzzle her neck and Serena sighed happily. Then she confessed guiltily, "But I wish Lady Elspeth would have arrived earlier. From what Catherine said, *she* could enlighten us all. Did you know that she caused quite a scandal at court four years ago?"

Gyles lifted his head and with a muttered oath rolled to his back. "Serena, you are impossible! Are you so taken with court life that you have no care for your husband? Cherie, we have not been man and wife for over two weeks, and . . . oh, what's the use?"

207

Serena tentatively touched his shoulder. "Gyles? Forgive me, I did not mean to run on so. Gyles, please. It has been such an enjoyable evening for me, let's not argue." Serena's hand moved in a circular motion over Gyles's chest and down his stomach.

Gyles's anger cooled and another, stronger emotion took its place. Gyles reached up and twined his fingers in a lock of delicately scented hair. "How can you bear to live with me, Serena? Since we were wed I have brought you naught but sorrow. Ah, lass, why do you stay?"

Serena laughed softly. "Because I love you, and I will keep telling you until you grow weary of hearing it. Because without you I would have nothing to live for. Because you are my life and I love and treasure you above all else. Because just looking at you fills my heart to such limits that at times I am sure 'twill burst in its joy." Gyles's arms went about Serena and pulled her effortlessly against him. Serena's hand reached up to lay against his cheek. "Shall I tell you more?"

"Nay," Gyles whispered just before his mouth slanted across hers.

9

"Serena!"

At the sound of her name, Serena paused in mid-step and turned. Catherine, her skirts lifted high above her ankles, was racing down the corridor in Serena's wake, her bronze hair escaping its ribbons and falling around her flushed face.

"Serena," Catherine gasped and rested a hand on her friend's shoulder in exhaustion. "I have been running all over this castle looking for you. Why weren't you in your room?"

Serena laughed. "Gyles was gone when I got there, so I decided to see more of the castle so I won't need a page to get around. Now catch your breath and tell me why you were looking for me."

Catherine took a deep gulp of air. "Matilda wants you. In her chambers. Immediately."

"But she told me I could have the rest of the day to myself!" Serena wailed, "Gyles and I planned to go riding this morning. Oh, Catherine, he'll be absolutely furious!"

"Well, it can't be helped. Matilda is selecting materials for her new gowns and insists upon you being there."

"I don't suppose I have the time to return to our chamber and leave Gyles a note?" Serena asked hopefully.

"Absolutely not, Serena. You've been at court two

weeks and you know how Matilda is. The queen is sweet, generous, and mild-tempered unless her orders aren't carried out posthaste. Hurry, Serena, you've kept her waiting long enough." Catherine's hands urged Serena forward.

"Oh, wait, Catherine, wait." Serena came to an abrupt halt. "You must do me a favor, Catherine. Go to our chamber and wait for Gyles and explain what has happened."

Catherine looked doubtful, but eventually nodded her consent. "All right, I'll do it, anything to get you back to the queen. Now hurry, Serena, please!" As Serena sped down the hall Catherine called after her, "Don't worry, I'll speak to Gyles."

Catherine started off at a more sedate pace in the direction of Serena's chamber. In the past fortnight, Catherine had grown quite fond of Bryan's sister and Bryan himself. Catherine's whole life had changed since she met Bryan—because for the first time she was in love, and if she understood Bryan correctly, he was falling in love with her. And all because of a chance meeting with Serena. A small frown darkened Catherine's features. She was truly fond of Serena, but Serena's husband was a different matter. So arrogant and cynical, Gyles had effectively intimidated Catherine since Serena had first introduced them. That had been the first common ground Catherine and Bryan had found. While Catherine stood somewhat in awe of Gyles, Bryan passionately disliked him. Both agreed that Serena would be far happier had she married a different man. Simply, Gyles was not good enough for Serena. And something more plagued Catherine. Gyles was the kind of man not easily forgotten and Catherine was certain she had met him before. Something had flickered in Catherine's memory that refused to be pushed aside—a vague uneasiness that she could not define. Catherine was afraid that Serena would be deeply hurt by her husband.

Catherine rapped on the door of the chamber Gyles and Serena shared. There was no response and Catherine glanced down the hallway, hoping that Gyles would come

210

into sight. She bit her lip nervously. If Matilda sent a page for Catherine, she would have no choice but to return to the queen's chambers, and then Gyles would never learn Serena's whereabouts; it would be Serena who would feel the full weight of his anger. Decisively, Catherine pushed open the door and entered the room. There was naught to do but wait, and Catherine irritably paced the room. Serena's tapestry stood in its loom by the window and Catherine stepped in front of it to admire Serena's handiwork. Serena had laughingly told Catherine that it would be a wedding gift for Bryan and herself and Catherine was amazed at Serena's tremendous undertaking. The tapestry was taller than Catherine and its width was more than Catherine could reach with outstretched arms. The scene was of Broughton, minute in detail and amazingly real—exactly as Bryan had described it to Catherine. How long it would take to finish Catherine could not guess, but she respected Serena's courage in her choice of subjects. If Serena meant it as a wedding gift, Bryan should not be in any haste to wed.

Catherine was startled out of her contemplation by the squeak of the door hinges as it swung open, and she had nearly stepped around the tapestry to declare her presence when Gyles's voice froze her to the floor.

"Come in then, if you must. I have no desire for Serena to find you here, so say what you will quickly."

A low, cultured laugh came from directly in front of her and Catherine moved backward until she felt the wall behind her.

"Gyles, you amaze me. Are you so afraid of your puny little wife that you dare not incur her wrath? *Mon homme,* you have changed much if that is the case."

"Four years is a long time, Elspeth. But you have not changed—still beautiful, still heartless."

"Not so heartless, Gyles. Remember? In the end I did as you asked."

A snort came from Gyles and Catherine heard him move around the room. Catherine's heart was thudding so loudly that they surely must hear it!

"Aye." The word sounded as if it were wrenched

from Gyles's throat. "You did as I asked, but only after I threatened to hold you in irons."

Again that humorless laugh. "And now our circumstances are reversed. I am free and you are wed—how ironic, don't you agree?"

"Ironic," Gyles agreed.

"You have been busy these past years; indeed, you have done quite well. Lord of Camden." The title rolled from Elspeth's tongue. Then with a touch of sarcasm she added, "How lucky for you that Serena's greed for a title overcame her natural reluctance to wed a bastard. But then, since she is a Saxon, I suppose she could hope for nothing more."

"You've sharpened your claws sufficiently, Elspeth, so would you mind getting to the point? Serena and I are to go riding in a short time."

"Do not fret so, Gyles. Serena will not be coming—I have seen to that—so you and I can enjoy a leisurely chat. Your first evening at court was far too short and then to be interrupted by William Rufus was really too taxing."

"Come to the point!" Gyles bellowed and Catherine clapped a hand over her mouth to hold back her startled scream.

Elspeth sighed loudly. "Still impatient as ever, Gyles. Very well. I wish to resume our former relationship and I wish to see Alan."

A shocked silence reigned until Gyles finally spoke. "Elspeth, you have taken leave of your senses!" he said incredulously.

"Not at all." Elspeth was quite calm. "I have often regretted giving Alan up into your care."

"You did not want him, remember?" Gyles's voice was strained.

"No. But my husband would have believed Alan was his—when he wasn't on a battlefield he was drunk—and Alan could now inherit the estates."

"And you would not be forced to marry again."

Catherine could sense Elspeth's shrug. "Yes, that is unfortunate, but I have a plan for that."

Gyles's tone was dry. "Which includes me?"

"But of course, cherie. Perhaps I misled you when I spoke of our former relationship. What I propose is a marriage. Ours. I have proven my ability to bear children, Serena has not. The Church will easily grant an annulment to you. Alan can return from Normandy and at last know a mother's love." The rustle of Elspeth's gown indicated her movement to the door. "Come, Gyles, think on my offer. But for now, accompany me to the stables and help me select a mount."

The door closed behind them and Catherine's breath exploded from her lips. Gyles and Elspeth! Poor Serena! Did she suspect? No, of course not. How could she? Catherine tiptoed cautiously from behind the tapestry. Gyles should be far enough away by now so that she could make her way back to the queen without being seen.

Catherine's hand fell on the latch to open the door, then she jumped back with a startled cry as Gyles loomed in front of her.

"What are you doing here?" Gyles boomed.

Catherine retreated a step and swallowed convulsively. "I . . . Serena asked me to . . . to find you. The queen summoned her back and she asked me to tell you that she wouldn't be able to go riding this morn." Gyles's green eyes bored into her with such intensity that Catherine began to tremble. "Well," she laughed shakily, "I must return to the queen. If you will excuse me?"

Gyles's fingers wrapped around Catherine's upper arm as he sent the door flying shut with a kick of his foot. "You are lying," he said in a dangerously controlled voice.

"Nay!" Catherine was thoroughly frightened. "I swear, 'tis the truth. Serena did not wish for you to wait vainly for her so she sent me."

Gyles relaxed his grip but remained firmly in Catherine's path. "And you only just arrived?"

"Nay . . . I mean, aye . . . I . . . I came a few moments ago, but you were not here, so I thought to wait for you," Catherine stammered.

"Then why were you leaving?" Gyles queried softly. "Know you this, Catherine, I do not tolerate those who would spy on me. You will not leave this chamber 'til you speak the truth."

Catherine dissolved into tears. "I have told you the truth, as God is my witness! Please, let me pass."

Gyles's hand fell limply to his side and his face softened. "I have no wish to frighten you, Catherine, for you are Serena's dearest friend. Am I so fearsome?"

There was a poignant note in his voice and as Catherine's fear subsided some small amount she managed a tremulous smile. "You are accustomed to dealing with Serena and I vow she fears naught." Relaxed now, Catherine passed by Gyles only to be brought up short by his quiet voice.

"You heard it all, did you not?" Gyles turned slowly until he faced Catherine.

Fear returned with a heavy hand as Catherine stared back into that emerald gaze. She licked her suddenly dry lips and managed to choke out, "Aye, Lord Gyles. I did not mean to spy, what I told you is the truth. Serena did send me. Lord Gyles, you are not considering the Lady Elspeth's offer?"

Gyles's dark head shook slowly from side to side. "Not for an instant. Think you I am so addlepated that I do not know Serena's worth?"

"That Serena loves your son I am fully aware, but she does not know who bore him, does she?" Gyles again shook his head and Catherine gained courage. "I have no right to say anything, but you should tell her of Elspeth's identity. 'Twill explain the looks Elspeth gives you. Serena has already asked me if I have noticed the way Elspeth watches you."

Gyles appeared not to have heard her as he took her arm and guided Catherine to the door. "Say nothing to Serena," he warned. "I will tell her if the need arises."

"Well, child, what think you of this one?" Matilda draped a length of royal blue velvet over her shoulder.

Serena studied the color critically, one slim foot tapping impatiently on the materials that were scattered over the floor of the chamber. "I would say no, Your Highness." Serena sighed at last. " 'Tis far too dark."

Some of the women murmured in agreement and the velvet joined its companions in a rumpled heap. Matilda stamped back to a rack that held those materials not yet examined, petulantly kicking at the materials littering the floor.

"Your Majesty, if I may?" Serena suggested and waved a hand toward the rack. Matilda had been at the selection process for the entire morning and the better part of the afternoon and Serena was growing weary. The queen unfailingly selected dark, muted colors that only served to turn her pure complexion a sickly white. Matilda nodded her consent and Serena stepped quickly over the piles of cloth to the rack. Serena indicated several bolts to the tailor along with an assortment of fur and lace.

"Now, Your Highness, if you would consider this one." Serena pulled a length of peach-colored material from its bolt and held it up for Matilda's perusal. "There is also a yellow, a lavender, and a gold brocade, Your Majesty." The tailor quickly unrolled samples of all three, then stepped back.

Matilda frowned, considering her lady's selections. "I think those colors are better suited for someone younger."

"Nonsense, Your Majesty," Serena retorted boldly, then flushed as Matilda laughed with delight at her outspoken comment. "I mean, Your Majesty, that these are perfectly suited for you."

Matilda lifted each cloth in turn and then nodded. "You are right, child, and you have excellent taste."

"Of course she does, Mother. You would not allow any of your women to have otherwise." A lilting voice called from the door.

"Insolent cub! Henry, when will you learn that you must wait to be announced before you enter?"

Henry picked his way through the rainbow on the floor and, grinning, brushed his mother's cheek with his lips. Matilda pushed him brusquely away. "You are interrupting, Henry. What do you want?"

"*Ma mere,* do I need a reason to visit the most beautiful woman in all England?" Henry tossed her an impish grin.

"Hah!" Matilda snorted, but her expression mellowed and she signaled for her ladies to leave. "Not you, Serena," Matilda called as Serena made to follow the others. Obediently, Serena halted and awaited her orders. "You may instruct the tailor that I will have gowns from the materials you chose. The decision of the trims I leave in your hands."

Serena did as she was bade, struggling to calm the tailor's sudden attack of nerves while at the same time subduing her own impatience to return to her chamber. As the tailor fluttered about gathering up the strewn materials, Serena bent her attention to selecting the trims for Matilda's new gowns. Serena's hand paused over a pelt of silver fox, and she lifted the fur to test its softness against her cheek. It entered her mind to ask Gyles for a few coins with which to purchase the pelt or one greatly similar, but she immediately pushed the thought from her mind. Gyles had been moody of late and Serena never knew from one moment to the next what small thing would fire his anger. At first Serena had thought Gyles's ire stemmed from the fact that she had little time to spend with him; but the few days she had managed to wheedle from the queen had given the lie to that, for Gyles had been irritable and restless, unhappy with any diversion they indulged in.

"You are far away from us, petite Serena." Henry's voice drew Serena back to her surroundings, and he smiled down into her warm blue eyes. "Or perhaps only as far as where your husband bides." The color rose in her cheeks, and Serena glanced about the room only to realize that Matilda had retired to her bedchamber and the tailor was maintaining a discreet distance. Henry's lean fingers stroked the fur near where Serena's hand lay. "My mother has grown most fond of you, m'lady. Indeed, the court has brightened much since your arrival."

Serena smiled uncertainly, feeling herself drawn once more by the force of Henry's personality. "You are too kind, Your Highness."

"Nay, I speak only the truth as I see it." Henry's fingers left the fur and he moved a space apart from her. "Have you ventured forth to see the city?"

"I have not had that pleasure as yet, Your Highness. It seems that whenever I have a day to myself, my lord does not; and the reverse is also true."

Henry considered her thoughtfully. "I had planned to visit an armorer in London on the morrow. It would please me greatly if you would accompany me—with your lord, if he finds himself free," he added hastily as an uncertain look flickered across Serena's face. "My mother would be most unwilling to spare your company, but I am sure I can persuade her to release you into my care. And you need not fear that Will shall intrude, I will see to it he is occupied elsewhere."

Serena gazed into Henry's soft brown eyes. How different were the two brothers born to the same parents! Since their first meeting, Serena found herself wary of William's attentions. While he made no overt moves, William managed to be present whenever Serena found herself separated from Gyles or Bryan, and he left no doubt in Serena's mind as to his motives. Even while William sneered his insults to her, his gaze boldly devoured Serena's delicate form, as if the clothing she wore was non-existent. How did one go about putting a prince in his place, Serena wondered. It would not be beneath William to convince his mother to demand that Serena remain in London when Gyles returned to Camden, and who then would protect her honor from that odious princeling?

"Lady Serena," Henry snapped his fingers beneath her nose. " 'Tis rude to ignore your prince."

Serena's already pinkened cheeks heightened in color. "Your forgiveness, I pray, Your Highness. 'Twas not my wont to be impolite."

Henry's silver laughter rang through the room. "Methinks, fair lady, that you take me far too seriously. Which in itself is a refreshing change from the rest of the

217

court," Henry remarked soberly. " 'Tis not often a third son is looked upon with more than pity, for when compared to his brothers, he has naught to commend him to others."

Serena's tender heart went out to the young man standing beside her. It was true; she found William more overwhelming in his manner than Henry; yet Henry bore himself with a regality William could never hope to match. What cruel twist of fate had decreed that William should one day rule England, while, at most, Henry could only hope for a purse and perhaps a small estate? None at court sought Henry's favor, but rather spent their time begging William's generosity—which to Serena's eye was buried so deeply no mortal could hope to find it. For a brief moment, Serena found herself pitying Henry, but then common sense prevailed. Henry wanted no friend because of that demeaning emotion, but rather he wished it to be given because of who he was, not what he was.

Henry was awaiting her answer and she gave him a fleeting smile. "I must speak to my lord, Your Highness. If he grants his approval, I should be most happy to tour the city with you. Indeed, I would be most honored."

As it happened, Serena had no opportunity to inform Gyles of Henry's proposal. Matilda was in a bad humor and Serena discarded half a dozen gowns before the queen settled on the one she would wear. Then Matilda's hair required dressing, and just as Serena patted the last curl in place, Matilda decided she wished it arranged differently. Out came the ribbons and the entire process began again. At last Matilda was satisfied and Serena heaved a sigh of relief as the queen released her for the remainder of the evening. Serena hurried from the chamber and raced through the passages, the skirt of her gown held high in her clenched fists.

Serena burst into the room and immediately began pulling the gown over her head, and in her haste Serena heard the rending sound as a shoulder seam gave way beneath her frantic efforts.

"Damn!" The word exploded from Serena's lips as she hurled the torn garment on the bed then threw open the armoire and pawed through it until she found the gown she wanted. The gown was a brilliant shade of red, which enhanced Serena's milky complexion while at the same time it lent a rosy hue to her cheeks. Serena had hoped to arrange her hair with matching ribbons, but there was no time left for that, so Serena nimbly tucked a few stray tendrils of hair back into the snood and with one final glance at her face in a hand mirror, she left the room at a rapid pace.

The meal was already in progress when Serena entered the hall and she slipped as unobtrusively as possible to her place beside Gyles. Bryan threw Serena a knowing grin at her flustered appearance from across the table while Catherine's expression was totally enigmatic.

Gyles poured wine in her goblet, then bent to Serena. "You are late," he accused his wife softly.

Serena took a sip of wine before answering. "It couldn't be helped." Her blue eyes sparkled up at Gyles. "But 'tis nice to know you missed me. Did Catherine find you this morning?"

Gyles cast a glance across the table at Catherine's suddenly tight face and nodded. "Didn't Catherine tell you?"

Serena swallowed a mouthful of beef. "I haven't spoken with anyone save Matilda, Henry, and the tailor all day. I don't know what's gotten into the queen today, but I didn't have a moment to myself. I am sorry about our ride, Gyles."

" 'Tis naught." Gyles's large hand covered hers briefly. "There will be another day."

The meal was completed and the tables swiftly cleared. Serena strolled leisurely through the hall with Gyles while they viewed the preparations being made for the coming Christmas festivities. A Yule log of gigantic proportions was being dragged the length of the hall, raising such a cloud of dust from the rushes that Serena began to cough and her eyes watered. Gyles guided her from the disturbance to a place where the air was cleaner, and laughed.

At Serena's questioning look Gyles pointed upward

to where a sprig of mistletoe had been hung on the wall. "We have had little enough privacy this past fortnight," Gyles sighed. "I would be much happier if the queen held you in lesser esteem. You rise when I do and often return late into the night." His green eyes burned into Serena with an intensity that left her breathless and trembling as his face lowered to hers. "I have been too much a monk of late, Serena, which is a situation only you can remedy."

Serena nearly melted against Gyles. His distressing behavior in their bed still continued and more often than not, Serena knew Gyles turned away from her even when his raging desire demanded fulfillment. Serena would have argued away Gyles's fear, if she had thought she could convince him that his fear was groundless, but she knew Gyles well enough to realize that that tactic would be useless. Her only salvation lay with the hope that in time Gyles's memory of the ghastly birth that haunted his thoughts would fade.

Gyles's mouth hovered near Serena's lips and, in fact, her closeness had driven all other thoughts from his mind. His passion flared deep within his loins and Gyles knew his insatiable desire as severely as a thirsting man feels the need for water. For the briefest yet tenderest of moments, their lips met and they stood apart from the rest of the world. Gyles drew back, allowing his darkened green eyes to leisurely caress his wife. Against the red of her dress, Serena's skin took on an alabaster translucence that caused Gyles's breath to catch in his throat. A pulse beat at the base of the slim column of her throat and Gyles stared at the spot, fascinated by that fluttering movement.

Serena leaned carefully against the wall, afraid that if she strove to move the effort would prove too great and she would collapse into Gyles's arms. What power he held over her, that a look, a touch could reduce her to a state of such utter weakness. She was as dependent upon Gyles for life as she was upon air to breathe or food to eat. How she longed to draw his head to her breast and hold him, wiping out all memories of pain he had ever suffered.

"So delicate. So fragile." Gyles's left hand curved around the back of Serena's head while his right lifted her face upward.

"Not so fragile, m'lord." Serena's lips parted in a smile. "I'll best you in a tourney yet."

Gyles's brows pulled downward in a frown. "You would not dare. Not again."

"Test my anger and you will discover the truth for yourself," Serena replied with spirit.

"How touching!" A sardonic voice beside them sneered, causing Serena to start; and without looking up, she knew that William had been observing Gyles and herself for some time.

Gyles's hands fell from Serena's face, but he placed his arm around her waist then moved slowly to her side, as if reluctant to allow William to gaze upon his wife.

"Your Majesty." Gyles's tone was barely civil.

William's eyes flicked derisively over Gyles before coming to rest upon Serena. "Ah, our fair Saxon maid, how enchanting you look. I had despaired of finding anything of note in this country 'til you ventured to court."

Serena colored. "You are most gracious, Your Majesty. But England has much to offer." An increased pressure at her waist warned Serena to silence.

"Indeed, Your Majesty," Gyles added, "there are parts of England that rival our native land in their beauty."

William dismissed the words with a wave of his ham-like hand. "All I have seen of this country is unpleasant—rocky, tempest-ridden shores; icy winds; treacherous men, and serpent-tongued women!"

Beside Gyles, Serena stiffened, and glancing down he could see the flinty sparks begin to fly from her eyes. Serena could barely restrain the words that flew to her lips. How dare he? How dare he! His father had come and nearly destroyed the best England had to offer, and now this pompous, blustering jackass dared to . . . Serena's eyes narrowed in anger and her lips parted to give voice to her thoughts.

"You must visit Camden, Your Majesty," Gyles smoothly intervened. "To my mind, 'tis the loveliest of places on this isle, though my wife would readily argue that Broughton claims that honor. Would you not, Serena?"

"Nay, Gyles, for both hold different splendors," Serena ground out.

"Perhaps that is true." William fixed Serena with a calculating stare. "But your Saxon wife has proved the last part of my findings—these women have tongues like knives. I much prefer our gentle Norman women. Is this not also true of you, Sir Gyles?"

A wry smile twisted Gyles's lips. "In truth, Your Highness, in the dark I have found no difference between the two."

Serena's first reaction to her husband's glib statement was one of anger, but then a far better idea took hold. She rested her hand lightly upon Gyles's arm and smiled pertly up at him. "Indeed, Gyles, 'twould appear to be the same between Saxon and Norman men. Though I vow the good Lady Diane could find fault with that statement. Indeed, Your Highness," Serena's vengeful blue gaze pierced through William, "save for my stalwart husband, I, too, have found the Norman men far lacking by our Saxon standards."

William's head reared back as if slapped and his face suffused with blood. It was common knowledge to the court that he dallied almost nightly with Lady Diane— one of his mother's ladies—and she had much to say on the subject of his performance—or lack of it—and she cared not who was her audience. William's mouth opened to retort, but the words caught in his throat when another voice joined their conversation.

"Surely, fair Serena, not *all* Norman men?" Henry asked with a teasing smile. "I will grant you that some of us are more crude than others, but I beg you not to form any hasty opinions."

His speech finished, Henry bore her fingertips to his lips before he turned to Gyles. "You have the good fortune, Sir Gyles, to have made the most beautiful woman in England your own. You have my congratulations . . . and my envy."

"Hah!" William snorted and stalked off.

"I really must teach him better manners one day," Henry mused as he watched his brother depart. Then turning back to Serena, he smiled.

Serena's eyes sparkled in return. "You have my thanks, Your Highness. It seems you are forever coming to my rescue."

Gyles observed the exchange with cold displeasure; finding Henry's attentiveness no less irritating than William's caustic comments. Serena was bantering lightly with Henry and Gyles's eyes flickered briefly as the prince bent closer to speak to Serena. Gyles studied Serena, unable to find any fault with her behavior save that the reserve he had felt in her of late seemed to have evaporated. Was it his imagination or did Serena's eyes sparkle more than usual, was her color a bit higher? And why should either William or Henry bother to pursue her when there were women at court far more willing and experienced to lead them a merry chase? That Serena was attractive Gyles could not deny, but surely she was far too delicate for William's taste and too quick-tempered. But Henry . . . there was a growing warmth in his eyes that Gyles did not care for and, with his easy manner, Henry had put Serena completely at ease.

"May I, Gyles?" Serena's hand was resting on his arm and with an effort Gyles brought his attention back to the conversation.

Henry took Gyles's silence as reluctance, so he hastened to add, "You need not fear for your lady's safety, Sir Gyles, on that point I can assure you. I shall borrow her only for the day and return her to you before evening."

Gyles bowed ever so slightly from the waist. "My lady is free to do as she chooses, Your Highness. And she often does," Gyles added beneath his breath.

But Henry had already raised Serena's hand in fare-well. "I shall send a page for you at mid-morning. Until then, fair Serena." And with a last smile, he was gone.

"I am sorry." Serena turned to Gyles, laughter still rich in her voice. "I meant to speak with you of Henry's invitation, but——"

"Henry?" Gyles raised one dark eyebrow. "How did you come to be so friendly that you may address him by other than his title?"

Serena was taken aback. "I do not address him with other than his title when we speak together."

"Of course," Gyles stated drily, "I had forgotten your fondness for titles. It took you what . . . five, six months before you called your own husband by name? What a pity you haven't that much time to spend at court. No doubt you would have both princes dancing attendance upon you."

Serena's temper flared beneath his accusation. "At least, dear Gyles, you need not contend with any former lovers of mine while I, it seems, meet your paramours continuously! Some day, sweet husband, you must gather them all at Camden so I may have a full accounting!" Serena whirled to leave, then spun back and her words lashed at his already jarred nerves. "And if 'tis of any matter to you, your pallet this night is beside the fire. See that you remember that."

Serena gained their chamber and for a long moment contemplated barring the door against Gyles. "Let him find some other place to rest his head," Serena sneered at the door.

There was an abundance of women at court who would be honored to share their bed with him. Serena was neither deaf nor blind and the whispered conversations and admiring glances had not escaped her notice these past weeks. 'Twas all very well for Gyles to strut and prance for the ladies of the court, but let her, Serena, say so much as a kind word to a knight and Gyles accused her of dallying. The more she dwelled upon the matter, the higher rose her ire, and in frustration Serena snatched up the earthenware pitcher from its table and sailed it across the room to shatter against the wall. The basin followed its mate to the wall and the next object to catch Serena's eye was the unfortunate table, and with a hearty kick it skittered along the floor to rest against the door.

The door opened slowly, paused, then was pushed wide and Serena faced it, breasts heaving in anger, blue eyes sending daggers at the man framed in the portal. Gyles placed one foot cautiously inside the room, and when no missiles flew at him, confidence returned and he stepped into the room and closed the door behind him. Serena gave a disdainful sniff then flounced about the room, folding away the gown she had worn during the day and giving her attention to her preparations for bed.

Gyles leaned lazily against the door, arms folded over his chest, enjoying to the fullest the glimpse he caught of a small, round breast, a shapely buttock and a slim leg. Serena felt his heated gaze upon her and turned to face Gyles as she laced the neckline of her nightgown.

"Is it your intent to stand there all night or were you planning to go out again?" Serena flung at him.

Gyles lifted his shoulders in a careless shrug while he gave Serena a mocking smile. "Which would you prefer, cherie?"

Blue eyes flicked brazenly over Gyles. "I," she stated clearly, "care not a whit. Do whatever pleases you."

Gyles sauntered toward her and Serena retreated, all too aware of what darkened his eyes to a deep emerald green. Gyles leisurely stretched out his arm and twisted a hand in Serena's hair. Serena gasped in outrage and her hands came up to tug at the lean forearm beside her cheek, but she had not foreseen Gyles's next move as his free hand locked in the fabric of her gown and tore it leisurely from her neck to her waist. This time it was Gyles's turn to have misread the extent of Serena's anger, for her knee was moving before he was aware of it and found its mark with amazing accuracy, if not with any great strength; and Gyles's hands quickly loosed their hold to assuage his pained groin. Serena spun out of reach, snatched Gyles's pillow from the bed, and hurled it at his head. The coverlet and a blanket followed quickly and as Gyles disengaged himself from their cumbersome folds he saw Serena shrug out of her torn gown and heave that at him as well.

"Enough!" Gyles bellowed at her through the material while his hands worked to free himself. At last his face emerged and his green eyes clouded in anger. "In the name of the saints, woman, what is the matter with you?"

"Me!" Serena shrieked at him. "You brainless oaf! You accuse me of playing you false and then have the nerve to ask me what is the matter?"

"Do you deny toying with Henry's attentions? Or William's?" Gyles advanced upon Serena. "Do you say you are true to your vows?"

"If you can even put such a question to me, then my answer will make no difference." Serena brushed by Gyles and after a moment's searching, slipped another nightgown over her head. "Since we wed you have done naught but accuse me of deserting my vows, first with Richard, now with Henry or William. That you can say such a thing to me proves you know me not at all." She pointed to the heap of bedclothes. "There is your bed. Take your rest upon it from now on."

Gyles snorted. "A typical woman's trick—denying her mate the pleasures of his married status."

"I have denied you naught—ever," Serena told him in a voice so cold Gyles hardly recognized it. "And since you will have this out, very well. I like Prince Henry and enjoy his companionship greatly. He asks nothing of me save that I be myself, and that he readily accepts. He does not set upon me at every turn and pounce on every word I speak. Learn now, Gyles, that I choose my own friends—man and woman—and I do not take kindly to your censure when you seem to think 'tis a fine thing to spread your favors among the women here. Choose one road or the other, Gyles, but not both."

"Are you demanding an apology, wife?" Gyles sneered down at her. "If so, be warned. For hell will freeze before you hear one from my lips." He reached

226

out, catching Serena by the shoulders and pulled her to him. "But I will enjoy my rights with you."

Beneath his burning lips Serena remained unyielding, her blue eyes dispassionate as she stared over his bowed head at the fire, while Gyles's mouth nibbled at her neck. His hands cupped her breasts and Serena thrust away the feeling of pleasure that surged through her blood.

"May I remove my gown before you render this one useless as well?" Serena inquired coolly.

Gyles's head snapped up and Serena felt little satisfaction at the hurt that showed momentarily in his green eyes. "Damn you!" Gyles hissed through clenched teeth. But his hands fell to his sides.

"For the way I feel about you, I am probably already consigned to hell," Serena answered softly. "I do not need your help to speed me on my way."

10

When Gyles woke—none the worse for a night spent on the stone floor—Serena was already gone. He rushed through his dressing in the hope of catching his wife still at table, halting momentarily as his gaze rested on the ruined nightgown. Gyles's mouth compressed into a tight line, that had been a mistake on his part, for Serena was not a woman who would forsake her anger and replace it with passion. Serena—even in anger she stirred him more deeply than any other woman in the throes of love. The door swung closed behind him as Gyles quickened his pace toward the dining hall, the tentative words of an apology already forming in his mind.

But once seated with a trencher in front of him, Gyles learned his efforts had been in vain.

"Serena left some time ago," Bryan informed him. "And were I you, I wouldn't go near her until she cools off a bit. She fairly snapped my head off when I bid her good morrow." Bryan hid a grin as Gyles pushed his food away. "I have already been told by Serena to mind my own business, but where her welfare is concerned, I will not hold my tongue."

"I need no advice from you on how to deal with my wife," Gyles told him bluntly.

"Nevertheless, you will hear me out." Bryan's eyes were grim. "If I must force you at swordpoint. I have never pretended that I approved my father's choice of you, but when Serena told me she loved you . . . her happiness has always been uppermost in my mind. Suffice it to say I wished her well, for the look in her eyes softened my heart.

"Then yesterday Catherine came to me in tears. I have seen you once before—several years ago—at court, with the Lady Elspeth. You hold an uncommon disdain for women, which I find most offensive, especially when it is directed against my sister. If you are going to return to that Norman harlot, do it in a manner that will cause Serena to replace her love for you with hate. Ruin as many lives as you please, but not Serena's. She is not ignorant, and the way gossip flies about this place, 'twill not be long before she learns of Elspeth." Bryan leaned forward and trapped Gyles's gaze with his own. "At least have the decency to tell her yourself before Serena discovers this secret from another source. Let her know why people snicker behind her back."

Bryan's words found their target in Gyles's heart, yet he resented the younger man's interference. "Serena can defend herself."

"Before she loved you, perhaps, but not now. Her love has left her vulnerable as never before. And I swear that if you cause her to suffer, I will personally separate your head from your shoulders."

Henry's slim hands clamped around Serena's waist and he swung her easily from her saddle to the ground. One hand rode casually at the small of her back as he signaled one of the royal guards to open the door to the armorer's shop and then return to protect the mounts. The heat from the forge hit Serena like a physical blow, making it difficult for her to breathe and the sound of a hammer beating relentlessly against steel was deafening. Henry shouted something in her ear and Serena shook her head and tilted her head upward to look at him.

Henry bent closer and tried again. "There is a bench over there." Henry pointed to the far wall. "Wait for me while I find the master."

Serena lifted her gold velvet skirt and made her way

toward the bench, casting a wary eye to the floor and often hopping to avoid the red-hot pieces of steel that flew from the hammers of the apprentices. Serena settled herself on the rough oak and surveying her surroundings, several pairs of eyes watched her covertly. Nervously, she smoothed the skirt of her gown and reached up to unclasp her cloak and throw back the hood from her face. Henry was striding through the room, a helmet jammed on his head, and a plump little man and several assistants struggled along behind with the various parts of Henry's armor.

"Your opinion, fair lady?" Henry turned in a circle in front of her and struck a pose.

"I think, Your Highness"—Serena tapped her chin thoughtfully—"that you should at least carry a shield. Of course, you would still need to worry about a rear assault."

Henry flipped up the visor and grinned. "A little more respect for your prince, woman, or I'll have you stretched on the rack."

"Oh, nay, I beg your mercy, sweet prince." Serena wrung her hands in mock horror, then slanting a glance at Henry from the corner of her eye she added, "But you still must guard your rear."

Henry threw back his head and laughed, his trim frame shaking with mirth. "Serena, your beauty is surpassed only by your insolence. My good man!" Henry motioned to the armorer. "The lady is of the opinion I have need of more protection. Come, let us see what wonders your forge has wrought."

It required four men to strap the armor around Henry; two worked on the leather straps that held the breastplate to the backplate, while the second pair concentrated on fastening the cuisse, kneepiece, and greave on Henry's legs. The only pieces missing were the sollerets, and Henry made an incongruous picture as he clomped about in leather boots beneath his full armor. Serena covered her mouth with her hands and laughed softly into them. Henry gave her a look of feigned anger and started forward, but the joint at the right kneepiece had not been well oiled, and when it locked, Henry lost his balance and fell heavily upon the dirt floor, raising a cloud of dust that choked everyone in the vicinity.

Serena could restrain her hilarity no longer—prince or not—and laughed outright. The master and apprentices were appalled, not so much by the distress of a member of the royal family as by the fact that anyone dare laugh at the prince. It was no easy task to help a man in full armor regain his footing: The apprentices' first priority was to turn Henry from his stomach to his back. Once that was accomplished, Henry's appearance resembled a beached fish ever more strongly, and Serena laughed until her sides ached. The men struggled gallantly to haul the prince to his feet, but the weight of the armor was too great and eventually Henry gritted out: "Take the damned leg-pieces off! I have no intention of spending the day on this floor!"

The apprentices rapidly complied and soon Henry was standing before Serena, while the remainder of the armor was unfastened. Serena had lowered her head to study the lap of her gown and to give her time to wipe the smile that still played on her lips from her face. When Henry asked curtly if she was ready to depart, Serena was able to meet his gaze with a sober countenance.

Serena rose and drew her cloak over her shoulders. "May I have a moment, Your Highness?" At Henry's nod she turned to the master. "I should like to view your swords—only the lighter, dress ones, if you please."

The master nodded and Serena followed him into the room at the back of his shop. The master led her to a low counter whereon were displayed an amazing assortment of dress swords. Serena studied each one in turn until after a dozen or so had been rejected, she halted at one whose hilt was not so elaborately scrolled. Instead a solitary emerald winked up at Serena from the crosspiece of the hilt, and in her mind grew a picture of a pair of eyes of much the same color set within a strong, angular face. Ever the good merchant, the armorer took note of the shadow of emotion that passed over Serena's face, and pressed his advantage.

"A fine choice, m'lady. I forged this one myself, and spent a great deal of time in its making. 'Tis a bit heavier than most swords of this type, but 'tis well balanced."

Serena hefted the sword with both hands and made a few desultory thrusts at the air while Henry watched from the doorway.

"Very good." Serena presented the sword back to the master, hilt first. "Wrap it carefully and then we shall discuss the price of such a blade."

Coins exchanged owners and the sword was presented to Serena in its wrapping of soft leather. With a wistful smile, Henry stepped forward and relieved Serena of her package. Once outside, Henry lifted Serena into her saddle and guided her knee around the pommel. The package he gave to one of the guards with instructions for them both to return to the castle. Henry swung onto his horse, then turned to Serena.

"The rest of the day is yours to command, as I am. What is your desire?"

Serena looked after the guards. "Is it safe for you to be abroad without them?"

"I am the third son, of no importance to anyone save my mother." Henry smiled. "Do not distress yourself unduly. 'Tis Christmas Eve and we will not be about when the sun sets."

Serena nodded. "Your Highness, it seems I must apologize for my . . . unseemly behavior. I meant not to cause you embarrassment."

Henry leaned over and covered Serena's hands where they held the reins. "I was not embarrassed, Serena, and your behavior was not unseemly." A chuckle began in his throat. "I can now see the humor in the incident, albeit at the time I did not. Never fear my anger, Serena, for of those I have met at court, you are the only one who has treated me with any kind of honesty. I would value it most highly if I could count you as a friend."

Serena's eyes misted. " 'Tis I who am honored, Your Highness, for of all the court, save for Catherine, you are the only one who I do not fear."

"And your husband?" Henry's brown eyes were sympathetic.

"I fear him most of all," she replied softly. They were silent for a moment, and then Serena shook herself mentally. It would not be fair to burden Henry's day with her problems. "Now, good prince," Serena lifted her nose in a haughty gesture, "since you are mine to command, I bid you find a place where I may ease my hunger."

"Your slightest wish, fair lady."

Henry preceded Serena through the crowded streets, glancing often over his shoulder to make sure they had not become separated. At last he stopped before a tavern where he guided her to a well-secluded table. Meat, bread, and a flagon of red wine were set in front of them and both greedily devoured the fare. Satisfied, Henry regarded her with soft, brown eyes.

"You puzzle me."

The statement was so unexpected that Serena nearly choked on her wine. "Do I indeed?" she retorted flippantly.

"Aye." Henry looked as if he might say more, but apparently changed his mind and pulled her to her feet and, after tossing a small purse at the innkeeper, out to the horses. "Would you prefer to ride or walk?"

"Walk, Your Highness."

Henry agreed, and one hand held the reins while the other kept a firm grip on Serena's arm. "You know a great deal about weapons. The sword is for your husband —in the way of an apology?"

Serena bristled. "I have nothing to apologize for, Your Highness. 'Tis Christmas, and I had no gift for him."

"Fair Serena, you needn't snap at me." Henry's lips twitched with a hint of a smile. "Tell me how you gained your knowledge of arms instead."

As they walked, Serena told Henry of her childhood at Broughton while in turn he regaled her with tales of Normandy. If any article in a booth caught Serena's eye, Henry insisted upon stopping and allowing her to view the displays at leisure; but at only one did Serena make a purchase. When she turned back to Henry she offered one of the two meat-filled pies she held.

" 'Tis not seemly," Henry began, "that you—"

"Do not offend me, Your Highness," Serena told Henry with a twinkle in her eye. "Besides, you are far too thin." Henry shrugged and bit into the pastry while Serena looked on.

"Too thin, eh?" Henry spoke around the meat.

"Yes, Your Highness. In fact, I think I shall rename you."

"Do you not think my parents will mind?"

Serena swallowed the last of her pie before answering. "I had not thought to have your new name legalized by the Church, but if you insist."

"Nay! At least tell me what name you have chosen," Henry teased. "Or is it too private to be said in the streets?"

Serena laughed softly. " 'Tis not all that private, but I doubt you would wish to be addressed in public as the Starving Prince."

Henry guffawed loudly, his slender shoulders shaking at Serena's humor. "You, who look as if you have yet to sit down to an entire meal, dare to call me thin? At the first strong wind you would blow away."

Serena gave him a secretive look. "That, I assure you, Your Highness, could never happen. But I am sure you have difficulty remaining astride your horse without benefit of armor," Serena challenged.

"Dear Serena, I shall prove you wrong. When we return to the castle, we shall stop at the tourney field and test our steeds."

"And our ability," Serena added.

Henry checked their progress, for the afternoon was waning and they had only a few more hours before they must make their way back to the castle. He lifted Serena onto her mount before swinging into his own saddle.

"Do you still wish to see Westminster Abbey?" Henry asked. " 'Tis not far."

Gyles paced restlessly from one corner of the chamber to another, pausing often to listen for the sound of a familiar footstep outside the door. The day had been sheer torture for Gyles, as it seemed word had spread that young Henry had taken a decided liking to a certain young Saxon woman and had offered his services as a guide to London. Gyles had fumed silently at the innuendos that had flown around the tables at the midday meal.

Where were they? What was so fascinating about London that Henry had not yet returned with Serena?

Gyles paced and fumed. It was folly to have allowed Serena to accompany Henry. Jealousy, bitter as bile, sprang to his mouth and coiled its malignant lengths about his mind.

Gyles halted his movement abruptly. Jealous? He? Preposterous! His mind cried out. Jealousy lives only where there is love and you do not love. The lass is your wife, 'tis all, and no other man, therefore, should gift her with his attention. Your wife! Your possession! No other's!

Why should Serena seek Henry's company? Prince though he be, what could Henry offer her that he, Gyles, could not? A position as his royal mistress? No, Serena would never agree to such an arrangement. His friendship? Possibly, but the look in Henry's eyes when he gazed on Serena held more than friendship.

Love? Gyles's mind caught and hung suspended on the word while his heart gave a sickening lurch. Was that what Henry offered that he could not? "I love you," Serena had told Gyles. "You are my life." But how long could a woman go on giving when she received nothing in return? Pain, swift and unrelenting, tore through Gyles's breast and he drove a clenched fist against the mantle. I do not love her! Love is for children and idiots. I learned that lesson long ago and it has oft been proven true in my life. I do not love! Gyles's mind raged. Fool! A small voice somewhere within him whispered. Will you deny Serena then? Will you set her from you—allow her to become Henry's mistress? Or Richard's? Will you petition for an annulment so she is free to marry whom she wishes?

"Nay!" Gyles's voice echoed in the room. "The lass is mine and no other shall possess her. Ever!"

The final notes of the Mass rang through the rafters of Westminster and faded away to silence. Her hood pulled forward to hide her features, Serena knelt beside Henry in prayer. Her entreaty to God ended, Serena crossed herself and immediately Henry's fingers closed around her elbow to assist her to her feet.

"The hour grows late, Serena," Henry murmured, as they moved beneath the towering arches of the sanctuary. "I fear our contest must wait lest your husband accuse me of kidnapping you."

As the chill night air enfolded her, Serena drew her cloak more closely around her. They mounted their horses in silence and Serena noted that Henry's hand rested upon the hilt of his sword and he looked constantly into the shadows around them.

Henry slowed his mount until Serena was abreast of him. "Stay beside me," he warned as he pulled his dagger from his belt and handed it to Serena. "Can you use this with any skill?" At her nod, Henry grinned. "I should never have sent the guards back, or at the very least I should have let you keep the sword you purchased to-day."

A shiver of apprehension coursed through Serena, and she gripped the dagger more firmly. "I'm sure I need not fear," Serena said defiantly. "Between the two of us we should be able to defend ourselves adequately."

Henry chuckled briefly. "Nothing daunts you does it, Serena?"

"Very little," Serena agreed airily, but her blue eyes strayed often to the darkened entrances of the buildings they passed. Viewing London during the daylight hours with a well-armed escort was all well and good, but to travel at night with only one poorly armed man was something else entirely.

Henry quickened the pace until the horses were cantering through the deserted streets; the sound of the hoof-beats vibrating loudly through the air and bouncing off the buildings to rebound against Serena's ears. Surely no one else was abroad at this hour, Serena thought. Even the worst villains required nourishment—no doubt they were now sitting down to their fare.

Through the darkness, Serena could just discern the flickering lights of the torches set on the palace walls. Not much farther now and they would be safe. Serena turned in her saddle to congratulate Henry on their good fortune when she caught the glint of moonlight on metal.

"Henry! Behind you!" Serena's warning rang clearly through the street.

Henry wheeled his mount sharply about and brought his sword upward just in time to parry the blow. Blue sparks flew into the air and then Serena had no chance to watch further as the reins were jerked from her hand and a hairy paw closed around one slim ankle. The horse reared as it felt Serena lose her balance and Serena slid helplessly from the saddle and into her assailant's arms. Serena squirmed and struck out violently with her fists, feeling an immense satisfaction when her captor gave a soft grunt as Henry's dagger tore its way down the man's arm and his grip loosened briefly, allowing Serena to twist around so that her feet touched the ground. The man growled incoherently, then swore aloud as Serena's heel came down hard on the arch of his foot while at the same time she drove the heel of her hand into the man's throat. Cruel fingers fastened in Serena's hair, tearing the snood from her hair and dragging her head backward until she could see the few stars that peeped through the clouds. With grim determination, Serena sank her long nails into the flesh of the man's cheek. A hand closed around her throat, choking off Serena's breath and causing brightly colored lights to dance before her eyes. Serena opened her mouth to scream but all that emerged was a harsh, croaking sound. Strength began to ebb from her limbs and each beat of her heart seemed to pound in her ears. In desperation, Serena forced the hand that still held the dagger upward; it was impossible for her to see clearly anymore, so she let instinct take over in the task of guiding the weapon toward her assailant. Inch by hard-fought inch, Serena's arm raised while the hand at her throat relentlessly tightened. One by one, the bright lights in front of her began to wink out, leaving in their place an ever-deepening blackness. The effort to defend herself became too great, and slowly Serena's fingers relaxed their grip on the hilt of the dagger and it fell uselessly to the ground. I'm going to die, Serena thought dully, and she gave herself up to the weakness that seemed to invade her entire being.

"Serena! Serena!"

Hands gently slapping at her face, her name spoken with quiet urgency, pulled Serena back to awareness. Her eyes flickered open to see Henry kneeling over her. Serena raised her hand and tentatively fingered the bruised flesh of her throat.

"Thank heaven!" Henry sighed. "Can you stand?"

"I . . . I think so." Serena felt Henry's arm come around her waist and lift her to her feet. She swayed dizzily for a moment before the world righted itself, half-leaning against Henry, as they made their way to his horse.

"Your mount bolted in the attack and there is no time to search for it now." Henry rested Serena against his horse's flank. "Lean back while I mount." Henry swung into the saddle then stretched out his hand. "Take hold, Serena, we must be away quickly before our friends decide to return."

Serena complied and Henry settled her before him in the saddle and urged the horse into a gentle canter. It required too much strength to sit upright, and with Henry's arm holding her securely, Serena allowed her head to rest upon his shoulder.

"You were not injured, Your Highness?" Serena asked above the clatter of hooves.

"Nay. Your warning was most timely on that part, Serena. Had you not cried out, I most certainly would be dead by now, and for that I owe you more than I can ever hope to repay. If I had been more alert, I could have come to your aid sooner. In that I failed you. 'Twould seem I am capable of nothing." Derision was heavy in his voice.

"But you did save me," Serena pointed out. "Were it not for you, God alone knows what fate would have befallen me."

"I should never have dismissed the guards," Henry criticized himself.

"But you did, and 'tis over, Your Highness. Neither of us came to any great harm, so do not berate yourself for what is past," Serena said, logically.

They passed beneath one of the high, stone arches that led to the castle courtyard; there a servant ran quickly from the stable to hold the reins Henry tossed at him. Henry dismounted and lowered Serena to the ground. Taking her arm, Henry led her into the castle.

"I must go to my chamber before I dine, Your Highness," Serena told him as Henry made to turn down the corridor to the great hall.

Henry stopped and considered her gravely. "Of course," Henry nodded. "I shall accompany you."

"There is no need, Your Highness, I do not wish to delay you any longer."

"Do not trouble yourself for that reason, for it does not trouble me." The tense lines in Henry's face had relaxed and he was once more his gentle, teasing self. "If your lord is angry because of the lateness of the hour, I shall explain the circumstances to him."

Serena smiled up at Henry as they walked. "That is most kind of you, Your Highness, but you needn't."

Henry dismissed the objection with a wave of his hand. "My fair Serena, after our adventure today, 'tis the least I can do. I must confess, the day did not end as I intended."

"Nor I." Serena laughed. "But I shall always remember it. How many others have had the honor of being saved by a prince?"

They reached the chamber and as Serena opened the door, Henry placed his hands gently on her shoulders. "Forgive me, Serena."

"For what, Your Highness?" Serena asked in puzzlement.

Henry pivoted Serena until she faced him and raised her hand to his cheek. "Do you always see the best in people, Serena? Will you forever believe in the good of men—failing to believe that some men harbor black thoughts?"

"Your Majesty," Serena nervously wet her lips, "this is not seemly . . ."

"Fair Serena," Henry's hand reached up to touch the soft coils of gold-streaked hair. "Lovely Saxon maid of my dreams. How your face haunts me day and night. When you enter a room, all others fade into nothing. How completely you trust me; so completely sure I will not bring dishonor to you. From the moment my eyes beheld you, I desired you . . . I held the hope that you bore no affection for your husband and would look favorably upon me. And you did, but not as I wished. You saw me as a friend, nothing more, yet you freely offered that to me." Henry's hand slid downward to cup Serena's chin. "I could insist upon your remaining here after your husband departs. Given time, I feel certain I could gain from you that which I seek. But you would never forgive me for that, and so, I fear I must be content with matters as they are . . . unless you bid me otherwise."

Henry's eyes trapped Serena's with the unspoken question until at last her gaze dropped away with a slight shake of her head.

"As I feared," Henry sighed. "You have my heart, dearest Serena, and I cannot reclaim it. How can a man live without that which he needs?"

"Your Highness . . ." Serena faltered; the title was incongruous in this situation. "Henry . . ." Serena pleaded softly.

Henry silenced her protests by placing a slim forefinger over her lips. "Love of my life; how I shall live when you are gone I know not, but I swear this: Never shall you have reason to fear me or suspect my motives. You need not fear ravishment from me nor seduction in my presence; if a friend is what you wish, then friend I shall be.

But should the time come when you have need of me, you have only to send word. 'Till the day I die, dearest love, I am yours." Henry raised Serena's hands to his lips. "I shall not speak of this again unless 'tis your desire. *Adieu*, Serena, be at peace."

Serena arrived in the great hall still shaken by Henry's revelation. Was it always to be her fate to be loved and desired by all men save for the one to whom she was truly bound by holy vows and her own heart? What would it be like to be loved in return? To know that her emotions were returned with the same intensity with which she gave them? Her blue eyes scanned the assembly, seeking—without appearing to do so—her husband's tall figure. Serena's heart lurched when she found him, standing beside the ravishing Lady Elspeth and paying particular heed to what she was saying.

Oh, Gyles, my love! Why must I be ever uncertain of you, always unsure? Will you cast me aside one day in favor of another? Will you never be mine as surely as I am yours? Sweet my lord, I fear for us. Dearest Gyles, will you never love me?

Tears stung her eyes, blurring her vision, and Serena turned quickly away to regain her composure.

" 'Twill do no good to run, Serena," Bryan's soft voice said in front of her as his hands deftly caught her wrist. "He has seen you and will soon be at your side. Dry your tears and stiffen your spine."

Serena nodded, and when Bryan released her hands, brushed hurriedly at her wet cheeks. Bryan chattered aimlessly of unimportant things, allowing his sister the time she needed to resolve the emotional torment within her. "Are you better?" Bryan asked at last.

"Yes." Serena's head lifted and she looked squarely at Bryan. "A momentary weakness, I assure you. Where is Catherine?"

"With the queen; they should arrive shortly. I must commend you on your matchmaking, sister. It is most effective." Bryan grinned down at Serena.

"I but introduced you, the rest was in your hands."

There was still a heaviness in Serena's heart, but for Bryan's benefit she forced a lightness into her voice.

"That is true," Bryan admitted. "And now I find myself torn in two directions: my love for Catherine and my love for England." Bryan's eyes took on a haunted expression.

"Why should the two conflict? Unless Catherine does not feel the same way toward you."

"That is not true, Serena. In fact I am thinking of offering for her hand, but . . . Serena, Catherine is Norman. I am Saxon and her people's sworn enemy! I wish for a Saxon king upon England's throne, yet I desire a Norman for a wife. Yet when I think of Catherine, I do not see an enemy but the woman I love and I forget all my noble goals. Serena, what am I to do?"

Bryan, always so sure of himself, begging for her help, touched Serena deeply. Often in the past he had comforted her and set her world aright. "You will do what your heart and mind tell you is right. It has been eleven years, Bryan. Eleven long years! The time for hate and revenge is long past, don't you see that? Norman, Saxon, wherein lies the difference? The years will pass, Saxon blood will mix with Norman and soon there will be no distinction between the two. Spare me your speeches and debates, Bryan, for you know I speak the truth. 'Tis time we start to build rather than destroy. With Catherine you can take the first step toward a new life—a happier life. You have hated for so long, Bryan, is it not time to begin to love?"

" 'Tis simpler for you, Serena, you are only a woman." Bryan shook his head unhappily.

"Only a woman!" Serena jeered. "And who, pray, do you think suffers the most during war? The brave knights? What do they sacrifice save their lives? They die gloriously—by their own choice—in the midst of battle. And when the victors come, 'tis the women who pay the final price of defeat. They pay with their bodies, their minds, their pride. Fathers, husbands, brothers, lovers, all slumber peacefully in their graves while the women give the victors their due. Any time you wish, brother mine,

I will exchange my lot in life for yours so you may have the simple task of being *only* a woman."

"No price is too great," Bryan began.

" 'Tis too great for me, Bryan, and I will not pay it. Nor will I allow Catherine to. Rebel if you must, kill if you must, but I will see to it that Broughton is taken from you, and with Broughton, Catherine."

Bryan paled. "You would not, Serena."

"I can and I will," Serena said firmly. "Throw your own life away, but no other's."

"Catherine would follow me anywhere, with or without Broughton." But Bryan was clutching at the wind, for Serena's arguments were invincible.

"You may be right," a deep masculine voice behind Serena said, "but is that the life you wish for Catherine? No priest will bless your union and nowhere will you be safe, for William hunts his enemies until they are dead." Gyles draped an arm casually over Serena's shoulder and felt her instant recoil. "And should Serena falter, I will assure you find no sanctuary with her."

A muscle in Bryan's jaw worked furiously at this unwelcome intrusion. It entered Bryan's mind to throw Gyles's own failings in his teeth, but he checked the impulse. If Serena was to be hurt, it would not be by her own brother, her own flesh and blood. No, the Norman bastard she married would have to deliver that punishing blow on his own. Bryan bent and placed a fleeting kiss on Serena's cheek.

"I must speak with Catherine. Perhaps what you say is true."

"And if Catherine agrees?" Serena sked softly.

A wry grin twisted Bryan's lips. "You will be the first to know." With a slight inclination of his head, Bryan was gone.

Gyles wasted no more thought on his departing brother-in-law but slowly exerted pressure on Serena's shoulders until she faced him. Serena did not raise her eyes to him and Gyles wondered at her strange behavior. Carefully, he tilted her head upward until he could see her face and still she would not meet his gaze. Leisurely,

Gyles allowed his eyes to wander over her face, down her throat . . . and stopped; for there, partially hidden by the collar of her gown, was a small, purple bruise like a delicate blooming flower. Serena noted where that green-eyed gaze lingered, but before she could speak Gyles lashed out at her, all the rage and frustration of the day pouring out in a vicious torrent.

"Henry should take better care of you in his bed. Does he not know you bruise most easily?"

Serena's eyes widened in outrage. "How would you know, sweet husband. It has been long since I have graced your pallet, bruised or otherwise. If your conscience plagues you with guilt, do not punish me because of it," Serena snapped.

" 'Tis your own guilt that makes you speak so. All the court knows that Henry dismissed his guards so he might be alone with you. Have you any idea of what gossip is now making the rounds? As far as the court is concerned, you became Henry's mistress today."

"Is that what you believe, Gyles?" Serena questioned softly. "Do you think I take my vows so lightly?"

"Do you deny it?" Gyles countered in a deadly hushed voice.

"There is nothing to deny. Believe whatever pleases you, Gyles, I am weary of defending myself and my actions to you."

Gyles's hands dropped to his sides as if their contact with her burned them. Serena's face was expressionless, her eyes veiled. "The meal is commencing, Gyles, we are becoming conspicuous."

Gyles hesitated, his features momentarily convulsed by what in another man Serena would have named pain, and then offered his arm to his wife. She has stopped loving me, something deep within Gyles cried in despair. Somehow, he managed to choke down the meal before him and his outward appearance gave no evidence of the inner turmoil raging in his mind. She's taken Henry in my stead because I took all she had to offer and gave her nothing in return. Gyles sipped at his wine, grimacing at its sour taste—no, not the wine, it was his own thoughts

244

that were bitter and sour. Serena was by his side, not touching her own meal, but managing to converse in fairly normal tones. Gyles looked away from Serena and straight into Elspeth's glittering black eyes. Elspeth looked from Gyles to Serena and back again and smiled mockingly, eloquently.

Most of the courtiers were on their feet now, moving about the hall and gathering in small groups to laugh and talk. High spirits prevailed—it was Christmas, the birth of our Lord Jesus Christ, a time of rejoicing, celebration, a time to forget the everyday cares of existence and be merry. The king set the Yule log ablaze amidst thundering cheers from his nobles and proposed the first toast of the evening.

Gyles stared morosely into his wine, trying to ignore the fact that Serena sat as immobile as a statue, not so much as glancing at him. Anger welled up within Gyles —what did Serena have to be miserable about? He was the injured party, after all; Serena had taken Henry as a lover while he, Gyles, stupid fool that he was, had remained faithful. Women! his mind spat contemptuously, and he had thought Serena faithful to him! But like all harlots, she had only waited for a better offer.

"Hadn't you better go to Henry, wife?" Gyles snarled. " 'Tis obvious you do not relish my company, perhaps his would suit you better."

Serena turned a fathomless blue gaze on her husband. "As you wish, Gyles." And she made to rise.

"Sit down!" Gyles's hand shot out and jerked Serena roughly back into her seat. "Have you no shame at all, no pride? Will you crawl after him like some bitch in heat?"

"I resent that slur, Lord Gyles." A silken, deadly voice intervened, which brought Gyles to his feet. Henry stood casually behind them, a goblet in one hand, but in his brown eyes flashed an anger that had not been seen there before and he seemed far older than his tender years. "Your lady wife has done naught to deserve your wrath, so if you must vent your spleen, vent it on me and me alone."

Gyles's green eyes flashed back defiantly at the young prince. Member of the royal family or not, this man was the cause of the rumors now flying about the court and Gyles was in no mood to allow Henry to defend Serena's actions.

"She is my wife," Gyles ground out from between clenched teeth. "So have a care, Your Highness, for prince or not I will challenge any man who would take her from me."

Serena's gaze flew from one man to the other. How dare they speak of her as if she were a piece of property!

"Am I to throw down a gauntlet, Lord Gyles? If we meet on the field of honor would that salve whatever wrongs you imagine have been done you? Would it soothe your ruffled pride to hack at me with a broadsword or tilt with a lance?"

"'Twould please me immeasurably, Your Highness," Gyles replied, his tone as icily calm as Henry's.

"No!" Serena whispered vehemently, but neither man paid her any heed. In fact, she might not have spoken at all.

Henry bent to place a hand beneath Serena's elbow and raised her to her feet. "Leave us, Lady Serena." His voice held a trace of warmth, but it was a royal command all the same.

Serena paused in front of Gyles, one delicate hand going up to rest upon his broad chest, and tried once more. "Please, Gyles, do not do this. What will be proved?"

"That your honor will be defended for one thing. Or do you intend to do that yourself?" Gyles mocked her.

"My honor has not been sullied, Gyles. There, I've denied it for you, is that not enough? Gyles, I beg you! Nothing will be served by—"

"Leave us, Serena!" Gyles caught her hand and thrust it back to her side. "Both your husband and your prince have commanded you, now obey!"

Eyes, green and brown, were united in one motive— to rid themselves of Serena's presence. This was not the time nor the place to defy either, and with an exclamation of disgust Serena whirled and walked away.

"The choice of weapons is yours, Your Highness." Gyles's voice was calm as he watched Serena's departure.

Henry turned to Gyles, all anger either faded or concealed in his brown eyes. With exaggerated patience he lowered himself into the chair Serena had vacated. The wood was still warm from her touch and for a brief moment Henry allowed himself the luxury of remembering how soft her hair had been beneath his fingers. One moment, that was all, for Serena's green-eyed husband still glowered down at him. "Sit down, Lord Gyles, and cool your anger with wine," Henry sighed heavily. "Aside from my brother, you are the most blind, vain, arrogant man I have ever met. Oh, sit *down,* I have no intention of fighting you."

Gyles subsided into his chair, every nerve and sinew in his body tensed with the desire to beat William's youngest son into a bloody, quivering mass of flesh. This man had touched his wife! Serena had lain with him, taken Henry within herself, allowed him to stroke her lovely gold-streaked curls and her breasts. Had he held her closely to him . . . afterward? Had Henry given Serena the words as well as the deed? Had Serena turned to him, molding herself against him as she did with Gyles himself?

"I would like to kill you . . . Your Highness," Gyles told the younger man.

Henry's eyebrows raised. "No doubt; were I you, I would probably feel the same. But I repeat, I will not fight you. Any other man who dares to dirty Serena's good name, yes, but not you. Oh, believe me, if I thought your death would send her flying into my arms I would not hesitate to have you killed. Yes, Lord Gyles"—Henry leaned forward when he saw Gyles's eyes narrow—"I would have you killed—in an instant, for I would not take the chance that you might kill me. But the question of that is moot, since that option would do me no good. Knowing Serena, at your death she would probably retire

247

to a convent for the rest of her life and what a waste that would be." Henry settled back comfortably. "Now we both know where we stand. I envy you your wife; I wish she were mine. You believe Serena has been faithless because of these idiotic rumors—"

"Nay, Henry," Gyles growled. "Because of the evidence on her person; no rumors made those marks."

"What marks?" Henry asked harshly. If William had found Serena alone after he had left her in her chamber, brother though he was, Henry would see that he paid.

"Do not play the innocent, Henry, Serena's pretense is enough for me to contend with. You know full well of what I speak. You should have been more careful, my wife's skin is most delicate and bruises easily." At Henry's still bewildered expression, Gyles curled his fingers around the arms of his chair lest his hands strike out of their own accord. "On her throat!" Gyles continued when he regained partial control.

Unexpectedly, Henry laughed, his brown eyes fixed intently upon Gyles. "You fool!" he said at last. "You ignorant fool. Be assured, that were Serena mine I would never misuse her as you seem intent upon doing. Do you know your own wife, I wonder? Have you troubled to look into those azure eyes and see the person behind them? I have—strong, tender, sympathetic, proud, stubborn—Serena is all of these and much more. I have watched her flay my brother with her tongue because he offended her; I have seen her cajole my mother out of a temperamental fit; I have watched the gallants at court fall at her feet for the wont of a smile or kind word. And I have seen the gentle look in her eyes when you are near. Serena would gladly surrender all she possesses for you; for you she would starve, kill, even die, if once, only once, Gyles, you would stir yourself enough to descend from that lofty pedestal on which you have placed yourself. By all that is holy, man, why do you torment her so? Why are you so willing to believe the worst about your own wife? She sees only the best in you, you know."

Gyles's hands clenched around the goblet he was

holding. "I do not need you to tell me the good points about Serena. I am her husband, after all."

"And her lord and master as well," Henry interjected with a note of sarcasm. Was it possible for one man to be so dense? "But I have fled the point of our conversation, have I not? You wish to know if I have bedded Serena." Henry continued brutally, feeling satisfaction as the scar that marred Gyles's face whitened. "No, I have not, though not for want of trying. I planned our time together today most carefully—my guards I sent away so that she would not feel ill at ease in their presence. I tried words both soft and teasing. I played the gallant suitor; I had every intention of seducing her, Lord Gyles. We are of an age, Serena and I; we are too young to carry a hatred for each other because one of us is Saxon and the other Norman. Were she free, I would ask her to be my wife—I would clothe her in silk and velvet and drape the finest jewels about her lovely neck and set dazzling rings upon her fingers. All this I had planned to offer her anyway—as my mistress. But then, before I could tell her, Serena looked at me and smiled, her eyes full of trust, and I knew then that no matter what I offered her she would never consent to be my mistress.

"As for the marks on her throat, they are my fault. 'Twas my lack of common sense that caused them to be placed there. On returning this eve, we were set upon by thieves. 'Twas Serena's warning that saved my neck and because of my foolishness she nearly lost her life. She was fairly strangled before my eyes by a great lout who dares call himself a man. She defended herself admirably, your noble wife, for she buried her dagger at least once in that swine's flesh, but Serena was no match for brute strength. When I was finally able to drive her assailant away, I was sure Serena was dead, she was so still and lifeless."

Gyles's face had set in an expressionless mask, the only sign he felt any emotion betrayed by the muscle that twitched in his cheek. "If that is true, Your Highness, why did Serena not tell me this herself?"

Henry snorted. "Did you give her a chance?"

Serena sat tensely beside Catherine, willing herself not to look in the direction where Gyles and Henry were cloistered. It was as if all emotion had been drained from her, no more feeling except a numbness that was creeping into every part of her body. Surely they wouldn't . . . they couldn't. Oh, Gyles, please, please . . . don't do this thing. Henry is no match for you and there is no reason for a challenge. Dear God! Please! If Henry is killed Gyles's life will be forfeit, don't let them do this!

A hand on her arm made Serena jump and she looked at Catherine, then followed the path her eyes had taken. Serena's heart hammered as she watched Gyles approach and Catherine rose to take her leave.

"Oh, no, Catherine, stay!" Serena clutched at her friend's hand.

"I dare not," Catherine whispered and quickly disappeared. Even when Gyles was in the best of moods, Catherine dared not stand between him and Serena.

Gyles eased himself into a chair beside Serena, casually reaching over and freeing one of the hands she pressed tightly together in her lap and holding it in his.

"Why, dear wife, you are trembling!" Green eyes caught blue and laughed mockingly. "For who, I wonder, Henry . . . yourself . . . me? Will you weep for me when I am dead, Serena?"

Serena paled and sought to free her hand. It was futile, Gyles's grip was too strong. "What have you done?" she asked breathlessly.

For an answer Gyles rose and drew Serena up with him. Without a word, his arm curled around her waist, Gyles led her through the hall, along the passageways and into their chamber. The door he closed with a kick of his foot, the bar Gyles easily lifted into place while Serena watched, silent and wide-eyed. Gyles crossed to the bed and raised one foot until it rested upon the curved footboard, all the while watching Serena intently.

"Take off your gown, Serena." His tone was so calm, so impersonal it made Serena gasp.

"What!"

"Take off your gown, Serena," Gyles repeated quietly, "or I will do it myself."

Serena's chin came up, her blue eyes huge, fearful and angry at the same time. For the first time since their marriage Serena was truly afraid of Gyles. His bellowing rages she could handle, but this hushed, nerve-shattering control Gyles was exercising made her shake inwardly. Well, she was not some cheap harlot who would do whatever he commanded.

"No." Serena's tone matched his.

"No?" Gyles cocked an eyebrow. "No, Serena? Are you disobeying me, defying me? My dear wife, that is most unwise. *Now take off that gown before I rip it from your back!*"

His words hit her like a physical blow and Serena took a step backward. Shakily, her hands worked at the bows at the shoulders and sides of the gown. At last all were untied and Serena crossed her arms over her breasts to hold the gown in place.

"Gyles, please," Serena begged in a whisper.

Apparently Gyles had lost his patience, for he swore, but still he made no move toward her. "Stop looking as if I'm going to beat you and remove the gown. I have never given you cause to think I would misuse you."

Serena's head drooped and she let the gown fall from her shoulders. Humiliated, she felt Gyles's eyes caress her, drinking in every soft rounded part of her that the thin undergarment clung to. What did he want? Why didn't he speak, move, do something, anything!

"Come here, Serena." Again that quiet command.

This time Serena did as she was told without argument and when she stood only inches in front of him, she raised tear-brilliant eyes to Gyles. His gaze was unreadable as he looked down at her, but there was a stillness about him that frightened Serena to the depths of her heart.

"Gyles, what is it you—"

Her words were choked off as Gyles's hand went around the slim column of her throat and closed swiftly and painfully on her already tender flesh. Just as abruptly,

Gyles's hold loosened and he studied the damage he had inflicted. Serena had unwittingly retreated from him and now through tear-blurred vision she watched Gyles leave the bed and come toward her. Suddenly the meaning of his actions were clear and Serena stood rooted to the floor. Gyles meant to kill her! He believed her unfaithful and meant to kill her! His huge hands were on her shoulders now; at any moment he would wrap them around her throat and slowly choke the life from her as the man in the street had tried to do earlier. She had fought then, with every bit of strength in her being she had struggled; but now she could not even raise a finger in her own defense. Better she should die than live with Gyles believing her to have sought another's arms. Far better . . .

But it was not Gyles's hands at her throat, but rather his lips kissing the red marks he had caused to be raised over the purple ones, his hands busily freeing himself from his clothing. Gyles's mouth traveled up the side of Serena's neck and caught at her mouth, bruising, demanding. In the recesses of her mind, Serena felt the fabric of her kirtle rend as it separated beneath Gyles's hands, and then he was molding her body against his, crushing her against his broad chest and hard manhood. Gyles half-dragged, half-carried Serena to the bed.

Without a word, Gyles followed her onto the mattress, his lips nibbling at the sensitive flesh down her side and stomach, then upward to tug the nipples of her breasts into taut peaks. It had been so long . . . so long . . .

Gyles dragged his mouth away from Serena and rose upward until he could stare down into the blue of her eyes. "When I die, will you pray for me, Serena?" Gyles demanded hoarsely.

Dear God! Serena's eyes flew open. Gyles *had* challenged Henry. Tonight might be the last time she would ever hold him in her arms, run her hands through the crisp, dark hair that matted his chest, feel him enter her and drive all else from her mind save the mindless, swirling passion that each evoked in the other.

"Oh, Gyles!" Serena whispered brokenly. "There was no need! I have ever been true to you. Oh, Gyles!"

"There was every need for what I did," Gyles murmured against her hair. "Every need, every reason. I want you to remember my lying beside you, holding you, taking you." Gyles's actions matched his words and laughter rumbled in his chest at Serena's gasp when his flesh penetrated her. "You will always be mine, Serena. Always! No man will ever give you what I can." Slowly, leisurely, Gyles began to move deep within her, eliciting the first sensuous responses from his wife. "And do you know why? Because you love me, Serena. *You love me!* To the end of your days, Serena, you will be mine."

Tears flooded Serena's eyes and she reached up to caress the smooth, rippling muscles in Gyles's back. He was right—she belonged to him as she would never belong to any other man. So different, yet she and Gyles were perfect for each other. Never could another man bring her to this point of total, mindless passion, nor could another cause her heart to pound by simply appearing. Love and desire, pain and remorse, all mixed together to form a bittersweet, haunting night of love. They slept fitfully and whomever awoke first reached out for the other.

Serena stirred in the early morning hours to find her head cushioned on Gyles's chest, his heart beating steadily beneath her ear. The fire was burning brightly; Gyles must have wakened some time before and added more logs, Serena thought. How comforting it is to be able to reach out and touch him. How good it feels to have his arms around me. Oh, Gyles, why couldn't you love me?

Serena hadn't meant to speak aloud, but in her anguish she had and Gyles stirred, his green eyes lazily watching her. It was as if he had touched her and Serena looked up into that fathomless gaze. All emotion burst into her soul: love, hate, anger, then love again, until Serena was sure she would go mad. Gyles should sleep, Serena knew; he would need all his strength for the morrow, but . . .

Wildly, Serena pressed herself to Gyles, her lips

prying his apart so her tongue could dart against his. Her hands worked feverishly; touching, arousing, demanding. Gyles writhed beneath Serena's touch and moaned softly, his breath coming in ragged gasps. Serena had become a vixen, no longer the gentle kitten who purred so contentedly in his embrace, but an uncontrollable, volatile woman who demanded kiss for kiss, caress for caress. Her hair fell in riotous curls about them both as Serena bent forward to catch his bottom lip gently between her teeth. Gyles's fingers tangled in her hair and pulled her even closer, his senses reeling and drowning in the taste, smell and touch of his wife.

There was no more time for conscious thought for either of them, only a dark, primitive need that had surfaced in both, which drove away time and place. Reality receded totally when Serena's fingers closed on Gyles's virility and guided his entrance into her. Gyles arched upward, filling her, feeling the light brush of Serena's breasts against his chest. His arms went around Serena's back and waist, drawing her ever closer while his hips thrust powerfully against Serena, driving himself deeper and deeper, while his mouth muted the cries that burst from Serena as the first waves of pleasure broke over her. Gyles found himself trapped in those waves as well; and heedless of all else he plunged recklessly onward, straining savagely until the spasms racked his body as he erupted with a force that left him spent and breathless.

Barely able to move, Gyles unsteadily smoothed Serena's perspiration-damp hair over her shoulders and down her back, luxuriating in its silken texture. Serena's face lay against his neck and Gyles could feel the soft sobs that shook her.

"Shh. Hush, cherie, there is naught for you to cry about." It was too much of an effort to speak, so Gyles settled Serena's head more comfortably against his shoulder. "Sleep, ma petite. The morrow will care for itself."

Gold trumpets with William's pennant hanging from them blared the entrance of the antagonists onto the field. Gyles's armor threw back the feeble rays of the winter sun time and time again, nearly blinding Serena. Strange how the smallest sound carried clearly from the field to where she sat. Serena could hear Gyles's mount give a snort of suppressed excitement, when the horse tossed its head, she could hear the jangle of its trappings in the clear, crisp air.

Henry was clad in his new suit of armor and tears sprang to Serena's eyes as she remembered the comical picture Henry had presented in the armorer's shop. Why did Serena imagine that from her vantage point she could smell the oil that softened the leather straps of the armor? Henry's steed was restive as well, and its hooves beat eagerly at the frozen turf. Ah, Henry, dear Henry, third son of William, you are far too young to go to your grave. And that is where Gyles will surely send you. Sweet, laughing Henry.

Gyles. My husband. Your life will be forfeit if you kill Henry, and I know you will. There is so much anger in you, so much pain. But good as well, I know that, too. The love you have given Alan proves that.

The trumpets howled again, the noise scraping across Serena's nerves and ears. All eyes were riveted to the field, Gyles and Henry caught the lances thrown by their squires and of one accord spurred their steeds forward. A lump rose in Serena's throat and try as she might, she could not dislodge it. Pray God Gyles would be satisfied with simply unseating the prince and would call a halt to the challenge. The drumming of hoofbeats beat against Serena's ears, obscuring all else; the roar of the spectators, the sound of her own breathing ...

The lances met and a splintering noise rent the air as Gyles's lance split and broke against Henry's armor while Henry's weapon found its way straight to its target. Even from where she sat, Serena heard the sound Henry's lance made as it sliced through Gyles's armor and into his chest. Oh! that strong, firm chest that Serena had so often used as a pillow. And the blood, staining the silver breastplate crimson as it gushed forth. Gyles toppled from the saddle and Serena was on her feet, running, crying, and screaming ... and screaming ...

"Gyles! Sweet, merciful God, no! Oh, Gyles! Gyles!"

Rough hands on her shoulders, holding her back, stopping her from going to her husband. William's hands bruising her flesh as he laughed down at her, his face contorted with desire.

"Oh, please, please. Let me go. Let me go to him, he needs me! Gyles, Gyles, you cannot die, you cannot! *Gyles!*"

"Serena! Serena, wake up, 'tis only a dream. Serena!"

Wild-eyed and crying Serena came bolt upright in the bed and strained to focus on the image in front of her. Oh, God, Gyles was dead, and Serena wished she were as well. Cold as death and then perhaps the pain in her heart would disappear.

"Serena!" Gyles shook her as hard as he dared, now truly frightened. Why didn't Serena awake? She was pale as death and just as cold, her eyes wide open, staring at him and seeing . . . what? "Serena, wake up!" She was gasping now, her breath coming unevenly, and Gyles hesitated only a moment before drawing back a hand and slapping her forcefully across the cheek.

Awareness seeped slowly into those huge sapphire eyes, while Gyles kept a firm grip on Serena's delicate shoulders. One last wrenching sob and Serena threw herself at Gyles, twining her arms so fiercely around his neck that he nearly choked. Gyles felt her tears wetting his shoulder and splashing onto his chest as he stroked the cold, shrinking flesh beneath his fingers.

"Here!" Gyles tenderly disengaged Serena's arms from his neck. "You are freezing. Let me get your robe. Serena?" Hesitantly, Gyles slipped from the bed, moving slowly so Serena could keep him in view. "You see, I'm only going to the chest."

Gyles found Serena's robe and his own and quickly belted the green velvet around him before returning to his wife. By the time he reached the bed, Serena had stopped crying and was simply sitting in the middle of the rumpled bedclothes looking lost and forlorn.

"Now, put your arms through the sleeves . . . there."
Gyles secured the sash at her waist, then brought her
back within the circle of his arms. "Are you better now,
Serena?"

Serena's head tilted upward until she could look into Gyles's eyes. "Gyles, do you . . . do you believe I dallied with Henry?" she asked tearfully.

Gyles took a deep breath and kissed Serena's forehead before answering. "No, Serena, I do not. I was . . .
angry 'tis all, and spoke before I thought. Were you any
other woman, I might have believed the gossips, but not
you, cherie."

"Then why the challenge, Gyles? Because of the gossip? That doesn't bother me in the least, nor should it
you. Let the old crows talk, what does it matter as long
as you and I know the truth? Refuse Henry's gauntlet,
Gyles. Please, I beg you. Think of Alan! How can I explain to him? Gyles, he's a little boy, he needs you. Oh,
Gyles, please!" Serena caught one of his hands in both of
hers. "I will do anything you ask, Gyles. Anything! I—
I'll return to Camden and never leave It again. . . . I'll
enter a convent. . . . Oh, Gyles, please!"

"Now why should you retire to a convent?" Gyles's
voice trembled with laughter. "Somehow I cannot picture
you spending the days on your knees or sleeping on a
hard pallet. No, cherie, 'tis far better you should stay with
me and warm my bed on cold winter nights."

In the corner of her mind a flicker of knowledge
began to grow. Serena pulled away from Gyles's arms and
watched a smile play on his lips; those green eyes should
have been clouded with concern but they were clear and
bright with just a hint of devilment.

"Oooh! You . . . you . . ." Serena rose to her knees,
azure eyes flashing. Gyles raised an eyebrow, inviting—
daring—her to continue her tirade. "You lied to me!
There is no challenge, there never was!"

"Serena," Gyles warned as he saw her gathering
rage. "I did not lie; you did not ask if Henry challenged
me."

"Didn't ask!" Serena fumed. "What in the name of heaven do you think I meant when I asked what you'd done? Do you have any idea what I went through?"

Gyles cupped Serena's face in his hands and grinned wickedly. "Oh, Serena, who better than I should know how you passed the night?"

His meaning was all too clear and Serena blushed. "I didn't mean that and you damn well know it!"

Gyles's eyes sparkled even more brightly. "Tsk, Serena, such language to use . . . and to your husband! I think perhaps I should turn you over my knee for that."

"Don't you lay a hand on me!" Serena flew from the bed in a single bound, her gold-streaked hair falling in a disheveled cloud around her. "You brute . . . knave!" She spat. Serena found Gyles's dress sword and brandished it in the air. "Come here, Gyles," Serena taunted. "Try to lay a finger on me. Try! I'll sever that member of which you are so proud from your body!"

Gyles sprang from the mattress and advanced upon his spitting wife. "Put that down, Serena."

"Nay! You've made a fool of me! You and your blasted pride—how could you? You pompous jackass, you horny goat!" Serena struggled to control her steadily rising ire. "And I was fool enough to believe you might come to some harm—I should have known better! You brutish Norman! What will you do if I _do_ take Henry as my lover?"

Gyles's features hardened, the whitened curved scar leaping starkly on his cheek. The humor of the situation had suddenly evaporated.

"Do not try it, Serena," Gyles advised harshly. "Henry I may not be able to deal with, but no one would fault me if I locked you in Camden's dungeon."

Serena's eyes glittered behind the sword. "Incarcerate me, will you!" She shrieked. "Only if I am dead!"

"What the devil are you so upset about?" Gyles roared back. "I thought 'twas your wish I not do battle with Henry!"

"I don't, you idiot! Do you think I want you dead?" Serena yelled.

"Then why are you holding me at sword point!?"

"Because I . . ." Serena gasped. What *was* she doing? Abruptly she hurled the sword across the room and began to sob.

Gyles relaxed against a bedpost. Serena with a sword in her very capable hands was nothing to take lightly, and for one brief moment he had feared Serena would use the weapon on him. By all that was holy, what had possessed him to play such a cruel trick on her? To hear Serena admit that she still loved him? To hurt her? To lay bare her emotions as his had been in front of Henry? Well, he had done that quite effectively, so where was the triumphant feeling he should be experiencing instead of this bleak sadness that was coursing through his soul. And why did Serena's broken sobs tear so at his non-existent heart?

Gyles walked to where Serena had thrown his sword and weighed it thoughtfully before crossing back to Serena and depositing the weapon in its scabbard. Serena presented her back to him. Determinedly, Gyles reached out to catch a thick lock of hair and wind it around his wrist until Serena had no choice but to follow the pull of her hair and move until she stood between Gyles's thighs.

Oh, why? Serena's mind screamed. Why this studied torture? Does he not know how he tears at my heart? Or is it that Gyles desired me only when I presented a challenge, an insult to his manly pride? And now, when he knows I seem to have no will of my own, does it please him to humiliate me by throwing my love in my face? What does it matter—I do love him and my pride be damned! God willing, I will bear his children and they at least will love me even if their father does not.

The play of emotion on Serena's face was too strong for Gyles to resist and he tenderly enfolded Serena in his arms. " 'Twas wrong of me to play such a trick on you, Serena. Had I known it would hurt you so, I would never have done so. Nay, lass, shed no more tears over this;

259

rather I would not blame you if you desired to strike out at me. I told you long ago that I would hurt you, Serena." Gyles's arms tightened. "Ah, lass, why didn't you listen?"

"Because what you said is true," Serena whispered into the lush velvet that covered his chest. "I love you, Gyles, but I cannot help wondering if it is enough. I cannot stop myself from wishing . . ."

Gyles sighed as he felt Serena give a small shake of her head. I will kill her yet, Gyles thought helplessly. If I do not draw the life from her body I will surely crush the spirit in her soul. And yet, I cannot send her away. Heaven help me, but I cannot.

11

The days flew by after the Yule celebrations. Serena found the queen more demanding than before and often the only time she saw Gyles was when she crept wearily into their bed. Unfailingly Gyles awoke upon her return, but never did he do more than fold her against his chest and stroke her hair until she fell asleep.

Serena had presented Gyles with his new dress sword after the evening meal on Christmas Day and had felt particularly pleased with her selection when after examining it closely he praised its workmanship. Then, surprisingly, Gyles had produced a leather pouch from one of his chests and, with a flourish, dropped it into Serena's palm.

Gyles grinned. "It has occurred to me I have never given you anything save the necklace that was your wedding gift."

With shaking fingers Serena loosed the drawstring of the pouch and tipped it so that the contents spilled into her hand. A soft "Oh" escaped her lips, for in her hand lay a ring of gold with an enormous emerald resting securely in the precious metal. Serena gaped unbelievingly at the treasure in her palm. Never had she received such a gift! What it must have cost Gyles, Serena could not imagine, but more important was the fact that Gyles had taken the time to search out a present for her.

"It . . ." Serena choked. " 'Tis beautiful, Gyles. Thank you."

Impatiently, Gyles lifted the pouch and tossed it aside. "Aren't you going to try it on?"

"Yes . . . of course," Serena said, hastily, and slipped the cool band onto the middle finger of her left hand.

Gyles lifted her hand from her lap and inspected the jewel critically. Apparently satisfied, Gyles drew Serena to her feet. "I sought to find a sapphire to match your eyes," Gyles told her softly. "But nowhere could I find a gem to rival their beauty. So you must be content with this poor bauble."

Tenderness washed through Serena and she twined her arms behind Gyles's neck and pressed her lips to his.

For a full week William held councils with his lords dealing with the troublesome Scots clans. Never willing to unite for a common cause, the fierce tribes had evidently decided they shared a common enemy at last and had turned to harassing William's outposts at every opportunity. There was no doubt in anyone's mind that the unruly Scots must be made to heel.

Among the Norman lords there was complete agreement with William's decision to send reinforcements to the border, while the few Saxon lords who remained from Edward's time exchanged meaningful looks. They knew all too well what would happen to those who contested William's power. One by one the barons stepped forward to pledge their appointed number of men to William. Broughton was called by the king's scribe who sat, quill poised above the roll, and Bryan hesitated momentarily.

It went against all Bryan held dear—his dreams of a Saxon king once more ruling England, seeing William and his band chased back across the channel. If it would make any difference in the outcome, Bryan thought, he would deny William Broughton's men. But forty knights would not dent William's force; indeed, the king could easily fill Broughton's pledge from his own household guard. And his Father had sworn sword-oath to William, and Bryan was at court only as his Father's representative.

An elbow jarred painfully against his ribcage and

262

Bryan swung upon its source to find Gyles had moved from the other side of the hall to stand at his side. They are waiting, Gyles's eyes told Bryan. Best to take your stand now and decide which side you will serve.

Resignedly Bryan stepped forward. "Broughton's pledge of forty men will be honored."

The scribe duly noted Bryan's words as he sullenly subsided into a chair. Silently, Bryan bade farewell to his ambitions. Perhaps Serena and Catherine were right; it was time to begin building, not tearing down. Broughton would eventually fall to him, but not if he were in exile or in William's dungeon. Inevitable. That was the word Bryan sought. His cause was lost, had been lost for a long time, although he had refused to admit it. Like his sister, Bryan was blessed—or cursed—with a will of iron and a stubborn nature that in itself could have repelled the Norman invasion. Had Bryan been born ten years earlier he would have undoubtedly yielded his life at Hastings and been happier for it. However, and here Bryan sighed, 'twas more important to survive than to shed one's blood in a futile effort. Which was another trait Bryan shared with Serena—both had inherited more than their share of common sense; their will to live far outstripped their willfullness. Well, sister, Bryan smiled wryly, it seems we were both destined to be disillusioned: you in love and I in my choice of causes.

While their men sat in council, the women contented themselves with conversation, needlework, and attending to the new ballads that were offered up by strolling troubadors. Serena perfected her knowledge of the Norman tongue with Catherine's assistance, and whenever Matilda did not require their presence it was not unusual to find them strolling about the palace grounds or riding in the royal forest.

Somehow, Henry escaped the councils—after all, he would not inherit the English crown, so none deemed his presence to be of any importance—and more often than not Serena and Catherine would find that Henry decided to make their outings his as well. Neither minded, for-

Henry was an entertaining companion and with his light-hearted comments kept both Serena and Catherine laughing until the tears streamed from their eyes. Never again did Henry attempt to single out Serena as the target for his attentions and no one could fault either the prince or the lovely Saxon wife for their behavior. If any tongues did wag or a few eyebrows raise, well, was not the Lady Catherine always present?

What Gyles thought of these arrangements—if he was even aware of them—no one knew, for that tall, darkly handsome knight silenced with a quelling glance anyone who dared broach the topic. Those foolish enough to hint that Gyles was being cuckolded found that death wore a grim countenance and viewed the world from behind clouded green eyes. It was only a short time until even the bravest of the courtiers ceased to bait Gyles—their lives were far too precious to be wasted over a morsel of gossip, no matter how juicy.

The councils dragged on and during that time Serena found that Gyles became withdrawn and preoccupied. His sense of humor, never in abundance in the best of times, had almost disappeared and Serena often wondered if that quality had existed solely in her imagination. Not that Gyles was ever impolite in his manner toward Serena, indeed the opposite was true; his bearing was so impersonally correct that at times Serena felt like screaming. But when they conversed, Serena had the feeling that Gyles's mind was occupied elsewhere.

Several times, Serena would sense she was being watched and would look around to find Gyles studying her. It was almost an appraising look Serena caught in those piercing green eyes—as if all her shortcomings had suddenly been brought to mind and Gyles found her lacking in everything he desired. Then Gyles's lips would twist in a brief smile and the sensation would disappear, leaving in its wake a nagging uneasiness that would not be laid to rest.

What Serena was most grateful for during her stay at court was that she had no contact with either Beda or Aurelia. The two sisters were seen together constantly, but they steadfastly avoided any contact with the residents of Camden and Broughton. Beda had, momentarily, even lost interest in seducing Gyles, which pleased Serena immensely.

Lady Elspeth was a constant visitor to the queen's chambers, her willowy figure drifting through the numerous ladies-in-waiting with a haughty arrogance that was, Serena found, surpassed only by Gyles's. But Serena had avoided any contact with Elspeth since their only confrontation shortly after Christmas.

Catherine had been admiring Serena's emerald ring when Elspeth had happened by. Unceremoniously, Elspeth had snatched at Serena's hand and bestowed a withering look at the gift and Serena.

"A bauble from Prince Henry?" Elspeth sneered maliciously.

Serena stiffened in outrage. "Indeed not, Lady Elspeth. 'Tis a gift from my husband."

Elspeth's black eyes narrowed into slits. " 'Tis odd," she looked meaningfully at Serena. "Lord Gyles used to be far more generous with his rewards for favors bestowed."

Catherine gasped audibly at the crude insinuation while Serena woodenly withdrew her hand from Elspeth's grasp.

"I am certain that you are well-versed in the matter of rewards for your favors, Lady Elspeth, but as of yet I have had no need to set a price for my husband. What he desires I freely give. Good day, Lady Elspeth." Serena bent into a mocking curtsy and presented her back before Elsepth had an opportunity to reply.

There was another who was not so fortunate as to escape Elspeth's wrath. That same night at table, by a pre-arranged signal, Elspeth invited her lover to come to her chamber, and smiled seductively when he silently agreed. Alone in her chamber, Elspeth unbound the flowing mass of her black hair and, dressing herself in a robe of stiff gold brocade sat patiently, awaiting the sound of the familiar knock at her door.

The knock sounded, followed swiftly by the man

265

and Elspeth rose at once to twine her arms about his neck and press her lips against his to meet his savage embrace.

"I feared you would not come," Elspeth breathed as she led the knight to her bed. "You have been so busy of late I was certain you had forgotten my presence. Ah, Gyles, why do you not visit me more often? I swear I am half-fainting for want of you."

Gyles gave a hard smile. "I come as often as I dare, Elspeth; and well you know it. I can hardly dance attendance on you in front of the court."

Gyles had risen from the bed to pour a goblet of mead and Elspeth followed him. "You dance attendance upon Serena well enough," Elspeth sneered up at Gyles.

"God's teeth, Elspeth," Gyles snarled. "She is my wife! Would you have me ignore her in favor of you?"

"Yes!" Elspeth spat back. "I would! I would have you at my side throughout the day *and* night. I want the court—nay, the world!—to know of our love, to know of our son."

"I offered for you once, Elspeth," Gyles reminded her in a pain-filled voice. "When you found yourself to be with child I begged you to allow me to seek the king's counsel—with him on our side your husband would willingly have divorced you and we could have married."

"I know, I know," Elspeth cried softly and hurled herself into Gyles's arms. "How often I have regretted my decision you cannot know. But you must try to understand how I felt: You had only two small lands, Gyles, one here and one in Normandy, while Roger——"

"While Roger had numerous estates, was wealthy beyond measure, and, above all else, his birth was legitimate," Gyles finished with a grimace. "Do you know, Elspeth, how often I have wished my mother had torn me from her womb before my time? How much less pain others would have endured had I never been born."

"But that is past now, dearest." Elspeth stroked his unmarred cheek—a fact Gyles marked with interest; she had never been able to accustom herself to what she considered his hideous disfigurement. "Roger is dead and your union is childless. Now, we can be together, you and I and Alan. Our son can be legitimatized, he can inherit my lands and yours; he will know a mother's love. Think on it, Gyles, I pray you."

"You would have me offer for you now?" Gyles lifted a raven tress from Elspeth's shoulder to his lips.

"Oh, yes, Gyles." Elspeth rested her head on his shoulder.

"Does honor mean naught to you, Elspeth?" Gyles forced her to look into his eyes. "I wed Serena, I took her to wife in all good honor, and I cannot drag those vows through the muck that would surely stain her if I did as you ask."

"Stain her!" Elspeth drew back with an arrogant toss of her head. " 'Tis not *her* honor that concerns you, but your own! What of my honor, Gyles, have you thought of that? I am the mother of your child, can you put that aside so easily? Is your memory so short that you have forgotten that you once declared your love for me upon your knees?"

"I remember," Gyles told her grimly. "And I also remember how you laughed and named me a fool—and I clearly recall a scene two months later when you told me you were carrying a child. My child, Elspeth, my seed. You killed my love that day with your words—have you forgotten that? Have you forgotten the names you used for me, the threats, the accusations? No vile, base-born, bastard's seed would ever find nourishment in your womb; those were your words were they not, Elspeth?"

"Yes," Elspeth whispered as she shrank from the strange light in Gyles's eyes. "But I was frightened, terrified of what Roger would do when he found out. Oh, Gyles, I was so terribly afraid, not only of Roger but of you—the way you threatened me drove me half out of my mind, I didn't know what I was saying or doing. But that has changed now, I am free to accept your offer."

Gyles turned his back on Elspeth and said in a harsh voice, "You killed something within me that day,

Elspeth. You made me less than human, incapable of any emotion save hatred. Serena's vibrant, happy life I have, in a few short months, turned into a living hell. I am slowly destroying her as you destroyed me four years ago and in all probability I shall cause her death. If Serena ever discovers the truth about you and me, Elspeth, God help us all."

Elspeth gave a haughty laugh. "Gyles, you are speaking like a moon-struck maid. Your Saxon slut will do nothing to either of us. Send her away and forget her! Did you not say she had a Saxon who once desired to wed her? Therein lies your solution, she can return to him. Or if that does not please her, mayhap Henry will install her as his whore—he finds her attractive, I know."

At the thought of Serena lying in another man's arms, Gyles's face darkened. "Serena is no whore, Elspeth, do not name her so. She has loved our son as if he were her own and defended him when he was attacked by one such as yourself, so do not seek to sully her name."

"A paragon of virtue," Elspeth jeered, then gasped as Gyles's hands closed over her shoulders.

"My wife," Gyles reminded her in a silken tone. "I do not take kindly to being told what to do with my life, Elspeth, and 'twould be to the betterment of your health if you never speak of my wife again. Catherine told me of the words you bandied with Serena today— and all over an emerald ring! You do not have the sense of a goat, Elspeth."

"You waste good coin upon a Saxon," Elspeth cried angrily, "while I receive naught from you! You could have given me that bauble, Gyles."

Gyles laughed and abruptly reached out to untie Elspeth's robe. "Nay, Elspeth, you taught me too well. Give me something worthwhile and perhaps I shall reward you. Perhaps," Gyles warned at Elspeth's pleased expression. "But you must please me well. Pleasure me, Elspeth! Play my harlot for this night."

"Whatever you desire, Gyles," Elspeth turned and led Gyles once again to her bed.

The councils spanned ten days and it was not until they were finished that Serena realized only a few days remained of their stay at court. By way of celebrating the completion of the councils, William ordered three days of festivities which would include hawking and a boar hunt. Serena was ecstatic because, save for the short forays she and Catherine had made, she had felt virtually a prisoner in the castle. Three days of glorious freedom! Well, almost. Serena would still have to attend the queen in the evenings, but the days would be her own.

"I can hardly believe it, Gyles!" Serena enthused as she shook out a lavender riding gown. "Matilda has excused me from my duties, so I will be able to ride for three days."

"Yes, well, take care you do not abuse that lovely seat of yours," Gyles warned with a trace of humor— the first he had shown in days. "You are hardly accustomed to living in a saddle."

"And you are, no doubt," Serena retorted with a grin. "Fear not, Gyles, I easily withstood the journey from Camden and I doubt a three-day ride will cause me any distress."

A playful slap on her buttocks brought Serena upright with a shriek and then she was lifted high in Gyles's arms and carried to the bed.

The sun, having been absent for the better part of a week, decided to lend its presence to William's festivities, and the day of the hunt promised to be crisp but clear and bright. The day lifted Serena's spirits even higher for during the past night, Gyles had lost his remoteness and been the tender husband she had long desired.

They broke their fast and then, with Bryan and Catherine, proceeded to the stables where their saddled mounts awaited them. Jocularity was the order of the day and as the courtiers set out, their laughter rang through the trees. Serena rode beside Gyles until a wild boar was sighted, then with a light admonishment to be careful, watched as he spurred his mount forward to be in on the kill. Catherine drew abreast of Serena and together they watched their men ride off.

269

"What pleasure they derive from this sport I fail to understand," Catherine said as Bryan disappeared.

"They are knights, men born to action and violent outlets for their feelings. They become restless when their tether is shortened and tempers flare when they are too long confined," Serena answered with a smile. "The king understands this. 'Tis far better they kill a boar than set upon each other."

"While we vent our restlessness on tapestries!" Catherine bristled.

"Catherine! Is that defiance I hear?" Serena asked in amusement.

Catherine ducked to avoid a tree limb. "No, not defiance, Serena, rather a sense of injustice at being dominated by men and restricted because I am a woman."

"Do not let Bryan hear that, or he will lay all the blame on me for your mood," Serena laughed.

" 'Tis amazing, Serena, but Bryan almost understands my feelings. He says what I feel is akin to what he does whenever he is slighted because he is a Saxon."

Serena nodded in agreement. "My brother is most observant." Then, with a sigh; "I only wish Gyles could understand as easily as Bryan does. But he tries, I know."

"Oh, yes, he certainly does try," Catherine commented drily. Immediately Catherine bit her lip when she caught the hurt expression on Serena's face.

"You do not know Gyles, Catherine. He is really a good man," Serena rebuked softly.

I know him only too well, Catherine thought bitterly, but aloud she said, " 'Tis only that he frightens me, Serena, you know that. I meant no insult."

"None is taken." Serena smiled. "Bryan tells me you will soon be visiting Broughton."

Catherine nodded, her face suddenly aglow. "Bryan plans to speak to your father and then offer for my hand. I have already written my mother and told her what to expect."

"Will your parents object?" Serena's brow furrowed briefly.

"No. They are most anxious for me to be wed. And

from what I have written my mother, Bryan sounds like St. George! Now what parent could reject such a suitor?"

Serena laughed along with Catherine. "You have made such a change in Bryan. He is far less angry now and takes to his wineskin less often. 'Tis a relief for me and I know Father will be pleased." From ahead came an excited shout and the high-pitched squeal of an animal in pain. Catherine and Serena exchanged a meaningful glance and then urged their horses toward the source of the excitement.

The clearing was ringed by a dozen men, some mounted, others on foot holding the reins of their mounts negligently in their hands. As Serena and Catherine entered the clearing along with the other women, Gyles was kneeling beside a dead boar from whose chest the shaft of his spear protruded. In one easy motion, Gyles pulled the knife from its sheath and slit the boar's neck, severing both arteries so that the life blood gushed onto the white blanket of snow. Savagely, Gyles lopped off the ears and tail as trophies of his conquest.

Serena had seen this sight many times before and normally it would not affect her, but there was a triumphant savagery in Gyles's actions and when he stood and his green eyes caught Serena in their gaze, she felt a shiver of apprehension course through her veins; for in Gyles's eyes there glittered a blood-lust and hatred that could not be denied. Even the lines of his face seemed to have changed; normally impassive, Gyles's features had hardened and set into a grim mask of barely controlled rage. A changeling, Serena's thoughts raced madly. No longer the gentle lover of the night past, but a brutal man possessed of ravening emotions. Within their locked gazes Serena felt a surge of emotion and she imagined she could hear Gyles's unspoken words. "I hate!" those eyes seemed to tell her. "There is too much vengeance within me to be appeased by anything in this world!" Fear ran icy fingers up Serena's back as she stared mesmerized at the gory prizes in Gyles's hands.

From Serena's left came a low, seductive laugh and

Serena swiveled in her saddle to see Elspeth, black eyes dancing, fixing Gyles with a provocative stare.

"Congratulations, Lord Gyles!" Elspeth's husky voice flooded the clearing. "As usual you are the first to draw blood."

Gyles's mouth twisted into a smile as he walked to Elspeth and dropped the bloody offering in her hand. "With my compliments, Lady Elspeth."

Elspeth leaned forward to murmur something to Gyles and Serena's chin lifted defiantly at the intimate gesture. If 'twas revenge for her behavior with Henry, Gyles was bent upon, Serena was not about to give him the satisfaction of seeing her jealousy. Elspeth's laughter rang out again and Serena felt several pairs of eyes turn to study her reaction. Serena carefully arranged her features into a mask of complete indifference and turned back to Catherine.

"If Elspeth doesn't remove her hands from Gyles," Serena ground out in a deadly voice but with an innocent smile playing on her lips, "I will scratch her eyes out."

Catherine's eyes registered alarm, but she sensed immediately Serena's purpose in the affected smile and let her crystal laugh carry over Elspeth's, drawing the attention of the hunting party. "You are toying with danger, Serena," Catherine warned softly. "Elspeth will not take kindly to our charade."

"Good!" Serena's smile widened into a grin. "Now why don't you go to Bryan."

"What are you planning?" Catherine asked fearfully.

"Why," Serena's eyes sparked with mischief and anger, "as our dear Henry would say, I intend to give Elspeth a lesson in manners! Now, do as I say and go to Bryan."

Serena waited until Catherine was safely ensconced by her brother's side and then with a light tap of her heel, Serena sent her mount forward. Gyles and Elspeth still conversed in hushed tones, oblivious to the looks they were drawing and both looked up in surprise when

Serena halted beside Elspeth. Elspeth regarded this intrusion with amusement, failing to see, as Gyles did in a shattering instant, the devil playing in Serena's flashing blue eyes.

Serena leaned across Elspeth and picked up one of the boar's ears, fingering it distastefully. "It seems too small a price," Serena mocked in a soft, thoughtful voice. "I thought you told me my husband was most generous in his rewards." Elspeth's face went white with rage but Serena ignored her and fixed her gaze on Gyles. "If your purse is lacking, m'lord, perhaps the Lady Elspeth would care for a golden necklace or emerald ring. She has long admired both." Serena made a show of dropping the blood ear back into Elspeth's shaking hand. "Next time, demand payment before the deed, 'twill place you in a better position to barter."

Another tap of her heel sent the horse crashing from the clearing and into the dense forest. Dimly, Serena heard Bryan calling her name and Serena hastened her pace, her wounded pride goading her away from the sound of the different hunting parties. She needed time— time for herself, time to cool the anger that was roiling inside her. Deliberately, Serena made her mind a blank, willing herself not to think, for if she did she would scream. Scream so loudly that all of London would hear.

The lovely Elspeth! Serena's mind spat. What had Catherine said? So beautiful on the outside, so evil inside! And Gyles, God rot him. Lusting after Elspeth even while Serena had bathed in the warm glow of the night before. No better than a prancing stallion after a brood mare. A cur fit for a bitch in heat. God rot his bastard soul!

"Well, our dear Lady Serena."

That harsh voice could only belong to one man and with a mixture of horror and anger Serena felt the reins being jerked from her hands.

"Your Highness," Serena saluted the prince formally, coolly, then gasped as hands went about her waist to lift her from the saddle. William Rufus held Serena suspended

273

in mid-air, his dark eyes glowing at her indignation. "Put me down . . . Your Highness." The last was almost an afterthought.

William Rufus grinned at his alluring captive. "There is a price for everything, sweet Saxon. Shall I name mine?"

Serena's eyes widened in disbelief. "Unhand me, Your Highness. Now!"

William's grin broadened as Serena pummeled at his shoulders with her delicate fists. "You did not struggle thus in Henry's embrace, I'll wager. Come now, Saxon, I can offer you far more than my brother. You would like to remain at court, would you not? I can arrange it. You need no longer wait upon my mother—I can arrange that also. There are apartments next to mine—they are yours!" William's breath was foul with wine and Serena twisted her head to avoid his mouth.

"No!" Serena shrieked.

"I command it!" William roared, and then crushed Serena against him.

William's thick lips twisted brutally upon hers, prying Serena's lips apart so that his tongue could rape the recesses of her mouth. Serena's stomach churned at the wet, unwanted pressure. Outraged, Serena brought a hand up to claw at William's face. Four deep gouges appeared across William's cheek and immediately welled with blood.

Furious, William released Serena and with a tremendous shove, sent her hurtling backward against a tree. The breath left Serena's lungs with a whoosh and before she could recover, William was upon her, his hands tearing aside her cloak to expose the creamy skin of her throat and breasts that rose above the neckline of her gown. William's eyes kindled with lust and he buried his face in the sweet curve of Serena's neck.

"You are beautiful!" William muttered hoarsely against her flesh as his hands slid around her waist and up her back to jerk the snood from Serena's hair. Obligingly the gold-touched curls tumbled into his hands

274

and William wound them around Serena's throat. "Small wonder Gyles kept you hidden away. The miser! He wished to keep you all for himself. But no more!"

Serena struggled vainly against William's overwhelming strength. This could not be happening! William would not dare. . . . But he did, he was. Those destructive hands had fallen from Serena's hair and had plunged into the neckline of her gown to fondle her breasts. Oh, no! Serena moaned helplessly and William mistook her fear for passion and pressed himself against her so that she could feel his rising manhood.

"I must have you. . . . I will!" William's voice was thick and his fetid breath fell upon Serena's cheek. William ignored Serena's feeble protests and cursing the strength of the material, ripped Serena's bodice diagonally from the shoulder to the waist, exposing the light fabric of her kirtle. "Ask for anything and it shall be yours. Jewels, furs . . . you will be the envy of every woman at court. Even when I take a wife, none will dare insult you. God's blood, but you will be lovely in my bed!" The kirtle went the way of her gown and with horror, Serena felt William's lips at her breasts, and then his teeth bit into her tender flesh.

Sheer terror lent strength to her voice and Serena's scream echoed through the trees.

William's blood-suffused face loomed above her and Serena shrank from the look in his eyes.

"Who do you think will hear? You ran away from your party and there are no others here. And if there were, the trees make it impossible to tell from which direction your cry came. No, my little Saxon, what you gave my brother you will also give to me. Here! Now!"

"I would rather die than have you touch me!" Serena spat at William. She kicked out at William and landed a telling blow on his leg. Serena was released, briefly, and she whirled out of William's grasp, clutching what remained of her bodice to cover herself. "Lay another hand on me and I will kill you!"

William bore down upon Serena, his dark eyes hard

as polished stones at her defiance. "You have defied me over much these past weeks, Saxon, and I will tolerate it no longer. I want you and I shall have you!"

Serena didn't see the meaty hand draw back; she only felt the stunning force that descended upon the side of her face and heard the resounding slap as the back of William's hand met her flesh. The force of the blow sent Serena sprawling backward in the snow and bright sparks of color danced in front of her eyes. Dazedly, Serena focused on William as he dropped on top of her. She tried to scream again only to find her voice cut off by another slap to her face. Dear God, Serena implored silently as William's lips traveled down her throat while he held her pinned helplessly beneath his weight. Serena twisted her head from side to side trying to avoid William's seeking mouth. Her hands came up to scratch at William's face and eyes. Serena's nails dug into his ears, tore into his neck and came away crimson with blood, which earned her a quick succession of four more blows. Abruptly, William's bulk lifted and with horror Serena watched as he fumbled at his short tunic and leggings. Her feet came up to strike wildly at him, but William seized upon the frantic movement to force Serena's legs apart and flip up the skirt of her gown. One small fist flailed upward and through sheer chance, made contact with William's eye before Serena's efforts were stilled once more by his brawny form. William's mouth descended with bruising force on Serena's lips, but his victorious chuckle was cut short as Serena's teeth sank with a determined vengeance into his bottom lip.

William's head reared back. "Saxon slut!" he snarled. "I'll . . ." The words died, his expression freezing into one of disbelief.

Serena lay half-panting, half-sobbing, staring up at William's inert form, the salty taste of blood in her mouth, wondering at the sudden change in her attacker. The next moment gave Serena her answer.

"Get up, Will." A quiet, deadly, masculine voice came from somewhere behind Serena. William didn't move, instead his bruised and bloodied features contorted into an ugly travesty of a smile. "Get up, Will," the soft voice repeated, "or I'll kill you right now."

Like a ripple in a pool, some emotion quivered across William's face and disappeared, and he slowly raised himself away from Serena. Serena promptly scrambled to her feet and with one hand clasping the torn material to her bosom, felt a hand close around her arm to draw her away from William. Only one man would dare address the crown prince as Will, and Serena raised her eyes to Matilda's youngest child, the third of three sons: Henry. A small cry escaped Serena and Henry spared a brief smile for her. One hand balanced a light sword and with the other Henry reached up to unclasp his cloak and drag it from his shoulders.

"Put this on, Lady Serena. My guards will be here shortly, and I would rather you were decently covered." Henry's eyes shifted back to William as the older brother rose and adjusted his clothing.

"You are bewitched, Henry. I was only doing as the lady bid me. If she prefers my embrace to yours"— William raised his shoulders in a shrug—"you are better off without her."

Henry's eyes flicked over William's bloodied face. "And you are a liar, Will. Arm yourself." Henry's voice was devoid of emotion.

William laughed. "Little brother, do you challenge me over this . . . this Saxon? Henry, put down—"

William made a step toward Henry and stopped in amazement as Henry's sword cut through his tunic.

"No!" Serena leaped forward and grasped Henry's free arm. "Henry, no! He didn't . . ." Serena faltered. "He didn't."

Henry studied Serena's pale face and tensed when he saw the purple bruises forming on her cheeks. One slender hand reached up to gently touch the now-swelling flesh.

"Please," Serena whispered. "He is your brother, Henry, you must not do him harm." Serena winced as Henry exerted a light pressure on her bruises.

At last Henry nodded. "I'll take you back to the

277

palace; get your horse." Serena hurried away and Henry returned his attention to his brother. "If you ever dare touch her again, brother or not, I *will* kill you." The point of Henry's blade circled William's bared neck. "Heed my words, brother, for your life depends upon your obedience to them."

Two of Henry's guards appeared, and Henry motioned them forward. "Prince William has met with an accident," Henry said blithely. "See that he returns safely to his chambers and that the royal physician tends to his wounds immediately."

William made to protest then thought better of the idea and stamped off to mount his horse. A grim smile played on Henry's lips as he watched his brother ride off.

"Henry?" Serena laid a hand on his arm.

"I will have to kill him one day," Henry said thoughtfully, then seeing the look on Serena's face he smiled coldly. "He must die, Serena, surely you above all others can see that? Do you want such a mad beast to rule England?"

Serena considered Henry for a moment. "I want what is best for England," Serena said slowly. "And I doubt England would be best served by bloodshed—we've had enough of that for several lifetimes."

Henry's eyes bore a far-off look. "Just one more life—only one. When he is gone . . ." Henry's voice trailed off and he smiled down at Serena. "Are you sure you can ride, Serena?"

"Yes, Henry. I wish only to get away from here as quickly as possible." Serena gingerly fingered her cheeks.

Henry carefully lifted Serena onto her saddle and swung up onto his own mount. "Your bruises will fade more quickly than William's torn flesh," Henry laughed. "I doubt he expected such a struggle."

A shiver passed over Serena as she remembered William's lips at her throat, and a new thought struck her. What would Gyles say at her battered appearance? She could not tolerate accusations, not after today, and Gyles would most certainly accuse her of something.

Serena weaved in her saddle, her limbs growing weak as reaction to her near-rape set in.

"Henry!" Serena could barely force the name through her stiff lips.

Instantly Henry was beside Serena, his arm going out to steady her.

"I'm going to be ill," Serena whispered shakily.

Henry bore her to the ground and held her shoulders while she retched and afterward, bathed her face with clean snow. Serena leaned her head gratefully against Henry's shoulder.

"How did you find me?" Serena asked when she found the strength to speak.

"My party was not far away, and I heard your scream. I didn't know 'twas you, of course, I thought someone had fallen under a boar's tusks; so two of my men and I began to search. I had almost despaired of finding the victim when I stumbled upon you and William. Whatever possessed you to ride out alone, Serena?" Henry's voice held a reprimand.

"I . . ." Serena hesitated, then shook her head. " 'Tis a private matter."

Henry stroked the willful gold-streaked curls back from Serena's face. "Your husband? No, you needn't answer, I know of no other reason that would cause you such distress." Henry gave a humorless laugh. "I know not who I hate more, Gyles or William. Right now I feel I could kill them both!"

Serena began to weep and Henry's arms went about her shoulders to offer what comfort he could. "I was so frightened, Henry! He . . . William . . . was like an animal—he wouldn't stop! I tried, Henry, truly I did, but—Dear Lord! he wouldn't stop! What will I do if he tries again?"

"He won't, I shall see to that," Henry replied grimly, then his agile mind took up a different point. "Where was your noble husband while all this was happening?" Henry gritted out.

"We argued . . . I ran away. . . It doesn't matter, Henry. I'm sorry, I did not mean to burden you." Serena

279

brushed at the tears that hung on her eyelashes. "I haven't thanked you, have I?"

Henry gazed down at Serena's tear-streaked, bruised face and felt his heart wrench. "Dearest Serena, you need not thank me. I only wish I had found you sooner . . . before William. But I shall make certain he does not trouble you again." Henry stopped as he felt a tremor pass through Serena. "Come, we must get you back before the hunting parties return."

This time Henry took no chances, but placed Serena in front of him on his steed. As he guided his horse through the trees Henry cursed Gyles as a thrice-damned fool for not taking more care with his precious wife; and William as a lecherous goat who deserved a slow, agonizing death for his actions. The scene he had witnessed flashed again and again through Henry's mind, and each time it repeated, Henry felt the cold rage build higher in his breast. There was no doubt—William had to be taught a lesson, punished; the only question was how. A thought struck Henry and he smiled inwardly— William had been relieved that their father had not ordered him to accompany the forces that were to patrol the Scottish border, but possibly, just possibly, the king could be persuaded otherwise. Indeed, William would be taught, but very subtly.

The horse shied, and glancing down Serena saw the prostrate form of an animal partially hidden by undergrowth. With a start Serena found herself in the clearing she had so recently fled.

" 'Tis the boar Gyles killed," Serena informed Henry. "Why would they leave—"

Henry clapped a hand gently over Serena's mouth and then pointed to the edge of the clearing where two horses aimlessly wandered. From the woods beyond came the sound of a woman's laugh mixed with the deep tones of a man's voice.

"I believe we have stumbled upon a tryst," Henry whispered in her ear.

"We had better not have," Serena returned fiercely, "for I know the rider of one of those steeds." Henry turned their mount to leave the clearing but Serena's hand stayed his. "Take me over there, Henry."

"Serena, I do not think . . ."

"I know I have demanded much of you already, but this one last thing I would ask." Serena raised her face to Henry's and the expression in her eyes destroyed Henry's resistance.

"Very well." Henry rolled his eyes heavenward and sighed.

Henry might have spared himself the debate with his conscience for at that moment two figures appeared near the horses. The smaller of the two paused to brush at something on her cloak and as her head lifted Serena gave a muted cry. Standing in front of them, dark eyes shining with laughter, stood Elspeth.

"M'lord," Elspeth called over her shoulder, "we have been found out."

The man moved from behind the horses and Henry felt Serena stiffen in his arms.

"Gyles, dear, should you not greet your wife?" Elspeth laughed. "Come, cherie, you are being rude."

Gyles stood rooted to the ground at the sight of his wife. What had happened to Serena's face? She looked as if she had been thrown from her horse or hit by a branch—which was not surprising considering the way she had bolted from the clearing. But the look in her eyes! Never had Gyles seen such pain reflected in those luminous eyes—it cut through him like a dagger and severed his soul into innumerable pieces. Serena, Gyles's mind cried out. I meant not . . .

"It seems, Your Highness, that we have intruded," Serena's voice was cold and remote, totally devoid of any emotion whatsoever, and it sounded strange even to her own ears. To Gyles it was unbelievable. Serena fought back, she always had! Never had she leashed her emotions so tightly where he was concerned. Serena shouted, raged, cried, shrieked—but never had she displayed such control, and this frightened him more than the night she had threatened him at sword point.

"Lady Serena," Elspeth sneered. "You look quite

281

bruised. Perhaps Gyles should take you back to your chamber?"

Serena's eyes were like chips of ice as she glanced between Gyles and his mistress. Norman honor! she thought bitterly. He would take me to task for breaking my vows when he thinks nothing of easing himself upon the first available female.

"I would not consider leaving you without an escort, Lady Elspeth," Serena replied in that same cold voice. "I am sure His Highness will not mind making the trip with me." Then turning to Henry she spoke in a voice that barely carried to his ears. "Take me away, Henry. Please."

Henry complied without hesitation and as Gyles watched their departure, he wondered that Serena did not spare him a backward glance.

Gradually, in the late afternoon, the hunting parties returned to the castle; some the worse for the energy expended on the hunt while others rocked unsteadily from too frequent use of their wineskins. Gyles was among the first to return—his impulse to follow Serena had been checked by the knowledge that she needed time to cool her anger before he could reason with her and Elspeth had offered the most entertaining diversion. But the day had waned considerably since their confrontation, and as Gyles strode through the corridors of the palace, he felt confident that Serena would hear him out. Serena loved him and she herself had often told him that her love could overcome every obstacle.

A frown marred Gyles's brow when he approached his chamber and saw the two guards posted by the door. The men bore the royal standard on their tunics and Gyles could think of no reason why his chamber should be placed under guard. The men stood impassively, appearing not to notice Gyles until he tried to enter his chamber. Before Gyles's hand could reach the latch the guards had crossed the weapons they held so that the entrance was effectively barred.

"This is my chamber!" Gyles protested.

282

"That may be, m'lord, but we have orders to allow no one to pass," one of the burly guards answered.

"Orders? Whose orders?" Gyles's anger was kindled and his scar began to whiten. Barred from his own chamber, kept from his wife—on whose authority?

"The orders are mine, Lord Gyles."

The soft voice spun Gyles around to see Henry leaning against the opposite wall, his face half-concealed in shadows.

"The physician is attending your wife—I wanted to insure he would suffer no interruptions. When the leech is finished, the guards will leave and you will be free to enter." Henry eyed Gyles calmly.

Gyles advanced upon the smaller man. "What happened to my wife?"

Surprisingly, Henry laughed, a harsh ugly laugh. "That should have been asked earlier, don't you think? When you first laid eyes upon your wife in the clearing? What stilled your tongue then, the presence of your whore? What will you do if Serena dies?"

Gyles's face blanched. "Die?" He echoed dumbly. "Serena die?"

Henry muttered an oath and with a shake of his head began to pace. "Your wife is bruised, nothing more. But in the time it took you to arrive she could have died twenty times over."

Gyles flinched guiltily under Henry's words. He, not Henry, should have carried Serena back to the palace. He did not know how badly Serena was injured nor how she came to be hurt. And had he cared? Had he gone to her and seen she was cared for? No! Instead he had gone to Elspeth and . . . The door swung open and the physician appeared, followed by two of his colleagues. The physician waved them away before approaching Henry for a whispered consultation. Henry nodded as the physician spoke and then dismissed the physician and motioned the guards to leave the corridor. Henry stood contemplating the door of Serena's chamber before turning to face Gyles.

"She is well," Henry said contemptuously. "You may now return to your harlot with a clear conscience."

Gyles brushed past Henry and burst into the chamber.

Serena heard the door open and knew Gyles stood watching her. Serena flicked the bed curtains closed and walked deliberately to the armoire to pull out a gown. The door shut and Serena felt Gyles's eyes bore into her as she seated herself and began to comb the snarled locks of her hair. Serena refused to look at Gyles or speak, but kept her back carefully turned toward him.

"Serena?" Gyles's voice startled her, and Serena's fingers tightened convulsively around the comb. Oh, damn him, damn him! Why couldn't he leave . . .

"Serena," Gyles coaxed. "Shouldn't you be in bed?"

"Matilda expects me to dress her hair," Serena replied in a cold voice.

"Surely you aren't going to attend her tonight!" Gyles was incredulous.

"I have no choice—the queen commands and I obey. 'Tis what my life is made of: duties and obligations." Serena dropped the gown over her head and began to tie the bows. "Do not fear, I shall be dining with Matilda in her chambers tonight. It seems she has taken a chill from the hunt and has retired to her bed until the morrow. So you will be spared any embarrassment I might cause by my appearance."

"I want to explain—" Gyles began.

But Serena continued relentlessly. "I think it would be best if I made my pallet elsewhere—unless you have already made such arrangements. Catherine will not mind if I share her chamber until you leave the court. Or I could request a chamber of my own, but that would start tongues wagging. Perhaps you should move into Elspeth's chamber, 'twould cause no surprise among the court. Discretion is most important, don't you agree?"

"Serena!" Gyles seized her shoulders and spun Serena about. His face paled, then contorted in pain when he saw her battered features. Tentatively, Gyles's fingers stroked the swollen, mottled flesh that shrank from his touch. "Your face," Gyles whispered raggedly. "How . . ."

Serena stared at him then gave a twisted smile that sent a fresh bolt of pain tearing through Gyles while her eyes remained impassive. "Will you release me, please?"

Gyles did so reluctantly but steadfastly remained in her path. "Tell me what happened."

Serena's laugh was dry and harsh. "I was thrown from my horse. What did you think—that one of your fine Norman lords attacked me?"

Gyles eyed Serena's bruises suspiciously. "Those marks were not made by a simple fall."

"No?" Serena feigned surprise. "Perhaps I should have told you that I was thrown against a tree."

"Tell me what happened—the truth, Serena!" Gyles demanded as he reached out to grab her shoulders.

Serena fled from his advance. "Don't touch me!" She cried, then quieted at the incredulous look on his face. "I have been mauled enough today. Now I have told you the truth and you have showed the proper concern for my state of health, so I see no reason to continue this discussion. Will you stand aside and allow me to pass?"

"You misunderstood what you saw today. Serena, Elspeth is—"

"Don't!" Serena spoke quietly but with such vehemence that Gyles's words died a swift death. "I have no wish to hear more lies and excuses for your lust. Take your ease with anyone you please, but spare me this . . . this humiliation. Leave me some dignity at least." Serena's chin lifted defiantly. "The queen is expecting me, so will you please stand aside?"

"Not until I have your word that you will hear me out." Gyles rested his broad shoulders against the door and fixed Serena with an inflexible gaze. "When I have had my say, then you may decide whether you share Catherine's chamber—but not before!"

Serena passed a trembling hand across her brow. " 'Twill do no good! I have already decided—"

"Your word, Serena," Gyles insisted.

"Or you keep me here?" Serena laughed raggedly. "Your Norman arrogance is not to be believed! I am not one of your men and I refuse to be ordered—"

" 'Tis your choice." Gyles shrugged. "When you regain your senses you can leave."

Serena whirled away to study the fire. "Very well," she sighed. "You have my word I shall not go to Catherine until we have spoken."

"Your word of honor?" Gyles would not release Serena until she reaffirmed her oath.

"I have told you," Serena said dully. "I have given you my word of honor."

Satisfied, Gyles stood aside and opened the door for Serena.

"Remember," Gyles warned as Serena glided past.

" 'Tis not likely I shall forget." Serena answered.

Gyles watched as Serena sped through the hallway and out of sight. Confident, Gyles crossed to the table, pulled parchment and quill toward him and began to write. Three pages were covered with his sure hand before Gyles paused and reread the lines he had penned. A wry smile played about his mouth as Gyles boldly fixed his signature and seal to the bottom of each page. Each parchment was quickly folded, a few additional words inscribed and a larger seal stamped into the soft wax on the edges of each page. Soon, Gyles thought as he strode off in search of his retinue. Soon his life would be set aright.

Gyles was in good humor throughout the evening meal and the entertainment which followed. To Catherine, Gyles played the courtly gallant, and she began to glimpse the virtues Serena had often defended. Toward Bryan, Gyles retained an air of respect, refusing to be drawn into any argument and even agreeing that his behavior during the hunt had been shameful.

"I have already been taken to task on that point," Gyles told them cheerfully. And Catherine and Bryan exchanged bewildered looks at his exuberance. "Tell me," Gyles leaned back in his chair and contemplated the workmanship of his goblet. "Do you think Serena would be pleased with the gift of a mount—or perhaps several pelts of silver fox for the trimming on the grey velvet you gave her?"

Bryan's mouth fell open then closed with a snap as he overcame his disbelief. Catherine was more direct. "I think 'twould please her more to learn the truth about Elspeth."

Gyles smiled indulgently. "Ah, Catherine, you have indeed learned much from my wife."

Bryan came to a blushing Catherine's rescue. "I cannot find any fault with that, Gyles."

"Nor do I, Bryan." Gyles raised his hands in mock defense. "But you may think differently when Catherine lets you feel the sharp edge of her tongue. Then, perhaps, you and I can comfort each other when we are flayed raw by our wives." Gyles drained his cup and rose to sketch a bow. "*Adieu,* my friends."

Gyles's high spirits prevailed as he whiled away the hours in his chamber awaiting Serena's return. The night drew on and Gyles banked the fire repeatedly to keep the chill from invading the chamber; he sipped sparingly from the mulled wine—and waited. He began a game of chess, playing against himself—and waited. The sound of a passing footstep would send him flying from the chair to the door and more than once Gyles was confronted by an astounded guard. With a muttered apology Gyles returned to his chair to continue his vigil. And Gyles waited. Gyles's patience had overflowed its boundaries when dawn lightened the midnight blue of the sky. Head pounding, eyes red from lack of sleep, Gyles hurled himself from the chamber and through the palace corridors until he stood in front of the door to Catherine's chamber.

When there was no response to his knock, one foot drew up and back, then descended upon the portal with a force that separated the timbers. Ignoring the jagged, protruding splinters, Gyles thrust his way into the chamber, the look on his face stilling the cry that trembled on Catherine's lips.

"Where is she?" Gyles growled, heedless of the frantic

effort Catherine was making to drag the coverlet about her shoulders.

"Wha—what do you mean?" Catherine shrank against the headboard as Gyles advanced upon the bed.

"Serena—my wife! where is she?" Gyles grabbed Catherine's wrist.

"I don't know!" Catherine cried.

"You lie!" Gyles's grip tightened.

"Nay!" Catherine sobbed. "I do not know of what you speak."

Gyles released her arm and struggled to bring his rage under control. "Serena did not return to our chamber last night after waiting upon the queen. I thought perhaps—"

Catherine's raised hand silenced Gyles. "Serena was not in attendance last night. Matilda was told Serena had taken ill and was resting."

Gyles shook his head as if to clear it. "That is not possible, Serena sent no message and she went to the queen before the meal."

"I thought it odd you said nothing at table," Catherine mused aloud, "but then I assumed 'twas not serious."

"Bryan!" Gyles's head snapped up. "Did Serena go to Bryan?"

Catherine shook her head. "He did not say, but if she had, I am sure Bryan would have told me."

"Will you go to the queen? See if Serena attended her after you retired?"

"Of course, immediately—if you would step outside so I may dress?" Catherine glanced meaningfully at the door and for a brief moment thought a blush rose in Gyles's face.

Gyles paced impatiently outside the queen's chamber as he waited for Catherine to emerge, his thoughts veering from rage over Serena's behavior to bleak despair over her whereabouts. When Catherine appeared and gave a shake of her head, Gyles drove a fist into the palm of his other hand; and when Catherine informed him that Matilda had received a second note from Serena begging permission to withdraw from court, his hand shot out and Catherine found herself dragged along in Gyles's wake to a different part of the palace where Bryan took his rest.

Roused out of a sound sleep, Bryan could do no more than glare at his sister's husband until he caught sight of Catherine waiting in the hall.

"Close the door, Catherine!" Bryan barked, then rose and began to pull on his clothing. "Now what the devil is so important that you find it necessary to disturb my rest? And what is Catherine doing with you?"

"Do you know where Serena is?" Gyles demanded bluntly.

"I do not make a habit of knowing my sister's whereabouts," Bryan snapped. "As you can plainly see, Serena is most certainly not here. Serena is your wife, Gyles, 'tis not my fault if you have misplaced her."

"Serena is not a piece of armor I mislay!" Gyles replied irritably.

"No?" Bryan retorted as his head emerged from his tunic. "It appeared differently yesterday. Mayhap if you spent less time dallying with Lady Elspeth you would know where Serena is."

"I waited the night through!" Gyles flung out.

"And how long has Serena waited?" Bryan threw back. "If Serena does not wish your company I cannot find fault with her, in fact I applaud her decision. Would to God she had made it months ago! You would have spared my family much, Gyles, had you refused my father's offer and allowed Serena to marry Richard."

Gyles stormed from the room and for the remainder of the morning haunted the places within the castle that Serena frequented. Solars, sewing rooms, music rooms, all were empty, for the courtiers were enjoying the second day of the hunt. In desperation Gyles descended to the stables and found Serena's horse still in its stall. If Serena had decided to join the hunt while awaiting Matilda's permission to leave the court, she would have ridden her own mount, Gyles knew; and had she already left William's court, her steed would also be missing. Frus-

289

trated, Gyles returned to the palace, his footsteps crunching hollowly in the light dusting of snow, when a startling thought struck him.

The corridors echoed as Gyles ran past the public rooms toward the royal apartments, ignoring the astonished guards he passed and at last halting and speaking to a knight who guarded the entrance to one of the royal chambers. The guard disappeared with Gyles's request and a moment later he reopened the door to admit Gyles.

The chamber was dimly lit by less than its full complement of candles and the fire in the hearth had been carefully banked so that while it warmed the room it emitted little light. Lustrous fur pelts littered the floor, tapestries sewn with gold and silver threads hung from the ceiling to the floor and in the semi-darkness they caught and reflected what light was available. Near the fire a shadow moved, then resolved itself into the form of a slender man.

"Your Highness." Gyles bowed.

"Lord Gyles." Henry's voice held a faint trace of amusement. "Rise, sit here by the fire. Wine?" Gyles shook his head and Henry settled back comfortably into his own chair.

"I have come—" Gyles began.

"I know why you are here, Lord Gyles. In truth, I expected you much later, but 'twould appear your wife underestimated the effect her absence would have on you. She was under the impression you would search here as a last resort."

"Then you know—" A slim hand silenced Gyles yet again.

A folded leaf of parchment appeared in Henry's hand and he extended it to Gyles. "She asked that I give this to you if you bothered to try and find her. Apparently she doubted your . . . fidelity." Henry folded his hands beneath his chin and turned to study the fire.

Wordlessly, Gyles unfolded the parchment and scanned its contents. His face grim and his scar white

290

when he had finished, Gyles carefully refolded the note and placed it inside his tunic before he spoke.

"Do you know where Serena has gone?" Gyles, too, watched the fire.

"Nay." Henry's eyes did not move from the flame.

"Did Serena tell you what was in this letter?"

"Nay." The quiet voice seemed to fill the room. At last Henry shifted to face Gyles. "Nor do I wish to know. She has fled from both of us now—I did not ask her reasons but did only what I could. All that she asked me for I would gladly have given ten times over."

Gyles drew a pouch from his tunic. "Serena asked that I repay you for that which she borrowed . . ."

Henry sprang to his feet with a disgusted snort. "Your lady owes me naught! Did you not hear? I freely gave that which she needed—all that I gave is hers, not mine! She is my friend! Between us there can be no debt."

"Will you tell me where Serena has gone? I must find her." Gyles rose also and moved closer to the fire.

Henry passed a slender hand across his eyes. "That in truth I cannot do, for she did not confide in me. She came to me before the evening meal to ask for a few coins. Did you know she had decided to run away alone? Without benefit of guards? When I learned she was determined to leave, I insisted she have a small escort. Four of my knights ride with her to her destination; she will return them to me when she is safe. I also gave her a steed, for she was determined to take nothing that belonged to you, and I would not see her walk."

Gyles nodded and closed his eyes briefly. He knew Serena's temper well enough to believe what Henry said was true. And the emotionless note Serena had left confirmed Gyles's fear that she had told no one where she had fled. "I would question your guards when they return, Your Highness."

"As you wish," Henry agreed. "It may mean prolonging your stay and I understand you must return to Camden to gather your men for my father's Scottish campaign."

"Then, Your Highness, if you would question—"

"No!" Henry wheeled toward Gyles. "That I will not do! Find her any way you please, but I will not aid you. Mayhap Lady Elspeth can help you in your search!" Henry brought his emotions under control with an effort. "I have done as your lady requested, Lord Gyles. My solemn oath to her is fulfilled. There is no reason for us to meet until my knights return. I will not strive to keep you from your wife, but I will not actively support your cause, for by all that is holy, you are not worthy of her. If you find her, remind your lady my offer remains should she ever have need of it. You are excused from my presence."

Gyles bowed from the room and returned to his chamber. Serena's tapestry frame still stood by the window, its very presence accusing Gyles of his folly. Gyles strode to the bed and tore back the curtains to stare at the pelt-covered mattress. Cushioned in the middle of the fur—exactly as her note had said—were Serena's gold chain necklace and emerald ring.

12

The greying, battle-scarred knight cast a wary eye at the growing cloud banks building in the evening sky. They foretold no good, he thought wearily. He could see the wind gathering in the clouds, which meant the castle was due for another pelting of sleet or snow. The knight drew his cloak tighter around his armor. Sleet, he thought unhappily. The weather had taken a decidedly evil turn since the young mistress had arrived several weeks ago. He glanced at the slight form that paced the battlements in front of him. He had not seen his mistress since she had been a lass of twelve and the promise of beauty he had seen then had come true over the past years. Although when she had hailed the guard the night of her return and he had first set eyes upon her, the sight of her bruised face had taken him aback. But the bruises had faded since then and the beauty had reappeared but with a lack of vitality. His mistress did not live, he reflected sadly, she merely existed, going through the motions of life without conscious thought. And where was her husband? Not once had his mistress mentioned his name or the fact that she had even wed.

"Sir Cyril!" The lilting voice broke through the knight's thoughts, and with a sigh he moved to his mistress's side. "Some of these stones have loosened." A slender hand picked at the mortar and held the crumbled mixture for his perusal. "On the morrow gather some of the men and see to its repair."

"Yes, m'lady." A gust of wind blew across the battlements, causing Cyril to huddle deeper in the folds of his cloak. " 'Tis likely to storm again tonight, Lady Serena. 'Twould be best if you retired."

Sapphire eyes turned upward to reflect the light of the torches. "Dear Cyril, still afraid I will take a chill?" Serena laughed at Cyril's embarrassment. "Rest easy, Sir Cyril, I have long since passed the time when I am hustled off to bed by my nurse. See that the guards receive mulled wine every two hours to warm them throughout the night."

Cyril's reply was lost to her as Serena descended from the battlements. Her chamber greeted her with an enveloping warmth and Serena spared a brief smile for the young girl who was filling a tub with steaming water. Serena quickly disrobed and sank gratefully into the tub. A cake of soap was offered and Serena leisurely lathered herself from head to toe, allowing the delicate scent and hot water to drive the tension from her body.

But while her body responded to the ministrations, Serena's mind busied itself with the repairs and changes that had to be made in the castle. Serena made certain that her thoughts were fully occupied during her waking hours, for in a moment's idleness her treacherous mind returned to Camden and a tall green-eyed man whose very memory could cause her eyes to fill with tears. Above all else, memories were to be stored away in a far portion of her mind, to be taken out later—years from now—and perhaps then remembrance would not be as painful.

Serena rose from the water and toweled herself briskly, bringing a rosy hue to her satiny skin, before slipping into a nightgown. Serena eased onto the bed and drew the covers over her shoulders, deliberately closing her mind to the thoughts that hovered near her consciousness. "I want nothing from Gyles!" she had angrily declared to Henry, and now, Serena laughed bitterly at the ceiling. How could she forget, pretend an entire year of her life had never been? How was it possible to shut away the memories, the pain, the love? No, Gyles was a part of her, more so now than he had ever been; a portion of herself Serena could not always hide away.

It had been easy at first; there was so much to be done to make her new home comfortable. The commonplace needs of her life had occupied Serena totally until recently. Repairs to the castle and buildings were nearly completed; logs, food, all had been prepared. But now time was heavy on Serena's hands and no matter how hard she tried, Serena's thoughts turned more often to her ill-fated marriage. Serena delivered a solid blow to the pillow then sank back and closed her eyes, resolved to find sleep.

It seemed only minutes later that a hand on her shoulder was shaking her from her rest.

"M'lady? Lady Serena?" Serena's eyes flew open and she stared at the white face above her. "Lady Serena, Sir Cyril told me to wake you."

The young serving girl was so obviously afraid Serena would take offense at being disturbed that she smiled reassuringly. " 'Tis all right, you need not fear. What is it Sir Cyril desires?"

"There is an armed force beyond the drawbridge demanding Sir Cyril allow them entrance."

Serena leaped from the bed and ran to the battlements, belting a heavy chamber robe around her waist as she went. Heart pounding, she found Cyril peering over the battlement and hurried to his side. No one knew her whereabouts save the men who had accompanied her, unless Henry . . .

"What standard do they wear, Sir Cyril, can you see?" Serena also leaned over the battlement to inspect the armed gathering below.

"Nay, m'lady, they have declared themselves to be from Camden. The one who leads them calls himself Edward." Cyril withdrew from the edge and turned to his mistress. "Shall I allow them to enter, Lady Serena?"

Her initial despair had lessened with the knowledge that Gyles was not present in this force, and Serena trembled in relief. For the first time Serena realized it had begun to sleet and sharp gusts of wind bit through her robe and whipped her hair around her face and shoulders. Serena's hands and feet stung from the cold.

"Lower the drawbridge, Sir Cyril. They are my husband's men and I will not have them freeze for lack of shelter. Do what you can for their mounts and their own quarters—they may have to sleep in the stables this night, but 'tis better than naught. I will have a light repast prepared for them before they retire."

Serena disappeared into the castle, leaving Cyril to deliver the necessary commands. In her chamber while she hurriedly donned a gown, Serena could hear the tramping of armored feet in the hall below. Serena paused in the midst of tying a bow—Why hadn't Gyles come himself? I should be glad he has stayed away, Serena told herself fiercely. But the thought of being delegated to Edward's care still rankled her pride. Aware she was postponing the inevitable, Serena hurriedly finished dressing and ran to the great hall.

Edward stood by the fire, conversing with Cyril; both looked up when Serena entered.

"I bid you welcome, Sir Edward." Serena extended her hand and smiled as Edward bent over it. " 'Tis a fearsome night to be abroad, Sir Edward, so I can only guess that your errand is most urgent."

" 'Twas not my doing that drove us through this weather . . ." Edward began, then subsided when he glanced over Serena's head. "M'lady, I should explain, I am not—"

But Serena had already turned toward the source of Edward's hesitation and her eyes widened in shock.

"Will you not bid me welcome as well, m'lady?" Gyles moved forward to take Serena's cold hand and raise it to his equally cold lips.

"You!" Serena whispered. "Why . . ."

A crushing grip on her fingers cautioned Serena to silence. "My men have traveled far these past days, m'lady. Is there wine and perhaps some meat that they may ease their hunger?"

Serena twisted from Gyles's grasp and motioned to one of the housecarls. In a short time the tables were loaded with platters and flagons and Gyles's men fell upon them ravenously. Gyles eyed the scene with satisfaction before turning to Serena.

"I assume your chamber is warm. I will have a bath and take my meal there. And you shall wait upon me." Gyles stretched his hands toward the fire.

"I will not!" Serena's eyes sparkled in indignation.

"You will do as I say, Serena." Gyles was adamant. "Show me to your chamber then bring me meat and wine."

Serena started to protest, then thought better of it. With a slight nod, Serena led the way up a winding set of stairs to her chamber. Inside she issued instructions to her maid, and the young girl hurried to do her bidding. Serena swung the kettle of hot water from the fire and poured it into the tub. The maid returned with three housecarls also bearing water, which was emptied into the tub as well. When the door closed behind them, Gyles lowered himself onto the bed.

"Since my squire is below, you shall have to act in his stead and remove my armor."

Her lips set in a grim line, Serena moved to the bed and started unbuckling the leather straps of the breast-plate. The metal was freezing to her touch and Serena involuntarily pitied Gyles for the long hours he had spent inside the cold armor. Even when covered by a warm cloak, armor offered little protection against the winter elements; while the knight within was sheltered from the harsh wind, the metal unfortunately assumed the temperature of the weather, which meant that if a man was away from a source of heat for too long a time he could easily fall victim to frostbite and chilblains. More than one knight had stripped off his gauntlets to find his fingers red and so painfully swollen that movement was nearly impossible.

Gyles thrust his arms over his head so Serena could pull off his mail shirt. As Gyles lowered his arms Serena glanced at his hand, then reached out and brought it upward for closer inspection. The flesh was fiery red with a slight puffiness, and Serena turned Gyles's hand over to examine his palm.

"Are your feet as bad?" Serena asked when Gyles pulled his hand away.

"I've hardly had the opportunity to examine them," Gyles replied sarcastically. "A saddle is not the place to—"

"All right!" Serena snapped out. "You didn't have to spend the day ahorse because of me."

Gyles stepped out of the remainder of his clothing and sank into the waiting tub. A blush colored her cheeks as Serena hurriedly set towels to warm by the fire and laid Gyles's armor aside.

"I have an oil that will help." Serena indicated Gyles's hands.

"I've survived worse," Gyles flexed his fingers. "Do not trouble yourself. But I would like some wine."

Serena filled a goblet and handed it to Gyles.

There was a knock on the door, and a servant entered with a tray of meat and cheese. Serena took the platter and set it beside Gyles before retreating to a chair. Gyles rose from the tub to wrap himself in a towel and stand before the fire. He bit into a chunk of meat and swallowed it before looking at Serena.

"Now, wife, I have driven twelve of my men and their best horses for three days and as many nights 'til they are close to dropping where they stand. I have wasted an additional week at court when I should have been gathering my forces at Camden to ride to the northern border. The weather has been abominable and your man kept me waiting 'til he could wake you." Gyles slammed his goblet down with a force that sent the wine splattering over the rim. "Now you will tell me exactly what you hoped to prove by this insanity!"

Serena lowered her eyes to her lap. "My servants are not accustomed to your rages. 'Twould be a kindness to me if you would not shout."

"*Your servants!* Must I remind you that these lands became mine upon our marriage?" Gyles paced irritably in front of the fire. "Have you any idea of the embarrassment your silly disappearance caused me? Questions were asked for which I had no answers, Serena."

"I will give the oil for your hands to one of the servants." Serena left her chair and crossed the room. "You may have this chamber if you wish or I can have another prepared for you. Which do you desire?"

"I *desire* that you sit down and listen to me!" Gyles reached Serena in a few effortless strides and returned her to a chair. "My men and I will remain for two days, at which time you will return with us to Camden. You will remain at Camden and not leave unless I give you permission."

"Like Lady Elspeth?" Serena asked softly. Gyles's face registered shock and Serena smiled. "That is what her husband did to her several years ago, Catherine told me. But her husband had a reason—Elspeth had foresaken her vows. Do you accuse me of that?"

Gyles collapsed into a chair, one hand going behind his neck to massage the tensed muscles. "You know I do not. And you know also why I am here."

"Oh, yes," Serena laughed harshly. "You have come to reclaim a . . . a missing piece of property!"

"No property, my wife!" Gyles shouted. "You ran from me because you believe I was unfaithful to you."

"Are you going to tell me that you have remained faithful?" Serena's eyebrows raised. Gyles's eyes dropped from Serena's penetrating gaze. "No, I can see that even you cannot bring yourself to perjure your soul with such a lie."

Gyles leaned forward to clasp Serena's hands, but she withdrew from his slightest touch. "Do you wish me to confess? Very well. I laid with Elspeth but not out of love or desire. I was angry with you, myself . . . Elspeth is a reflection of myself, of all that I am, all that is evil and malignant within me. In truth, Serena, I myself am not certain why I laid with her. I took her out of hate, revenge . . . put any name to it you will, but try to understand, Serena. Elspeth . . ."

"I do not want to hear about you and Elspeth!" Serena cried as she jumped from her chair. "I do not care . . . bed whomever you desire, but stay away from me!"

"Serena!" Gyles implored, his hand outstretched in supplication. "Elspeth is Alan's mother."

"I know!" Serena cried, her eyes filling with tears. "Do you think me such a fool? Did you think I could see both you and Elspeth and not recognize the blending of both your features in Alan? I have known since the first time I saw you together."

"Why did you not tell me?" Gyles's hands caught Serena's shoulders.

Serena jerked away, blue eyes flashing. "What would you have had me say? 'Gyles, I know your secret? If you wish to bed Elspeth again you have my blessing?' You speak of your embarrassment, your pain. What of mine? My humiliation? Elspeth and all your fine Norman ladies whispering when they thought I did not hear. Why did you not come to *me*, husband? Why did you not open your heart to me as I opened mine to you? Did you think me a stone that I would go wherever you kicked me?" Serena's breasts heaved in anger. "I loved you, Gyles! I would have died for you had you asked it! You have said that you detest women, well allow me to share my feelings with you for the last time, dear, sweet, *loving* husband mine. To my mind, men are vermin, they are selfish, rutting, disgusting beasts whose very presence turns my stomach—you above all!"

Before Gyles could control his reaction, he saw his hand snake out and with sick horror watched Serena's head reel from the impact of his blow. Her face averted, Serena covered her stinging cheek as a humorless, almost hysterical laughter bubbled over her lips.

"Oh—what a perfect Norman you are, husband mine!" Serena gasped when she could finally speak. "What happens next—rape? But I had forgotten, there can be no rape between husband and wife, can there? Holy vows were spoken over us, so you may do with me whatever you wish. Rape only happens when a Saxon stupidly defies the advances of a Norman prince!"

Gyles went rigid first with shock then anger and the torrent of Serena's words abruptly halted when she realized what she had said. Had that been the reason for Serena's battered appearance—no fall, but a brutal attack by one of his countrymen? Gyles reached out to touch Serena's cheek but she danced away, anger flashing brilliantly in her eyes.

"No!" Serena stepped behind the chair Gyles had vacated. "Come no closer, I want no more tender Norman caresses. I have had more than my share of Norman honor and love."

Gyles threw the chair out of his path with careless ease. "Henry did that to you? That sniveling little whelp dared lay a hand upon you? I will kill him! I'll tear the heart from his body while he still lives!"

" 'Twas not Henry!" Serena cried. " 'Twas your glorious crown prince, William. And you will do nothing —you cannot, he will one day be your king so you dare not lay hands upon him. William will continue to do as he wishes, whether it be humiliating his lords or attacking helpless women. So speak not to me of what you will do to avenge my honor for all that you say will never come to pass."

"He took you?" Gyles roared, oblivious to all Serena had said. "He laid with you against your will?"

"What do you care, Gyles, you can always go back to Elspeth. So go to her, lay with her, get another child upon her—stay with your whore and be damned to you both!"

"Answer me!" Gyles's scar gleamed wickedly in the firelight.

Serena's chin tilted defiantly and she lowered her voice. "I will not answer your questions, now or ever. You forswore your right to question my behavior when you took your ease with Elspeth. And it would seem I never had the right to take you to task for anything."

"I have explained . . ." Gyles shook his head wearily. He could explain the night through and he knew Serena still would not forgive his deed. He had erected a wall between them that Gyles doubted he could ever bring down. There was no love in Serena's eyes as she steadily returned his gaze and Gyles felt something unborn die within him. Serena had once told him she had only duties and obligations, well that was all that was left to Gyles now, and he girded himself against the outburst he knew would come after his next words. "My men will bide here until the weather clears; when that happens we will return to Camden, yourself included. On the morrow you will begin making what preparations there are."

Serena stared at Gyles, astounded, and her fingers meshed together until the knuckles whitened.

"I will not accompany you—I refuse to go back to Camden!" Serena said fiercely. "There is nothing for me there."

"You are my wife!" How familiar that sounded—how often in the past Gyles had thrown that fact at her when Serena dared defy him. "You will do as I say!"

"No!" Serena whirled to face the fire so that Gyles would not see the tears that filled her eyes. "The only way I shall ever return to Camden is if you drag me there. Will you do that? The brave Norman conquering the defenseless Saxon—how like William Rufus you are. Am I to remain secluded in my chamber while you welcome your harlots in your bed?"

Gyles motioned impatiently. "After all I have experienced at a woman's hands, you need not fear I will take a mistress. I prefer celibacy to the subtle form of torture you women practice. But make no mistake, Serena, you will return to Camden if I have to tie you across my saddle!"

"I will run away again!" Serena warned.

"Then I will be forced to set a guard upon you," Gyles retaliated, his patience exhausted.

Serena turned to face him and Gyles was shaken by the pain and grim determination that showed in her eyes. "My soul will be free even while you keep my body prisoner."

The words fell so quietly that it was some time before their full impact penetrated Gyles's brain. "You would not!" Gyles managed to force the horrified whisper past his dry lips.

Serena eyed him steadily. "I will not return to Camden of my own free will. I will not bide there for the rest of my life. The choice, dear husband, is entirely yours."

"Alan will come home this summer." Gyles floundered desperately.

"Then he can place flowers on my grave. You are reconciled with Elspeth, let her give him the love that should have been his from birth. There is nothing left of me, Gyles. All that you said you would do, you have done. Are you pleased? All the hate you have nourished for women because of a moment's weakness by your mother has borne its fruit. I am destroyed. Does that please you? You have had your revenge upon my kind—you have torn me to bits and I can no longer repair the damage you have wrought." Serena's eyes dropped to the floor and she glided to the door. "You may have this chamber during your stay here. I do not wish to speak privately with you again, so do not seek me in my chamber unless you are prepared to use force to make me listen to your words, for that is the only way you will stay me. I will send a girl with the ointment for your hands and feet—use it or not, as you please."

Gyles rose late the next morning, gratified to discover the painful swelling and redness had all but disappeared from his extremities. Certain that Serena's anger had cooled during the night and he could easily reason with her, Gyles dressed hurriedly and upon leaving his chamber stopped one of the housecarls to inquire the location of Serena's chamber.

"M'lady is in the great hall." The man looked shocked by Gyles's inquiry. "She has been tending your men the night through, m'lord."

Gyles found his wife kneeling before one of his knights, her hands gently kneading the salve into the man's obviously chilblained feet. The knight made to rise when he saw his lord approach, but Gyles waved him back.

"The storm has lifted, Lord Gyles." The young man shifted nervously, embarrassed that Gyles had found his wife engaged in such a menial task. "We can be away for Camden whenever it pleases you."

Gyles nodded, his eyes following Serena as she rose, rinsed her hands at the washstand, and moved through the hall to take her seat at the table. Gyles took his place beside Serena, openly watching as Serena picked listlessly at her food and obviously relishing her discomfort.

"I have decided," Gyles said at last when Serena pushed her trencher away, "that I do not wish you to return to Camden. But you cannot remain here," Gyles added when he saw the hopeful light in her eyes. "I will deliver you into your father's care. You told me he is ill and desires to see you. I will allow you to stay at Broughton 'til your father wishes to return you to my care or you yourself want to return. Make your preparations, Serena, you have one hour."

{ BOOK III }
The Letters

13

My most gracious husband, Lord Gyles of Camden,

I am honoring my vow; the promise that you extracted from me before your departure to write once every fortnight and thereafter in reply to your letters will be fulfilled.

My father is the same, he has no strength to rise from his pallet but lies abed throughout the day. I read to him often, but he enjoys listening to the gentle strains of the lute far more. Aurelia's presence seems to disturb him greatly, so I restrict her visits as much as possible. Yet when he tries to speak of her, he falters, so I know not whether my actions please him or not.

My father knows not of our estrangement and I must ask you not to enlighten him. He will go to his grave anon and I wish his last days to be as carefree as is possible.

I remain,

> Your obedient wife,
> Lady Serena

My lawful wife in God, Lady Serena of Camden,

I am pleased that you have remembered your oath.

The border lands are not in the state of unrest that was prevalent upon our arrival some two months ago. For the most part the clans are poorly organized and have begun once again to quarrel amongst themselves. The danger here is minimal, yet I hope you have remembered me to God in your prayers.

The crown prince is in command of our army. For all his youth, he is an excellent warrior. 'Tis most unfortunate that an accident befell His Majesty a few days ago. Rumor has it he was set upon by a fierce clansman while our detachment of men razed a village. 'Tis odd, but Prince William refuses to answer any questions put to him about the assault. Yet as we bore him back to the encampment, in his madness, he raved and said 'twas I who caused his beating. 'Tis strange, is it not, wife, that he should lay the blame on my head? Why would I have cause to treat my prince in such a manner? But—thanks to God—Prince William will live. His Majesty will be bedridden for at least a week—the bruises about his face are terrible to look upon.

You need not fear your father will learn anything from me. Tell Lord Geoffrey I hope for his recovery.

I remain,

Your loyal husband,
Lord Gyles

My husband, Lord Gyles of Camden,

Catherine has arrived from Normandy. She and Bryan were wed a fortnight ago. I have taken the liberty of gifting them with a stallion and mare from your stables. They are a well-matched pair and Bryan is most pleased with their bloodlines.

My father is weakening rapidly; he has barely the strength to eat. Aurelia rarely visits him any longer, which is a blessing. He cannot bear the sight of her.

Beda has arrived from Camden for a visit of unknown duration. She asks for news of your arrangements with Sir Arthur for her hand. What will you have me say?

I remain,

Your obedient wife,
Lady Serena

My wife, Lady Serena of Camden,

Inform Beda that had she remained at Camden she would have learned several weeks ago the outcome of my preparations. Sir Arthur will not have her despite the richness of her dower. She may remain at Camden 'til autumn at which time Beda may retire to her dower estate or a convent. The choice is hers. My patience is at its end with the woman, for when Sir Arthur visited her last, she rudely insulted him and made mock of his offer. I wash my hands of her entirely.

My felicitations to Bryan and Catherine. May their marriage be long and fruitful. I am most pleased with your choice of gifts for them—'tis most fitting and proper. But then, you have always known what is best.

Summer has not yet hit with any great force here as I imagine it already has at Broughton and Camden. The nights and early mornings still carry a chill and the days, though clear, are not as warm as could be wished.

I have sent Edward to Normandy with orders to return with Alan. By the end of July I will be back at Camden and I wish Alan to stay with you until that time. 'Twill be only a matter of a fortnight's visit and I entrust my son to your gentle care. 'Tis good to know that in less than a month I shall be in my own home.

Kiss Alan for me, Serena, again, you were right. I do love him.

I am as always,

> Your loyal husband,
> Lord Gyles

My gracious husband, Lord Gyles of Camden,

Beda and Aurelia have gone to Camden to make preparations for Beda's departure. She is retiring to her dower lands 'til such time as she marries again.

Alan's arrival is eagerly awaited by all. You may

depend upon Catherine to make your son feel most welcome at Broughton. Though why you did not send him to Elspeth to await you I cannot understand.

If my letter appears stilted, m'lord, I must ask your pardon. Lord Geoffrey, my most beloved father, has been dead these ten days past and in my grief I find I cannot honor my vow to you beyond these few lines.

I am,

Your wife in God,
Lady Serena

My most precious wife, Lady Serena of Camden,

I am most sorrowed by the news of your father's death. Were there words which could ease your grief, I would write them, but your heart must find its own path out of the darkness into which it has descended. Lord Geoffrey was a good man, Serena, and you must believe that he felt no sorrow for himself at his death. He led a rich, full life—and he was blessed with a son and daughter who brought him much joy. If I could be so blessed, I would indeed gladly seek my grave for such wealth as that is beyond measure. And such contentment and joy as he found in you and Bryan I long for, yet know I shall never find.

I would not send Alan to Elspeth for the simple reason that she is not his mother. You are. You did not bear Alan in your womb, but rather in your heart, and that, most assuredly, is where a child is born.

What of you, my wife? Are you happy with the path you have chosen? 'Tis not too late, Serena, all is not lost. One word from you will end this tragic mockery between us. Think upon this.

As ever, I am,

Your faithful husband,
Lord Gyles

My husband, Lord Gyles of Camden,

I have thought much upon your last letter. The bitterness of my father's death has passed and in its place are the tender memories of him as he was when I was a child. My memories cannot be torn from me by anything on this earth; they are warm and sweet, comforting me greatly when my thoughts dwell bleakly upon my father's end. Bryan has worn out many steeds trying to outrun his grief. Bryan's grief was far worse than my own for he felt—at last—guilt at his actions, which have sorrowed our father these past two years. I cannot tell Bryan that what he knows to be true is false, yet I know Father would not want Bryan to blame himself for his rashness. 'Twould seem my brother and I both inherited our share of that trait.

Catherine is a great consolation for Bryan; she comforts him more than I ever could. We are too alike, Bryan and I, each of us sees the guilt in the other for our treatment of our sire. 'Tis good that Bryan has Catherine to pour his heart out to. I wonder how Father bore it when our mother died— he had no one to turn to then as Bryan does now. How alone he must have been!

We had word from Edward yesterday. He and Alan are in England and will arrive in three days time. All is ready to receive them; Catherine is a most efficient lady of the manor.

I have read again and again your last letter. In truth, I cannot say that the decision I made in the midst of a February sleet storm has brought me happiness; but it was wise, considering the circumstances. All joy is fleeting, transitory—I believe happiness to be beyond my ken now; all I desire is a measure of peace and that I have not found at Broughton.

I would ask that you not press me for an answer but allow me to weigh this decision carefully. I ask also that you not come to Broughton when you return from the border. I shall assure Alan's safe return to Camden; Bryan has already offered to deliver him into your care.

I pray daily for your safe return. God keep you, Gyles.

I remain,

Your most obedient wife,
Lady Serena

My gracious wife, Lady Serena of Camden,

Of necessity this letter needs be short, we are breaking camp and first light tomorrow will see us on the road to Camden.

I shall press no decision upon you, Serena. If time you need, time you shall have. Send Alan to me when you wish; I know how he must enjoy being with you again. With luck, Alan will not have to return to Normandy.

Dear Serena, I have missed you much these past months—more than I believed I could ever miss someone. Camden will be a lonely dungeon without your presence; I know not how I shall endure it. God watch over you, Serena, 'til I am there to take you from His care.

I am, as always,

Your devoted husband,
Gyles

My lawful husband, Gyles, Lord of Camden, Wolcott, and St. Clair,

As you can plainly see, I have returned Alan to your protection. The letter enclosed within mine should explain fully my reasons. Lady Elspath knew not where to send a message to you, so she sent it to me that I might pass it along to you. So I have done.

How you must have laughed at my last letter! What manner of man are you that you can practice such cruelty on another? It matters not, for I have reached the decision you so urgently desired.

You need not worry about imprisoning me at my dower castle. I have petitioned for an annulment of our marriage—I am sure you agree 'tis best we end this laughable union which should never have been.

You have won—you have your son, your son's mother, and your lands. Enjoy your victory.

Soon I will never more be,

Your wife,
Lady Serena

BOOK IV

The Fleeting Promise

14

"Bryan, are you certain you were right?" Catherine twisted her hands nervously in her lap.

"No," Bryan sighed as he seated himself heavily beside his wife. "But what else could I do, Catherine? She cannot continue as she has these past months—and Gyles does have certain rights."

"Rights!" Catherine jumped up and began to pace the room. "After the way he has treated your sister, you dare speak of *his rights*? What of Serena—what . . ."

" 'Tis Serena I am thinking of!" Bryan roared. "Mayhap if they meet—"

"She does not wish to see him! Not now! You know that," Catherine interrupted.

"You read his letter, Catherine, the annulment Serena has petitioned for upset him greatly. What possessed her to do such a thing?" Bryan went to the window and studied the road below.

Catherine rested her head on Bryan's shoulder. "There was no petition, Bryan," she said quietly. "How could there be? What grounds would the Church accept?"

"Oh, God!" Bryan swung on his wife. "How could she make such a mess of her life? And why be so cruel as to tell Gyles what was not true?"

"Because she loves him and she can no longer bear the pain he brings her." A cloud of dust caught

Catherine's attention and she clasped Bryan's hand in hers. "He comes."

Bryan nodded slowly and placed a light kiss on Catherine's lips. "Prepare her, Catherine, and offer up a prayer. 'Tis all we can do now."

Catherine ran lightly to her sister-in-law's chamber and rapped on the door.

"Enter." Serena's voice carried softly through the panel. Serena's room was flooded with light from the August sunshine and the gold streaks of her hair shimmered brightly. Serena looked up from the sewing in her lap and smiled briefly. "Catherine! You needn't request entrance to my chamber, you are welcome any time."

Catherine glanced uneasily about the chamber, unable to steady the wild beating of her heart. "Serena, I . . ."

Serena laid her sewing down and studied Catherine with concern. "Catherine, do you feel well? You are quite pale."

Catherine knelt beside Serena. "Bryan and I have been worried about you, Serena. What you are doing is unfair to yourself as well as to Gyles."

Serena's mouth tightened into a thin line. "I do what I must, Catherine, I thought you understood that."

"I do, but . . . but neither Bryan nor I can bear to watch you wither and die like this."

"Wither? Hardly that, Catherine!" Serena laughed.

Catherine's anger flared at Serena's humor. "Laugh if you wish, but we have taken matters into our own hands. Were I you, I would change my gown and freshen my hair— Your husband is here!"

Serena's eyes flew open and she said accusingly, "You told him!"

"No. Bryan only summoned him so that you could try to mend whatever is wrong between you." Catherine rose to her full height.

"Bryan has no right to interfere with my life!" Serena cried.

"He has every right—he is your brother! 'Tis time

you stopped being so stubborn. You could be mistaken about Gyles."

"Not in this!" Serena retorted. "Why do you suddenly feel the need to defend Gyles to me?"

"Because he is your husband and you have a duty to him."

"Do not presume to tell me where my duty lies, I know—"

"Then prepare yourself," Catherine snapped. She whirled and left the room without another word.

Resignedly, Serena rose to change her gown and dress her hair. To her chagrin Serena found herself taking special care with her appearance, glancing often into a small looking glass to insure her face was not too flushed and her hair hung exactly as it should. She had no choice —at least that is what she told herself—if she refused to go downstairs and meet Gyles, Bryan would bring her husband to her chamber and Serena preferred to meet him in more neutral surroundings. As she descended the stairs, Serena heard Gyles's voice coming from the school-room she and Bryan had used as children.

It shouldn't be like this, Serena thought as she leaned miserably against the wall, listening to the resonant play of Gyles's voice. 'Tis not fair that just the sound of his voice makes me long for his embrace; not when he has played me for a fool with Elspeth. The tears that had remained unshed for so long threatened her, and Serena drew a deep breath to compose herself before crossing the threshold to where Bryan and Gyles waited.

"You wrote that she was ill," Gyles was saying, "and now you say she is not! Which is the truth?"

"The latter, Gyles." Serena answered from the door-way, enjoying the way her husband sprang to his feet at the sound of her voice. As quickly as he moved, she might have just seared his flesh with a torch. "I am in the best of health."

"Then perhaps you will explain—" the sneer died on Gyles's lips, his green eyes clouded first with anger then growing horror and disbelief, as Serena walked slowly to a chair and eased into it.

Bryan murmured an excuse and closed the door behind him. Serena kept her eyes carefully averted from Gyles, while he stood mutely watching her, his hands flat upon the table in front of her chair. Gyles's skin had turned the deep bronze Serena remembered from the summer before, his short tunic exposed the firm muscles of his arms and shoulders that rippled under the suppressed violence of his emotions. He had grown leaner during the months of the campaign; Serena saw when she raised her eyes to him, his cheekbones more pronounced, the sensuous lips that had so often pressed upon her own now tugged downward into a frown, the dark hair Serena had so often toyed with curled slightly at the nape of his neck. He was all she had ever desired; this dark, remote, silent man who stood watching her as if she had the plague. Yet she could not utter a single word, for those piercing green eyes held her trapped in their depths.

Fear, overwhelming and urgent, constricted Gyles's throat. Innocent Alan! He had told his father Serena had eaten too much and become as large as Nellwyn, and Gyles had thought no more about it. Oh, God! Not this! Gyles's heart rebelled against the evidence before his eyes.

"You . . . Serena, you are with child!" Gyles managed to force through his dry throat.

"How observant!" Serena stated drily. "Have you nothing more to say?"

Gyles slumped into a chair, all emotion save fear driven from his mind. Gyles indicated her swollen belly. "W-when will the babe be born?"

Serena rested her slender hands protectively over her rounded figure. "Soon—the child has dropped this past week, and the midwife is certain 'twill be no longer than a fortnight. You need not tarry here, Gyles, if that is what concerns you. My child can enter this world quite easily without your presence."

"Your child! 'Tis my child as well!" Gyles bellowed, goaded into anger by Serena's calmness. Had she no idea of the ordeal she was facing? Gyles thought as his hands tightened around the arms of the chair.

"Are you certain, Gyles?" Serena directed a pointed look at him. "Perhaps 'tis Henry's or Richard's or William's or any other man's—you accused me of faithlessness often enough, why are you now so sure you are the father of my babe?"

"Don't, Serena!" Gyles's whisper was anguished. "You were ever true to me, I know. Why did you not tell me?"

"I had planned to, and then I received Elspeth's letter. Do you really believe I could have told you after that? I will not live on the scraps from your whore's table, Gyles. I would rather name my child a bastard before the world than grovel at her feet or yours. Elspeth wanted you and Alan—she is welcome to you! Dissolve our marriage and take your vows with Elspeth. 'Tis what you have always wanted. I will make no claim either for myself or my child." Serena rose to pour a goblet of wine, which she sipped thoughtfully before continuing in a small voice. "Is Elspeth at Camden?"

"No." Gyles shook his head. "She came to see Alan a few weeks ago. That was what she requested in her letter, Serena. She wanted only to look upon our son. I will not deny she asked me to end my marriage to you, but if you had once listened long enough to me I would have told you what I told Elspeth—I would never annul our marriage. She did not believe me at first, but when she stayed at Camden I forced her to see the truth. I laid with her at court 'tis true, but out of anger, not desire. I used her then as she used me four years ago. God's truth, Serena, she wished only to see Alan; and the ironic part is that he spoke constantly of you. Elspeth stayed two days, then she left, vowing never to return."

"And what of your other harlot?" Serena asked in a strangled voice.

Gyles turned at her odd tone and found Serena's back presented to him. "Beda, too, is gone. Lydia is planning to retire to a convent and Mara will soon be pledged in marriage. Christ in heaven, why must we speak of this now? You must return to Camden where Nellwyn and I can care for you."

Serena's laugh grated across Gyles's nerves. " 'Tis impossible, my time is too close at hand. I cannot travel such a distance now." Oh, Gyles, love me. Love me! Serena cried silently. Please! *Please!* The goblet dropped from her nerveless fingers as Serena forced away the pain that was starting again in her back and sides. Not now! Not now! Please, God, wait 'til he is gone. Do not let him see this, I beg you! He is afraid, and I love him and would spare him this.

"Serena?" Gyles scooped up the fallen goblet. "Serena, you are white as linen! What is it?"

"Naught." Serena answered when she was sure her voice would not betray her. "You will excuse me, I know. I was sewing some things for the babe when you arrived and desire to return to my chamber to complete the task."

Gyles accompanied Serena to the staircase; above all he did not wish to upset her in any way before the birth. His initial shock had receded somewhat, and Gyles watched Serena carefully. The six months of their separation had sharply defined her in his memory, yet now she seemed far more beautiful than he had remembered; the heaviness of her body did not detract in any way from the delicate oval of her face, and the generously fringed sapphire eyes had gained a brilliance Gyles had not seen before

"Serena," Gyles captured one of her hands in both of his, "would you like me to send for Nellwyn? If the messenger leaves now, they can be back in three days."

Blue eyes turned up to green and Gyles found himself propelled back through time to the day when he had first beheld this maid who had come so unwillingly into his life. Just so had she looked at him at their first meeting: wide, clear eyes gazing steadily at him, reflecting a mixture of apprehension and sadness. And in their time together, Gyles suddenly realized, Serena had demanded nothing for herself, but had given all she could to him, lending him strength when he felt his world was crumbling, loving him . . .

With dreadful accuracy, pain swift and sure cut deep into the heart Gyles had so long denied possessing. I

322

love her! Gyles thought in wonder. I love her now and forever, and now the cruel game I played on her because of Henry has borne its fruit and will take her from me. Until that night he had taken such care that his seed not take root within Serena, but he had forgotten his fear in that sweet night of passion. Now his love, his wife, would die because of his weakness. For in Gyles's mind there was no doubt that Serena could not give life to his child and still live herself. Take me in her stead, Gyles prayed, 'tis I who deserve to die, not she.

Serena's nails dug into the palms of her hands as she wondered at the reflective look Gyles had assumed; curious yet grateful as well, for his silence granted her the time she needed to fend off this fresh wave of pain. Serena drew a shaky breath. "I have no need of Nellwyn, the midwife here delivered Bryan and myself, and Catherine is here if I need her. But you needn't stay, Gyles, in truth I would prefer it if you would leave."

"I think not." Gyles traced the line of his scar with a bronzed forefinger. "If my son cannot be born in his own home, his father will at least be in attendance."

"No, no, no and no!" Serena stamped a tiny foot in frustration. "I don't want you here! My daughter will be born in the room where I first saw life and I will not have her frightened by her sire!"

"Our child, wife," Gyles corrected silkily, "will not be frightened of me. Tiny babes rather like me, in fact, though 'tis to be hoped our child has not inherited your willfullness."

Serena rose to the bait, not realizing that Gyles was deliberately provoking her into anger, for he would not be able to bear it should she retreat into the icy control he had encountered at her dower lands. She must not fear this birth! Gyles told himself vehemently.

"My willfullness?" Serena spat out, angered even further by the smile that tugged at the corners of Gyles's mouth. " 'Twas not my willfullness that caused your faithlessness! 'Twas—"

Gyles reached out to place a hand on Serena's abdomen, feeling the life he had placed within her stir vigorously beneath his touch. Serena was mute, her eyes welling with tears at the tender expression that softened Gyles's features as the child she had so happily carried made its presence known to its father.

"The babe moves constantly," Serena told Gyles hesitantly. "The midwife says 'tis a good sign."

Gyles nodded in agreement. "Our child will be whole, Serena, do not fear—" He stiffened when Serena abruptly brushed his hand away and began to slowly climb the stairs.

"I fear nothing," Serena called back to Gyles, her words ringing through the hall. "Not the king, queen, that abominable knave William Rufus, not hell, and not you—so why in God's name should I fear giving birth to the only thing in the world that can return my love?" Before Gyles could reply, Serena had vanished from sight.

Once out of Gyles's vision, Serena collapsed against the wall, biting hard on her knuckles until the height of the contraction passed, then made her way carefully to the chamber that had once been her parents' and was now occupied by Bryan and Catherine. Her light knock was answered immediately by Catherine.

"Gyles is staying, Catherine, so you can stop frowning at me and arrange for his chamber—next to mine if 'twill set your mind at rest," Serena teased gently.

"Then all is well between you?" Bryan came forward.

Serena shrugged. "Nothing has been decided yet and 'tis none of your concern anyway. Now, two things I would ask of you both. Bryan, will you help me back to my chamber? And will you, Catherine, find the midwife?" Serena turned to leave, then glanced behind her to find Bryan and Catherine staring at her. Slowly, as if speaking to small children, Serena said, "It has begun and unless you wish to give up your bed for my confinement, may I suggest you make haste?"

Bryan didn't bother to reply but instead took his sister's arm as Catherine ran from the room.

"Are you in much pain?" Bryan questioned softly.

"Not as much as I will be." Serena laughed gaily.

"Do not look so worried, Bryan! I have been waiting for this all these long months—"

"What is going on?" Gyles's roar overrode Serena's voice and before the echo had ceased, Gyles was framed in the doorway. "Catherine just ran past me muttering a prayer and the servants are scurrying abou—"

"Bryan, take Gyles into the schoolroom and keep him there, will you?" Serena's calm gaze contrasted strongly with the grin on her lips. "And, Gyles, stop shouting— you are frightening the servants and my child."

"My God!" Gyles paled beneath the sun-touched skin as knowledge smote him. "Why are you here? You should be in bed! You . . . oh, bloody Christ!" Gyles bent to raise Serena in his arms. "Do not stand there gawking, Bryan, do something!"

"Have you a suggestion?" Bryan shouted, angered at Gyles's presumptive manner and Serena's calmness.

"I would like to go to my chamber," Serena put in lightly, grinning widely as she tapped Gyles on his chest, thoroughly enjoying their confusion. "Is that possible?"

"Of course 'tis possible!" Gyles stopped when he realized he, too, was shouting.

"Turn left, the door at the end of the corridor." Serena directed Gyles as he strode through the hall. Then, as he made to deposit her on the bed, "No. I must change first."

"Serena!" Gyles groaned helplessly.

Serena laughed, her thoughts lighter than they had been in months. She should be afraid, but she was not, she had only an overwhelming sense of relief and joy. Soon now . . . her waiting was at an end. She slid behind a dressing screen and as quickly as possible changed into a summer nightdress. Gyles was impatiently waiting and when she emerged, he sprang from the chair on which he had perched to turn down her bed.

"That is not necessary, Gyles, 'twill be some time yet." Serena settled into a chair and picked up her sewing.

"You cannot mean to simply sit there!" Gyles was dumbfounded.

"I can hardly go riding, Gyles." Laughter bubbled

up again and Serena gave vent to it. "But we could play a game of chess if you wish. There is a board some-where . . ."

"You are insane, Serena!" Gyles towered above her.

"Not in the least, Gyles." Another cramp began and Serena's fingers tightened around her sewing.

Gyles felt his throat constrict at the sight of Serena's tensing features. "How long?" Gyles managed to force out.

Serena closed her eyes briefly, humor evaporating rapidly as the pain of the contraction lasted longer than the previous ones. "They began this morning." When she could finally speak, Serena's voice was weak.

"You should have told me immediately, Serena, rather than going through that scene below." Gyles's eyes softened to a gentle emerald green that trapped Serena in its depths. "I would take the pain from you if I could."

"But you cannot." Serena could feel her anger at Gyles's betrayal ebb from her heart to be replaced by the love she had tried so diligently to bury. "There is naught in life that does not bring pain at times. My love for you brought pain, the first time you took me was painful; this is only a passing moment in my life, which will soon be over and forgotten and my child will be here for me to love. Life will continue, it always has, it always will." Gyles's eyes had dropped, his face buried in his large, strong hands as the broad shoulders that had borne so much shuddered with the fear and misery he could no longer contain. Serena rose and gently pried Gyles's hands away and down to her belly, holding them with her own and smiling through the tears coursing down her cheeks. "You are remembering what you should not. I know what troubles you—not all women are the same, Gyles, you above all should understand that."

Her kindness undid him completely and Gyles pressed his lips into her soft, fragrant hair. "Serena, love. Ah, love, what have I done to you?"

Serena tilted her head upward to give him a tender smile. "You have done no more and no less than any other man. And yet much more."

"Serena . . . love." Gyles caught her face between his hands. "I do love you—don't leave me, Serena, I could not bear my life without you, love! All my life, wherever I offered my heart, 'twas returned to me in pieces, cast aside . . ." his voice caught. "I vowed never to give it again, but . . . my love, my love, how can I live if you do not?"

"Hush!" Serena told him sharply. "You believe that because one woman died I shall, too. Well, I shall not! Do you think I shall conveniently die so Beda or Elspeth can feel free to test your manhood? They will both learn to keep their distance from my husband. You are mine—only mine. When you are angered, tell me rather than trying to find solace in another's bed. If I act unwisely, tell me, and I shall give you the fight you are spoiling for. Only do not turn me away. I am your wife and—"

"Aye." Smiling, Gyles interrupted Serena, the knuckles of his hand stroking her cheek. "You are my wife, my love, my life." Serena would live, he thought hopefully, she was far too stubborn to do otherwise. Gyles bent to place a tender kiss upon Serena's lips.

"Do you love me?" Serena asked in a tight voice.

"Always." Gyles smiled, then froze as Serena's nails bit into his forearms.

"Then . . . will you go . . . and find Catherine?" Serena managed to grit out between clenched teeth. "She went . . . for the midwife. My child is . . . impatient."

"Our child," Gyles corrected automatically as he helped Serena toward the bed.

"No!" Serena struggled when she saw where Gyles was leading her. "Not yet, please, back to the chair."

"Serena, you should be abed," Gyles remonstrated.

"No!" Serena was adamant. "Please, Gyles, 'tis not time for that yet." Despite her brave words Serena was beginning to dread the signs that told her another contraction was starting—not fear, but the knowledge that something far worse was still to come put a dent in her courage. "Go . . . find Catherine."

"You should not be alone." Gyles carried Serena

to her chair, depositing his precious burden gently on the cushion. "Let me send one of the servants or Bryan."

Serena managed a smile. "As you wish, Gyles."

The second summons was unnecessary for Catherine entered a short time later, the wizened midwife close behind, her grin as toothless as a newborn babe's. She went immediately to Serena, her wrinkled brow furrowing as she deftly examined the young woman.

" 'Twill be a time yet, m'lady." The midwife rose and spotted Gyles. "Who be he?" The indignation she felt at this intrusion was plain.

"My husband." Serena laughed softly. "Does his presence disturb you?"

"Aye—he should be gone. 'Tis not his place to be here." She eyed Serena shrewdly. At last she said, "But he may stay . . . if he keeps out of me way. If you wish it."

Oh yes! Serena thought. I wish it dearly. But she said, "You should leave, Gyles. She is right, 'tis not your place. Go with Bryan."

Gyles knelt beside his wife. "If you have need of me, Serena love, send someone."

Serena nodded, her hand going to the scar that marred Gyles's cheek. "Do not fear, for I do not."

Gyles kissed Serena's fingertips and withdrew along with Bryan, the door standing open behind them so Gyles might hear Serena if she called for him.

The midwife gave a brief cackle of laughter then turned her bright eyes on Serena. "Now we begin. Walk, m'lady."

Bryan and Gyles sat in the great hall, several pitchers of wine and ale on the table between them. The night was cool for August and Bryan had caused a fire to be lit while Gyles had paced restlessly until Bryan had pressed a horn of ale upon him. Now husband and brother sat in silence, each thinking of the woman upstairs whom they both loved. They waited for a sound, a sign, anything that would tell them how near they were to the end of their vigil. Bryan stole a glance at Gyles's grimly set features and was surprised to see a muscle tic in his cheek. He must care, Bryan thought, or he would not be so silent. The silence—it invaded every part of the castle, so that even the servants spoke in hushed tones.

Catherine appeared, briefly, to give them an encouraging smile, but that was all. Gyles rose, and when Catherine retreated he stared numbly at the space she had vacated. With a soft curse Gyles drained his horn, refilled it, drained it, and filled it again. Should it take this long? The pains had begun in the morning and the sun had long since left the sky. How long had Elspeth labored with Alan? Half a day? Longer?

Gyles passed a hand over his face. So many years had passed and yet so few, and at that time Gyles had not cared about the woman laying on the narrow bed, moaning and screaming like some demented creature. Only the child had mattered then, so Gyles had ignored the cries and whimpers and removed himself from their source to wait in the chapel; wait for the screams to stop, wait for the wail of his child. Gyles sprang from his chair with an oath—that was what was missing, there was no sound coming from Serena.

"She is strong," Bryan comforted softly.

"Aye," Gyles replied, his eyes fixed on the stairs. Still he would have been easier had Serena at least been crying.

"Then worry not." Bryan rose and clapped Gyles on the shoulder. "Serena and I were delivered by that selfsame midwife and our mother was of the same build as Serena."

Somewhere above them a door slammed and both turned expectant gazes to the stair. Catherine ran halfway down the steps then paused and motioned for Bryan. Husband and wife held a brief, whispered consultation, each casting anxious glances toward Gyles as they spoke. Catherine whirled to flee back up the stairs while Bryan stood, head bowed, before drawing a deep breath and returning to Gyles.

Gyles wrapped his fingers tightly around his drinking horn, stilling the trembling that shook him while he searched Bryan's face anxiously.

"There is not much time," Bryan began slowly.

"Oh, God!" Gyles sank weakly into a chair.

Bryan recognized his mistake instantly. "Nay, Gyles, 'tis not what you think—there is no difficulty for Serena." Bryan wet his lips nervously before continuing. "While Serena has been here, 'twas obvious that all was not well between you. Serena said very little, 'tis not her way to confide her troubles to others, but she was so unhappy, so terribly controlled—as if she had locked all her emotions away—and Catherine and I—" Bryan spread his hands helplessly "—we couldn't reach her.

"Then one day Richard came for a short visit. He had no way of knowing Serena was here, of course, but . . . Richard made her laugh, Gyles."

"You are telling me that Richard visited Serena?" Gyles's scar went white. "And you allowed this?"

" 'Twas not a matter of allowing or disallowing, I haven't that control over Serena's life! I want—have always wanted—only happiness for my sister. They talked, played chess, even rode until Serena was certain she was with child. She needed . . . something, someone in her life." Voices sounded from the entrance and Bryan spared a look toward the disturbance. "I only wanted you to know before you misunderstood what is about to happen. From Serena's window Catherine saw him approaching—Richard is here."

Gyles stiffened as footsteps carried into the hall, then inclined his head slightly. "I will not shame you, Bryan, for I, too, desire Serena's happiness. And I thank you for your tender care of her in my absence." He moved with a horn of ale, to a shadowed portion of the hall, to wait.

"Bryan!" Richard came forward to embrace his friend. "No one is about; where are Catherine and Serena?"

Wine was offered and Bryan waited until Richard settled himself before he answered. "Serena is in travail; Catherine is with her."

Richard started, then relaxed. "Well, I shall be glad when this is over. She is well, I take it?"

"As well as she can be under the circumstances," Bryan snapped. "I am glad to see you are not upset by this."

"Bryan, Bryan," Richard clucked his tongue chidingly. "I am concerned about Serena, but I have had months to adjust to her condition. As for the bastard's whelp I care not a fig. 'Twould be a blessing if it died." He smiled at Bryan's gasp. "Surely you agree with me, Bryan. After all, what would Serena do with a babe and no husband? She hasn't one, you know, the bastard returned a month ago and hasn't yet been to see her, though he entertained the Lady Elspeth for a few days."

Bryan's eyes glittered coldly as he studied the shadowed corners of the hall. "How do you know this?"

Richard tossed his blond head. "Your dear step-mother, Aurelia. She has been most helpful." Richard shrugged. "What does Serena plan to do with the brat once 'tis whelped?"

"Do?" Bryan repeated stupidly.

"Yes, Bryan, do!" Richard snarled. "She cannot mean to keep it. I fail to understand why Serena insisted upon nurturing that seed in her belly when I knew of a woman who could remedy that embarrassment, but I allowed it because for some reason 'twas important to her. But I will not allow her to keep the brat if it lives. She can send it to her bastard husband if she wishes, but 'twill not be brought into my home. You look shocked, Bryan, you shouldn't be. When Serena is recovered I will come for her, she will be mine as she should have been from the first. She is not untouched, I have accepted that, but I'll not accept another man's child—especially not his!"

Bryan stared. "Has Serena agreed to this?"

Richard laughed. "Agreed? What choice does she have—go back to Camden? Hardly. Serena's pride would never allow that. Stay here? Impossible, for she knows you would release her to the bastard whenever he asked. Nay, Bryan, she need not agree, just see where her only escape lies."

A drinking horn shattered against the stones of the

hearth and Richard found himself sprawled full length in the rushes as his chair was kicked from beneath him. Strong hands grasped his tunic and Richard was lifted upward until his toes brushed the floor.

"I gave Bryan my word," Gyles ground out, his eyes throwing green sparks, his face set grimly, "that I would not disgrace his home. I will honor my word because Bryan wishes it so." For a brief instant Gyles nearly cast honor aside when he saw the sneer on Richard's lips, and his fingers tightened around Richard's throat. Despicable pup!

"Gyles!" Bryan's voice was horrified. "Gyles, you're choking him!"

Reluctantly, Gyles loosened his grip, allowing Richard to fall gracelessly back into the rushes. "Because of my word, but listen well. Stay away from Serena—my wife and child are not your affair."

Richard sprang to his feet, his eyes dilated wildly. "Serena is mine! She has always been mine!" Richard's hand fell to his sword. "You will never claim her again, I swear it. Be on your guard, Lord Gyles, for you will not know your wife and child long—I'll see you food for the worms first." He turned and ran from the hall.

Sinking back into his chair, Bryan stared after Richard, his brow furrowed with worry. "Richard doesn't mean what he said, Gyles. He only said those things to anger you."

"Richard didn't know I was here, Bryan, remember?" Gyles folded his arms across his chest, then his voice sharpened. "Is what he said true? Did he ask Serena to deny our child life?"

"If he did, Serena made no mention of it. Mayhap he suggested it and Serena gave him such a tongue-lashing for his trouble that she decided 'twas best forgotten. Had Richard been insistent, Serena would not have continued to receive him."

"Then his jealousy has driven all reason from him," Gyles muttered. "And if he tries to see Serena again I will see him whipped."

"Understand, Gyles—" Bryan started to plead.

332

"Nay! Richard believes he loves Serena. I do not like it, but I can accept the fact. But I will not tolerate his interference in my life or Serena's any longer. He should long ago have accepted our marriage." Gyles slammed a fist on the table to accent his words.

"Cease your bickering." Catherine shrilled from the steps. "Are you both mad?" Catherine's face was ashen, the hand that rose to her wildly disarrayed hair trembled violently.

Bryan went to Catherine and led her to a chair, shaking his head as Gyles made to speak. Catherine buried her head in her folded arms and began to cry wretchedly as Bryan smoothed the auburn hair back from her face.

Turning from the scene before him, Gyles felt a cold helplessness surge through his veins. Don't think! His heart screamed. If she were dead Catherine would have told you. A hard labor, 'tis all, and Catherine had not known what it would be like. Serena, Serena, do not give in, I need you.

Bryan cradled Catherine in his arms while her weeping quieted. "The midwife . . . she made me leave. I . . . I couldn't bear it any longer. She's not human—making Serena walk during the pain, and now when she cannot walk alone, the midwife keeps pulling her around the chamber. And Serena hasn't made a sound, just sets her jaw and shakes her head when the midwife tells her to walk."

"The babe?" Gyles questioned Catherine in such a dispassionate voice that she longed to claw at his green eyes with her nails. "It lives?"

"Yes," Catherine replied stiffly. How *could* he be so coldly unfeeling? Did he care nothing for the woman who was going through agony to give life to his child? Catherine was about to give voice to her thoughts when Gyles presented his back to her and stalked through the hall and up the stairs.

The door to Serena's chamber had been left open to permit what breeze there was to circulate freely. Her hair had been tied hastily on top of her head, but a few wisps had escaped and now clung damply to her face and neck as Serena wrapped shaking hands around the bedpost for support. How long could this go on? She moaned inwardly. As if she were a tiny cork, wave after wave of pain picked her up in its swell and hurled her forward toward release only to trap her again and again in its depths. How did my mother bear this, how did she go through this twice and still survive? Another pain was starting and Serena ground her forehead against the bedpost.

"Walk!" The midwife was tugging at her again, trying to loosen Serena's grip.

"I—cannot," Serena snarled down at the midwife.

"You must if you wish to hasten this birth!"

Hasten! Serena jeered silently. She had been walking for hours and the babe was no closer to being born than it had been before. "Nothing will hasten this!" Serena choked out as the crest of the pain hit.

"It must be done," the midwife insisted in a wheedling tone. Demands had not reached the girl she had delivered nineteen years ago, so a different attack must be used. "When the next pain comes, we will walk and soon you will hold your babe—"

"I cannot!" Serena was adamant.

"Why can you not, wife?" Gyles's form stood in the doorway. "Are you so weak you cannot give my son life?"

"Weak?" Serena screeched in disbelief. "You dare accuse me—you blackguard, knave!"

Gyles smiled in the face of Serena's rising anger while inwardly his heart wrenched at the sight of her trembling form. He glanced briefly at the midwife and saw the growing concern in her eyes as she skillfully pressed her hands against Serena's abdomen. The babe had to be delivered soon, Gyles knew, and Serena seemed to have lost the strength to carry the labor through. Grim resolve bolstered Gyles's flagging courage, and he strode forward to pull the midwife's hands from Serena.

"At the next pain, you will walk as you have been told." Slim fingers tightened painfully about his upper arms and Gyles hardened himself against the pleading he saw reflected in Serena's wide azure eyes. Gyles gave her a gentle shake. "You will do as you have been told."

"I cannot!" Serena whispered, then set her jaw as another pain began.

"Walk!" Gyles roughly dragged Serena's hands from his arms. "Or I will drag you if I must to see my son safely born."

Sheer stubbornness came to her aid and Serena forced herself to keep pace with her husband. At last it was over as Gyles realized from the decreased pressure on his hand and he guided Serena toward a chair.

"No, 'twill be easier if I remain on my feet."

Gyles nodded and passed a cool cloth handed him by the midwife over Serena's face and throat. " 'Twas not so bad, was it?" he asked gently.

"It hurts, Gyles!" Serena cried softly.

"I know, cherie." Gyles smoothed the wisps of hair from Serena's forehead. " 'Twill soon be over if you—" he had almost said "if you can hold on a bit longer" but checked himself in time. Gyles continued, "If you but bend your willfullness to the task."

A spark of humor gleamed in the depths of her eyes as Serena replied, "My willfullness, sir knight, has naught to do with—" she broke off with a quiet gasp as another spasm bent her in half and a gush of liquid soaked her gown and the floor.

With each pain, Gyles guided Serena about the boundaries of the room and when she felt she could stand no longer he did as he had threatened and dragged her mercilessly beside him.

"No . . . no more," Serena gasped. The candles had burned themselves out once and had been replaced with fresh ones that were now burned nearly halfway down. Serena collapsed against Gyles. "I . . . cannot. M-my legs . . . will not hold me any longer."

" 'Tis good!" The midwife pronounced with relief. "Now you will help me, m'lord."

As he was directed, Gyles carried Serena to the bed, watching in horror as the midwife proceeded to tie strips of linen first to the bedposts and then to Serena's wrists and ankles. A roll of several thicknesses of leather was thrust between Serena's teeth and Gyles retreated a step before the starkly primitive twist her features had taken.

"You go now!" The midwife jabbed a forefinger at Gyles. "And tell Lady Catherine she is needed."

Catherine returned to the chamber, unwillingly, and Gyles slumped in a chair, his courage gone. He worried no longer about Serena's silence, for now her agonized groans floated down to the two waiting men. Gyles had spent most of his life controlling his emotions and reactions in front of others and he did so now, maintaining a rigidly imposed impassive expression while his eyes stared blankly at some indefinite point in space. Inwardly, Gyles's heart twisted with every sound; Serena's cries beating against his ears like sword against armor. Soon, God, please, Gyles found himself praying, make an end to this.

But his prayer was unanswered and night dragged on into morning with the servants reappearing to go quietly about the task of preparing the morning meal for the knights who would soon be coming to break their fast. Gyles shook his dark head brusquely at the girl who offered him a platter of food and glanced at Bryan who toyed with his own meal. Bryan met Gyles's look and abruptly pushed out of his chair. A blood-curdling scream clawed through the air and Gyles felt the hair on the back of his neck prickle with fear. In back of him, an earthen pitcher fell to the floor and shattered, the servant who had carried it stood round-eyed, eyes fixed on the staircase.

Hard on the heels of the dying echo of the scream came a second, prolonged wail—that of an infant hardily enraged at being brought from the security of its mother's womb. Gyles took the stairs three at a time, his powerful legs bringing him swiftly to Serena's chamber where he paused, uncertain whether to enter.

"Come!" Catherine, laughing and weeping, beckoned to him. "Come, Gyles, see your son!"

A tiny bundle of squalling humanity was thrust into his hands and Gyles carefully pulled the swaddling back to expose the face. Hair black as night, eyes the color of pure sapphire, Gyles's second son screamed his protest at his father, while Gyles grinned stupidly at the red face. Catherine gently took the babe back into her arms and smiled at Gyles.

"You may see Serena if you wish, but do not tarry overlong, the midwife has instructed she rest." Catherine and the midwife retreated to a far corner of the room to deposit the babe in his cradle.

Gyles padded softly to Serena and eased himself onto the side of the bed. Serena's eyes flickered open and she managed a weak smile, which he returned.

"You have your son," Serena whispered.

"Aye." Gyles raised both of Serena's hands to his lips. "Our son, Serena, and I thank you for him. He is much the image of his mother."

"And his father," Serena added sleepily. Bringing Gyles's hand to her cheek, Serena fell into an exhausted slumber.

"What say you!" Aurelia exploded at her stepson. "You and Catherine had no right to take my chamber!"

Bryan closed his eyes wearily, it had been a long, trying evening and he wished only to see his sister and her child and retire to his pallet. Bryan sighed, "Aurelia, you are no longer lady of the manor. I have allowed you to stay at Broughton because I believed my father would have wished it so, but you will remember your place! Catherine will arrange for you to have any chamber you desire, but for now, cause no further trouble, the night has been long and I am weary."

Pale blue eyes bored into Bryan. "I care not for your problems nor for what ails you and I demand——" Aurelia gasped at the sight of Gyles striding arrogantly through the hall. "You! What are you doing here?"

A smirk played about the corners of his mouth as Gyles bent over her hand. "Lady Aurelia, as always your charm leaves me breathless. You have seen your dear sister safely to her dower estate?" Aurelia snatched her hand away and Gyles laughed as he turned to Bryan. "Look in on Serena if you like, but do not wake her."

"Wake her!" Aurelia spat. "Has day become night and night become day of a sudden?" Then with a speculative gleam. "Has Serena taken ill?"

Bryan ignored her, so she focused her attention on Gyles. "She is well then? And the child?"

Gyles laughed again at the eagerness in Bryan's face. "Serena is well, needing only sleep and time in which to recover. And I have a son, a fine healthy son who already promises much." At the hissed intake of breath behind him, Gyles turned. "Will you not extend your good wishes, Aurelia?"

Aurelia lowered her eyes before Bryan or Gyles could see their malevolent glitter. All my plans! She thought. "But of course, Gyles, 'tis a shock to me is all. Had I known, I would have stayed here to aid Serena during her confinement."

Bryan snorted, "I am sure Serena would have been most grateful!" The sarcasm was heavy in his voice. "I will inform Catherine you have returned."

As he watched Bryan depart, Gyles was conscious of Aurelia's careful regard, but when he turned, her gaze had shifted elsewhere. Idly, Gyles asked, "Lady Beda is well?"

"She is as well as can be expected, having been cast out of her home to make her way as best she can. How could you do such a thing to one of your own country-women? Even Bryan, base Saxon though he is, has decreed I may stay at Broughton as long as I wish; while you, a Norman—"

Gyles raised a hand in an imperious gesture for silence. "Had Beda acted less shrewishly toward Lord Arthur she would have been married this summer. I had set her in a most favorable light to that good man and she saw fit to destroy that which I had carefully labored to build. Do not blame me for your sister's stupidity, 'twas only when she deliberately set those plans awry that I ordered her return to her dower lands."

"Feel you no guilt?" Aurelia persisted.

"Guilt? Nay, not for my actions toward your sister. I have my father's wife to care for as well as my half-sister, and I have been most lax in my duty to them, which I shall remedy as best I may."

"But you love Beda!" Aurelia sputtered.

Clouded green eyes coldly appraised Serena's step-mother. "What portion of that emotion I still retain after dealing with those such as yourself and your sister is given fully to the woman upstairs and my two sons. I never thanked you for arranging my union with Serena, did I, Aurelia? 'Twas indeed the finest plot you ever turned your hand to, and had it not been for you and Beda, I would never have found the contentment I have now."

Aurelia repressed the angry words that sprang to her tongue and walked haughtily away from the mocking smile Gyles bestowed upon her. The sanctuary of her chamber gained, Aurelia paced restlessly, her white brow lined in thought. At last her expression brightened and Aurelia hurriedly set quill to parchment, scratched a few lines and sealed the missive. Descending to the great hall, Aurelia sought out one of the knights who had accompanied her to England from her home in Normandy. His obedience and loyalty had been tested often, and Aurelia had no doubt where his allegiance lay.

"Sir Cavell," Aurelia murmured when the knight was at her side. "I must bid you return to my sister and deliver this letter safe into her hands."

Sir Cavell slipped the note inside his jerkin and nodded. "As you wish, m'lady."

"Understand," Aurelia warned sharply, "my sister only must receive this letter, entrust it into no one else's care. And tell none of your comrades where you are bound."

Sir Cavell inclined his head once again. "I understand, m'lady. I shall leave anon." With a bow, he departed.

As soon as he had finished the midday meal, Gyles made his way again to Serena's chamber. At the midwife's urging—for she was uncertain as to the duration of Serena's recovery—a wet nurse had been obtained and now sat beside the infant's cradle, waiting patiently until the child would need her. Gyles knelt beside the cradle and extended a long forefinger to stroke the velvet skin of his son's cheek. The babe stirred in his sleep and Gyles hastily withdrew his hand and crossed the room to Serena's bed.

How small she looked; how tired and frail with purple shadows ringing her eyes. Carefully Gyles placed one of her hands in his and seated himself on the bed. A small sound issued from Serena's throat and she turned her head toward Gyles, a hint of a smile on her lips as if sensing his presence.

"Still sleeping?" Catherine's quiet voice startled Gyles and he looked up to find her standing beside him.

"Aye." Gyles glanced again at Serena as he framed his next question. "The birth . . . was it . . . difficult?"

" 'Twould be a lie if I told you 'twas easy." Catherine spread her hands in front of her. "You saw part of it yourself, Gyles—'twas a long labor, exhausting for Serena because the child was backward. Had it been me, I would have given up, but not Serena."

"No," Gyles looked at the delicate hand laying in his. "Serena would fight to the end for the child. The midwife, did she say . . . another child . . . could Serena endure it?" Gyles's sight blurred for his fears had not abated, and if another child would mean Serena's life then he would absent himself from Serena's bed, completely this time so there would be no possibility.

"You do care for her!" Catherine's surprised voice broke into Gyles's thoughts. Then with a reassuring smile she said, "The midwife proclaimed her most fit, Gyles."

"I cannot help fearing . . ."

"Your fears are much of your own making, Gyles," Catherine told him roughly. "There are risks for every woman who bears a child, Serena included. But she is in no greater danger than any other—look for yourself! Serena is alive and quite well and when she fully recovers I doubt she would take kindly to your pleasuring yourself on another." Catherine sniffed and flounced from the room.

Gyles stared after her in slack-jawed amazement.

Sweet, docile Catherine had gained a barbed tongue since he had last seen her. Serena's influence no doubt, Gyles thought wryly, a smile teasing his lips when he recalled how often he had exchanged heated words with his wife. And how pleasant had been their reconciliations! Gyles shrugged off the last of his fears, feeling his heart lighten immensely. At long last he had a family; a wife, two sons who would know the love of a mother and father, which Gyles had been denied, and there would be more children, of that Gyles was certain. Gyles looked down at Serena and was startled to find Serena awake and watching him with wide sapphire eyes.

"The child?" Serena murmured.

"Sleeping," Gyles replied, brushing a light kiss on her forehead. "And his mother?"

Serena smoothed the covers over her stomach with a small laugh. "Much lighter and flatter! Gyles . . . I am glad you came."

"Even though you did not ask me?" Gyles teased.

Smiling at his bantering tone Serena pulled a second pillow beneath her head, her efforts aided when Gyles lifted her upright and fluffed the pillow into place. "I believed you did not want me—and certainly not my child. Your letters told me nothing of your feelings."

"And your letters, madame, were full of love and warmth?" Gyles rebuked her. "Better I should have written to Bryan in your stead, I would have known of the babe much sooner. I warn you now, Serena, the next time you find yourself with child I will not be so put off."

"Aye, Gyles, the next time I shall be safe within Camden's walls," Serena assured him. "Have you any name in mind for our son?"

Gyles's eyebrows raised. "Serena, I barely knew of his coming, how could I have chosen a name?"

"Then, if you have no objection, Gyles, I would like to name him Evan. 'Tis a good name, in the Welsh it means a highborn young warrior."

"You have given much thought to this, I can see. What if I do not agree?" Gyles laughed, then instantly was sorry as Serena's face fell. "Cherie, you may call our son by any name you so desire, I did but jest with you. Evan it shall be."

Evan was christened the same night, held securely in his father's arms, while his mother watched from the bed, her blue eyes blazing with love and triumph.

Three days after the birth Nellwyn returned to Broughton with Alan in tow. Her face flushed with exertion, Nellwyn burst into Serena's chamber with a glad cry.

"Where be the wee lord, lamb? I daresay there be none here who could properly care for him no matter what ye say, so I came with or without Lord Gyles's leave. Alan I brought along, for 'tis none too soon for him to meet his brother." Nellwyn pointed at the wet nurse in outrage. "You! What be ye doing here? Lady Serena will have no need of ye, will ye, lamb?"

Gyles looked as if he were trapped in the midst of a sudden storm and Serena smothered a laugh.

"Nellwyn, I am most pleased to see you as well, but Evan's wet nurse is here at my request and you will treat her kindly. Evan is in his cradle, sleeping, so you and Alan may see him if you wish."

Nellwyn descended upon the cradle in a flurry of skirts, while Alan followed more slowly. Cautiously, Alan peered over the carved wooden side and examined his sleeping brother. Behind him, Serena and Gyles exchanged a knowing look before Alan turned and hesitantly approached the bed.

"What do you think of your brother?" Gyles inquired.

Alan darted a look over his shoulder to Nellwyn who was still exclaiming over the babe, then lifted his shoulders in a shrug.

"I know not how I shall manage when we return home, Gyles," Serena began thoughtfully. "Catherine has been so helpful with Evan—and you know I haven't regained my strength yet."

"Wha—" Gyles started to protest. Serena's health had rapidly improved in only three days. In truth, the young wet nurse was proving unnecessary since Serena insisted upon nursing Evan herself. He caught Serena's warning frown and gave a slight nod of understanding. "Well, perhaps we could find someone at Camden?"

"Someone extremely trustworthy," Serena agreed, teeth tugging at her lower lip.

"What's trustworthy?" Alan piped up. He clambered onto the bed beside Serena, smiling happily when her arm went around his shoulder.

"It means I need someone I can depend upon, someone who will help me take care of Evan. Your brother, Alan, is too small to care for himself like you do; Evan has to be fed, dressed, held, played with, so he can grow to be as strong as you."

Alan cast a wary eye at his father who smiled and tousled Alan's hair. "Am I trustworthy?"

"Indeed you are, son," Gyles replied. "Did Nellwyn not entrust her life to your care for the journey here?"

Alan pondered that for a moment—the babe had caught him unaware, for Alan had never thought there would be another child who would rival him for Serena's and his father's affections. It had been painful to be separated from them and sent to Normandy, but Alan had endured that stoically, for Serena had promised he would soon return to Camden. And so he had, Alan thought with a quick flash of joy, Serena had kept her word. Alan glanced once more over his shoulder to the sleeping Evan. His little brother *was* terribly little and helpless and Serena *did* appear awfully pale and weak.

"You will not have to find anyone, Serena." Alan scrambled off the bed and drew himself up manfully. "Evan is my brother and I shall care for him."

"Thank you, Alan." Serena looked at him seriously. "With your assistance we shall manage admirably."

His mind greatly eased, Alan returned to Nellwyn to tell her of the important duty he had been charged with. Gyles watched Alan peer again into the cradle, feeling the tension ebb from his mind and body. His own past had repeated itself in Alan and Evan—but in Gyles's case Lydia had not been Serena, and in any event perhaps he had already been so embittered by his own bastardy that no amount of coaxing could have persuaded Gyles to give Kier the devotion or love Alan would eventually display for Evan.

"A babe every year, Gyles?" Serena's soft voice brought Gyles from his musings.

"As many as you wish, as often as you wish, cherie." Gyles grinned, then bent to whisper in Serena's ear, "I shall do my best to comply with your demands."

Serena looked up from the babe at her breast to Gyles, lounging beside one of the arrow slits that illuminated her chamber. "Where is Alan?"

Gyles turned with a smile. "Bryan and Catherine have taken him riding. Don't tell me you miss the little scamp, love, he's been under foot for the past fortnight!"

Evan gave vent to a raucous belch and Serena laid him in his cradle then joined her husband. "I had no idea he would take his role as Evan's protector so seriously!" Serena laughed. "But at least Alan doesn't resent Evan, for that I am very grateful."

"I, too." Gyles brought Serena into his arms and captured her lips with his. "I have much to be grateful for, Serena, you above all else," Gyles told her when at last he could speak.

Serena rubbed her nose playfully against Gyles's chest. "So grateful you are already planning your departure," she laughed softly. "You really shouldn't discuss your plans with my brother, Gyles, I have long been able to find out whatever I wished from him."

"Vixen!" Gyles nipped Serena's ear then studied her earnestly. "But I fear I must return to Camden—I have been away far too long and the harvest will soon begin."

"I know, Gyles. Oh, how I long to go with you!" Serena said fervently.

"That is impossible, cherie, you are not yet well enough to consider such a journey," Gyles stated firmly. "I will not have you endangering yourself, much as I want you beside me. Give yourself another month, Serena."

344

"A month, Gyles! I do not need that much time," Serena protested.

"You do!" Gyles was implacable. "I nearly lost you because of Elspeth and now that I have you back I will not run that risk again. Four weeks is not so long."

" 'Tis easy for you," Serena grumbled. "At least at Camden you will be free of Aurelia and Beda. How I loathe them! Slipping in here when I am gone on the pretext of playing with Evan. Nellwyn caught them yesterday taking Evan out of his cradle—I do not like it, Gyles!"

"Nor do I," Gyles agreed, "but you can hardly deny them access to the babe."

"I can and I shall!" Blue eyes sparkled angrily. "I won't allow Aurelia to kill my son as she did my father."

"What did you say!" Gyles turned Serena back to face him. "What do you mean?"

"Exactly what I said—Aurelia murdered Father!" Serena spat. "I don't know how, but I am certain she had a hand in his death. And Father knew it too, at the end; he didn't even want her in his room, but of course she insisted, saying it was her *wifely* duty. Hah! That one wouldn't recognize a wifely duty if the priest dangled it before her nose!"

"Can you prove this, Serena?"

Anger departed as quickly as it had arrived and Serena gave in to the gentle pressure of Gyles's arms. "No, I cannot prove it," she replied dispiritedly, "I only know what I've told you is true. I could see it in Father's eyes. Do you understand now why I do not wish to remain here?"

"Aye, love, I understand, but that alters nothing. Evan can travel well enough, but you cannot and surely neither Aurelia nor Beda can mean Evan harm. 'Tis not uncommon for a woman, once safely delivered, to imagine—"

Serena tore away from Gyles's embrace. "I am imagining nothing!"

But was that entirely true? Serena wondered as she pressed a hand to her eyes. Ever since Beda had arrived,

345

Serena had had a sense of impending doom. She would awake in the middle of the night with a feeling of terror so great that her throat was constricted to the point where Serena could barely swallow or breathe. At such times Serena would take Evan into the bed with her and weep silently as the babe's breath fell on her cheek. Was she the only one at Broughton who felt this dread of tomorrow? Gyles saw nothing amiss, nor, apparently, did Bryan or Catherine—perhaps it was merely a phantom of her own creation. Was it her imagination that Aurelia and Beda watched her every move?

For herself Serena was not afraid, but there was Evan to consider now, sweet little Evan who trusted all who held him in their arms. Innocent Evan who was helpless against the evil Serena felt invading Broughton.

"When . . ." Serena's voice caught in her throat. "When will you leave?" Why did it seem she was always bidding Gyles farewell?

"I had planned to remain for two more days." Gyles toyed with a strand of Serena's hair. "But if you wish, cherie, I will remain a bit longer."

"No!" The word came out more sharply than she intended and Serena bit her lip in vexation. "Do not alter your plans, but one thing I ask of you: Take Evan with you."

"Serena, you cannot be serious!" Gyles trapped Serena's face in his hands. "Take Evan to Camden without you! The babe must eat—"

"I'll have Nellwyn find a wet nurse. Please, Gyles, take Evan from here."

Sighing inwardly Gyles reflected upon the complicated woman who was his wife. Serena was not given to wild imaginings, but since Beda had arrived, Serena's mind had taken a sinister bend. If taking Evan to Camden would bring her peace . . . "Very well, Serena, I shall do as you ask."

"Thank you," Serena whispered.

Gyles would long remember the look in those azure pools when he agreed to Serena's request.

The day of departure was warm and clear as Serena bade a tearful farewell to her son.

"Take care of him, Nellwyn, be sure he does not catch a chill the two nights before you reach home." Serena tucked a small blanket more securely around Evan.

"Now, lamb, didn't I see ye and Bryan safely grown?" Nellwyn clucked her tongue disapprovingly. "There still be time to change your mind, ye know. 'Tis not good taking the wee one away from his mother this soon. I'll gladly stay with ye 'til ye can travel."

"No!" Hastily Serena deposited Evan's basket in Nellwyn's arms and retreated to where Gyles stood with Bryan and Catherine.

"Godspeed, Gyles." Serena handed him the stirrup cup when they were alone.

Gyles drained the cup and set it upon a tray carried by a page. "Serena, are you certain this is necessary?"

"No, I am not at all certain." Serena's eyes filled with tears. How handsome Gyles looked, the gentle breeze ruffling his hair, the helm carelessly held under one arm, those emerald eyes so bright and clear that they fairly pierced her soul. It was as if she were seeing him for the last time and the premonition caused Serena to tremble. "Take care, my love, guard yourself and the children. And love them, Gyles, for they are precious beyond words."

A shadow of emotion chased across Gyles's features. "You know I will, cherie, but you speak as if we were going to be separated for years rather than a few short weeks."

With an effort Serena pushed the nagging fear away and forced a light tone. "What nonsense! 'Tis simply I find separation from those I love intolerable, and those few weeks you speak of will truly seem years to me. Pay me no heed, Gyles, you said yourself I have been moody of late. Now come, kiss me as a husband should and quickly, your men are waiting."

"As a husband and quickly?" Gyles teased a curl that fell over Serena's shoulder. "The two are quite

347

different, but I shall do my best." And he did with such vehemence that the embrace lasted far longer than intended, leaving Serena breathless and Gyles cursing his binding clothing. Against her lips, Gyles whispered, "Recover soon, love, I have been celibate far too long."

"I shall. God protect you, Gyles."

15

Serena's days fell into a listless pattern—Bryan was busy with the upcoming harvest, Catherine ran Broughton's household affairs with an efficiency that required no aid, so Serena was left to her own devices most of the time. Beda and Aurelia prowled the castle like two hounds who had suddenly lost the scent of their prey, watching, it seemed, Serena's every move until she felt she would scream. Serena's only escape was her chamber and she took to barring the door when she retired for the evening. But Serena told no one of her precautions, fearing Bryan would laugh at her as Gyles had done.

Letters from Camden arrived often, which made Serena think the messengers in Gyles's livery must soon drop from exhaustion. Serena replied to every letter, filling her own missives with inquiries about Alan and Evan and light anecdotes of life at Broughton. If her letters held a forced gaiety, Gyles appeared not to notice, which increased Serena's determination to put aside her private fears. After all, three weeks had passed since Gyles's departure and nothing had come of Serena's forebodings —indeed, she was becoming bored with her indolent existence.

"But, Bryan," Serena pleaded one morning when they had broken their fast; Aurelia and Beda having quit the table to go riding. "Gyles did not mean for me to be denied all forms of exercise!"

"You are not denied *all* exercise, sister mine." Bryan reproved her with a grin. "You have your walks."

"Walks!" Serena gave a snort of disgust. "It has been five weeks since Evan's birth, I am fully able to sit a horse now—and were you not so stubborn I could have left for Camden by now."

"Gyles said four weeks and four weeks it shall be," Bryan insisted.

"Oh, heavens, Bryan, let Serena ride!" Catherine put aside a piece of tapestry and glared at him. "It won't hurt her in the least, she's not made of parchment after all. And either you allow Serena to ride or she'll bully your men into letting her take sword practice again."

Bryan slammed a fist on the table and Serena hurried to placate him. "It wasn't sword practice, Bryan, 'twas archery and I bullied no one."

"I ought to lock you in your room!" Bryan roared. "Of all the harebrained stunts—"

"Oh, do be quiet, Bryan, you are giving me a headache." Serena made a wry face. "And Gyles wouldn't like that either."

"You are—" Bryan stopped as a familiar figure entered the hall.

"Richard!" Serena was on her feet in an instant and across the hall. "How wonderful to see you! Where have you been?"

Bryan restrained the urge to pull Serena away from Richard's arms and instead greeted him levelly. "Welcome, Richard. This is a most unexpected surprise."

"I would have come sooner, but we have been plagued with a band of thieves these past weeks." Richard smiled easily, yet Serena sensed an undercurrent between the two men. "Serena, my dear, you appear fully recovered from your ordeal."

Serena decided to ignore the endearment—Richard was an old family friend. "So I am, Richard, as I have been trying to convince Bryan. Do you know he won't even allow me to ride?"

"For shame, Bryan, how can you be so heartless? You can see for yourself how well Serena is." Richard's arm fell to Serena's waist and he dropped a kiss on her cheek, causing her to recoil slightly.

"I am following Gyles's instructions," Bryan glowered. "He wants Serena in the best of health when she returns to Camden."

Richard stiffened briefly. "I can well imagine. However, that is of no concern now—what is important is that Serena wishes to ride, so . . ." He turned to Serena with a smile. "Shall we indulge your whim, m'lady?"

Her eager consent was overriden by Bryan, and Serena glared wrathfully at her brother.

"Short of clapping Serena in irons there is little I can do to prevent her acceptance, however I do have one condition. Postpone your outing 'til this afternoon and I shall accompany you."

"But of course!" Serena exclaimed, relieved that Bryan had conceded defeat. "And, Catherine, you must come, too."

"I thank you, but no." Catherine laughed. "I have far too many things here that need to be done. Mayhap tomorrow."

"By all means, tomorrow," Richard murmured distantly as he looked blankly at Catherine. With an effort he collected his thoughts. "A game of chess, Bryan? My father isn't nearly the opponent you are. Serena, love, why don't you rest 'til our ride, I don't want to overtax your strength."

Serena eyed Richard curiously, bridling under the patronizing tone in his voice. "That won't be necessary, Richard, I—"

"My dear, of course it is." Richard sounded shocked that Serena should defy him, and he placed a hand beneath her elbow and propelled her to the staircase. "Rest well, Serena."

Alone in her chamber Sarena mused over Richard's odd behavior. He acted as if the past year and a half had never happened! As if she were a maiden still with no marriage vows, husband, or child. Child! Richard had not asked about her child—he hadn't asked if she'd given birth to a boy or girl, hadn't asked to see the babe. . . .

A cold finger of terror crept up Serena's spine and she tried to shake it off. Oh, but I'm being silly! Serena told herself. If Gyles could see me now he would laugh at me. Gyles would say my imaginings are besting me. Richard didn't ask about Evan because he already knew—Bryan undoubtedly wrote Richard immediately after I gave birth. As for Richard's manner, well, he is an old friend and is acting much as Bryan has been behaving. Nothing odd or suspicious in that.

Serena found herself gazing through the same arrow slit that Gyles had stood before three weeks earlier. Three weeks? It seemed more like three years since Gyles had left. Leaning against the wall, arms hugging her sides, Serena drove all bleak thoughts from her mind, concentrating instead on Camden and Gyles. Gyles, my own love, my heart, mine! Serena's heart fairly sang as she shaped a mental image of her husband. The black hair that curled ever so gently at the nape of his neck and was so soft to the touch of her fingers; a straight, slim nose set between green eyes that clouded to a muted shade when Gyles was angry, threw shards of brilliant emerald when angered, or softened to fathomless green when he held Serena in his arms. Serena closed her eyes, imagining the gentle, insistent pressure of Gyles's lips against her mouth, throat, breasts. Gyles's hands slowly removing her cumbersome garments; caressing, arousing, lifting her against his hard chest.

A few more days, Serena reminded her willfull body as she dragged her thoughts back to safer ground. A short nap—as Richard had suggested—Serena reflected wryly. Her dreams were sure to be pleasant.

Flanked by Richard and Bryan, Serena cantered happily through the gaming woods of Broughton. Richard's odd behavior persisted, but in her newly regained freedom Serena ignored it, concentrating instead on the delightful autumn day. A doe, fawn by her side, left her grazing to study the source of laughter that reverberated through the forest. A red fox crouched beneath a fallen tree, sensing danger in the appearance of this trio of humans.

Abruptly reining her mount to a halt, Serena laughingly turned to Bryan and Richard. "I challenge you both: a race to the place where the trail forks. Are you game?"

"God's blood, Serena!" Bryan exploded. "Gyles will have my head for letting you ride, I refuse—"

"A truly marvelous idea," Richard put in softly, brown eyes probing the trees for . . . what? "We'll allow you a head start—in the interest of fairness."

"Bah!" Serena gave an arrogant toss of her head, setting her gold-flecked curls bouncing. "I wouldn't take advantage of either of you in such a way. But if you insist . . ."

Serena drove a slippered heel into her mount's flank and the horse leaped forward, then stretched out into an even pace.

"Damn it, Serena!" Bryan roared futilely. "Halt right where you are!"

"Catch up—if you can!" Serena merrily called back.

Bryan muttered a curse and set off in pursuit, Richard beside him. But Serena was well ahead and her lighter weight lent her a slight advantage, so when her two self-proclaimed guardians rounded the last curve that led to the fork, Serena was waiting, mocking them with a huge grin.

"Serena, I'm going to flay your deceitful hide," Bryan threatened as he drew rein.

"How you carry on, dear brother mine," Serena pouted. "Poor Catherine, I pity—"

Of a sudden, her mount started, prancing to one side; as she strove to quiet the normally gentle filly, Serena caught a flash of color in the wood.

"Bryan? There is some—" Too late Serena recognized the glint of sunlight on metal, too late she noticed the deathly silence of the game forest, she was too far from Bryan's side to grab his dagger for her own protection. Serena's scream was torn from her throat even while she sent her mount forward. "Look to your left, Bryan! Your left!"

His sword half pulled from its scabbard, Bryan wheeled his steed to meet the danger head on. Five men descended upon the once-frivolous party and, even while he defended himself, Bryan knew this was no motley group of bandits. Their arms were too fine, their movements too well trained to be other than men who made their living through use of weapons.

Bryan's sword pierced one man's neck, a pink froth spewing forth when the point was withdrawn. Another attacker was on him immediately, and Bryan swung around, catching a glimpse of Serena from the corner of his eye.

"Ride, Serena!" Bryan managed to yell before he was forced to concentrate solely on his defense.

"Richard, help him!" Serena cried as she drew abreast of her childhood friend. "He'll be killed! Richard, draw your blade, for the love of God!"

Why was Richard simply sitting there? Why didn't he help Bryan? Why—why were the men only intent upon Bryan! Richard shifted his gaze to Serena and smiled, the soft, gentle brown eyes ablaze with such bloodlust and hatred that Serena had never seen.

"First Bryan, then Gyles," Richard intoned as he grabbed the bridle of Serena's mount when she made to flee. In a harsh, rasping voice Serena barely recognized he continued, "I could not kill Bryan—we were once very close—but I swear I shall run your precious bastard through myself, with pleasure."

Serena made a choking sound and hurled herself from the saddle, snatching Richard's sword while he tried to control two restless mounts.

"Serena, no!" Richard's anguish carried to her ears as she buried the blade deep into one man's back.

Chivalry be damned! Serena thought grimly as she wrenched the sword free of the body. In his madness Richard was of no value—indeed he must have planned the attack himself—and Bryan alone could not stand off the attackers.

Bryan swayed in his saddle as an alien blade found a home beneath his upraised arm and he cried out as his sword fell from his grip.

"Bryan! *Bryan!*" Serena dropped her own weapon and rushed to catch her brother as he plummeted to the earth.

"Not the girl!" Richard's inhuman shriek pierced the air. "I was promised—not the girl!"

Arms outstretched, Richard's voice was the last sound she heard, Bryan's crimson stained tunic the last sight Serena focused on before the relentless steel of a blade landed flat across the side of her head, then turned and bit into her side.

Gyles, my darling, my love! Serena's bones dissolved and she slumped to the ground, not knowing that Bryan's body covered hers almost at once.

Something moist nuzzled at her hand and the slight girl stirred at the touch. Eyelids flickered open, blue eyes searched the source of the disturbance. She tried to pull herself up, but a great weight hampered her and looking down she saw the hazy form of a man. What? . . . Memory flared briefly and she cringed away, managing finally to drag her skirts from beneath the body.

Blood! Her stomach churned, but she forced down the bile and weaved a hesitant path toward the small mare that had awakened her. The mare stood quite still, very willing it seemed, to be ridden.

"I must . . . get help." The girl spoke softly to the mount. "Then we must . . . ride . . . get . . . warn . . ." She dropped the reins as if they burned her fingers and groaned. "I cannot . . . take you. They would know . . . I am . . . I should be . . . dead? He's dead!" She pointed unsteadily at the man on the ground.

Her head began to spin and she closed her eyes to steady herself for a moment. "Thieves . . . and Richard . . . Richard planned? Who? I . . . I do not remem—" The girl began to laugh hysterically and she stumbled blindly from the clearing. "Gyles . . . there was . . . Gyles? Must warn . . ." Blood dripped from her scalp, matting her hair and soaking the right sleeve of her gown. Her side was on fire and she pressed her arm tightly over the gaping wound, vainly trying to staunch the flow of blood.

How long she walked the half-crazed girl did not know, but somewhere in the vast wooded area her strength deserted her and she crumpled onto a pallet of dead leaves.

{ BOOK V }

A Castle
Under Siege

16

Gyles smiled approvingly as Alan, under Nellwyn's watchful eye, struggled to exchange Evan's soiled napkin for a clean one. The task completed, Alan proudly stepped back so Nellwyn could inspect his handiwork.

"Aye, lad, that be . . . fine, just fine." Gyles could sense the grin the old nurse was holding back and scooped Evan into his arms to critically appraise Alan's task himself.

The napkin slipped haphazardly down one of Evan's hips and Gyles ducked his head so Alan would not see his smile. "I agree, Nellwyn. Alan, 'tis a fine job, you will be a great help to Lady Serena when she returns."

Alan's chest swelled visibly under his father's praise and he strutted importantly between Nellwyn and Gyles.

"Will m'lady return soon, Lord Gyles?" Nellwyn asked after she had deposited Evan in his cradle.

"Aye, Nellwyn. In her last letter my lady said she is fully recovered and eager to join us." Alan was tugging on his arm and Gyles obligingly swung Alan onto his broad shoulders.

"She'll be most pleased with the changes ye've made." Nellwyn gave an approving nod. "Lady Mara's wedding —'twas most kind of you to find her a husband—and Lady Lydia beaming at the idea of going to live with her rather than joining a convent."

Gyles chuckled. "Do not praise me overmuch, Nellwyn, 'twas Sir Arthur's doing entirely. Upon his last visit —when Lady Beda treated him so shamefully—he became taken with my sister and she with him. I did but fall in with their plans."

"That's one I be glad is gone, that Lady Beda." Nellwyn sniffed distastefully. "She were naught but trouble. Why the way me lamb used to cry herself to sleep over that one—oh! I be sorry, m'lord."

"No need, Nellwyn, that lady will cause your mistress no further hardship." Gyles threw the nurse a lame smile. "I wasted much of the months of our marriage, a mistake I shall not make again. Was she very unhappy as my bride, Nellwyn?"

The nurse was not surprised at the question, for during Serena's absence Gyles had grown fond of Nellwyn, and she in turn was pleased to find the Norman lord did indeed have a heart. Gyles spent as much of his days as was possible in the nursery, which Serena had instructed Nellwyn convert out of an empty chamber. And it was only natural that the nurse and the husband should fall to discussing Serena, who was so dear to both their hearts.

Nellwyn delighted in regaling Gyles with tales of Serena's childhood, recounting the willfull ways of the young child, who from birth had twisted both father and brother about her fingers. Serena's mother had been of a different mold, however, for mother and daughter were of the same nature and she recognized early the independence that manifested itself in Serena. Far from being unhappy with the event, Serena's mother encouraged it and from childhood Serena was taught to value her mind above the dowry she would one day bring her husband.

"At first me lamb was more angry than unhappy," Nellwyn answered slowly. "Went against her nature, being forced into a marriage that way; aye, ye should have seen the fit of temper she gave way to when Lord Geoffrey told her about you. 'Twas all that Norman woman's doing of course—begging yer pardon—after Serena all the time, telling her she had better wed before she turned so ugly no man would look at her. Fairly tossed Serena into bed with every knight who came to court Serena, that witch did. And she spent all of Serena's dowry money, every coin! But me lamb fixed her proper, she did." Briefly, Nellwyn described Serena's revenge upon her step-mother.

"I wish I could have seen that!" Gyles grinned. Alan was asleep on his bed and Nellwyn and Gyles had long since availed themselves of two of the chairs in the nursery. "She has a fiery temper, my little Serena."

"That she does." Nellwyn chuckled in agreement. " 'Tis the best thing ye did, giving her a babe. Heed me words, m'lord, keep her busy raising yer wee ones, that will keep her out of trouble."

"You only say that because you love being a mother hen." Gyles's eyes gleamed devilishly. "And Evan and Alan cannot defy you the way Serena does." He sobered. "Nellwyn, are you bound to Serena?"

"Aye, but only by me heart. The old lord granted me freedom after Serena was born." Nellwyn's face softened with an inner glow as she looked into her past. "I was married—ye did not know that, did ye?—to a freeman at Broughton, once I had me own freedom. James his name was, a good man, kind and gentle; the best smithy in all of Broughton's lands. We had a small cottage, in the castle's shadow, and Bryan and Serena oft came to see us in the evenings. James and me, we were not blessed with children—four babes I lost before they even stirred in me womb." A single tear rolled down Nellwyn's cheek, and Gyles squeezed her hand gently. "But we loved each other, and Serena and Bryan kept our cottage lively enough. James even forged Serena's first suit of armor and a wee sword—she came crying to us one day because Bryan had laughed at her and said he wouldn't play with such a puny little girl.

"Well, when James finished those arms, ye've never seen such happiness! Serena picked up her sword, put on her armor, and stamped off to find Bryan. Laid him flat on his face, me little lamb did, took that sword and hit him hard on his rump! Bryan couldn't sit proper for a week—and neither could Serena, for when Lord Geoffrey found out what she'd done he gave her the hardest part of his hand. Then he told Serena that if she was going to play with weapons she'd best learn how to use them—and she did."

"A happy childhood," Gyles murmured absently.

"Aye, but it did not last." Nellwyn's expression turned bitter. "The bastard Will—yer pardon—King William's invasion ended it. I lost me James at Hastings."

"I am sorry." Gyles studied Nellwyn's seamed face.

Nellwyn gave a quick shake of her head. " 'Tis the way of things, m'lord, and 'tis best forgotten. I have me memories." She looked at the cradle. "And now . . . now there be Alan and Evan, and if I know me lamb we'll be needing a larger room for a nursery."

There was a light tap on the door and Edward entered before Gyles called his permission. Gyles frowned at this breech of etiquette and then caught the slight blush that colored Nellwyn's cheeks as she swiftly averted her gaze. Edward and Nellwyn! Gyles laughed to himself. Who would have guessed? I must tell Serena of this when I write next.

"Yes, Sir Edward?" Gyles raised a speculative eyebrow.

"A messenger below, m'lord," Edward said in a strained voice.

"From Broughton?" Edward nodded but did not meet Gyles's eyes, keeping his gaze fixed slightly above Gyles's head. "Splendid!" Gyles sprang from his chair and out the door, Edward on his heels.

"Forgive me, m'lord, for having been the one to bring you these tidings." The young squire stood in front of the table on which lay the message he had delivered.

Gyles rested one muscular thigh against the table and fingered the paper beside him. "How fares your lord, good squire?" Gyles asked in a calm voice.

"Lord Bryan was close to death when my lady sent me hither. The priest had been sent for and a Mass was being said." The squire swayed on his feet.

"Bring this man a chair!" Gyles shouted and eased the squire into the seat before softly continuing. "You will feel better when you have rested and eaten. You rode without stopping?"

"Yes, m'lord." He swallowed a mouthful of wine. "Lady Catherine told me to make haste."

"I will commend you to Lord Bryan, lad, and I will tire you no further. Seek your chamber and when you are rested, return to Broughton." Gyles rose wearily. "Sir Edward, come with me."

The night was old when Edward finally left his lord's chamber, the door closing softly behind him. A short while later Gyles appeared and made his way slowly to the nursery.

"Nellwyn?" The old nurse was kneeling beside Alan's pallet and she got stiffly to her feet as Gyles walked to Evan's cradle. His eyes never leaving Evan's face, Gyles questioned, "You have heard?"

"Aye." The word was a choked sob. "Edward . . . Sir Edward was here . . . is it true?"

"I do not know—all that is certain is that Serena has disappeared, and so has Richard." Gyles closed his eyes. "Is it possible, Nellwyn, could she and Richard—"

"Nay!" Nellwyn said sharply. "She ran from ye once, 'tis true, but not . . . not like this."

"No, of course not," Gyles sighed. "In a way, I wish it were true, at least I would know that she is safe, that . . . Oh, God! what has happened to her?"

"Shh. Ye'll wake the babes. Come." Nellwyn tenderly guided Gyles back to his chamber and pressed a goblet of wine into his hand. Using the stern tone that so intimidated Alan, Nellwyn ordered, "Drink."

Nellwyn turned away from the stark anguish in Gyles's eyes as he numbly obeyed her.

"I know what ye be thinking, m'lord, and ye be wrong. Me lamb is alive—I know. If she were . . . dead, I would have felt it. Here." Nellwyn touched her left breast. "I would have known and so would you."

"I am leaving for Broughton at dawn, Nellwyn. I know I needn't remind you, but guard the boys. Edward will be in charge while I am gone. See that there is a man with each of my sons at all times. Never, under any circumstances, should my sons be left alone with anyone unless Edward, Justin, or yourself are also present. Do you understand?"

"Aye, m'lord." Nellwyn's eyes were round with alarm.

"I shall find her," Gyles promised grimly. "I had to tell one of my sons his mother was dead; I will not tell my other son the same thing. Evan will have his mother if I need search all of England. Goodnight, Nellwyn."

Alone, Gyles snuffed out the candles and retired, but sleep did not come immediately. Instead, Gyles's mind dwelled upon the way he had laughed at Serena's fears when she had pleaded for his understanding. She had been afraid; had known, sensed, the danger that waited for her. And I laughed! Gyles swore to himself, damning his own arrogance.

"Take care of the children . . . love them, for they are precious." Her sweet voice floated to him from the darkness, and Gyles could almost imagine Serena was beside him.

"Serena?" Gyles whispered into the darkness. "I will find you, Serena, do not fear. The children are safe and soon you will be safe as well. I love you, Serena."

Gyles closed his eyes, fighting off the bleak despair that had threatened to overpower him when he first read Catherine's hasty letter. Life without Serena? Intolerable! Unthinkable! Gyles would not allow it to happen. And in order to find Serena, he must be rested, in full control of his mind and reactions. The many hard years of campaigning served Gyles well. He forced himself to think of nothing and within minutes he was asleep.

Catherine heard the drumming of hoofbeats before the knight in charge of the watch reached her with the news of approaching visitors. She slipped quietly from the room, nodding her approval to the squire who immediately took his place in front of the door to her chamber, and descended to the hall at the same instant that the group of armed men entered.

The tallest of the knights detached himself from the party and strode toward his hostess. "Catherine. How is Bryan?"

"He will live, God be praised!" Catherine smiled as her hands were kissed. "And you, Gyles?"

"Weary. Dirty." Gyles's lips twisted into a parody of a smile but the muted green eyes were cold. "Is there any news of Serena?"

Catherine's smile faded and she drew Gyles up to her. "Bryan wanted to see you the moment you arrived. I will warn you now, say naught of this . . . this tragedy if Aurelia is near. Bryan feels he can see her fine hand in all of this."

"I noted you have doubled the men on the battlements," Gyles commented. "Are you as well protected within?"

"Yes. I have guards patrolling the courtyard, grounds and corridors, also men posted at our chamber door day and night. Yourself, Evan, and Alan?"

"I left orders, they will be well-guarded."

They paused before entering the chamber and Catherine turned to Gyles. "It has been a week and for most of that time Bryan hovered between life and death. Try not to react to his appearance."

Bryan had lost weight and dark circles ringed his sunken eyes, but when Gyles approached the bed, Bryan's eyes flew open, revealing the life that flared within. "Gyles . . . good to see you."

Gyles grasped Bryan's outstretched arm. "Are you well enough to tell me what happened?"

Bryan pulled himself upright with a groan, and Catherine hastened to push several pillows behind his back. "Leave us, Catherine."

"But—" Catherine protested.

"Now, Catherine!" Bryan barked, then softened at her wounded look. "Please, Catherine."

Bryan waited until he was certain Catherine was

365

safely away. "I am sorry, Gyles. I shall spend the rest of my days regretting my weakness in giving in to Serena's request. Had I been more firm, she would be alive today."

"Are you so certain Serena is dead?" Gyles availed himself of a chair and stretched his long legs in front of him.

Bryan's face registered surprise. "If she were alive, Serena would have found a way to return here, or at least get a message to us. Her mount was found grazing near the place where we were attacked, but there was no sign of Serena. Surely you do not believe Serena simply walked away?"

"What of Richard?" Gyles ignored Bryan's question.

"God alone knows that." Bryan raised his hands in a gesture of helplessness. "He has vanished without a sign —Catherine sent a rider to his father but he hasn't seen Richard since . . ."

"Do you believe him?" Gyles asked sharply, then sighed when Bryan nodded.

"Gyles," Bryan carefully phrased his question. "How fared . . . I mean, Serena and yourself, there were no . . . problems?"

"If you are wondering if Serena ran away with Richard to escape me, the answer is ño. There was no need—we were reconciled. But we are making no progress, tell me as much as you remember about the attack."

Slowly, painfully, Bryan set about explaining the day of the attack, beginning with his argument with Serena and culminating at his own wounds and loss of conciousness. Bryan spared not himself, for he was convinced he had missed some signal that should have warned him of the trap. And Richard's treachery was disclosed for the first time—a revelation far more painful to Bryan than the injury he had incurred. Bryan's tale of Serena's bravery brought a smile to Gyles's lips; he could well imagine his wife using a sword on those so foolhardy as to think a woman would stand by and watch her brother murdered.

"I do not understand." Bryan fell back against his pillows. "I have done naught to earn Richard's hate and

God knows neither has Serena, yet he would not raise a hand in our defense."

Gyles mulled Bryan's recital over thoughtfully before he responded quietly, "Oh, but you did. I told you upon my last visit that I thought Richard had taken leave of his senses—I am certain of it now. You were an obstacle that stood between himself and Serena. You were quite willing to return Serena to her husband, and to Richard that was unforgivable."

"Then why not wait 'til Serena was on her way back to you?" Bryan argued. "Even if I died, Serena would still be married to you, she would not be free to wed Richard."

The two men were silent for a time before Bryan suddenly swore and Gyles started.

"Did Serena ever speak to you of Father's death?"

"A bit," Gyles admitted. "Why?"

"I'm not certain but Serena felt Aurelia murdered Father. I don't know why, she would never tell me, but Serena was positive Aurelia had a hand in it. What I am trying to say is, just before I passed out I heard Richard shout: 'Not the girl. I was promised.' "

"Then 'twas you the men were after, not Serena?" Gyles said slowly. "But why?"

Bryan frowned. "If I die without issue, Broughton goes to Serena." Gyles shot out of his chair. "You did not know? Of course, there was no reason for Serena to tell you—I am young, there was little chance of my death. So Aurelia saw to it that I should meet with an accident."

"But she would not gain Broughton even if you died. By your own words, 'twould go to Serena."

"And through Serena to you," Bryan stated calmly. "You would benefit through both our deaths." Bryan waved Gyles back to his chair as he began to advance to the bed, "I know you had no part in this. But somehow, Aurelia stands to benefit if you inherit Broughton."

"How?" Gyles snarled angrily.

"I do not know." Bryan sighed. "At that point my reasoning fails. But I know this—my sister is dead."

"No!" Gyles bellowed. "She lives! *She lives!*"

Bryan studied Gyles compassionately. " 'Tis hard, I know, Gyles, but you must accept it."

"No!" Gyles repeated quietly. Then, unconsciously, he mimicked Nellwyn's words and gesture as he touched his hand to his chest. "I would have felt her death here. I will not believe 'til I see her body with my own eyes."

Bryan closed his eyes. "You may never find her body, Gyles, there are wolves in the forest. You know as well as I what a pack of wolves can do to a body."

"Then I had better organize searching parties." Gyles rose. "Have I your leave to make use of Broughton's men?"

"Of course, Gyles. Take as many as you need." When Gyles left, Bryan turned his face to the pillow and wept as he had wished to do since he had become aware that Serena was dead.

17

The search began immediately, men from both lands who once would have spent their time squabbling were now united in one goal. Not only Broughton's knights, but freeman and serf alike gathered in the courtyard to see if the arrival of Lady Serena's husband would effect any changes in the pall that had hung over the castle for a week. If Gyles was surprised by the turnout of manpower, he hid it well, sending only an inquisitive look to a gnarled old man standing near the steps of the castle.

"Will you look for the lass?" Rheumy eyes fixed themselves on Gyles intently, blinking rapidly when he nodded. " 'Tis time, too. The lass saved me from death once— I pray I can do the same for her."

Gyles clapped the old man's shoulder, barely able to speak over the thickness clogging his throat. "Thank you."

Then he was once again in control of his emotions and in a cool, deliberate voice Gyles explained what was required of the assembled men. Broughton's stables were emptied and mounts of various sizes and descriptions were supplied by the freemen who were lucky enough to own them. Speed was utmost in Gyles's mind and mounted men covered more ground than those afoot. The sea of humanity broke into small groups, two knights to a group, and started for the gaming forest—they would begin where the attack had taken place and from there spread out into a circular pattern, like a spider spinning a giant web.

Gyles swung lightly into the saddle he had vacated so recently and set off with his own party. He was a knight, a man of deeds in place of words, and he doubted not that he would find Serena—it was easier on his soul to have a physical task to occupy his body and thoughts; there would be no time for brooding.

From that day forward Broughton was alive with activity, men arose and left their pallets at dawn not to return 'til the sun gave way to the moon. No man complained at the pace that was set, for if Gyles drove them hard, he drove himself with a merciless determination that seemed to stem from inhuman strength. The pattern of the search grew, the circle widening day by day; a hundred eyes seeking, probing, looking for a sign—any sign—that would mean Serena still lived.

All that was uncovered after a week's time was a scrap of blood-stained cloth that Catherine identified as having come from Serena's dress. Silently Gyles folded the scrap and placed it inside his tunic.

"Surely you realize what this means, Gyles." Bryan had regained his strength sufficiently to allow him to join the others at table.

"It means Serena was able to walk to the edge of the forest," Gyles replied, turning from the fire.

"It means she is dead!" Bryan shouted, his patience at an end partly from Gyles's obstinance and his own inability to join in the search. "Give it up, Gyles, for my sanity if not your own."

"No," Gyles answered curtly and stalked off to his chamber.

The days and weeks plodded forward. The search parties varied in composition, crops had to be harvested, which meant the serfs returned to their land. Armor, weapons, saddles, all had to be repaired at times, so freemen returned briefly to their forges. Knights grew weary, as did their mounts, and Gyles worked out a rotating schedule so that each knight searched for one month and rested the following month. But not Gyles—the little excess weight he had gained during the summer melted quickly away, the muscles that had grown lax from disuse were stretched and worked until they were as tautly drawn as a bowstring, the arrogance that was so much a part of his features was refined with a grim determination that was seldom broken by a smile. Above all else there was a haunted bitterness in the depths of Gyles's emerald eyes, which Serena would have despaired at had she seen.

Too late Gyles had learned to love, too late the man had given freely of his heart and his lesson had brought an unending sorrow. Once every fortnight Gyles rode to Camden to insure that all went well during his prolonged absence. The first words from Alan's lips were always the same: questions of Serena and her return. And Gyles's answer was automatic: soon. Nellwyn would turn away so neither father nor son would see the tears that sprang to her eyes.

One night in November, Alan unexpectedly forced the truth of the situation painfully into Gyles's soul. They were seated on the floor of the nursery arranging Alan's wooden knights into battle lines while Evan gurgled happily on a pelt in front of the hearth. "When Serena comes home do I have to call her Serena, Father?"

Gyles picked up an elaborately carved mounted knight. "What will you call her instead?" Gyles teased with a smile.

"Well!" Alan moved an archer to a different position. "Could I call her Mother?" The toy dropped from Gyles's numbed fingers and Alan, fearing he had angered his father, hurried to explain. "I know my mother is dead, but . . . couldn't we . . . I . . . pretend? Serena wouldn't be angry, would she?"

Gyles stared mutely at his son, the power of speech completely deserting him as his mind raced back to the day he had found Alan and Serena swimming in the pool. How angry he had been that day, how furious because he thought Serena had taken a lover. Oh, God, Gyles thought wretchedly, am I to spend the rest of my life being reminded of the short time I had with Serena? Evan emitted a particularly happy sound and Gyles shifted his gaze to the babe. All my life, to the end of my days.

Nellwyn came to Gyles's rescue. "Come, lad, 'tis time ye had yer bath so Evan can have his supper."

She bustled Alan from the room as the wet nurse entered, then hesitated when Gyles placed Evan in her arms.

"Go ahead," Gyles instructed gruffly. "Can you not see the babe is hungry?"

"Aye, m'lord." But she eyed Gyles hesitantly.

"Then feed him!" Gyles exploded. "And stop looking like a frightened cow!" He left the chamber with a slam that fairly shook the stones of the castle.

Nellwyn found Gyles standing on the battlements, his cloak billowing around him in the wind. Summoning up her courage, Nellwyn touched Gyles's arm.

"The boys are nearly asleep, m'lord; that is, Evan be sleeping and Alan wants ye to hear his prayers. And I've calmed Evan's nurse, poor lass."

Gyles sighed. "I shall apologize before I leave tomorrow. I must have frightened her half to death."

"Aye, that ye did." Nellwyn heartily agreed. "Have ye decided what to tell Alan?"

"That I believe Serena would be honored if he addressed her as mother. No argument, Nellwyn," Gyles told her sternly.

"'Twill be worse later, when ye cannot hide the truth any longer," Nellwyn remonstrated. Gyles stiffened and started to walk away but Nellwyn caught his arm and spun him back to face her. "Ye tried, Lord Gyles, no man could have done more, but give it up now! She's gone! Ye have the babes to think of. Do ye want Evan to grow up without a father as well as a mother?"

"Evan shall have both."

There was nothing to be gained by arguing further and Nellwyn turned sadly away to seek her chamber.

Gyles did not return to Camden again until Christmas, when he stayed for a week, recovering from a severe case of frostbite. The search had progressed far beyond the point where men could return to their homes each night so the serfs and freemen were no longer involved. Only knights and squires remained and when evening fell, pavilions were erected so they might take their rest in relative comfort.

Frostbite was common among the men, as was congestion of the lungs, and both men and steeds wearied as the seemingly endless search continued. When the new year was a month old, even the staunchest of the men had admitted defeat.

Gyles was Bryan's guest as he passed through Broughton on his way to Camden and now, his hunger eased, Gyles leaned back to enjoy his wine and he raised his goblet in a toast. "Catherine, you set a splendid table. I thank you."

Catherine beamed. "You are most gracious, Gyles, and you are welcome here anytime. Now tell us, how are the boys?"

"Fine." Gyles swirled the wine thoughtfully. "Alan received a bow for Christmas and he is quite a marksman already. Evan has discovered his legs, so naught is safe now that he can crawl to whatever catches his eye. Nellwyn swears he is as much a trial as Serena was."

Bryan and Catherine glanced nervously at each other, but wisely held their tongues. Attending to a piece of stitchery nearby, Aurelia had no such qualms.

"Serena was always a trial," Aurelia snapped. "You needn't glare at me, Bryan, nor you, Gyles. Who should know better than yourself—look at how she acted, running away from court as she did. Disgraceful! And the way she twitched her skirts at Prince Henry while she was at court . . . I can tell you, Serena was the talk of all the ladies."

"I am certain you could tell us a great deal, Aurelia," Catherine retorted. "But none of us wish to hear what you have to say."

Aurelia tossed her head arrogantly. "She was a Saxon, of no importance. I say we are well rid of her."

"And I say, if you do not hold your tongue, I shall cut it out of your lying mouth," Gyles said conversationally.

"How dare you!" Aurelia gasped.

"Oh, I dare." Gyles favored her with a cold smile. "Every word you speak makes it that much easier for me. Pray continue."

The sound of scuffling in the entrance hall cut short Bryan's laughter and he rose from his chair only to collapse back with a sharp intake of air.

"Dear God in heaven above!"

That from Aurelia as she shrank against the back of her chair. Gyles swiveled toward the disturbance and went deathly still, the curved scar jumping into relief against his cheek.

An emaciated, bearded man stood alone in the center of the hall, his overly bright eyes fixed upon Aurelia.

"Bryan?" Catherine reached for her husband's hand for reassurance. "Who is he? A hermit?"

Bryan shook his head. " 'Tis . . . 'tis Richard!" He whispered.

Richard raised his hand and pointed at Aurelia. "I am come for you, lady. 'Tis time you pay for your sin— and pay you shall, to the eternal damnation of your immortal soul and mine, for I am to be the instrument of your penance."

"The man is insane!" Her sewing fell from her hands and Aurelia looked wildly about her. "Kill him—kill him!"

"Have you not had your fill of killing?" Richard hurled the words at her and began to advance relentlessly upon Aurelia. "Will your lust for blood never be satisfied? How many must die because of you?" A dagger appeared in Richard's hand and he paused when Aurelia placed herself behind Bryan. "Do not defend her, Bryan, I beg you. 'Twas she who plotted your death."

Richard swung about as Gyles tried to approach. "You! You above all should understand, Lord Gyles. She swore . . . swore! . . . that Serena would not be harmed. But she lied! Her villains struck down Serena when she had dropped her sword . . . a defenseless girl, and Aurelia had her killed. Murderess!" He swung back to Aurelia.

"Tell them, lady. Tell them where I have been these past months. Tell them!"

"I—I don't know what he means, I—"

"Her dower estate! In her dungeon. But I escaped!" A dry, cackle of a laugh tore from Richard's throat. "Your penance, lady. Your life for Serena's."

Later no one would be able to say precisely how it happened but Aurelia—for reasons known only to herself —stepped from behind Bryan and in that instant Richard saw and took his advantage. With a wild cry Richard launched himself at Aurelia, the force of his impact carrying them beyond anyone's reach. Richard's dagger found its way into Aurelia's hands and she sank the long, thin blade into Richard's back. Seemingly unmindful of the pain, Richard dragged himself to his feet, pulling Aurelia with him. He grabbed a handful of her blond hair and smashed Aurelia's face against the stone wall . . . again . . . and yet again until Aurelia's features dissolved into a froth of red pulp and Catherine's scream broke the spell that held everyone motionless.

Richard flung Aurelia's limp body from him and sank to his knees as Bryan reached him. Gyles examined Aurelia briefly then with a shake of his head covered her with a cloak handed him by one of his knights.

Bryan cradled Richard's head in his arm, and while he watched, the madness faded from Richard's eyes.

"Forgive me . . . my friend." The sound of death rattled in Richard's lungs. "But I . . . I loved her . . . so much. And . . . I killed her."

"Serena is dead?" Gyles knelt beside the dying man. "You are certain, man, Serena is dead?" Gyles grasped Richard's ragged tunic and shook him.

"Gyles," Bryan gently lowered Richard's head. "He can tell you naught."

Richard's body was sent to his father the following morning and the next day Aurelia was laid to rest at Broughton. Only Bryan, Catherine, and Gyles were present to hear the priest read over her body, for Aurelia had not been loved by Broughton's inhabitants. Bryan had desired to return his step-mother's remains to her kinsmen, but after much discussion with Catherine, relented to his wife's reasoning. Such an insult would not be taken lightly by Aurelia's family so to avoid further strife, Aurelia was buried in the family cemetery, but her grave was in the section reserved for Broughton's less noble kin, far away from Lord Geoffrey's side.

Gyles moved through the days like a sleepwalker, answering automatically when a question was put to him and overseeing the preparations for his return to Camden. The eve preceeding Gyles's departure, Bryan—a skin of ale under each arm—sought out Gyles in his chamber.

"I came to bid you good luck upon your journey." Bryan dropped a skin unceremoniously into Gyles's lap and folded himself into the chair opposite Gyles.

Gyles looked at him. "Thank you."

"We wanted you to be the first to know—Catherine is with child." Bryan raised his skin in a salute and drank deeply.

"My congratulations." Gyles turned to study the blaze that warmed the chamber.

Bryan took a deep breath and tried once more. "What are your plans, Gyles?"

"Plans?" Clouded green eyes suddenly pinned Bryan to his chair. "I have none."

"Damnation, Gyles!" Bryan lost his temper. "How does anyone reach you?"

"I don't know what you mean," Gyles stated blandly, but an impatient spark flared somewhere within him.

"The hell you don't. Look at yourself, take a good look. I hardly think Alan will be overjoyed to see you this way. But then, he may not even recognize you, after all you've not been to see him in well over a month. By now he probably thinks Edward is his father. But that shouldn't concern you—all you want to do is wallow in self-pity and the rest of the world be damned!"

"Bryan," Gyles warned softly.

"The great Lord Gyles!" Bryan sneered. "Mighty warrior! What of Evan? His mother is dead and his father might as well be."

In the blink of an eye Gyles was out of his chair and holding Bryan against the wall by the front of his tunic.

"You have no right—"

"I have every right," Bryan ground out. "Serena was my sister, I loved her, too. But she is dead, Gyles!"

"No!" Gyles howled and smashed his fist into Bryan's jaw. "She lives . . . you know she lives!"

Bryan picked himself up from the floor, fingering his jaw tenderly before quietly repeating, "Serena is dead, Gyles."

Gyles made a low keening sound far back in his throat. "She lives!"

"No, Gyles, Serena is dead. She has been dead these many months." Bryan guided Gyles back to his chair and wiped a trickle of blood from the corner of his mouth. "Accept it, Gyles, I have. All these months, the searching; the meanest hut was not overlooked, every man, woman, and child was questioned. You did all you could, and all the time Serena was dead. Gyles, no man could have done more! 'Twas hopeless from the beginning."

"But we cannot be certain, Bryan," Gyles whispered brokenly. "We never found her body. Only a scrap of cloth."

Bryan longed to run from the anguished, torn man before him, longed to withdraw the sharp blade of pain he was, of necessity, inflicting upon him. Yet he could not.

"Serena could be at Aurelia's estate," Gyles grasped desperately at his final hope. "Richard was carried there, why not Serena?"

"Gyles." Bryan eyed him sadly. "Richard himself told us Serena is dead. If they were both prisoners, Aurelia would have seen no harm in allowing them to see each other. Why would Richard have come for Aurelia unless he *knew* Serena was dead? He knew! Aurelia's penance he called it; her life for my sister's. You know Serena, if she were alive she would have found some way to get word to us."

"I know . . . oh, God, I know." Gyles buried his face in his hands. "What do I do now, Bryan?"

"You live," Bryan told him firmly. "You take each day that is given you. If 'twill make you feel better, get drunk right now—that is why I brought you that skin—but that won't solve anything except to give you a sleep without dreams."

"I cannot forget her—I doubt I ever shall." Gyles had leaned back in his chair and closed his eyes, all emotion apparently locked away, his voice cold and without inflection. "Oh, God! Bryan, I had so little time with her."

"I know. You won't forget. But one day you will be able to think of her without feeling that a dagger is being twisted in your vitals." Bryan quietly left the chamber.

"I wish there was something we could do." Catherine and Bryan watched the last of the knights depart for Camden. "He's changed, Bryan, he's become unreachable —like he was when I first met him."

"Dear Catherine." Bryan smiled sadly. "We can do naught. Gyles must find his own path out of this darkness."

18

Duty. Duty to his sons, to the old lord's wife and daughter, to the people of Camden, to his retinue of knights. Responsibility for the lives and lands that had been placed in his hands. Obligation, responsibility, duty —all bore Gyles through the final winter days when his grief threatened to overpower him. Pain shared drew Gyles even closer to Alan and often the boy crept into his father's arms to seek assurance.

Gyles dried the tears and cradled Alan's head against his hard chest, crooning tender words that Alan could not understand, but the tone of Gyles's voice comforted the lad. Evan, too, sensed a difference in his father and often in their play the babe would abruptly sit back and stare at his father, his blue eyes wide and serious. Serena's eyes, Gyles would think. Oh, God, Serena's eyes looking at me through our son. Then Evan would laugh and the spell would be broken, leaving Gyles almost limp with the force of his emotions.

Gyles changed—a heart once opened and laid bare is not stored away as easily as a faulty piece of armor— the arrogance, pride, that were so much a part of him fell away when he was safely away from the prying eyes of those who did not know him well. If Gyles had indulged in drinking bouts, if he had taken other women to his bed, perhaps his men would have been less uneasy in his presence—but he did not, and where before there had been only a natural reserve in Gyles's manner, there was now an aloofness, a detachment that alternately stirred pity and fear in the hearts of those who saw him.

Gyles ate, slept, issued orders, rode, played with his sons, and occasionally accepted a challenge for a game of chess with Edward. As Bryan had said, he faced each day as it came, and Gyles even managed to find a portion of happiness in Alan and Evan—but it was a bittersweet joy tinged with the knowledge that Serena was lost to him forever. Infrequently, Gyles would retire to his chamber for an entire day, seeing no one and refusing the food that Nellwyn brought to the door and at such times Nellwyn would quietly withdraw, understanding that Gyles's sorrow had become too great for him to bear in the face of others that day. To Gyles, his life seemed an endless agony, an earthly purgatory from which there was no escape.

Spring arrived at Camden and with it Mara's wedding. Three days before the ceremony was to take place, guests flocked to the castle—the ladies in gaily-colored gowns giggling demurely at the swains dancing attendance upon them. Gyles was the perfect host to all, but stayed much in the background, allowing Mara to play the lady of the manor, to be the center of attention.

Gyles was on his hands and knees, doing his best to imitate a ferocious steed, while Alan, both arms wrapped securely around Gyles's neck, shrieked with glee. Infected with his brother's high spirits, Evan chortled and let fly one of his toys in the general direction of his father. Gyles raised his head at a knock on the door and the toy caught him squarely in the eye.

"Ouch! little scamp!" Gyles laughed and tumbled both of his sons onto the pelt covering the floor to tickle them mercilessly. "Enter, Nellwyn, and take these two monsters back to the nursery."

" 'Tis . . . 'tis I, Mara," her voice came shyly from the doorway as Gyles rose to his feet. "I am sorry, I did not mean to intrude."

" 'Tis all right, Mara," Gyles gave her a weak smile. "We . . . the boys and I . . ."

He is embarrassed! Mara thought, wonderingly, as she watched her half-brother straighten his clothing and thrust his long fingers through his hair. And he—he loves his sons, he truly does! I can see it in his face and eyes. Mara's heart wrenched. How much unhappiness Mother and I have given him—not once in these past years have we given him a single chance to be a part of our own family. How lonely we must have made him feel! Mara's heart, having been softened by love, had become sensitive to the feelings of those around her, and she had gradually realized that Gyles was not the ogre her bitter mind had painted him. Nellwyn appeared to take her charges in hand, her eyebrows lifting at the sight of Mara.

"Take the boys to the nursery, Nellwyn," Gyles instructed. "And, Alan, if you can remember your manners, perhaps Lady Mara will allow you to dine in the hall tonight."

Alan's face lit up and he turned pleading eyes to Mara. "I shall be good, I promise."

Mara smiled. "But of course, Alan; how could I possibly celebrate such an occasion without my nephew at table? I should be most honored."

"See that he changes his tunic." Gyles wagged a finger at Alan's soiled clothing and with a nod, Nellwyn hurried from the chamber. "Now, Mara, is something amiss that brings you to me?"

"No, not at all," Mara blushed—how terrible to remember that since his arrival she had avoided Gyles as much as possible. "I only wanted to thank you for . . . for arranging my marriage, this celebration, everything!"

Gyles's face relaxed into a smile. "You are entirely welcome, Mara. Did you believe I would force you to remain here forever?"

"Much to my shame, Gyles, yes I did," Mara replied truthfully. "I ask that you can find it in your heart to forgive my actions and words. I fear I was all too willing to believe the worst of you—to allow others

381

to fill my head with what I now realize were vicious lies and rumors. I am truly sorry, Gyles. And, I would have you know that I am proud to call you brother."

A smile so kind it twisted Mara's heart curved Gyles's lips. " 'Tis my turn now to thank you, Mara. I wish you as much happiness with Arthur as I knew with Serena." Gyles paused and cleared his throat, adding to himself, "I seem to discover everything too late."

"Gyles, I did have a question." Mara was uncertain how to continue.

"Yes?" Gyles prompted with a frown; Mara had grown quite serious.

"Did you—I don't really mind—but, why did you invite Beda to my wedding?" Mara blurted out. "If 'tis not my concern, then I don't expect an answer, but . . ."

"I did not ask Beda to attend!" Gyles broke in. "Good God, you mean to say she is here?"

"Yes!" Mara burst into tears. "Downstairs with Arthur, flirting and teasing. I know I was his second choice, but why does Beda have to throw it in my face?"

Cold rage built in Gyles's breast, but he spoke gently to Mara. "Dry your tears. You do not wish Arthur to see you with red eyes, do you?" He brushed a tear from her cheek and smiled. "Now go, splash some cold water on your face and arrange your hair. And, Mara, remember, Arthur was not forced into this union—he chose you."

Beda rubbed a hand across Arthur's chest, oblivious to his embarrassment and the efforts he was making to be free of her company. "You really are terrible, Arthur! Surely you knew I was only jesting when I refused your offer. There is still time—tomorrow could be our wedding day instead—"

"Beda! How good of you to come." Gyles grasped her hand firmly and pulled her from Arthur. That good man threw Gyles a look of eternal gratitude and hurriedly disappeared.

"Ah, my sweet knight." Beda fairly melted against Gyles. "I have so missed your company."

Gyles resolutely pushed Beda away, his voice a low

growl. "What are you doing here, Beda? Mara did not invite you."

"That twit!" Beda scoffed. " 'Tis my right—she is my sister-in-law."

"What you have done is unforgivable, but for Mara's sake I shall not ask you to leave. Only keep your distance from Arthur."

Beda smiled wickedly. "And you, Gyles? Must I also keep my distance from you, or is this warning your way of telling me that you still desire me? Could it be that you are jealous."

Gyles thrust her cloying hand away and walked off in disgust, Beda's laughter following him.

Mara's wedding day was an ideal day for early spring —warm, sunny, with a gentle cooling breeze that kept the air in the castle fresh and clean. It was generally agreed that Mara was a beautiful bride, so lovely in fact, that Arthur did not take his eyes from her the entire day.

Gyles retired early, the merrymaking too reminiscent of his own marriage for Gyles to be at ease with the revelers. His chamber was dark, and Gyles lit a solitary candle before disrobing and going to stand before the window. It was a clear night and above him Gyles could see the winking lights of the spring stars. Serena, Gyles sighed bleakly. I never imagined 'twould be so difficult without you. He closed his eyes, summoning instantly the mental image of Serena as he did so often during his lonely nights. Dearest love, why can I not accept what all others do? Why do I feel that you still live? My mind screams at me to accept your death, yet my heart tells me nay. My only love, were it not for the babes I think I would hasten from this earth. But I fear I am destined to live to an old age.

Sighing again, Gyles moved from the window and slipped into bed, only to fling himself from the pallet a moment later with a shout.

"What the devil?" Gyles brought the candle to the bed and his face went rigid with anger. "What are you doing here?"

Beda raised herself until she leaned against the headboard and laughed. "Gyles, you astound me! You are acting like a lad with his first girl; now stop being coy and come here."

"Get out, Beda!" Gyles gritted. Beda allowed the linen to fall from her shoulders, exposing her white abundant breasts to Gyles's gaze. With an oath, Gyles turned away and shrugged into a robe, his stomach churning with revulsion. "What do you want?"

Beda laughed. "You needn't play the bereaved husband with me, Gyles. I know you far too well. And I would think 'tis obvious what I desire."

"You have an odd way of displaying your grief," Gyles said harshly. "Have you prayed at Aurelia's grave of late?"

"Bastard knight!" Beda hissed and swung the open palm of her hand across Gyles's cheek.

Gyles viewed her calmly as he checked his seething desire to throw her bodily from the room. "I know full well my lineage—what of yours?"

"I came because you are now free of that distasteful marriage." Beda refused the bait and settled more comfortably against the pillows, her eyes glittering. "We make a splendid match, Gyles—I will even allow your two brats to stay at Camden if you so desire. 'Twas brilliant of you to charge Arthur with Lydia's care upon his marriage to Mara. Camden will be so pleasant when free of their ugly faces. I am given to understand that the nursery is next to this chamber and I am afraid that will not be satisfactory, put your . . . sons in a different wing of the castle."

Gyles had stared open-mouthed during the recital, but when Beda quieted and smiled up at him, the months of frustration and sorrow burst through his control. Without warning Gyles's hand closed around Beda's wrist and he jerked her from the bed with such force that Beda was hurled against the wall.

"Whore! Think you that I would soil myself with your body?" Gyles's lips pulled back from his teeth in a snarl. "Slut! I would rather clasp an asp to my breast!"

"You will wed me," Beda spat back, "or I will see you dead. And you have two sons now, remember that, Gyles. Who will see to them if you die? Soil your hands?" Beda sneered. "You should be grateful I have kept my silence! You should be honored that I will share your pallet! 'Tis rumored Serena displeased you so you arranged her untimely death."

"You are brave to risk the same fate." Gyles eyed her contemptuously. "But then you are the sister of a murderess."

"And you are a murderer. You have no choice, sweet bastard; marry me or I shall tell the world of Kier's death." Beda quickly donned her gown and left the chamber.

With trembling hands, Gyles poured a measure of wine and downed it in a single swallow. God, oh, God! Gyles laughed weakly to the empty room. The past two years might never have been; I am back where I started. No Serena, no love, no . . . For the first time since Serena's death a cry tore from Gyles's throat and he collapsed in a chair, his shoulders heaving with the uncontrolled sobs that racked his body.

Mara settled herself in the saddle, smiling at Arthur when he inquired as to her comfort. A movement from the castle steps caught Mara's eye and she glanced up to find Beda watching the departure, a satisfied smile on her face. Mara flushed guiltily when their eyes met, and she hastily averted her gaze as Beda laughingly disappeared into the castle. Arthur's affection and their marriage had given Mara the confidence in herself that she had so sorely lacked and now she raised her head defiantly. Beda had made her life a trial while she had lived at Camden and Mara was determined to put an end to Beda's infamous plan. Mara's eyes narrowed in defiant anger. Oh, Beda, you will sorely regret allowing me to know your secret.

"Arthur!" Her husband was immediately at her side. "There is something I have forgotten. I must return to the castle."

"I can do it for you, Mara," Arthur smiled. "There is no need for you to disturb yourself."

"Perhaps," Mara said thoughtfully, " 'twould be best if you accompanied me—I may need your strength."

Arthur looked questioningly at his bride. "What is it, Mara? What is it you have forgotten?"

"Something I thought I should never have cause to speak of." Mara slid from the saddle into her husband's arms and gave him a solemn smile.

Beda stepped lightly into the small chamber from which Gyles conducted the affairs of his lands. Wooden shelves lined the walls and were strewn with leather-bound volumes, scrolls, and loose papers. Gyles rested against the table, his hands clenched so tightly against its edge that his knuckles had turned white. Beda gave him a triumphant smile and swept into a deep curtsy.

"I had not expected your summons this quickly, dear Gyles, but may I admit it pleases me greatly?" Gyles remained watchfully silent so Beda plunged recklessly onward. "I have seen much that displeases me, Gyles, so I shall begin immediately to set things aright. Mara's and Lydia's chambers and solar will make an excellent nursery for your boys—and I do not want them to dine in the hall, Gyles, last evening was bad enough with Alan constantly underfoot and asking questions. Really, Gyles, 'twas quite intolerable!

"Now, I plan to move into my old chamber immediately so what shall I do with those rags of Serena's? I had thought of burning them—"

"Touch one item in that chamber and I will break your neck!" Gyles spoke the words so casually that it took a moment for their full impact to hit Beda.

"I don't understand, Gyles, what—"

"He knows the truth, Beda. I told him." Mara and Arthur stepped into the center of the room. "It does not speak well of me that I held my tongue for this long, but then I have been much the fool of late. I, for one, hope you are drawn and quartered!" Mara spat out.

"Mara," Arthur pulled her gently away from Beda. "Gyles, should you have any further need of us, send a messenger at once."

They departed and Beda, her face drained of all

color, turned to face Gyles. His green eyes raked her from head to toe, his features impassive save for the whitened scar on his cheek. Braced for Gyles's wrath to explode, Beda returned his stare arrogantly. From the window came the sounds of the guests taking leave: laughing voices, the jingle of harnesses, the impatient blowing of the mounts as they waited for their riders. And still Gyles remained silent, his eyes like green flames burning into Beda.

"Beda, you are the most lying, deceitful bitch I have ever known; and I am most tempted to end your rotten existence." At Beda's outraged gasp Gyles smiled faintly. "You have long said I lacked breeding—shall I prove it?"

"I don't know what you mean." Beda retreated towards the door, then shrieked when Gyles grasped her wrist and thrust her into a chair.

"You murdered your husband, Beda," Gyles stated in a flat voice. "Mara followed you that day—odd as it may seem, she felt Kier might turn his wrath on you and she did not wish any harm to befall you. She was hiding in the woods when I found you."

" 'Twas Kier's plan," Beda admitted breathlessly. "He wanted you out of the way—"

"After he discovered I was cuckolding him or before?"

"After . . . no, before, he was jealous of you; he knew I loved you, wanted you, he thought—"

"He thought if he could kill me, you would be faithful? Poor Kier—I can almost pity him. But why did you kill him? You were the lady of Camden; you had Kier wrapped around your finger, he denied you nothing."

"Nothing!" Beda spat. " 'Tis exactly what Kier was —nothing. A weak, puling imitation of a man, the sight of him turned my stomach! Yes, I killed him! He was bending over your body—we both thought you dead— and I found a tree limb and smashed it against his head.

"Had you awakened more quickly you would have seen me drag his body beneath a tree so 'twould appear

387

his steed had carried him into a branch. Then, when you awoke I made you believe Kier's death was by your hand. Oh! how you believed me, Gyles. You were willing to do anything to keep your precious freedom. You even helped me weigh down his body and throw it in the river."

Beda laughed harshly. "You were to wed me—not Serena. But Lord Geoffrey feared for his daughter—no dowry only a small estate—who would accept such a bride? And then Aurelia made a mistake, she mentioned to Geoffrey that you would take a wife. 'Twas a godsend to Geoffrey; you had no need for greater wealth, all you needed was a woman who could give you a legitimate heir.

"We thought, at first, your marriage would make no difference to our plan. You were estranged from Serena, there was no chance for an heir." Beda jumped to her feet and began to pace wildly. "Then you took her to your bed, Aurelia failed to conceive and Geoffrey began to suspect that his sickness was unnatural—as indeed it was. The herbs Serena tended so carefully were most useful to us. One is particularly poisonous when administered in small doses over a long period of time. 'Twas easy enough for me to steal the herbs from Serena's chest and send them to Aurelia. Aurelia was certain Bryan would take her to wife when Geoffrey died."

Beda turned with a snarl. "We are Normans! While we beggared our lands, Geoffrey's power increased—he gained the king's favor—and you, a baseborn bastard gained Camden. Camden should have been ours—William swore to my father that a vast estate of England should be ours upon his victory. But he lied! My father died in poverty, Aurelia and I were forced into loathsome alliances. Why should we not claim these lands? 'Twas ours in all fairness!

"Your marriage forced us to rethink our plan—but you really made it quite simple. With Geoffrey's blood already staining our hands, shedding more could make no difference. All of Broughton's natural heirs must die— Broughton would come to you through Serena, and when she was gone, you would marry me."

"And then I would meet with an untimely end?" Gyles forced his hands to remain at his side. They had planned it so well, all of Broughton's heirs would die, including Serena. They had never intended for him to live out his life with Serena.

"Yes, you would have to die as well, but only after I gave birth to your heir. I truly wished you could live, but you see, if I was to control the lands, you had to die. We nearly succeeded—Bryan nearly died and Serena . . . if Richard hadn't lost his nerve . . . he thought we would allow Serena to live, to run away with him. But Serena had borne you a child, an heir . . ."

"Evan." Gyles eyed Beda coldly.

"Evan," Beda repeated dully. "We had to be rid of him as well, but Serena became suspicious, she never left the babe alone, and then she sent him to Camden with you."

"You would murder a helpless babe!" The bile rose in Gyles's throat.

"Yes!" Beda snarled. "The lands should have been mine. Mine! No one else had the right to them. No Saxon and not you!"

Beda flew at Gyles, her nails raking his neck, leaving four deep paths that welled blood. She twisted and turned as Gyles sought to control her wildly flailing limbs while avoiding her nails. Beda screamed and hissed, spat full into Gyles's face and wound her fingers in his hair. Gyles grunted as Beda jerked a clump of hair from his head and with an oath he slammed a large fist against her jaw.

19

Nellwyn bustled into the great hall, a mother hen in search of her errant chicks, her color high and her eyes sparkling. "He be here, Lord Gyles, below in the courtyard. These old eyes have never seen such finery—looks like one of them ancient gods me lamb was always reading about. Alan, you come along now, 'tis time ye were back in the nursery. Where be Evan?" Evan's head appeared between his father's legs and he gave a merry gurgle to his old nurse, crawling with amazing dexterity beneath a table when Nellwyn made to pick him up.

"Aye, ye little rascal, ye would choose to play yer games now!" Nellwyn scolded as Alan ducked beneath the table to join his brother. "Ye two will be the end of me—that be what ye wish?"

"See what awaits you?" Bryan grinned down at Catherine from his place behind her chair.

"Leave the boys, Nellwyn," Gyles ordered with a smile. " 'Twill do no harm. Alan, bring Evan out from there immediately!"

The visitor entered and for a moment no one spoke, and then Catherine sank into a curtsy as Gyles and Bryan bowed. The voice which broke the silence was familiar, a thread of humor coloring the tone.

"Rise, my lords and lady." Henry, youngest son of the royal family, dropped his sword onto a table and strode forward to greet each in turn. "Lord Bryan, you look well. And dear Lady Catherine—ah! my congratulations to you."

Henry turned to Gyles, their eyes clashing in remembrance before Henry smiled and clasped Gyles's forearm. "As ever, Lord Gyles, you appear to enjoy the best of health. From the missive you sent my father, the king, I expected to find Camden a haven for carrion crows. And your lady, Lord Gyles, is she not present?"

Catherine gave a muted cry and Henry looked at her sharply, noting the pallor of her face, which was not caused by the babe she carried.

"We . . . I thought word had reached the court," Gyles said in a quiet voice. "My lady was killed September last."

A spasm crossed Henry's face. "We had not heard —my condolences, Lord Gyles. May I ask—"

"'Tis the reason I wrote the king." Gyles indicated a chair. "Will you not be seated, Your Highness? 'Tis a long tale and, I fear, a most unpleasant one."

Catherine withdrew as the three men arranged themselves at a table. Bryan spoke first, beginning with the attack upon his riding party that had culminated in Serena's death and his own injury. Richard's part was explained, his murder of Aurelia bringing a pained expression to Bryan's eyes as he remembered his friend dying in his arms.

"Will Balfour be taken from Richard's father?" Bryan asked of Henry. "He has no other heirs—not even a daughter—and he is an old man. Richard's death has broken him, the loss of Balfour would kill him."

"He knew naught of Richard's plan?" At the shake of Bryan's head, Henry sighed. "In that case, I see no reason to bring an innocent man more sorrow. Balfour's lands shall remain intact. Proceed."

Gyles took up the tale, his deep, melodious voice relating the plot Beda had revealed to him. Not sparing his own guilt, Gyles explained Kier's death and his own part in disposing of the body of his brother. His liaison with Beda Gyles kept to himself, for it had only a slight bearing upon the whole. He said only that he was to

391

have wed his brother's wife. Henry said little during the narration, interrupting occasionally to ask a question, but otherwise he silently contemplated the coats-of-arms hanging on the wall.

Justice—his father had sent him to Camden to mete out justice. How could justice be delivered to the dead? William Rufus should have been sent instead; he would one day rule England, not Henry. And he, Henry, was to sit in judgment, for when such wealthy lands were involved, William insisted upon discretion. Land! Henry sighed inwardly when Gyles rested from his narration to take a drink of wine. Two—no, four, Henry corrected himself—four people sacrificed for a few acres of land. Four lives wasted; offered up on the altar of greed. Wanton destruction: disgusting and unavoidable.

Henry's well-ordered mind rebelled against the illogical, improbable facts Gyles was so calmly delivering. Was it for this William had crossed the channel? So that innocents could be slaughtered, brave men had fought and died? This was the kind of legacy William Rufus would bestow upon England, Henry thought angrily. His brother would like nothing better than to have families displaced so the crown would fall heir to the lands and their richness. How William would enjoy destroying Serena's husband . . . and son. Oh yes, Serena's son, of that there could be no doubt. Henry studied the babe now playing quietly with his brother, a babe who in a different time and a different place might have been his own. Henry drove that disturbing thought from his mind and returned to his perusal of the coats-of-arms while Gyles concluded his story.

"May I see Lady Beda?" Henry requested when Gyles had finished.

"As you wish, Your Highness, but—" warned Gyles, "—'twill serve no purpose. Lady Beda will not answer any questions you may put to her and she will deny any charges I make."

Gyles led his royal guest through the second level of the castle and up a narrow, winding staircase to a turret chamber on the side of the castle farthest away from the family wing.

"I felt 'twas best," Gyles explained as he lifted the bar from the door. "You can appreciate my plight, I am certain, Your Highness. I have no desire for my children to have any contact with Lady Beda. And 'twas for my own sake as well; had she freedom of my home I believe I would have killed her."

The door swung open to reveal a small but well-appointed chamber, the spring sunlight lying in bright pools on the worn stone floor. Henry stood to one side as Gyles closed the door and leaned back against the panel, placing himself between his prisoner and freedom.

"Beda, I have brought you a visitor." Gyles's voice was cold, the hostility he felt barely concealed.

Beda rose from her seat near a window. "Gyles, I must insist again that you release me immediately! I—" Beda's eyes widened when Henry stepped forward and she fell to her knees. "Your Majesty! How glad I am someone has come to my rescue. I have been kept here by this—this beast against my will."

"On a mere whim?" Henry did not raise Beda to her feet but instead rested a hip negligently upon the table, his eyes hooded.

"No whim, Your Majesty." Beda cast a scornful look at Gyles. "I cannot imagine what he has said that would bring you to Camden, but I pray you, do not leave me to his devices. He bears a hatred of the old lord's family and myself, and I do fear for my very life at his hands." Henry gave no sign that he believed her and Beda felt a moment of uncertainty before rallying her courage. Surely Gyles would not have mentioned Kier's death, for if he did, Gyles would also have to implicate himself. Beda resolutely squared her shoulders and pointed a shaking finger at Gyles. "He is responsible for the death of my husband, Your Highness. I dared not speak before now for he would surely have taken his revenge upon me."

"You were at court two winters ago, were you not,

Lady Beda?" Henry asked as he toyed with a goblet. "Why did you not approach the king with this matter?"

"I-I dared not, Your Majesty!" Beda gasped. "He . . . I was watched constantly."

Gyles snorted in derision. "No doubt you were, Beda, but undoubtedly by whoever shared your bed, not by me."

Beda's hissed intake of air brought a lifted eyebrow from Gyles and a quickly hidden smile from Henry.

"Your Majesty, must I listen to insults from one such as he?" Beda turned an imploring gaze on Henry. "I appeal to you, Your Majesty—I have no one to turn to in my time of need, save the king's well-known justice."

"And justice you shall have, Lady Beda," Henry told her with a winning smile. "I desire only the truth in this matter and would have your side of the tale I have been told. Please, rise, be seated. I wish you to be comfortable in the telling." Henry deposited Beda in a chair and waited, an expectant look in his eyes.

Beda shifted beneath the prince's direct gaze. What had Gyles told Henry? Had he admitted his part in Kier's death or had Gyles merely laid the blame for Serena's death on her shoulders? Beda glanced nervously at the two men and suddenly wished she had never returned to Camden.

"I . . . I do not know what you have been told, Your Majesty," Beda said sullenly. "May I know the charges against me?"

Henry drew back in surprise. "But, Lady Beda, what charges could possibly have been levied against you? You have said you fear for your life at the hands of Lord Gyles—I but wish to know why."

"I saw Gyles murder my husband, Your Majesty," Beda repeated. " 'Tis because of that he wishes me dead."

"If what you say is true—" Henry gazed thoughtfully at Beda "—in his place I would have killed you also. Immediately. Why do you suppose Lord Gyles waited so long?"

"He . . . he used me most vilely, Your Majesty! He made me his harlot—Lady Mara and Lady Lydia will testify to that."

"Even after his marriage?" Henry glanced incredulously at Gyles. "M'lord, have you no shame? You preferred this—" he waved a hand at Beda, "—to your wife? I fear, Lord Gyles, your many years of warring have left you addlepated. But, Lady Beda, I have it within my power to set aright the injustices done to you." Beda's features brightened only to darken at Henry's next words. "You shall marry Lord Gyles and regain the position you were so shamefully deprived of."

The look in Gyles's eyes stilled Beda's acceptance. Oh, no, Beda thought desperately. Where before her plans had centered around once again being the Lady of Camden, Beda now knew that if she agreed to Henry's offer she would be going willingly to her own execution. Gyles would not really kill her, of course, but his face told Beda he would like nothing better than having her at his mercy for the rest of her life. Gyles knew she was in part responsible for Serena's death and Beda would pay dearly for that guilt. Her life was far too precious to be wasted because of one Saxon's death.

"I . . . I thank you, Your Majesty, b-but I do not . . . cannot wed Lord Gyles."

They returned to the great hall and Gyles calmly poured a goblet of wine for each of them.

"Beda has never repeated her story?" Henry inclined his head in thanks as he accepted the wine.

"Nay." Gyles relaxed in his chair. "Since admitting her guilt she has not uttered another word about the plot."

"And no one else heard her confession?"

Gyles shook his head.

"What a coil!" Henry groaned. "A crime such as this should be tried at court."

Gyles contemplated his goblet. "With no witnesses, a woman who refuses to acknowledge any conspiracy as the accused, and a bastard knight? With all respect, Your Highness, do you think that is wise?"

Henry swore and began to pace. "You are right—naught would be gained if we aired this at court. Beda could be punished for Kier's death, but that would entail a scandal I do not believe England should be subjected to at this time, and Richard and Aurelia have already paid with their lives."

Gyles raised his eyes to Henry. "And my sentence, Your Highness? What is my punishment for my part in Kier's death?"

A child's laugh rang out from the nursery.

"You also have paid for your crime. I would not have exacted so cruel a price." Henry returned to his chair. "No one else will know—whoever attacked Bryan's party will not dare to admit to it—though I shall have to tell the king all that has transpired. He will agree with my decision. 'Tis precisely this my father hoped to avoid; overlord murdering overlord for land can only tear England apart. I shall speak with Bryan and Catherine and you should instruct your sister and her husband thusly: There was no plot, Aurelia was murdered because Richard's crazed mind believed her guilty of Serena's death. Serena, unhappily, fell prey to a band of thieves. Beda has become ill and has returned to Normandy—I shall arrange that myself and see to it she remains there. And Kier's death was purely accidental, his horse dragged him into the river and his body was never found."

"You are most generous, Your Highness."

"Nay, I am not; I am doing only what is best for England." How glibly you lie, Henry's mind taunted. Best for England? Most assuredly, but also best for Serena's son, the son that could have been yours; for you would never forgive yourself if you denied him his inheritance. "The guilty have found their punishment and the innocent have also suffered enough. Naught can be gained by re-telling the story. I bid you good day, Lord Gyles."

{ Book VII }

Our Lady
of Sorrow

20

The cloister of Our Lady Of Sorrow lay cradled amidst the ancient oaks and yews that had witnessed the rites of the druids, the invasion of Roman legions come to subdue the war-like Celts and, as evidenced by the chapel and surrounding buildings, the introduction of Christianity to a heathen England. The cloister had survived for nearly three centuries; far back from any well-traveled road, visitors were a rare occurrence as were thieves, for there was no great wealth in the nunnery. The river from which the member of the convent carried the water for washing, cooking, drinking, and cleaning was too shallow to admit any but the lightest crafts, so Our Lady of Sorrow had been spared the destruction the Vikings and Danes had so carelessly wreaked upon the lands.

But for all its seclusion, the cloister had its ties with the secular world. Well-born widows often retired within the high stone walls—some joined the order while others chose merely to live out their remaining years in the privacy accorded by the cottages provided by the order. The youngest daughters of impoverished freemen as a matter of course joined the ranks of the order for lack of a dowry. Noblewomen frequently retired to the cloister for weeks of contemplation, meditation, and renewal of their soul. But the spiritual solitude of the cloister—while available to all—was also balanced with worldly cares.

Buildings fell into disrepair, cloth was needed to sew the order's habits, and while the sisters tilled the soil to provide their own grain, meats had to be procured from the outside world. So when the titled women took their leave, their purses were lighter by a good many coins. With the establishment of a small orphanage, finances were even more pressing, so the good sisters took needle in hand and fashioned tapestries, altar cloths, coverlets, and eventually as word spread of the fine workmanship, ladies' marriage gowns and babe's swaddling.

Idleness was the enemy of the soul and the black-robed sisters saw to it the novices quickly learned the inadvisibility of sloth; those who did not were scourged and when the weals on their back faded or their knees ceased to ache from the long hours spent kneeling on the unrelenting stones of the chapel floor, the novices had been thoroughly chastised and went about their duties with renewed vigor.

The scourge was used with less frequency since Sister Theodosia had become abbess upon the death of Sister Agatha; although in her own way Sister Theodosia was as implacable as Sister Agatha had been. The quiet tongue-lashing delivered by the abbess was far more painful and humiliating than the scourgings had ever been; yet the abbess was held in tender regard and respect where Sister Agatha had only been feared. A woman of gentle temperament, the abbess trusted in God to attend to the spiritual needs of her flock, and herself for their daily survival.

But on this day in early summer, the abbess's normally clear brow was clouded as she watched a young novice, an iron kettle in each hand, start down the path leading to the river.

"She is an asset to the abbey, our Sister Anne."

The abbess turned and smiled at the tall, spare nun beside her. For the past five and twenty years since Sister Theodosia had joined the order, she and Sister Marcella had been as close as the rules allowed, until now each knew what the other was thinking.

"How has Sister Anne spent her day?" The abbess

glanced once more at the grey blur vanishing into the trees.

"She has attended all the Offices and spent the rest of the time with the children. The babes especially seem to fascinate Sister Anne." Sister Marcella fell into step alongside the abbess. "You should speak with her again, Reverend Mother, her appetite has all but disappeared in the past few weeks and she rarely sleeps. I believe she spends most of the night in the chapel."

"Praying?" The abbess questioned with a smile.

"Mayhap, but I think not."

" 'Tis sad—she would make an excellent addition to our order." The two nuns stepped from the brilliant sunshine into the enveloping shade of the abbey.

Sister Anne filled the kettles with water and then, on impulse, knelt and bent over the river to lave her face. There was a slight breeze and she sat back on her heels, lifting her eyes to watch the tree tops dance against the sky. How peaceful it was with only the sighing of the wind and the chirping birds for companions. Sister Anne studied the light playing over the water, turning the small waves into brightly tipped daggers that stabbed at her eyes and brain, bringing to mind memories of another sun-washed day—a small boy, laughter, a cool, refreshing pond . . .

The impression faded and Sister Anne pressed tapered fingertips against the ache that was beginning in her temples. "When you are ready God will reveal all," the Reverend Mother had said when she was strong enough to walk to the abbess's office.

Sister Anne recalled the terror that had swept over her when she awoke to find two black-gowned sisters hovering over her pallet. Though it seemed to take hours, it was in fact only a few minutes until Sister Baptista and Sister Madeline had quieted her screams and calmed her down sufficiently to ask her name.

Sister Anne had stared at her questioner blankly. "I do not know."

"Where is your home, child?" Sister Baptista had smoothed back the hair from her face.

"I do not know!" Sister Anne's eyes had widened in horror. "I . . . I cannot remember. Oh! please, tell me . . . where am I? What has happened?"

"Child, child," Sister Madeline had soothed. "Calm yourself, my dear. Can you remember anything at all?"

"I . . . no . . . I must leave." She had tried to sit up but fell back with a small cry at the pain that knifed through her head and side.

"You must rest, child." Sister Madeline had pressed her back to the pallet. "You are hurt, you have been ill for three weeks and you must regain your strength."

"Sister, you . . . you do not understand . . . I must warn." The flickering image in her mind had died and she began to sob helplessly.

She could recall nothing; no face, no name. It was as if she had been born again at the moment she awakened in the cloister. While she lay in her cubicle day after day, her wounds healing, she would try to remember who she was and where she came from. But when she did, a dull ache would begin in her head and the harder she tried to envision people and places, the sharper the ache became. Only at night when one of Sister Judith's potions brought sleep to her did vague pictures flare into her mind and torment her dreams. Upon awakening in the mornings she would try to recall what she had dreamed, but that, too, was futile, and she was left with only a feeling of deep loss.

When Sister Madeline proclaimed her strong enough, she had been escorted to the abbess. The black robes of the order no longer frightened her and she herself wore the grey robe of a novice, the rough cloth rubbing painfully against her skin and causing her to wonder if she was accustomed to finer material. She had been spared the wimple that completed the habit and her hair was freshly washed and tied back with a scrap of cloth. She had examined the shining locks curiously—she had no remembrance of what she looked like, had no idea of her coloring or features, and mirrors were forbidden within the convent walls lest the good sisters be taken with their looks and fall prey to the sin of pride.

The abbess had smiled kindly and indicated that she should be seated. "Well, child, how are you feeling?"

"Much stronger, Reverend Mother, thank you. I am most grateful for the care the sisters have given me—I wish there was some way I could repay your kindness."

"Do not trouble yourself with such matters." The abbess had settled herself behind a table. "We must now consider you—your future. Sister Madeline has told me you remember naught of your past."

"That is true, Reverend Mother. I do not even know how I came to be here!" Unconsciously she had copied the abbess's movement and placed her hands within the wide sleeves of the robe.

In her quiet voice the abbess had recounted how a band of mummers had found the girl wandering from the forest, her side and head seeping blood and delirious with fever. The band had cared for her as best they could and though they managed to staunch the flow of blood, an infection set in and her fever worsened, sapping even more of her precious strength. They had realized that if the girl were to live she needed shelter and rest, something their way of life did not permit. One of the band remembered the cloister and they changed direction immediately and brought her to the abbey. The rest the girl knew. She had fought the infection threatening her life for three weeks and had won—but when she awoke her memory was gone.

"Then they knew nothing of me?" The girl had asked softly. "I had hoped . . ."

"Nay, child, none of the mummers knew you or had seen you before you happened upon them," the abbess had continued brusquely. "But you are well now and must decide what to do."

"Do?" she had repeated. "I . . . I had not thought . . ." Tears pricked her eyes and she lowered her head. "Would it not be possible for me to remain here?"

The abbess had smiled. "You may remain as long as you wish, child. Aah, we cannot continue to call you that. Have you a name you favor?"

"Anne," she had promptly replied without knowing

why. How could she? She did not remember her mother nor the fact that her name was also Anne.

The abbess's eyebrows had raised a fraction at the swift answer but she made no comment.

So an identity had been created for the bewildered girl—she was no longer "child" but Sister Anne, she was dressed as a true novice of the cloister and performed the required duties. To those who entered the cloister after her arrival she was simply Sister Anne, a nun who preferred not to speak of her past and her privacy was respected. Sister Anne was pious, obedient, rarely angered, tireless in her devotion to her work, and throughout the winter months she seemed to have completely adjusted to and accepted her fate. But along with renewal of life, spring had also brought a depression to Sister Anne's spirit.

Her appetite declined and Sister Anne soon lost the pounds Sister Madeline and Sister Judith had labored so diligently to replace. She spent long hours in the chapel, her fingers moving ceaselessly over her rosary, her blue eyes wide open and staring blindly at the statue of the Virgin. Sister Anne's repose was once again invaded by the demonic images that had not plagued her for many months, until now in early summer she avoided her pallet; making her way to her cubicle only when she was so weary that her vision blurred. With increasing frequency, however, even that strategy was not entirely successful and her sleep continued to be riddled by disturbing dreams. She found the visions of her sleep returned to haunt her days as well.

Sister Anne wrenched her thoughts back to reality. The sun would set in a short time and she would have to return to the cloister for Vespers and Complin. As she had done every day since the ice had thawed from the river, Sister Anne knelt on the grassy bank and leaned forward until her watery reflection stared seriously up at her. Large eyes made even more enormous in the delicate, thinly refined face studied the alien features as her trembling fingers touched her hollowed cheeks, the slender nose, the rosebud mouth. My face, she thought in a mixture of wonder and confusion, and I do not even recognize it.

Her hands moved to the wimple and in one easy motion Sister Anne pulled it from her head. Gold-streaked brown hair spilled out of the wimple, tumbling around her face, down her shoulders to her waist. Her hair had been left uncropped—unlike the other postulants'—at the abbess's insistence, for in all good faith the abbess could not allow the woman known as Sister Anne to join the cloister, not until her identity was fully revealed. Now Sister Anne drew her fingers thoughtfully through the soft curls—and was immediately struck by a dim memory of a pair of strong, lean hands twining themselves in the same locks, fingers meshing at the back of her head, lips slanting across her own . . .

Almost, almost she could picture another face beside hers in the pool. The pain in her temples increased unbearably and with a smothered cry Sister Anne closed her eyes, allowing the image to slip away. Please, God, Sister Anne prayed as the throbbing diminished, please help me to remember. I know 'tis selfish of me. You must have a reason, but . . . Despair rose within her and Sister Anne began to weep as she had not done since coming to the cloister. As her sobs quieted she heard the sound of the chapel bell. Vespers! She had forgotten. Her hands flew to the discarded wimple and she hurriedly tucked her hair into the veil and secured it around her head.

Having delivered the water to the kitchen, Sister Anne raced across the courtyard to the chapel. The service had already begun and she slipped as unobtrusively as possible into her seat on a hard wooden bench. Without conscious thought, her lips began to move through the psalms and antiphons of the Office, but Sister Anne's mind returned to the disturbing thoughts that had touched her—surely they had been a man's hands, not a woman's. Of that Sister Anne was certain as she was of nothing else. But who was the man? Husband? Lover? Had they been happy together?

The Vespers' Canticle began: *Magnificat anima mea*

Dominum, My soul doth magnify the Lord. And Sister Anne felt the music flow soothingly over her confused and heavy soul. Her eyes turned to the soft glow of the candles and, mesmerized, she watched the flickering flames. The chapel had always been a comfort to Sister Anne, as had the sweet sound of the sisters chanting the lessons or lifting their voices in the canticles, but tonight the usual all-pervading solace was missing and in its place a vague uneasiness.

Sister Anne's gaze traveled about the chapel as if seeing it for the first time. Unlike the order's residence, the chapel was constructed entirely of wood; the altar, walls and pews having darkened and warped over the years so that even on the brightest day the sanctuary was shadowed and dark. Candles burned in profusion, casting all the occupants of the chapel into a curious relief, their silhouettes dancing against the walls. The silver crucifix on the altar was the center of the chapel, catching and reflecting the uncertain light in gleaming rays. A small chapel, it could hold no more than fifty people, yet the massive pillars that supported the ceiling lent an impression of height, so that when the sisters gave voice to the hymns of praise the sound appeared to be heard in heaven. The chapel enfolded the worshipers as a mother hugs her child to her breast: loving, peaceful, serene.

And I do not belong! Sister Anne thought a trifle wildly, and with the thought, sadness at the realization that her life lay outside the cloister's walls, not within, stabbed at her heart. I thought I did; I was certain that whatever my past I would not have to search for it, but I must. I must know!

"Sister Anne," the soft touch on her sleeve caused her to start and she flushed as she realized that all save the abbess and herself had left the chapel. "Are you well?"

"I . . . yes, Reverend Mother, I am well." Sister Anne rose from her knees.

"You have lost weight again." The abbess surveyed the thin face and body critically. Even through the copious folds of the habit it was a simple matter to see the girl was becoming too thin. "Sister Madeline is worried."

"Forgive me, I shall try to do better." Sister Anne bent her head. "Reverend Mother, I must speak with you."

"Of course, my child. You have prayed on what disturbs you?"

"I have prayed, but there has been no answer." The abbess drew the girl down to the bench alongside her as Sister Anne continued. "I have fasted and prayed—I have tried to do as you advised, Reverend Mother, and wait for God to reveal all in His time. But all has been for naught! I do not belong to the cloister and I do not belong to the world beyond these walls. What am I to do?"

"You must be patient, Sister, and have faith in His ways. There is a reason for your being here." The abbess smiled gently into the drawn face.

Sister Anne buried her face in her arms. "You cannot understand, Reverend Mother! You have no way of knowing what it is like not to remember your name, your past, even what you look like or what foods you enjoy! I didn't even know I could sew until Sister Claudia thrust a piece of tapestry into my hands. 'Tis as if I am a blank page of parchment awaiting the touch of a quill. I am afraid to remember the past and I am afraid not to and I do not know why I fear either!"

The abbess was silent. No easy words of compassion sprang to her mind, though she ached for the emptiness Sister Anne was experiencing. The abbess, too, prayed daily that Sister Anne's memory might be restored to her, but beyond prayers, there was naught that could be done.

"Come, Sister," the abbess rose from the bench, "the repast is waiting as are the others. Ask Sister Judith for a potion before you retire, I am told you are not sleeping well."

Sister Anne sighed inwardly as she walked to the kitchen. The abbess did not understand, she could not know the helpless confusion that swam through her thoughts. She forced back the tears that threatened and managed somehow to choke down a portion of her meal. Looking at the familiar faces at the table, Sister Anne felt a rush of shame. How could she be so ungrateful to these kind women? They had nursed her back to health, given her food and shelter, and now she wanted to desert them, to find the part of her that was hidden. She owed them so much . . . her very life!

But I do not belong here! Sister Anne raged silently. I feel like an outsider, like one of the ladies who retreat here for a time then take their leave. Surely inquiries could be made somehow of these visitors—young women did not disappear without people knowing of the event! Someone must be concerned with her whereabouts. Sister Anne decided she must ask the abbess about the possibility of questioning their guests tomorrow. Sister Judith placed a goblet in front of her and she drank it all obediently, smiling slightly when she returned the goblet.

"Thank you, Sister."

Sister Judith looked pleased. " 'Twill grant you a peaceful night. Reverend Mother has excused you from Matins so you need not rise 'til Prime."

"Will your elixir also spare me from my dreams, Sister Judith?" Sister Anne questioned with wide eyes.

The older woman lowered herself onto the bench near Sister Anne. "Are they unpleasant, your dreams?"

Sister Anne shook her head. "Nay, Sister, not unpleasant but rather disturbing, as if something is trying to reach out and touch me but cannot. And there are people in my dreams now—people without faces in strange rooms but I cannot hear their voices and when I try to touch them or see their faces, the dream stops and I awake. Sister Judith, what am I to do?" she pleaded.

The nun had no answer beyond a reassuring pat on the hand and Sister Anne wearily sought her pallet.

The following day found Sister Anne more relaxed than she had been in the past few weeks, her wide sapphire eyes had lost their haunted expression though a sad emptiness still remained in their depths. Shortly after the midday meal Sister Anne found the abbess alone in her office and she tapped softly on the open door.

"Yes? Oh, Sister Anne, come in." The abbess motioned her into one of the chairs. "What is it, child?"

"Reverend Mother, would it be possible to make inquiries about me . . . my identity . . . to the outside world? Or question the guests that come here for retreat?"

The abbess sighed, "Child, child, do you know what you are asking? Our guests retire here to separate themselves from the outside world. They do not wish to bring their cares behind these walls. As for any of our order venturing beyond the abbey, you are fully aware of our rules."

"But, Reverend Mother—" Sister Anne broke in.

The abbess continued as if the girl had not spoken. "There is an additional barrier, which I did not wish to reveal. You assumed—and we did nothing to dissuade you—that you had been injured in a fall from a horse, but I must tell you now that is not true. When William invaded England, many of our brave Saxon knights found their way here and for a time our cloister was engaged solely in healing the wounded. I, along with many others, saw a great many wounds inflicted in the heat of battle and I say to you now that your injuries were caused by a sword.

"If you look to your side, you will see that what I say is the truth—no tree limb, rock, horse's hoof, nor even a dagger can inflict that type of wound. And no thief would allow his victim to live, so you cannot hope to explain your injuries thusly. Sister Judith, Sister Madeline, and I had thought to keep this from you, but is now impossible. Whoever you are, wherever you were found, you were set upon by a well-armed force. Assassins, dear child, who for some unknown reason left you alive when they made good their escape. You can see now why, until you regain your memory, your presence here must remain a secret. Why do you believe we did not tell the novices how you actually came to us? You must have powerful enemies, Sister Anne, for them to go to such lengths to secure your death."

"But you can only guess at that, Reverend Mother!" Sister Anne insisted. "You cannot be certain that my death was plotted. It could have been a band of thieves—they could have been well-armed, 'tis not unheard of."

"I would indeed not be so certain if I had not heard from your own lips what I guessed. You spoke when the fever raged within you, child. You spoke of murder and blood; of destruction, an ambush in a wooded place. For months we dreaded the sound of the bell above the gate to our cloister—every day we waited for a party to descend upon us and ask if we had heard or seen you. We dared not question any of those who retreated here out of fear that should your presence be revealed we would have been condemning you to death. To regain your memory is the only safe course for all of us."

"You mean I must remain here 'til such a time?" Sister Anne displayed the first burst of anger toward another that the abbess had seen. "I will grant you that what you say could be true, but I cannot believe that whoever wishes to kill me would harm you or any of the sisters. You have done naught to warrant such harsh treatment."

"To your mind—and mine—perhaps not, but to others . . ." The abbess raised her hands in a helpless gesture.

"Surely all who knew me must believe me dead now," Sister Anne stated boldly. "So wherein could lie the harm? A few subtle questions . . . please, Reverend Mother!"

"I shall pray for guidance," the abbess relented with a sigh. "Now, Sister, you must excuse me."

With a sense of wonder Sister Anne suppressed an impatient retort and left the abbess's office. During the first months of her stay the only emotion she had experienced had been confusion and a tinge of fear, fear of the unknown. But recently she found herself chafing under the order's restrictions, becoming impatient with herself and others though she managed to conceal it. But last night, she mused while she strolled through the courtyard, last night the dreams had come again and had not frightened her. Rather she had welcomed the vague images and the contentment they brought, and when she sought to recapture the dreams today, her head did not throb as badly as before. Could it be possible that her memory was returning? Sister Anne smiled to herself; perhaps her prayers had been answered at last. Caught up as she was in her own thoughts she failed to hear the gate of the cloister swing open and barely avoided being trampled beneath the hooves of a massive steed. She stepped quickly aside, making certain that her head remained lowered when a deep, masculine voice called down to her.

"Sister, are you injured?"

She gave a slight shake of her head and hurried off in the direction of the orphanage.

"Cloisters!" The dark man snorted as he watched the novice disappear. "Women so engrossed in their prayers they do not attend to where they are." He settled back into his saddle. "I still fail to understand why you had to drag me along, Bryan."

The young lord of Broughton laughed as he dismounted. "You heard Catherine, Gyles. She insists upon having this cloister prepare swaddling for the babe and I cannot refuse her. And since you are a father twice over I thought your opinion to be of value."

Gyles of Camden swung from his steed and grimaced. "I know naught of cloth and trimmings, those matters were attended to by Alan's nurse and——" he hesitated briefly "——and Serena prepared all that Evan needed."

It still hurt after all these months to think of his wife. The pain had not diminished but had changed from the sharp, twisting sensation in his belly to a poignant yearning in the heart he had once denied having, when he remembered the loss of his wife.

Bryan ignored the shadow that passed over Gyles's face. "Nonetheless, 'tis a job I could not undertake alone, and since Catherine is unable to travel, you were the best at hand. Besides, I thought you might enjoy a visit to Broughton before your guests descend upon Camden for the tourney."

"And you and Catherine will be able to spoil my sons 'til there will be no living with them," Gyles responded with a laugh, then sobered as his laughter drew the attention of the sisters in the courtyard. Once again Gyles's impatience returned. "We have probably frightened the nuns, Bryan, how long is this going to take?"

"Presently," Bryan chuckled, "I believe that must be our escort to the abbess."

The abbess studied the two men seated before her and restrained the flicker of amusement she felt. It was obvious they were both uncomfortably out of place within the quiet isolation of the order, particularly the dark knight whose gaze seemed to mock the piety surrounding him.

Ah, well, 'twas not his coins that would find their way into the order's purse. The abbess returned her attention to the younger man. "We have a fine selection of materials, Lord Bryan. I have sent several of the sisters for those best suited for your purpose, you may view them here if you wish. Now, the threads and trim . . ."

Gyles withdrew his attention from the conversation and watched through the window as a band of children and nuns surrounded his and Bryan's mounts to admire the trappings. The smaller children playfully darted beneath the horses' bellies and between the hooves, skillfully evading the sisters' hands when the women tried to snatch them away from the potential danger. Gyles muttered an oath under his breath and ungraciously stalked from the abbess's office, not even bothering to turn and answer Bryan's question as to where he was going. The mounts were well trained to be sure, but with a group of squealing babes underfoot Gyles was not about to trust Demon's volatile temperament to any great length. As he approached the steeds, the children fell back, hurrying into the relative safety of the sisters' arms when they glimpsed the white curved scar on Gyles's cheek. Gyles surveyed them silently for a moment, his green eyes flickering over the clean but patched clothing of the children while they measured him in turn, their eyes round with fear at the awesome figure standing before them.

Sister Anne stood at the rear of the group, her heart beating so wildly at the sight of the tall stranger that she felt she would swoon. How handsome he was, in spite of the scar that marred one cheek; but when his gaze was about to fall on her, Sister Anne lowered her head, for there was a coldness in those green eyes that caused her to tremble. Surely he was not angry with the children for wanting to touch the steeds and their finery— they had naught in their lives that even hinted of such splendor.

In fact, Gyles was not angry in the least, rather he found his heart melting in the face of the innocent, wide-eyed urchins. Were these rags all the children had to wear? Gyles wondered. Serena would have deplored these conditions; would, in fact, probably have prevailed upon him to bring these children to Camden. Or perhaps . . . A plan began to take shape in Gyles's mind and he suddenly smiled as he scooped the nearest child into his arms and onto Demon's saddle. Within a short time all the children had had a turn on Demon's back accompanied by a short ride around the courtyard. When the last of their number finished his ride, the children and nuns thanked Gyles warmly and retreated to the orphanage. Gyles retied Demon's reins to the pillar and made his way back to the abbess's office.

Bryan looked up from the long table of materials and smiled as Gyles entered. "I am nearly finished, Gyles."

Gyles nodded then turned abruptly to the abbess. "How many children do you care for here, Reverend Mother?"

The abbess was slightly taken aback. "Why . . . at the present time we have fifteen children. I noticed some of the smaller ones by your steed, I hope you are not angry, m'lord, I am sure they meant no harm."

Gyles waved away her apology. "I should like to see the children better cared for." The abbess made to protest but Gyles silenced her with a gesture of his hand. "I have no doubt the good sisters do the best they can, but the children's appearances are wanting. Surely with all the materials you have here, the order could fashion new clothing for them."

"I am afraid not, m'lord, these materials are made up and sold to the nobles. We are a cloister, m'lord, and we are not wealthy; the gold our work brings in barely provides for food we cannot supply ourselves and for the building repair that is essential. 'Tis rare indeed if we have any coin to spare."

"Then determine what the children need and I shall see you receive what is required," Gyles directed the nun. "If the orphanage is in need of repair, I shall send you masons and carpenters from Camden. Make your list, Reverend Mother, I shall take it with me when we depart. Bryan, I am sure the Reverend Mother needs time to make her list. Will you join me in a short stroll?"

The abbess announced the convent's good fortune to the nuns at the evening meal. For a brief moment the members of the order sat in stunned silence—then the normally sober faces broke into smiles and quiet laughter and excited chatter ensued.

Sister Anne remained silent, but a joyous warmth suffused her mind and heart. What a generous gesture for the tall lord to have made! The children would have new clothes; shoes for the cold winter so their feet would not have to endure the icy floors of the cloister; the roof of the orphanage could be repaired, there would be no further need to place wooden buckets beneath the cracks in the ceiling to catch the water that seeped into the building when it rained or snowed.

"Why would he do such a thing, this Norman lord?" Sister Anne questioned the abbess abruptly. "When he first saw the children he appeared angry."

"Out of kindness, Sister." The abbess smiled. "And as for appearing angry, the young man who accompanied Lord Gyles informed me that he is grieving over the recent loss of his wife. Lord Gyles has asked that after the orphanage has been seen to, a monument be raised to the memory of his wife."

A wave of sympathy swept over Sister Anne. "How sad—Lord Gyles must have loved his wife very much

Do you think—could we perhaps pray for him, Reverend Mother? Perhaps God would grant him a measure of peace."

"An excellent thought, Sister." The pleasure the abbess felt at Sister Anne's new interest in others she did not reveal, but inwardly she thanked heaven her prayers had been answered. "And I think you should pray for him since you retire to the chapel so frequently." The abbess rose to leave, but halted, a puzzled frown drawing her brows together. "How did you learn Lord Gyles was a Norman?"

"I—I do not know," Sister Anne stammered, her face coloring slightly in her confusion. A dull throb began in her head and she pressed her fingertips to her temples. "He just . . . looked as if he were a conqueror. I . . . he was so arrogant, so . . ."

"Do not trouble yourself." The abbess drew Sister Anne's hands from her temples. "Now go to the chapel and pray for the Norman lord."

Within the week the items the abbess had listed began flowing into the cloister. Yard after yard, bolt after bolt of materials were carried into the sewing room to be stacked neatly on the open shelves while the children were also brought in to have their measurements taken and recorded. To everyone's shock—her own not least of all—Sister Anne discovered she could read and write, so she was delegated the task of recording the children's sizes as they were paraded before her.

This accomplished, the sisters set their hands to the task of fashioning clothing and new linens. The children were delighted with their new clothing, exclaiming over the rich yet durable fabrics until the sisters had to take them firmly in hand and calm their excitement to a more acceptable level.

Sister Anne reveled in the children's happiness, laughing with them and at them whenever her duty took her to the orphanage. She taught the little girls simple embroidery, delighting in their uncertain stitches and praising their efforts. She worked tirelessly in the laundry, scrubbed the stone floors of the chapel until they glistened and she prayed nightly into the small hours of the morning. Sister Anne's dreams were no longer ghastly, but they still tormented her because the face of Gyles of Camden intruded upon her. Why should I dream of him, she asked herself fiercely. I do not know him, indeed I have never met that good lord. So why do I think of him, dream of him—why do I imagine his face as it looks when he smiles? Why do I see his eyes turn cloudy green when I think he is angered? I must ask the Reverend Mother to have one of the other sisters pray for this man, he touches me too deeply.

But she did not. Instead, Sister Anne found herself thinking more about the man she had seen but once, and her prayers for him became more intense. And the more she prayed the more she thought and dreamed of Lord Gyles, and Sister Anne found herself eagerly awaiting his next visit so that she might find out for certain if his eyes were really green. Sister Anne did not have long to wait.

Three weeks after his first visit Gyles returned to the cloister of Our Lady of Sorrow, bringing with him the promised stonemasons and carpenters. Gyles groaned inwardly as he saw the abbess walking toward him. What had possessed him to lend support to a convent? Priests, nuns, monks, the Church—Gyles had little use for any of them. He was a man born and raised in the harsh realities of life, not sheltered from the cruelty by high walls and Masses. What was he doing here amid a group of withered, sanctimonious old women? There would be a tourney at Camden in a fortnight; Gyles should be home making preparations for the event. But his heart was not in it as it had been nearly two years ago, Gyles mused. A mental image of Serena strutting across the field of combat cut into Gyles like the dull blade of a dagger. Serena. Their time spent together had been less than a year if he took the time to count the days. And of that short time too many days, nay weeks, had been wasted in arguing. Why does it still hurt, Gyles sighed as he dismounted. Why can I not close my eyes and see blackness rather than her face?

"Welcome, Lord Gyles." The abbess smiled as he bowed slightly. "As you requested, we have readied a cottage for you. But the workmen must stay outside our walls."

"Of course." Gyles nodded. "I understand. But my plans have altered, I shall remain only for the night." If I could leave right now I would be happier, Gyles added to himself, but aloud he said, "I hope I have not caused you any inconvenience."

"Nay, m'lord," the abbess quickly assured him. "For all you have done for our cloister we are deeply grateful. In fact, we are offering up prayers for you daily. But come, would you like to see the children before the evening meal? They, too, would like to thank you for your generosity."

Sister Anne saw the knight and abbess approach the orphanage as she gave a final adjustment to the gown of the small girl in front of her.

"Now then, quickly, little one, into line with the others. You remember what to say to Lord Gyles?" The little girl nodded vigorously. "Good. Remember, give him your prettiest smile and do not forget to curtsy. Now go."

Retreating into the nearby shadows, Sister Anne watched as Gyles received the solemn gratitude of the children, his stern features twisting into a smile when the girl she had so recently dressed forgot the words of her speech.

"Sister Anne!" The small girl wailed and burst into tears, then turned and ran to where Sister Anne was standing.

Sister Anne knelt in front of the small girl, placing herself between the Norman lord and the child. A few whispered words as she quickly dried the girl's eyes and Sister Anne stepped back and the ceremony continued without mishap. How tall Lord Gyles was, Sister Anne thought as she watched him. His features proud, yet when she looked closely, Sister Anne detected a sadness in his brilliant green eyes, and she felt an urgent desire to go to him and cradle his head against her breast as she did so often with the children. How deeply he must have loved his wife, Sister Anne thought with a sudden pang. At least she had died knowing who she was and where she belonged while I know neither. The dull throb in her temples which had begun when she first set eyes upon Lord Gyles increased in intensity until she felt her head would burst. I must get away from here! Sister Anne gathered the skirt of her habit in her hands and ran from the courtyard to the chapel.

21

"Dearest love, how I have missed you!" Strong, gentle hands traveled along the woman's unclad body as her lips met the man's above her and each tasted the other's sweetness. "We have been parted so long . . . so long. My darling, why did I not find you sooner?"

The man lowered himself onto the woman and in a convulsive movement she arched upward to meet him, a small cry escaping her parted lips. The massive, postered bed, its curtains partially drawn, stood squarely in the center of a huge chamber, the only light coming from a fire blazing in the hearth. Lush tapestries decorated the walls, rich fur pelts were carelessly strewn upon the floor, beside the bed stood a table upon which rested wine and two silver goblets. The entwined couple moved slowly as if savoring each other's closeness; the man whispering soft endearments against the woman's gold-touched hair . . .

Sister Anne came awake with a jolt, blue eyes staring fearfully at the ceiling while she strived to calm the wild beating of her heart. She struggled from the narrow rope cot to the washstand where she splashed water onto her burning cheeks and pounding temples.

Lord, forgive me my unclean thoughts, Sister Anne prayed as she returned to her pallet and hid her face in her hands. She recognized all too clearly the figures in her dream—herself and Lord Gyles. Sister Anne

shivered in the early morning coolness and hurriedly retreated to the warmth of her bed before continuing her
musings.

Lord Gyles had been a frequent visitor to the convent during the past three months and each time Sister
Anne had learned of his impending visit, her dreams of
him became as impassioned as no nun's dreams should.
She had long ago given up trying to force him from her
waking thoughts and dreams, for to do so only meant that
his image plagued her more intensely. And her dreams
left Sister Anne with a warm glow tempered with a sharp
pang of loss. She confided to no one the course of her
thoughts, though at times Sister Anne felt certain the
Reverend Mother knew the visions that flashed through
her mind.

The man was a magnet and Sister Anne was
inexorably drawn to him. During his visits to the cloister
Sister Anne followed Lord Gyles about the grounds like
a puppy trailing its master. How badly she desired to
speak with him, to gaze fully upon that handsome yet
arrogantly closed face, to look deeply into the green eyes
that had haunted her from the first. But she hadn't—Oh!
She had been tempted, without a doubt. Lord Gyles often
strolled to the river on hot afternoons and Sister Anne had
followed, secreting herself among the trees while Lord
Gyles knelt by the river and thoughtfully trailed his
fingers through the cool water. He had also taken to
haunting the chapel when the sisters were finished with
Offices and Sister Anne—secluded once again by the
shadows of the chapel—observed with a mixture of pity
and surprise the stark anguish that twisted Lord Gyles's
features. Poor man, Sister Anne had thought sadly, you
poor unhappy, lonely man! She had begun to weep silently
and had fled before a sound could betray her.

Bits and pieces of what Sister Anne believed to be
her past began to flare during Lord Gyles's visits—always
just enough to tantalize her before eluding her grasp completely, scenes of rooms, castles, even a tournament, but
rarely any recognizable faces save that of Lord Gyles.

And when he left, the brief flashes would lessen in intensity so that Sister Anne despaired of ever remembering her past. She considered directly confronting Lord Gyles—since he occupied her thoughts in the extreme it was quite possible that they had known each other in what Sister Anne privately referred to as her "other life." But the abbess's warning, given so long ago, stilled Sister Anne's impulse. What if in the past she had been a threat to Lord Gyles or the younger man who had accompanied him on that first visit? Judging from his haughty bearing and cold gaze, Sister Anne was certain Lord Gyles would have no qualms over removing anyone or anything that thwarted him.

In all, Sister Anne was confused; alternately torn between fearing the tall, grim knight and desiring to be held in those strong arms, she felt caught up in a whirlpool of questions that threatened to drown her sanity in its roiling fury. As her anxiety increased, Sister Anne's appetite decreased in direct proportion until dear Sister Judith was frustrated beyond belief. Sister Judith plied the young girl with tempting morsels from the convent's kitchen to no avail, so that now Sister Judith had to be content with assuring herself that Sister Anne did not succumb to any illness.

Sister Anne roused herself from her thoughts and slipped out of bed to dress. Her mind had already flown to the day ahead, to the arrival of Lord Gyles. Today he was coming to inspect the repair of the orphanage and consult the abbess on the matter of his dead wife's memorial—Sister Anne would be able to observe him for the greater part of the day. Once again, she had turned from fearing Lord Gyles to caring, caring so deeply that she prayed the anguish that unfailing overwhelmed Gyles during his stay in the chapel would be absent this time.

Gyles pushed the trencher containing the remnants of his morning meal away with an exasperated oath. What a time for the abbess to take ill! He had arrived at the convent shortly after noon yesterday, hoping to conclude his visit swiftly and depart on the morrow, only to find that the abbess was indisposed and would not be able to receive him. Mayhap in a day or two, the sour-faced Sister Marcella had told him. So now he had to delay his departure indefinitely.

With a curse, Gyles lowered his aching head to his hands. He had slept poorly the night before, falling asleep only to be wakened by the chapel bell during the night, and what rest he had found had been haunted by dreams of Serena. God! What he would give for a flagon of hearty ale. Of late Gyles had taken to indulging in late-night drinking bouts that commonly ended with Edward dragging his overlord from the great hall and up to his bed. If Edward had been puzzled over the sudden change in Gyles's behavior, the situation was clarified by an indignant Nellwyn. Lord Gyles, it appeared, was being pressured by the king to remarry—his bride was an orphan of sixteen and as such the king was her guardian until she was wed. Gyles, widowed with two small children, was an ideal prospect as a husband.

When the royal messenger had delivered the king's note some six weeks ago, Gyles had immediately declined the match, stating as cause his still unfinished period of mourning. This William had deemed unacceptable and a fortnight later had instructed Gyles to think more on the matter—unless he had a different bride in mind for himself? Gyles knew further protests to be futile and had gone to inspect his future wife. Gyles had come away from the meeting filled with loathing, for his bride had watched him with limpid brown eyes as if she expected to be violated by him at any time. She had not spoken unless Gyles addressed her directly and spent her entire day in her solar embroidering or working on tapestries. On the last night, Gyles's bride-to-be, Lady Margaret, had at last spoken her mind. She had no wish to marry, she quietly informed Gyles, but to enter a convent, for she felt she had a true vocation. But she would agree to the marriage if Gyles agreed not to consummate the vows. Also she wished to bring her priest to Camden and have

422

a private chapel installed in her new solar so she could have Mass said daily.

Gyles had been ready to agree to all Lady Margaret's requests—he would have readily agreed to anything in order to escape from Margaret's presence—when she stated her final demand. Under no circumstances were his children to come near her. For the first time Lady Margaret's eyes gleamed with a fanatical light; she wanted no bastard's spawn to soil her pure soul and perhaps ruin her chances for salvation. Gyles had coldly turned his back on Lady Margaret and proceeded to his chamber. He did not speak to her again save to inform her before departing that he would send a messenger when the king decided upon a wedding date.

Gyles's lips twisted into a travesty of a smile as he gazed derisively around the cottage. His future wife wanted to become a nun and he was the one in the convent! What irony! It was upon his return to Camden that Gyles had begun to drink to excess; the stony silence he had retreated into after Serena's death gave way to brutal surliness and a vicious temper that lashed out at everyone save his sons. Even Nellwyn and Edward felt the sting of his tongue when they were unfortunate enough to do something that offended Gyles.

Gyles thrust himself away from the table and walked to the open doorway of the one room cottage he occupied; his green eyes narrowed into slits as the glaring sunlight slanted across his face. He would have to urge the workmen to finish the repairs to the orphanage quickly. Gyles wanted them back at Camden by harvest, and he hoped to finalize the arrangement for Serena's memorial with the abbess during this stay. Gyles could not tolerate more than one last visit to this place.

The courtyard, Gyles noticed, was deserted at this hour. The bell had rung for Sext as his meal had been delivered, which meant the nuns would be about their duties until the bell tolled at midafternoon for Nones. Gyles braced his hands against the door post above his head—if the abbess had recovered, word would have been sent to him, so it appeared he must endure yet another day and night at the cloister. Gyles groaned despondently and stepped into the sunlight.

As Gyles strode toward the river a slight figure in the gray robe of a novice stepped out of the shadows by the cottage and rapidly followed in his wake. Gyles knelt at the bank and splashed the cool water over his face and arms. Then, thinking better of such a brief ablution, Gyles stripped off his tunic and plunged into the river. Secluded on the bank, Sister Anne watched unashamedly as the Norman lord swam easily to the center of the stream. Blue eyes sparkled appreciatively as Gyles circled aimlessly, pausing occasionally to dive beneath the surface or float lazily on his back, the bronzed skin of his back and shoulders rippling with each stroke of his powerful arms.

"Am I so ugly, Serena?"

"Oh! nay, Gyles, I never knew a man to be so magnificent!"

Sister Anne blinked rapidly and searched the water for the woman whose voice she heard. Save for Lord Gyles the river's surface was unbroken and Sister Anne knew none of the order had followed her from the abbey, so then who . . .

"I am a selfish man, Serena. Do not leave me."

"Never, Gyles! I shall stay with you always. Where else do I belong? You are my husband."

The words beat at Sister Anne's temples and she pressed her hands over her ears to still the voices.

"Four weeks, Gyles! 'Tis so long a time for me to wait!"

"Regain your strength quickly, Serena love. We have been parted overlong."

Fear and confusion overwhelmed Sister Anne and she cried out against the taunting voices. The soft cry floated over the water to where Gyles was lazily floating and he turned quickly to the bank, his eyes probing the trees and undergrowth.

"Who goes there?" Gyles called. "Show yourself!"

Sister Anne shrank against the tree trunk, the sound of Gyles's command driving the voices from her mind, leaving her dizzy and half-fainting from fear of discovery. While Gyles studied the shore line Sister Anne remained motionless, scarcely daring to breathe. Only when Gyles struck out for the bank did Sister Anne turn and flee back to the abbey where she sought comfort in the flickering light of the chapel.

Gyles gained the shore and hurriedly donned his clothing, his eyes alertly flicking to his right and left as he cursed inwardly at his carelessness in leaving his sword and dagger at the cottage. Yet what had he to fear? Gyles chided himself. He was in a cloister, not a battlefield, and none of the sisters could possibly wish him harm. 'Twas probably some poor novice who had come to collect water for the abbey and having stumbled upon his bath, had run to say a penance for having seen a nude man. Gyles's lip curled in contempt as he strode through the still deserted courtyard. Nuns! A bunch of females unable to accept the fact of their own womanhood who preferred withering in a convent to ripening in a man's arms. By the chapel door Gyles paused—his guest cottage would be unbearably hot by now, whereas the chapel was always cool and restful.

The heavy leather soles of Gyles's boots slapping against the stone floor announced his presence in the chapel but the novice saying her rosary at the altar did not move. The prayer rail groaned under Gyles's weight and he stared balefully at the cross behind the altar. Prayers—what good had they ever done him? The merciful God these demented women worshipped had destroyed the sweetest creature ever to grace the earth. When Serena was lost Gyles had been praying for the happy day not a fortnight hence when they would be reunited. Even through the agonizing months of that fruitless search Gyles had prayed; during the weary hours spent riding through rain and snow he had beseeched God to help him find his wife. All had come to naught—Serena was dead and he would soon be bonded to another in a fashion that made a mockery of the sacred vows. For the first time in a long while Gyles felt the urge to weep and he buried his face in his hands.

Sister Anne finished her rosary and after making the sign of the cross turned to withdraw. During her prayers Sister Anne had resolved never again to seek out Lord Gyles if only God would see fit to allow the dizziness and voices she had heard to pass. Moving thoughtfully down the aisle, her head bowed, a small movement caught her attention and Sister Anne halted. Lord Gyles knelt in one of the pews, his handsome face obscured by his hands. His shoulders were heaving, Sister Anne saw, as if he were fighting all the demons of hell—or perhaps only the grief he kept so deeply buried. All of Sister Anne's brave resolutions fell away in the face of Lord Gyles's sorrow. Surely God would want her to offer comfort to one so sorely in need; Sister Anne could not ignore such pain as the Norman lord was bearing.

Without knowing quite how it was accomplished, Sister Anne found herself seated on the pew in front of Lord Gyles, her slender fingers brushing his hands as she spoke.

"God's way is not always clear to us, m'lord, we can only accept His will. You must believe, m'lord, that there is a reason for—" Sister Anne gasped in pain as the long fingers of the knight closed over hers so tightly that the bones were nearly crushed.

Gyles's face was deathly white, the green eyes so brilliant it pained Sister Anne to look at them. "M-m'lord? Please . . . I . . . you are hurting me!" Sister Anne managed to stammer out. Why was he staring at her as if she were a ghost? Sister Anne's fear of having known Lord Gyles returned with a vengeance and now she struggled to free herself from his grasp. "Please, m'lord," she sobbed as the dull throb in her temples began and the dizziness washed over her again.

The entire world narrowed for Gyles until only the delicate face with its hollowed cheeks and wide sapphire eyes remained. Serena! Gyles's heart thudded against his

426

ribs and he shook his head to clear his vision. It wasn't possible, not here, not now, after all these months! Gyles studied the tearful face within inches of his—Serena's face without a doubt, but thinner, far too thin; and there was an emptiness in those blue eyes he loved to gaze into, a blankness Gyles had never seen before. But it was Serena, his wife, his love.

"Serena," Gyles finally croaked. "Dear God, Serena!"

Sister Anne stiffened at the name the voices had spoken. Who was she, this Serena? Lord Gyles's wife? The bruising grip had relented, but he still held her hand in his.

"If it please, m'lord, my name is Sister Anne," she told him in a steadier voice. "I know not of Serena."

Gyles's eyes widened briefly and he raised a shaking hand to the veil covering Serena's head. What if she had taken the vows of the order? What . . . The veil came loose and Serena's hair spilled over his fingers as she gave a small gasp and recoiled from his touch.

" 'Tis not me, m'lord, you must not—"

"You are not of the order? You have taken no vows?" Gyles's hands fell to Serena's shoulders and he shook her gently. She was so thin, so terribly fragile.

"N-nay, m'lord." Sister Anne was truly frightened now and she began to quake. What possible difference could it make to this man whether she had taken her vows, unless . . . unless he knew her and her past! Her spirits soared and, momentarily forgetting the abbess's warning, Sister Anne's eyes flashed happily as she caught eagerly at his hand. "M'lord, please, m'lord, do you know me? Have we met? Who am I? Please, m'lord, can you tell me . . ."

Serena's questions brought a strange light to Gyles's eyes and he quelled the impulse to crush Serena to him as he stared at her in disbelief. Serena's face showed no sign of recognition, no sign that she knew him, indeed had ever known him, while she pelted him with questions. With great reluctance Gyles took his hands from his wife.

"How—" Gyles's voice caught and he cleared his

throat of the lump that had formed there. "How long have you been here, Sister?"

"I am not certain, m'lord, but I would guess since harvest time last. 'Tis said I was waylaid by thieves and sorely injured and left for dead. A group of mummers found me wandering from a forest and brought me here." Sister Anne cautiously related the story the abbess had told her to give if questioned, for Sister Anne was not entirely certain how much faith could be placed in Lord Gyles. "The sisters saved me from certain death, m'lord, and allowed me to stay as a lay member of their order. You see, my wounds had become infected and I succumbed to a fever, which cost me my memory. So please, m'lord, if you know me, I pray you, speak to me of my life."

"I do indeed know of you, Sere—Sister." Gyles gave his wife a crooked smile. "I have known you and your family for some time—you have a brother whose first child will soon be born. You are wed to a noble lord and you have a son who will shortly be a year in age."

Sister Anne's eyes shone. "Truly, m'lord? A husband and a son? Oh, 'tis more than I hoped for. Tell me—"

"Nay, Sister." Gyles stood and gestured for her to do likewise; struck when she did so by the fragility barely concealed by the rough gray robe. " 'Twould be best if we speak to the abbess before I tell you more."

"Oh, yes, m'lord, Reverend Mother will be so pleased." Sister Anne started to replace her veil, then laughed softly. "I shall not need to wear this any longer thanks to you. And I am most grateful to you, m'lord. When I am restored to my husband I shall ask him to grant you any reward you desire." Gyles's laughter caused her to frown at his uncalled for levity and she said in a sterner vein, "But come, Reverend Mother is better today and she should be in her office. I will take you there."

The abbess was not in her office but was overseeing the work on the orphanage, Gyles and Sister Anne were informed in icy tones by a stern-faced Sister Marcella who cast disapproving looks at the young woman's bare head.

Before Sister Marcella could say more, Sister Anne had pulled Gyles out of the room and through the corridor leading to the orphanage.

The abbess watched them approach, the delicate beauty of the woman she knew as Sister Anne a dramatic contrast to the dark masculinity of Lord Gyles, and she, too, frowned at the unbound, waist-length tresses; but before the abbess could upbraid Sister Anne, Lord Gyles spoke to her and proceeded alone to the Reverend Mother.

Sister Anne wandered about the orphanage's court-yard, tilting her head back occasionally to observe the masons as they worked at bringing down sections of decaying wood and replacing it with more durable stone. The children darted about, making a game of dodging the falling lumber. Sister Anne called out a sharp reprimand then returned to her own happy musings.

Soon she would be back with her family—it mattered not that she did not remember either husband or son, Sister Anne had faith that once reunited with her loved ones her memory would return.

Her brows drew together as Sister Anne recalled her dreams of Lord Gyles. Now that it was confirmed that she was wed she must set aside all thoughts of him and speak to no one of her dreams in which Lord Gyles played such a major role. The thought brought Sister Anne up short—what if Lord Gyles meant to escort her back to her husband? If so, Sister Anne must have a chaperone, for she doubted any husband would look kindly upon his wife undertaking a journey with another man, no matter how good a friend he proved to be!

Sister Anne had become oblivious to her surround-ings and had inadvertently wandered into the shadows she had previously warned the children from. Odd, she thought, how after she had recovered from her initial fear of Lord Gyles his presence had been comforting, warmly protective, serene. In the same instant she heard the rending sound of wood giving way, Sister Anne also heard Gyles's call; warning her, calling her "Serena" with a horror in his voice that lifted the veil she had labored under during the past months. As Gyles lunged across the courtyard, her name still on his lips, she remembered. Sister Anne was gone, Serena had returned.

"Gyles," Serena whispered and then the world exploded in a brilliant flash of pain as a section of wood struck her head and she descended into blackness.

22

The abbess quietly entered the guest cottage, a bowl of warm water and clean linens in her hands, and made her way across the room to the bed. The dark knight appeared not to notice her presence and she cleared her throat discreetly to announce her entrance. "Lord Gyles? 'Tis time I cleaned her wound, m'lord."

Gyles glanced up, then returned his gaze to the woman in his arms. "Do what needs be done, Reverend Mother."

"Lord Gyles!" The abbess sighed, "Will you not release her? Just for a time while I bathe the cut—I can send for a tray so that you may sup when I see to your wife."

"Nay." Gyles's voice was ragged. "Twice before I was parted from her when she had need of me, once when my child was torn from her body and then when she was nearly killed by those black-hearted sons of satan who—" His voice broke and he shook his head violently. "Nay, I will not release her! Serena is where she belongs, here safe in my arms, and here she will stay 'til she awakens. Do what you must; my presence will not hinder your work."

As the abbess carefully washed the matted hair and dried blood away from the cut on Serena's head, Gyles's thoughts turned back to the day they had first set eyes on each other. How beautiful Serena had been, her eyes so wide with fear and anxiety they looked like sapphire flames when she stared up at him. What manner of man had he seemed to her then with his grim demeanor and the implacable hatred he had carried for all women?

Serena cried out softly despite the abbess's gentle touch and Gyles drew her closer to his chest as if to ward off the pain with his own body. The joy he had felt at finding Serena had long since vanished and as the day passed and she had not awakened, Gyles's fear increased. Surely fate would not be so cruel as to take Serena from him a second time. How could he live with the knowledge that had he payed more attention to the community of nuns, he would have discovered Serena months ago and she would now be safely at Camden. True, she would not remember their life together, but would that be so terrible? Their marriage had been forced on them both and the union had only begun to hold promise after a long year of misunderstandings and separations. What would it have been like had they loved each other from the beginning? Gyles groaned inwardly. To turn back time, to go back to the day they met, to their wedding night—to give Serena all the love that should have been hers from the start but which Gyles was only now capable of giving her.

The abbess finished her duties and collected her things. "One of our order will remain outside the door. Call out if you desire anything or if your lady awakes."

When she was gone Gyles smoothed the hair from Serena's face and tenderly traced her features with his fingertips. "Open your eyes, my love," he whispered. "Do you not wish to see your husband? And Alan and Evan— they have need of you as well. It matters not that you have no memory of us . . . perhaps 'tis best this way. How many people wish for a second chance at finding happiness here on earth such as the one we have been granted?" Gyles pressed a kiss on Serena's unmoving lips. "We shall begin again, you and I. You will return to Camden as my bride and I will court you as I should have done so long ago. I have caused you much pain in the past, that I know, and, my dearest love, I would willingly sell my soul to the devil if that would buy back your sorrow. But such bargaining is futile now—I can only pray that you come back to me." Gyles fixed his emerald stare on the cross above the bed, willing his own strength to flow into Serena.

A black cloud seemed to have surrounded her mind and body; a warm, comforting, black cloud that wasn't frightening in the least. There was an ache in her right temple, but that magically diminished when something moist and warm was drawn over her scalp. She stirred, moaned, felt herself held more tightly within the gentle cloud. Memories buried for so long came flooding back as well as the vision of a tall, dark knight praying in the darkened chapel. Abruptly the cloud around her was no longer comforting but terrifying, for it threatened to keep Serena from Gyles for all time and she fought against it, crying out her fear and distress.

"Serena! *Serena!*" Gyles caught her flailing arms, pinning them between his chest and Serena. "Be still, my love, all is well. Cherie, please, you will do yourself harm this way."

Serena's eyes flew open at the sound of his voice and she stared, transfixed, at the sun-bronzed face just above her own. Tentatively, afraid she was still dreaming, Serena freed one hand and touched the scar that was so familiar to her.

"Gyles?" He took her hand and pressed it to his lips. "Oh, Gyles, I feared you were a dream."

"Nay, love, no dream. Flesh and blood only."

With a sob Serena threw her arms around his neck, heedless of the tears that streamed down her cheeks to dampen Gyles's tunic. Again and again she murmured his name, clinging fiercely to him while Gyles lavished kisses on her hair and throat.

"We thought you dead," Gyles choked out, his own eyes bright with unshed tears. "Dear God, Serena, we thought you dead!"

"We were attacked," Serena cried. "Bryan and

433

Richard and I, when we went riding. They killed Bryan, Gyles, I remember seeing his body—and they wanted to kill me as well! Oh, Gyles, I was so frightened I could not move; I let them kill my brother! Why, Gyles, why? Neither Bryan nor I have done anything to deserve death."

"Serena, love, hush." Gyles cupped her face between his hands and ordered firmly, "Be still, I say, and calm yourself. Bryan is not dead; he is alive and well, and he and Catherine are awaiting their first-born."

"Truly?" Serena gripped his forearms, afraid to release him lest her world suddenly crumble.

"Truly," Gyles assured her. "How do you feel? Does your head pain you?"

Serena shook her head. "Nay, Gyles, a slight ache 'tis all. Tell me of you, of Camden—our sons, are they well? Gyles—"

"Hush." Gyles placed a finger across her lips. "Are you hungry?" Serena nodded and Gyles smiled approvingly. "So am I. I vow I have not enjoyed a meal since you disappeared." Gyles strode to the door and asked the sister waiting outside for a supper tray, then returned to the pallet and took Serena in his arms.

"Gyles—"

"Hush," Gyles said sternly. "For nearly twelve months my bed and arms have been empty; allow me the pleasure of simply holding you again. There will be time later for your questions."

Serena did not argue, instead she touched his hair, shoulders, face; allowing her hands to remember the texture of him while her mind recalled their life together. 'Twas this she had missed all this time in the convent without realizing it—the wonder of holding her love to her breasts. Of all the things in the world, how could she have forgotten Gyles, Serena wondered. He was as much a part of her as her very soul; without Gyles she was incomplete. Looking back, Serena bitterly regretted having fled from Gyles in London. How much unnecessary pain she must have caused him then. Had she but known what would happen . . .

"Promise me we will never be parted again," Serena whispered anxiously.

"I promise," Gyles answered. And then, as if he could read her thoughts, "There will be no more partings for you and me. I intend to keep you safe beside me for the rest of my days, despite wars or princes or dark ladies from the north country. And if you ever try to escape me again, I swear I will chain you to me day and night."

"I would not blame you for that," Serena replied and snuggled closer to Gyles. "In truth I would enjoy it, for I have had my fill of separations."

Gyles tilted Serena's head backward and fixed his lips upon hers, recapturing in an instant the burning passion that had always been theirs. Serena responded eagerly to his kiss, her body growing warm and pliant as it molded against Gyles. Strangely, in spite of her willingness, Gyles did not press his suit, but gently ended the kiss. "That, too, I have missed," he told Serena in an odd voice.

Serena smiled and opened her arms invitingly, but Gyles only shook his head and chastely kissed both her hands. " 'Tis not meet, Serena."

Any protest Serena might have made was effectively silenced by the return of the sister with their meal. Puzzled by Gyles's actions Serena did not speak when they were alone once again, but she covertly watched her husband as he applied himself to his food. Gyles had changed in the time she had been gone, Serena thought as she toyed with her own food. Once he would not have refused her obvious offer; once Gyles would have taken her in his arms regardless of the surroundings. A sudden thought caused Serena to lose what was left of her appetite. The only reason Serena could think of for Gyles's behavior was too awful to contemplate—she swallowed hard and studied his profile in the wavering candlelight. Gyles had found another; that was why he had not touched her.

"Gyles?" Her voice shook and when he looked up

to meet her eyes Serena discovered she could not ask the question that had jarred her out of her newfound joy. Serena dropped her gaze and steadied her voice. "Will you tell me now about Alan and Evan?"

"They are well." Gyles finished his wine. "Both have grown so much you may not recognize them—especially Evan, he was just a babe when you saw him last. He has your eyes, but in all other ways he favors me."

His pride in both sons was plain to see and Serena felt tears sting her eyes. "And the others? My family?"

Gyles smiled at her across the table. "Bryan and Catherine are well, as I told you. Nellwyn, too, enjoys good health; Sir Arthur has something to do with that I think.

"We discovered the reason you were attacked, Serena. 'Twas a plot hatched by Aurelia and Beda to inherit Broughton and Camden. Aurelia poisoned your father; you were justified in your suspicion of his death. Had the attack on your party succeeded, Evan and I would have fallen beneath their greed."

"But they arranged our marriage," Serena said in a disbelieving tone. "Aurelia practically forced my father into arranging it and Beda seemed to have no objections, aside from being banned from your bed. Do you tell me now that those elaborate preparations were made solely because they wanted the land?"

Gyles nodded grimly. " 'Twas all for the lands, Serena. Your father, Bryan, you—all of us were merely pawns to be used and discarded as they saw fit. Richard, too, was a tool they used out of sheer desperation." Briefly, Gyles described Richard's part in the attack and the fatal confrontation between Richard and Aurelia. "I am sorry, cherie, that I must bring you such news in this way, but 'tis best you know all that has happened now, before you leave the cloister."

Serena's heart froze at his words. What else had transpired that she was not aware of? Had Gyles found another woman to take her place? Serena fearfully pushed the thought away—if Gyles had, he would soon tell her. "Was Balfour taken from Richard's father?"

"Nay. Prince Henry decided 'twould be best if such news was not spread across England. He came to Camden and made his judgment there."

Serena sighed and left the table to gaze into the dead fireplace. "Poor Richard. Were it not for me, he would still be alive. Why did he not do as I asked? Why could he not have married another and been content at Balfour?"

" 'Tis not hard to understand. Richard loved you, Serena; for him there could be no other."

Tears scalded Serena's cheeks as she mourned for him. She wept not for the Richard who had willingly led her and Bryan into an ambush, but for the gentle, innocent friend of her childhood and the ardent rogue who had first captured her heart. Suddenly Serena felt very old and weary—the world she had known was gone; all the familiar, comforting things had disappeared along with her father and Richard.

"Have you more to tell me?" Serena asked tiredly. "The bell will ring soon for Complin—"

"There is more." Behind her, Serena heard Gyles shift in his chair. "You have not asked how I fared, Serena. Why?"

Serena shook her head fearfully, feeling her mind go numb with the shock of what she would surely hear. "You are here," she answered uncertainly. "I thought 'twas evident you fared well."

"You are wrong; I did not. 'Twas pure hell for me, Serena, the endless months of searching for you, afraid to find you yet more afraid that I would not. 'Twas hardest to return home and face our son, knowing that some day I would have to tell him that his mother had disappeared. But worst of all was having to agree to a marriage arranged by the king. I wanted to die, my love, as I was certain you had. Only the thought of our sons stayed my hand."

Gyles's voice was soft but it seemed to reach every corner of the room, surrounding her with his presence.

" 'Twas different for me, not knowing who I was or where I belonged. I only knew that something important was missing, and when I would try to remember my head would ache so badly I had to give up." Serena sighed. " 'Tis not the life I had planned."

"Nor I." Gyles came to stand behind her. "Do you remember how it was with us in the beginning? The anger, the accusations, the wounds each of us inflicted on the other? I have had a great deal of time to remember, Serena, to wish our life together had been different. 'Twas not your fault, nor mine. We were strangers then and though we did not know it, there were other forces that also worked against us. I want you to know I never blamed you for running away or wanting a divorce."

"I wished only for your love," Serena managed to say. "I wanted our marriage to be a happy one, Gyles, I could never have gone through with a divorce."

Impatiently Gyles swung Serena around to meet his gaze. "Because of Evan?"

"Nay, for myself," she told him in a small voice. "If I did not love you I would have raised Evan by myself."

"And now it seems I must take new vows." Gyles framed Serena's face with his large hands when she tried to look away. "When I return to Camden I must do so with a bride—will you marry me, Serena?"

Serena's legs nearly gave way and she swayed weakly. Gyles's arms fell to her waist to support her, his eyes full of concern. "What is it, my love? Why are you so pale?"

"I . . . I thought you meant you had to wed another." Serena leaned against his chest. "Gyles, you frightened me half to death with your talk of brides and vows. 'Twas cruel of you to jest with me in such a manner."

"I did not jest, Serena," Gyles replied seriously. "Since your father is dead I should more properly ask Bryan for his permission and your hand, but that would take time and I have lost too much time with you already. So I ask you, Serena, to be my wife."

Serena's eyes widened in confusion. "Have you taken leave of your senses, Gyles? We are wed—"

438

" 'Twas a ceremony to satisfy the laws of the Church and the laws of the king. It united two people who had no wish to be wed. 'Tis not the way I want our lives together to begin, Serena. I want our vows to join our hearts and I want our children to know that 'twas the love we bear for each other that gave them life, not simply a moment of lust. You must know, too, that the love I have for you is deep and abiding and will not end no matter what befalls us." Gyles's eyes glowed brilliantly. "Will you take your vows with me now? Will you willingly link your heart and soul with mine?"

"Surely you must know I will." Serena threw her arms around his neck. "Oh yes, Gyles, yes."

Tenderly Gyles drew Serena to the one window in the cottage and there, with the moon bathing them in its light, they clasped hands and sank to their knees. Hesitantly, almost shyly, Gyles began speaking, not the formal words he had once recited but the vow he had made to himself nearly every day since Serena's disappearance.

"Now and forever I take thee unto me. I pledge my right arm to protect thee and my love to surround thee through all the tomorrows we will share. Never again will thy heart wander alone and afraid, for mine shall walk beside it into eternity."

If her voice had wavered when she had first taken the vows that bound her to Gyles, now Serena's voice was strong and clear.

"Thy life is mine; wherever thy path shall lead I shall willingly follow for that way lies my love. All that I deem of value—my heart, my soul, my honor—all do I lay at thy feet, and in doing so their worth is increased ten-fold. My love goes out to thee as thy love flows unto me, timeless, unending, eternal."

Only the moon watched as Gyles rose and pulled Serena into an embrace as sweet and tender as any bride could wish. Happily content, Serena rested against his broad chest, listening to the steady, even rhythm of his heart. Tomorrow they would return to the outside world with all its obligations and duties; but the night with its velvet cushion of stars was theirs to share, as was their love. What better way, Serena wondered dreamily as Gyles swept her up in his arms, to begin a new life of memories.

{ EPILOGUE }
Camden

The pennants above the castle walls were snapping proudly in the early autumn breeze, proclaiming to one and all that Gyles, Lord of Camden, was in residence. Below in the freshly harvested fields pavilions were being erected, squires hurried about rubbing down lathered mounts and polishing armor. Knights owing their allegiance to Camden greeted their equals as they arrived in their lords' retinues and high born ladies fell into each other's arms, exclaiming over the unusual turn of events that had led to Lord Gyles holding two tourneys in one year.

In his chamber Gyles donned a tunic from his coffer and smoothed the material over his broad chest. Turning, he delivered a lusty whack to a pair of softly rounded buttocks.

" 'Tis your own fault, cherie—" Gyles laughed to forestall an outraged protest "—for placing temptation within my reach."

Her blue eyes sparkled as Serena laughed up at her husband in complete agreement, and went eagerly into the circle of his beckoning arms.

Gone was the dismal pall which had hung for so long over Camden and Gyles in particular. Unparalleled joy tinged with disbelief had greeted Gyles when he first returned to Camden with Serena held lovingly but securely before him in the saddle. Nellwyn had wept copious tears,

Alan had shrieked with happiness, while Evan curiously eyed the stranger who was his mother.

It had taken less than a fortnight for Evan to completely accept Serena and he was soon toddling into her outstretched arms with delicious abandon. Nellwyn had declared her young mistress to be naught but skin and bones and set about preparing the most appetizing meals she could concoct while Gyles merrily composed a letter to the king informing him that the Lord of Camden was no longer free to wed a certain Lady Margaret.

Serena herself was euphoric. Gone were the days and nights during which she had lived in a void and in their place was a delightful world where she was surrounded by those who loved her. Serena could not get her fill of Alan and Evan, so that when word reached Camden that Catherine had been safely delivered of a son, Serena sent a note of congratulations along with a gold christening cup to Bryan, but declined the invitation to visit Broughton. She was home, at Camden; at long last her life was as she had always dreamed it would be.

Gyles rarely allowed Serena out of his reach or sight during the first month she was home. After nearly a year of agonizing loneliness, Gyles was determined to keep his wife by his side lest she be torn from him once again. He was starved for the touch, sight, and sound of his wife, and while Nellwyn plied Serena with food, so, too, did Gyles tenderly nurture her with a love as vibrant and vitally alive as he was. By day Gyles played the courtly suitor who laughed and wooed his gentle maid and at night he held Serena and gave proof of his love 'til both nearly fainted with pleasure. Only now, nearly two months since her return, could Gyles bear to be separated from Serena for a few minutes, and finally Serena had been able to persuade him to participate in the lists he had planned in celebration of her return.

"May I be assured Godwin will not appear on the field this time?" Gyles now raised Serena's chin with his finger and smiled, but his eyes were serious.

"You may indeed, Gyles," Serena replied, a teasing light in her eyes, then she sighed. "Poor Godwin, I fear he will never more take part in the lists, so you, my dearest love, must carry my standard."

"With the greatest pleasure, love." Gyles bent to place a lingering kiss on her lips. "And with the greatest honor."

ROMANCE... ADVENTURE... DANGER...

DUCHESS IN DISGUISE
by Caroline Courtney   **(94-050, $1.75)**
The Duke of Westhampton had a wife in the country and a mistress in town. This suited the Duke, but his young wife, whom he'd wed and tucked away on his estate was not pleased. So, being as audacious as she was innocent, she undertook to win his attention by masquerading as a lady he did not know — herself.

WAGER FOR LOVE
by Caroline Courtney   **(94-051, $1.75)**
The Earl of Saltaire had a reputation as a rakehell, an abductor and ravisher of women, a dandy and demon on horseback. Then what lady of means would consider marrying him — especially if she knew the reason for the match was primarily to win a bet? When he won a wager by marrying her, he never gambled on loosing his heart!

SWEET BRAVADO
by Alicia Meadowes   **(89-936, $1.95)**
Aunt Sophie's will was her last attempt to reunite the two feuding branches of the Harcourt family. Either the Viscount of Ardsmore marry Nicole, the daughter of his disgraced uncle, or their aunt's inheritance would be lost to the entire family! And wed, they did. But theirs was not a marriage made in heaven!

PHILIPPA
by Katherine Talbot   **(84-664, $1.75)**
If she had to marry for money and Philippa knew she must — then it was fortunate that such a very respectable member of The House of Lords was courting her. It would be difficult, though, to forget that the man she loves would be her brother-in-law. . . . A delightful Regency Romance of a lady with her hand promised to one man and her heart lost to another!

LILLIE
by David Butler   **(82-775, $2.25)**
This novel, upon which the stunning television series of the same name is based, takes Lillie Langtry's story from her girlhood, through the glamour and the triumphs, the scandals and the tragedies, to 1902 and Edward VII's accession to the throne.

ROMANCE...ADVENTURE...
DANGER...

SKARRA
by Henry V. M. Richardson   *(91-221, $2.50)*
Highland lord of a large and noble clan of Scotland,
SKARRA is a soldier of fortune, an eloquent scholar and
a fiery lover whose fierceness at battle and tenderness at
love blaze a legend across 17th Century Europe—and
through the hearts of two very different women.

LADY OF SKARRA
by Henry V. M. Richardson   *(81-493, $2.50)*
Tatti is THE LADY OF SKARRA and her tumultuous story
takes her sailing the high seas, bound unwillingly for the
colonies. Her beauty, her spirit, her tenderness sweep
the granddaughter of SKARRA into adventure and love!

MY LADY BENBROOK
by Constance Gluyas   *(91-124, $2.50)*
The Earl of Benbrook had schooled Angel Dawson well.
The street accents were gone from her speech when he
presented her as a gracious lady at the court of the King.
And Angel had taught Nicholas, too, the lessons of love.
They had earned her an even more precious honor; she
was now his wife, the Lady Benbrook!

THE KING'S BRAT
by Constance Gluyas   *(91-125, $2.50)*
The Earl of Benbrook gazed at the waif who had been kind
to his dying sister. With a mixture of guilt and gratitude,
he vowed to turn the street wench into a lady. It was a task
that would involve him with Angel far more deeply than
he guessed, and would change her far more than she
dreamed! The tempestuous tale of Angel Dawson's rise
from the streets of London to the court of Charles II.

ROMANCE...DANGER...ADVENTURE...

THIS TOWERING PASSION
by Valerie Sherwood   *(81-486, $2.50)*
500 pages of sweet romance and savage adventure set against
the violent tapestry of Cromwellian England, with a magnificent
heroine whose beauty and ingenuity captivates every man who
sees her, from the king of the land to the dashing young rakehell
whose destiny is love!

THE KING'S BRAT
by Constance Gluyas   *(91-125, $2.50)*
The Earl of Benbrook gazed at the waif who had been kind to
his dying sister. With a mixture of guilt and gratitude, he vowed
to turn the street wench into a lady. It was a task that would
involve him with Angel far more deeply than he guessed, and
would change her far more than she dreamed! The temptestuous
tale of Angel Dawson's rise from the streets of London to the
court of Charles II.

MY LADY BENBROOK
by Constance Gluyas   *(91-124, $2.50)*
The Earl of Benbrook had schooled Angel Dawson well. The
street accents were gone from her speech when he presented
her as a gracious lady at the court of the King. And Angel had
taught Nicholas, too, the lessons of love. They had earned her
an even more precious honor; she was now his wife, the Lady
Benbrook!

WARNER BOOKS
P O Box 690
New York, N.Y. 10019

Please send me the books I have selected.

Enclose check or money order only, no cash
please. Plus 50¢ per order and 20¢ per copy
to cover postage and handling. N.Y. State and
California residents add applicable sales tax.

Please allow 4 weeks for delivery.

_____ Please send me your free
mail order catalog

Name_____

Address_____

City_____

State _____ Zip_____